Praise for *The Nesting Doll*

The Nesting Dolls is a vividly rendered, sweeping historical novel. Alina Adams deftly portrays three generations of women, beautifully weaving their coming-of-age stories about love, sacrifice, family, and ultimately survival. I absolutely devoured this compulsively readable gem of a novel."

—Jillian Cantor, *USA Today* bestselling author of
The Lost Letter and *In Another Time*

"A moving saga of three generations of women determined to triumph over the forces of history no matter the cost. *The Nesting Dolls* is a memorable story of courage that is both inspiring and bittersweet."

—David R. Gillham, *New York Times* bestselling author of
City of Women and *Annelies*

"Utterly rich and satisfying. *The Nesting Dolls* by Alina Adams takes us on the complicated path through the fascinating history of Communist Russia and Russian immigration to the United States in that rarest of literary treats: a multigenerational saga in which each character feels true, each turn of circumstances rings both surprising and inevitable, and the final page leaves you wanting to turn back to the first and read it again."

—Meg Waite Clayton, *New York Times* bestselling author of
The Last Train to London

"Adams's finely detailed historical romance . . . follows five generations of headstrong, passionate Jewish women. . . . The author's wry Soviet-Jewish humor enlivens the well-developed characters, who make fatal mistakes as well as selfless sacrifices. This is a satisfying, life-affirming saga."

—*Publishers Weekly*

"Mesmerizing. . . . Adams's sweeping tale offers captivating explorations of her characters and their complexities, particularly when it comes to their struggles between the pull of the heart and the realities in which they live."

—*Booklist*

"A fascinating multigeneration tale. . . . Adams combines rich historical detail with an engrossing narrative."

—*World Magazine*

The Nesting Dolls

THE
NESTING
DOLLS

A NOVEL

ALINA
ADAMS

HARPER

NEW YORK ● LONDON ● TORONTO ● SYDNEY

HARPER

A hardcover edition of this book was published in 2020 by HarperCollins Publishers.

THE NESTING DOLLS. Copyright © 2020 by Alina Sivorinovsky. All rights reserved. Printed in the United States of America. No part of this book may be used or reproduced in any manner whatsoever without written permission except in the case of brief quotations embodied in critical articles and reviews. For information, address HarperCollins Publishers, 195 Broadway, New York, NY 10007.

HarperCollins books may be purchased for educational, business, or sales promotional use. For information, please email the Special Markets Department at SPsales@harpercollins.com.

FIRST HARPER PAPERBACKS EDITION PUBLISHED 2021.

Designed by Leah Carlson-Stanisic

Photograph by OrkiCu/Shutterstock, Inc.

Library of Congress Cataloging-in-Publication Data has been applied for.

ISBN 978-0-06-291095-0

21 22 23 24 25   LSC   10 9 8 7 6 5 4 3 2 1

In memory of . . .
Igor Khait (1963–2016)
He was the best of us all. . . .

The Nesting Dolls

Prologue

═══

2019

"Love is not a potato," Zoe's great-grandmother Alyssa had been telling her since before Zoe was old enough to know for certain what either word meant.

Zoe hoped her confusion was merely a language barrier. Her great-grandmother spoke Russian—and some German. Zoe spoke English—and some Russian. Neither spoke Yiddish. Her great-grandmother was very proud of this.

"Because," Zoe's great-grandmother explains, in Russian, "when love goes bad, you cannot throw it out the window." In Russian, *okoshka* (window) rhymes with *kartoshka* (potato).

"What Balissa means," Zoe's mother, Julia, chimes in, using the portmanteau Zoe gave her great-grandmother as a baby. This is what happens when three generations of women—and one so-genial-they-sometimes-forget-he's-in-the-room man—share a three-bedroom apartment in Brighton Beach, Brooklyn. There's no such thing as a private conversation. *For this we left the Soviet Union?*

Then again, this is the neighborhood where a faded metal sign off the elevated subway welcomes you to BRIGHTON BEACH: A WHOLE NEW WORLD!, while the majority of residents are doing their best to turn it into the old one. Want to buy something in a restaurant or store and don't speak Russian? Good luck with that! On the other hand—sales tax? What's that? To paraphrase Leona Helmsley, in Brighton, only the English speakers pay taxes.

You'd think, with her mother having been born in America, and Zoe having been born in America, they'd speak the same language. You'd be wrong. Mama jokes that she's stuck between languages; she's starting to forget Russian but hasn't learned English yet. Mama communicates in Russian, at home and at work, with a few English words thrown in, like "okay," "parking" (rather, a hybrid, *za-PARK-ovat*), and "mobile phone" (aka *MOBIL-ney*).

"What Balissa means"—Mama's lips flatten against each other and purse out. She resembles a platypus in a pink housecoat, needles stuck through the lapel, ready for any sewing emergency—"is there's nothing more important than choosing the right person to spend your life with."

"She is right." *Oh, good, another nation heard from.* It's the first thing Zoe's grandmother has said since Zoe arrived to help plan her grandparents' forty-fifth-anniversary party.

Baba Natasha is in a snit, shuffling from living room to kitchen, silently sliding a stack of cherry *pirozhki* the size of an open hand onto the lacquered coffee table alongside marmalades of many colors that look like orange slices with sugar shells. Snits should never prevent eating.

Zoe asked Mama, when they began planning the big day weeks ago, why Baba is so against a party in her honor. She's usually all about being venerated. It doesn't take much to get her talking about the academic gold medal she almost earned in school, if a vengeful instructor hadn't decided to teach Baba a lesson. There was also anti-Semitism involved. In Baba's stories, anti-Semitism is always involved. She is equally happy to boast about how she's circumvented the Americans' tax system, using their own rules against them. "So easy! Why does everyone not to do this?" Problems begin when Baba feels the family isn't gushing over her *enough*. At

Zoe's NYU graduation, Baba made a point of telling everyone she wasn't some ignorant, immigrant grandmother, but, "I hold the degree in mathematics, also!" And God help anyone who forgets to call, email, or send flowers on March 8, International Women's Day. And then again on American Mother's Day.

"I deserve both!" Baba says.

Zoe lives in terror of Baba discovering Grandparents Day is a thing.

Baba's birthdays are major celebrations, necessitating more flowers, a gift (with receipt included; she says it's so she has the option to exchange it, but Zoe suspects Baba needs to know how much it cost), a dinner in her honor (where she always snatches up the bill; she says it's so she can make sure they charged the table properly and no one overcalculated the tip, but Zoe thinks it's so the assembled can chime in about how she can't be expected to pay, please, let us, it would be an honor), and several toasts that extol the unparalleled wonder that is her.

So this antipathy toward an anniversary party is not like Zoe's Baba.

On the other hand, Zoe doesn't need to ask Mama why, in the face of Baba's resistance, Mama is still so adamant about going through with it. When your bickering parents are running the clock out on forty-five years of marriage the same way they entered it, her haranguing and his amicably agreeing, you throw them a shindig in a Russian restaurant on the Brighton Beach boardwalk, complete with a house band; a mirrored dance floor; aspic-covered fried foods; a variety of shredded, colored cabbages; and many tipsy toasts, at least 50 percent of which are required to be in rhyme. That's just what you do.

Mama claims to have no idea as to the origin of Baba's negative stance. Neither does Deda. Neither does Balissa.

They keep claiming this right up until the night of the party.

Zoe gives up and shows up as mandated, along with maybe a hundred other people who had no choice in the matter. When your bickering friends are running the clock out on forty-five years of marriage, you show up. That's just what you do.

Zoe, however, shows up with a date that, on any other occasion, would have been the talk of Brighton Beach, and still might be, provided all live through the scheduled festivities.

For now, though, Baba is at the center of the tables, and the attention. Baba and her immobile frown. The earsplitting festive music isn't doing it for her. Mama and Deda's cajoling also does no good. Mama moves on to hissed threats. Deda throws his hands in the air and pastes on a twice as wide smile, to make up for her lack of one. That's when the night takes a surreal turn even Zoe's millennial cynicism couldn't have predicted. Her grandmother is handed an anniversary gift, some kind of civic license in a fancy frame.

Baba's frown fades, melting like a coat of armor dissolved by a stealth acid attack. It's replaced by an almost punch-drunk bewilderment. Baba, who prides herself on remaining in control and on top no matter what the situation, suddenly looks helpless and lost.

She turns to Zoe and whispers, "Why would you to do this?"

Zoe doesn't know what to say. Because Zoe has no idea what Baba means. Why would she to do what?

As Zoe's confusion deepens, Baba's passes. She forces it to pass.

Without waiting for Zoe to answer, right there, in front of all her guests, Baba raises the frame above her head.

And hurls it to the floor.

===

Book I

Daria

1931–1941

===

Chapter 1

═══

ODESSA, USSR

Signing the marriage license brisked by so quickly, Daria missed the exact moment when she moved from seventeen-year-old girl to married woman. One minute, she was standing between her mother and her groom at the shabby ZAGS office in front of an official stamping the couples through, the next she was kissing Edward, being kissed by Mama, receiving an embrace from Edward's papa, and it was over. As Isaak Israelevitch declared how delighted he was to have Daria for a daughter, Mama scrutinized the license she'd snatched from the officiant's hands, making certain Daria had done as instructed and signed her new legal name as Daria Gordon, not the Dvora Kaganovitch she'd been registered at birth.

"Come with us back to the house," Edward urged his new mother-in-law as they were ushered toward the door, past the line of couples waiting their turn to wed. "We have friends dropping by to celebrate."

"*Neyn, nyet,*" Mama stammered, first instinctively in Yiddish, then forcing herself to switch to Russian.

When laws were changed seven years earlier, mandating all Soviet children were now required to attend secular schools, Daria's mother had overruled her husband's edict that girls belonged at home. In their ramshackle shtetl of Valta, old men wept into their beards about all-boy, rabbi-led *cheders* replaced by a coed Yiddish-language school teaching Communist ideology. But that wasn't good enough for Mama. She dragged her daughter away from her friends, whom Mama pronounced provincial, to a school in the neighboring village. Let others limit their future by clinging to Yiddish. Mama's only child would learn Russian, and have the entire world at her feet. Mama lectured it didn't matter if Daria's fellow pupils were the same grubby Ukrainian hooligans who came to Valta each Easter to throw rocks and howl how *zhidy* killed Christian children and used their blood to bake matzoh. They were living in modern times, and Daria would be a modern woman. Stop bawling and do what your mother tells you!

As soon as Daria had absorbed an acceptable amount of Russian, Mama dictated a letter to Comrade Stalin, which Daria translated and transcribed, thanking him for this opportunity he'd granted them. Mama's next step was pushing Daria to speak Russian without those back-of-the-tongue-rolled *r*'s Daria's teacher had thoughtfully encouraged the other children to laugh at, until Daria exorcised her last telltale bit of Yiddishkeit. The same, however, did not apply to Mama. Her Russian stalled at the level of a child. Nonetheless, she refused to speak Yiddish to the worldly Gordons.

Mama demurred at their invitation to join the celebratory supper. "I do not wish to cause trouble. I must not embarrass you in front of your friends." She ducked her head, as if her mere provincial proximity might somehow tarnish them.

"You wouldn't embarrass us, Mama!" Daria looked to Edward and his father for support. They dutifully echoed Daria's denial. Even as their furtive glances told her otherwise.

"Do what your husband tells you"—Mama severed the reins she'd held tightly over her daughter for seventeen years—"and everything will be well, my Daria."

═══

MAMA HAD BEEN so eager for Daria to begin her new life, she'd insisted her daughter bring her solitary travel bag to the ZAGS. Isaak Israelevitch carried it for Daria.

"Edward must protect his fingers," he explained unnecessarily as, all around them, placards proclaimed Edward Gordon's upcoming piano concert series at the Odessa Opera House.

It had been these posters, still wet from paste, that inspired Mama to effectuate a match between her raven-haired, ebony-eyed, voluptuous girl and the tall, dark, handsome, and accomplished Edward Gordon. They'd come to Odessa from Valta specifically to land a fellow worthy of Mama's treasure.

Since the repeal of the New Economic Policy, NEP, allowing individuals to own small businesses, Mama pronounced the shopkeeper a man with no future. She said the same about the clerks and local government administrators who'd expressed interest in Daria. Mama knew a Jewish boy could rise only so far in politics, no matter how shrewd, ambitious, enterprising, or dynamic. Especially if they were shrewd, ambitious, enterprising, and dynamic.

"Men are to be tortured," Mama had instructed Daria as they stood outside the opera house late one March evening, at the cross streets of Lastochkina and Lenina, across from the towering arched doorway topped by a golden balcony surrounded by two pairs of Roman columns. There was a decorative level even higher than that, framed by gold statues, the most prominent of which was a topless woman on a half shell, one arm raised in salutation, the other embracing a torch while trying to ride three panthers taking off in different directions. Two more statues, marble this time, flanked the stairs leading up to the front entrance, representing comedy, tragedy, muses, operas, and ballets. While the woman up top was half naked, the figures below were wrapped in flurries of marble cloth. Daria wondered if any of them were cold. Daria certainly was cold. March in Odessa could be windy and inhospitable to standing around this close to midnight, wearing a virginal white dress that demurely draped down to Daria's ankles and up to her chin, yet was so tightly fitted above the waist that shivering was out of the question. She'd burst right through.

"We can't torture Edward Gordon, Mama, if he can't see us. He's in there. We're out here."

"On the stage, he doesn't live. He will need to exit eventually."

Music lovers streamed out of the opera house, buttoning coats, wrapping scarves around their necks, and pulling on gloves Daria envied from afar. Mama hooked her elbow through Daria's and pulled her around the crescent moon shape of the opera house, toward the rear exit along Teatralny Lane.

And there he was! Edward Gordon! In the flesh!

He was thinner than Daria had expected. All angles and lines, from the narrow cut of his shoulders to the jut of his elbows. His ebony eyebrows appeared drawn in, as did the two slashes of trimmed mustache below his equally symmetrical nose and cheekbones. He stood chatting with a group of admirers, half turned toward Daria. Their eyes met over the blond head of a woman who somehow managed to keep touching Edward—first on the forearm, then on the shoulder, then on the cheek, brushing off a nonexistent speck. Daria perceived that, unlike his hair, brows, and mustache, Edward's eyes might be not black but wintergreen, a striking contrast in a face paler than the rest of his coloring. She took a step in his direction.

Edward noticed her and smiled. Daria started to smile back.

Which was when her mother gave Daria's arm a firm tug, redirecting her trajectory away from Edward. Instead of stopping, they walked blithely past him and his entourage, Mama looking straight ahead, making it clear Daria had best do the same. They continued walking until they'd rounded the corner and were back at the front entrance, blending into the crowd of exiting citizens.

Daria threw both arms out to her sides, dress be damned. "I

thought we were here to meet Edward Gordon. What are we supposed to do now?"

"Now," her mother said, "we go home."

HOME WAS MOLDAVANKA. Part suburb, part ghetto along the
city's northern rim, it was a onetime Moldovan colony that, by the
turn of the century, had expanded to house nearly seventy thousand of Odessa's poorest Jews. They came to work in factories,
as laborers, as tailors, and as buyers of secondhand clothes. They
stayed because laboring in factories, tailoring, and selling secondhand clothes didn't pay much. Mama made it clear she and Daria
were just passing through. Mama had no intention of settling down
amid squalor that looked like a fire had recently crumbled entire
blocks. They rented a room on the top floor of a house otherwise
occupied by a bearded Jew who still clung to Old World nonsense,
and his wife, who spent her days trying to disguise that. The room
was barely large enough for the single bed it came with. They'd
dragged it against the wall to give themselves a sliver of space for
the chest of drawers, on top of which stood a basin to wash in. The
height of the bed made opening the middle drawer impossible. If
they wished to reach the one below, they had to wriggle along the
floor until they lay face-to-face with the chamber pot. Their landlord asserted there was no space for a coal stove. His concession
had been to sell Daria and her mother a pair of threadbare rugs
they could hang on the walls to keep out the cold.

As she and Mama undressed in the dark, scurrying under the
blankets, Daria whispered, "If you wanted me to meet Edward
Isaakovich, why didn't you let me speak to him? He wanted to
speak to me, I could tell."

"Men disdain easy women. We will make him work, so he understands your value."

IT TOOK SEVERAL DAYS. Several frustrating, nerve-racking, endless days, during which Daria pestered her mother, suggesting

they should try again, walk past the opera house again, slower this time, maybe actually stop and speak to the man.

"No," Mama said. "If there is no effort in the chase, there is no triumph in the victory."

Not even a week after their stroll, word came from a neighbor, who'd heard from a customer of her husband's who'd been queried by the friend of the father of the boy who delivered coal to the Gordons, whether anyone might know the identity of a certain girl who fit a certain description. Edward wished to meet her. He'd left a ticket for his evening performance, along with an invitation to visit him in his dressing room, afterward.

Daria was about to shout, "Tell him yes," when Mama interrupted. "Please inform Edward Isaakovich that my daughter will be accompanied by a chaperone. We shall require two tickets."

Chapter 2

That night, the pair of them shared box seats, looking down at Edward onstage. To Daria, it appeared the artist glanced more times than was absolutely necessary in their direction. But what did Daria know? She'd never been to a piano concert before. She'd certainly never been inside a place as grand as the opera house. Each seat felt wider than the bed she and Mama shared—softer and warmer, too. And the rugs were on the floors, not the walls. The walls were taken up with gold lining, sparking beneath radiant chandeliers. Daria was so preoccupied manipulating her miniature, secondhand binoculars to look up at the lights and down at the glamorously dressed orchestra audience, she barely found time to pay attention to the music, much less the man making it.

Edward took his final bows following four encores triggered by enthusiastic applause and bouquets of roses tossed onstage by giggling teens and blushing dowagers. Daria's mother rolled her eyes. *Those poor souls, did they have no one to teach them?* Then Mama made Daria wait until every last guest had left the theater.

Twenty minutes after the hour they'd been invited, Daria raised her hand to knock on Edward's dressing-room door. Mama slapped it down and stepped in front of Daria so that when Edward opened the door, he saw not Daria but her mother.

Edward instantly rearranged his features from surprise to welcome. He bade them to come in, expressing how pleased he was to see them . . . both. A table, topped by a silver samovar the length of Daria's arm, had been set by the window. It made Daria think of a lightbulb that had sprouted potato buds. Based on the way her mother was beaming, Daria guessed it was the latest fashion. Next to it stood a ceramic white plate piled with a dozen slices of rye bread, a small cup of butter, and an equal-sized portion of black caviar.

"May I offer you some tea?" Edward inquired.

Daria waited for Mama to speak first. When she didn't, Daria shot her a queer look and filled in, "Yes. Please. Thank you."

Edward poured, offering Daria a close-up look at his hands. She'd noticed how fluidly they moved over the piano keys, but now that she wasn't sitting multiple meters up, every finger appeared to possess an extra joint, so limber were his movements. Each gesture manifested like a precise piece of a seamless whole, caressing the air and sending an electric current flying through the room, piercing Daria and causing her to shiver for no discernable reason. Edward's smile suggested he knew precisely the reason.

He respectfully handed Mama the first cup. *"Möchten sie zitrone oder zucker?"*

Daria burst out laughing. "Where did you learn such terrible Yiddish?"

"Not Yiddish!" If they weren't in public, Daria didn't doubt Mama would have slapped her, and not on the hand. "German! Edward Isaakovich speaks beautiful German." She then awkwardly stammered, *"No ya govaru po Russki."* But I speak Russian.

Only then did Daria understand what Edward already had. Her mother's uncharacteristic silence was due to embarrassment over her accented, grammatically shaky Russian. Edward had asked if she would like lemon or sugar in German, due to that language's similarity to Yiddish.

"Of course," Edward switched from German to Russian as

smoothly as he'd earlier shifted his facial expressions. "Please forgive my error."

Mama magnanimously did. She also forgave Edward his subsequent mistake, when he presumed that the next time they saw each other, Edward would be alone with Daria.

Mama insisted on chaperoning them everywhere. At the cinema, it was all three of them watching Alexander Dovzhenko's film *Earth*, about tragedy striking a collective farm in the form of a jealous kulak unwilling to give up his private land for the good of all people. Mama was enthralled by Edward's scandalous gossip about how he'd seen an earlier version of the film in Moscow, before censors removed a sequence featuring a female nude. Not out of bourgeois prudishness, obviously, that wasn't the Soviet way. For political reasons. The great Sergei Eisenstein believed a naked body too sensual and individually abstract. It lacked social realism and so was counterrevolutionary. Daria's mother proved so enthralled by Edward's tittle-tattle, she failed to notice that, while Edward addressed Mama, sitting in the seat to his left, his right palm was, in the dark, creeping under Daria's skirt and to the inside of her thigh. In return, Daria slid her fingers beneath his shirtsleeve for a tantalizing burst of skin on skin.

Later, Mama realized she'd forgotten her glasses inside the theater, leaving Edward and Daria alone long enough for him to steal a kiss in a dim corner, his hand rising from Daria's waist to graze against her breast for an encore of the electricity that had shot through her the first time she'd glimpsed his sensual fingers.

As far as Edward was concerned, every brush of his lips against Daria's, every sweep of his hand across her bodice or along her thigh all happened outside Mama's vision, knowledge, or even suspicion.

"Let the boy believe he's in control," her mother dismissed. "What does it hurt us?"

The only thing hurting Edward was his inability to go any further than the furtive kisses and allegedly chance caresses. Daria sensed his frustration, but, as Mama pointed out, the solution was up to Edward. "He knows what he needs to do."

"Shouldn't he have done it by now?"

After all, Daria had followed Mama's instructions. For nearly six months, she'd kept Edward waiting; she regularly stood him up. She smiled cryptically as she swore there was no one else in response to his jealous inquiries, and she let his hands wander only so far before teasingly pulling away.

Mama didn't appear concerned that their efforts had yet to bear ultimate fruit.

And yet, one night in September, Daria woke to her mother mumbling something distantly familiar into the slit where their bed met the wall. And the next day, Mama claimed not to be hungry while preparing breakfast for Daria. It wasn't until their landlord snarled at Daria about daring to eat on this holiest of holy days that Daria confronted her mother. "You're fasting? For Yom Kippur? Last year, you called it superstitious nonsense. You said we're all better than that now. Were you praying last night, Mama?"

"Let the boy believe he is in control," her mother said. "But just in case someone else is . . ."

Edward proposed that evening.

AFTER BIDDING GOODBYE to Mama at the train station, Daria, Edward, and Isaak walked to the Gordon apartment on Karl Marx Street, Isaak still carrying Daria's suitcase, Edward holding Daria's hand, her wedding ring pressed between their linked fingers. Edward stroked the back of her palm with his thumb. She shivered at the knowledge that they were almost at his home. Their home.

Isaak apologized for taking Daria in via the courtyard, but it was a more direct entrance than from the street on the other side.

"Prior to the Revolution, my late wife, Edward, and I lived in the front apartment on the third floor, the one with the large window. Afterward, as a show of their esteem for Edward's talents and his vital work representing the glories of the Soviet Union to the rest of the world, they allowed us to keep two of the rooms in the back. The ones facing the courtyard. It was the most they could do. How would it have looked if bourgeois exploiters like us had been given the better spaces over a worker's family? But we were fortunate—don't mistake my gratitude for complaining. When they partitioned the apartment, instead of the front rooms getting to keep the toilet and kitchen for themselves, we were allowed to share with the new families. Communal living, the way it should be. Fair to everyone. Not like some places with the outhouses and no running water. We have a Primus, too. Runs on kerosene. So if the bathroom or the kitchen is in use, we can still heat water, stay warm."

The tunnel entrance to the courtyard was so dim, Daria heard, rather than saw, swarms of pigeons nesting overhead. Splatters of guano dotting the cement walls and floor confirmed her inference. The three of them were just emerging toward the light when a hulking figure loomed in the foreground, blocking the sun and them from going any farther.

"Adam Semyonovitch," Isaak's voice conveyed heartiness, wariness, exhaustion, and warning. Though Daria couldn't quite tell whom the latter was for. "Meet my new daughter-in-law."

Daria moved obligingly into the path of a man who she realized was not, in fact, a giant. He stood barely taller than Edward. But while Daria's husband's slender frame suggested a cultured, poetic delicacy, like a prizewinning stalk of wheat sketched by a sensitive artist, the man in front of them was built more broadly. Daria wondered if the width of his shoulders matched her own height. The muscles of his forearms strained against a shirt a wash or two away from tearing. It had already been patched, surprisingly neatly, along the elbows. Red hair covered his head, drifting south into a matching beard, stray tufts protruding from his collar and on the backs of his hands. Unlike Edward's, his fingers looked as if they'd been forged out of steel by a blunt hammer.

"How do you do?" Daria remembered her mother's edict that

you could tell a person's breeding from how they never lost their manners, no matter the circumstances.

No reply. No indication he'd even heard.

"Adam Semyonovitch is our *dvornik*," Isaak went on.

Now the heartiness, wariness, exhaustion, and warning made sense. Although on paper, a *dvornik* was a combination porter and janitor, over the past decade, it had become a much more important position. A *dvornik* didn't just sweep the sidewalk, empty the rubbish bin, mop the hallways, and lock the front gate in the evening. Because he did those things, he also kept track of every resident's—and their guests'—comings and goings, not to mention made himself familiar with the contents of their refuse, those items they attempted to shred and burn, such as personal letters, newspapers, pamphlets, and books. He saw what rationed foods they ate and made note of those they must have acquired illegally. He could also choose to bolt the gate earlier than scheduled and pretend not to hear their frantic ringing of the bell, thus locking residents out of their homes for the night. And he could, on a whim, share everything he knew with the local authorities.

No wonder Isaak faked being happy to see Adam, even as his tone betrayed how tired he was of appeasing this domestic tyrant who, theoretically, worked for him. Though, in the USSR, all men were equal. No one worked for anyone. Isaak's warning, Daria now realized, was for her.

"I hope you'll make my wife welcome." Edward's tone encompassed the same affableness, with a touch of pleading, and yet a bit of arrogance, too. No matter how powerful Adam may have been, Edward was still Edward Gordon, international musical sensation.

"Welcome." Adam's voice sounded like crushed glass soaked in vodka, then run through the mud and used to coat his throat. Daria felt as if she were being sliced by it.

Edward took Daria by the elbow and guided her past Adam, into the courtyard. A circle of greenery surrounded by a waist-high, cast-iron fence, dandelions struggling to breathe among the choking weeds, occupied the center. It was dwarfed on three sides by gray, five-story buildings, their patched brick facades crumbling, their balconies trembling. They were used as storage. Most feared setting foot upon the rickety structures. The deeper they entered, the more the air smelled of feline urine, stagnant soapy water, rotting fish, and fermented pickles.

It wasn't until they were heading upstairs to the third floor—Isaak apologized again; the elevator was for those who lived in the front—that Edward lowered his voice and, glancing around to make sure no one could overhear, told Daria, "Adam got his position by informing on his own mother. She died in prison. Tortured, they say. Becoming *dvornik* was his reward."

Chapter 3

━━━

Daria and Edward's first child, a daughter named Alyssa, was born the next year, followed by a second, Anya, two years later, in 1934. Both girls had their mother's luxurious waves of ebony hair, their father's glittering green eyes and his slender build, down to those aristocratic fingers. Neither showed signs of having inherited the hooked, incriminating nose Daria's mother had taken great care to breed out of their bloodline. Mama pronounced the offspring acceptable. Though she did wish Daria had waited longer and spaced them out in more upper-class fashion. Mama accused Daria of dropping litters like a peasant. Genteel women, she insisted, gave birth once.

"You are not a broodmare," Mama lectured. "You are a queen, a lioness."

Daria bit her tongue to keep from pointing out that lions were cats. Who delivered litters.

Daria also didn't feel the need to explain to Mama that it was difficult to space out children when your husband spent every moment he wasn't at his piano looking at you as if you were the most alluring thing he'd ever seen. When he could barely wait for the door to the room his father had graciously conceded to the newlyweds to close before he was reaching for Daria, stripping off her clothes along with his own, and, from their first night together, taking care to ensure her pleasure matched his own, instructing her in what he liked as well as encouraging her to explore and direct him. Under circumstances like that, having two children in three years was not that prolific.

Edward did travel a great deal. Daria went with him at first, but it became difficult once Alyssa was born and impossible by the time Anya came along. Comrade Stalin unveiling his battle against enemies wishing to destroy the socialist state via infiltration of foreign elements, and curtailing international travel as a result, proved a relief to Daria, though she expected Edward to be incensed. His father certainly was. As soon as he'd ensured no one could overhear, Isaak defiantly whispered about stupid decisions made by stupid members of stupid committees. Edward declined to throw a tantrum like his father and many of his colleagues. Unable to perform abroad, he displayed an unexpected pragmatism, making no fuss about limiting his appearances to traveling among the Soviet republics.

"It's like music, Papa. You have to let it flow where it wants. You can't force it. All you can do is adjust the key and find your rightful rhythm within it."

Edward insisted on seeing the silver lining. He said the limits on traveling left him more time to practice, which he did for hours each day, his delicate, precise fingers caressing the keys in a manner not dissimilar from the one that made Daria sing her own high notes. Rather than tiring, Edward drew energy from his playing. While other musicians might battle their pieces, frequently ending up defeated in the process, Edward followed Bach or Rachmaninoff's lead to inevitable triumph. Daria watched the familiar electricity charging up his hands into his brain, the resultant light radiating from his eyes like an addiction.

"He was like this as a youngster," her father-in-law boasted. "Never had to force him to practice. My burden was to make him stop! If I didn't, he would forget to eat, to sleep. The foolish boy told me once he thought he could live on music alone!"

Daria's mother approved of no third child appearing after Anya turned two and then three. Mama assumed Daria had heeded her sensible advice. But, in fact, it was because both girls were now sharing a bedroom with their parents. While neither Daria's nor Edward's ardor or enthusiasm had dimmed, timing became increasingly complicated.

They forced themselves to wait until the children were asleep, gambling that neither would wake unexpectedly. One night, after pleasuring Edward in the "French" manner he'd introduced her to, the pair struggled to stifle their laughter, imagining a bleary-eyed Alyssa or Anya catching them in the act and turning her parents in for the crime of engaging in cosmopolitan and foreign anti-Soviet activities.

They were joking, of course; anything else was ridiculous to contemplate. Except that, a few years earlier, a thirteen-year-old boy named Pavlik Morozov had reported his father, chairman of the village soviet, as a criminal who forged documents and sold them to enemies of the state. Pavlik's father was tried, sent to a labor camp, and later executed. In return, Pavlik's uncle, grandparents, and cousin killed the heroic child—and his younger brother, too. Now Pavlik was a martyr and a role model for good Soviet children everywhere. In their nursery school, Alyssa and Anya sang "The Song of the Hero Pioneer," chirping, "Our comrade is a hero / He did not allow his father / To steal the property of the people . . . To all youngsters, Morozov is our example / We are a squad of heroes / Morozov is dear to us / The Pioneers will not forget him."

Daria had lost track of how many times she'd heard the children perform it for parents at holiday concerts on May Day, Red Army Day, even New Year's Day. It sounded most peculiar when they belted it out, including the gory details of Pavlik's murder, next to a white-bearded, red-suited, jolly Grandfather Frost, beneath a *yolka* decorated with ornaments and tinsel. Edward cringed every time he heard it. Daria hoped people would assume it was due to the dreadfully tuned piano on which the nursery-school teacher hammered out her accompaniment, and not something that could be branded political. Because anything could be.

Just last month, there'd been a disturbance in their own courtyard. In the building across the way, on the fifth floor, two families who shared a communal apartment had gotten into a row. From what Daria could glean via the screaming that screeched out their window and ricocheted against anything within hearing range, one of the wives had stretched her clothesline across their shared kitchen, leaving soiled socks and underpants to drip water into the soup the second wife was preparing for her husband's midday dinner on the stove. The second wife responded by yanking down the laundry, which she called filthy and disgusting, and flinging it out the window onto the frozen mud. In retaliation, the first wife grabbed the cooking pot and dumped its contents out the window—onto her own laundry. That's when at least one husband got involved. Arriving home to find either his dinner or his unmentionables in a sodden heap on the steps, and hearing the screaming from above, he chose to join in.

Throwing his head back, he howled, "Fuck your Comrade Stalin, and your Comrade Lenin, too. Gypsy thieves! Stealing my home, squatting in my kitchen. I worked for it, I earned it, and you just come from your stinking Romania and take it! Moldovan, my ass. Gypsies, that's what you are!"

"Close the window!" Edward's father, catching Daria peeking, pulled her back and reached for the shutters. "You don't want them to know we heard and didn't say anything."

The final round of name-calling brought Adam out from his underground room beside the gate. Looking bored, he shoved the cursing husband toward the street, ignoring how "Fuck Stalin" and "Fuck you, gypsies," turned into "Fuck you, you motherfucking informer."

At this point, one wife came flying down the stairs, tripping over the coat she'd had time only to throw on, not to button.

"No, please, Adam Semyonovitch, let him stay. He didn't mean it. Everything is fine now."

"Everything's not fine!" her husband roared. "How much are you going to let these Red bastards keep taking from us? First our home, then our food, now our honor!"

"Shut your drunken mouth about your goddamn honor!" She screamed at her husband while turning to plead with Adam, latching onto his forearm, which did about as much good as if she'd been trying to stop a chopped tree from falling. "He doesn't know what he's saying. He's been ill. His fever must have returned. Please, Adam Semyonovitch, let me take him upstairs. We'll settle it ourselves. We won't be any trouble ever again; you have my word, please, Comrade."

The appeal proved unappealing. Adam kept moving, shaking the hysterical woman off like melting snow on his sleeve and dragging her husband through the tunnel and out the gate, locking it. He ignored the man's now contrite pleas from the other side, his promises to behave, his assurance that he hadn't meant what he said—it was a joke between dear friends; all Soviet peoples were dear friends now, even the thieving Gypsies . . .

The Chaika limousine came three days later. In the morning, like always. Four a.m. They whispered it was because that's when the accused were in their deepest state of sleep and would have the most difficult time launching a defense. Not that anyone was listening to what they were saying. The family was caught by surprise. It had been over seventy-two hours since the inciting incident; maybe they believed that they were safe. That the outburst, like Daria's father-in-law wanted, hadn't been observed by anyone. No one reported them. They'd gotten away with it.

They hadn't.

They took the husband and the wife. Herding them out to the car wearing the nightclothes they'd found them in. No coats, no hats, not even a shared shawl. They would be fine for a while. It was less freezing in the car. And later, there weren't enough wraps to keep you warm in the isolator on Marazly Street, where political prisoners were kept separate from common criminals. Unless, of course, these were important enough to be processed straight through to Kiev. Or worse, Moscow.

They took the children, too. No one was sure where they'd end up. After all, could ten-year-old twins, a boy and a girl, be enemies of the state? Then again, they'd heard what their parents said and, unlike Pavlik Morozov, hadn't informed. That would be counted against them.

The rest of the tenants were spared this time. Daria suspected her father-in-law had been holding his breath throughout the entire operation, looking around their rooms, speculating about what he'd be allowed to keep with him in exile.

Once the crisis had passed, within ten minutes of the Chaika pulling out of the courtyard, the primary communal neighbors took over the abandoned space, rifling through the departed's things, keeping what they liked, tossing the refuse into the street for the rest of them to fight over. Through the window, Daria spied a clothesline now snaking along the length of the kitchen.

After that, even the bravest inhabitants stopped looking Adam in the eye. Those, like Daria's father-in-law, who, in the past, had attempted to make jokes, thinking they could josh the sullen giant into good humor through their own example, or, at least, a polite "Good morning, Adam Semyonovitch," "Good evening, Adam Semyonovitch," "How pleasant that the rain has stopped, Adam Semyonovitch," now scurried by him, heads down, shoulders hunched, practically groveling along the ground in a dual attempt to court his favor and escape his notice.

It made Daria furious. Because it reminded her of her mother. Her brave, clever mother, who'd disobeyed Daria's father to send her to school, who'd ignored their neighbors preaching about the dangers of the city, who'd set out to make her own luck where her daughter's marriage prospects were concerned, and who'd stuck to her guns even when it looked like all her planning might prove for naught, turning to God only as a very last resort. And then Daria was forced to recall how Mama had acted in front of Edward and his father. Like she was afraid of them, like she wasn't good enough for them, like she owed them an apology for not having had their advantages, like she wasn't deserving of being treated like a person.

Daria had convinced herself to forgive Edward and Isaak for making Mama feel that way. She'd rationalized that it wasn't their fault, that the inferiority was in Mama's mind, that they'd been as polite as could be expected under the circumstances. But Daria would be damned before she'd give Adam the satisfaction of making her feel that way.

So while everyone else crawled, Daria stood up straighter. While everyone else feigned a fantastic interest in their watches or making certain they didn't slip on a patch of treacherous ice by keeping their eyes peeled to the ground at all times, Daria made sure to look Adam square in the face. She bade the girls to wish him good morning and good evening in Russian and, once, when her mother was visiting, in Yiddish. With a patronymic like Semyonovitch, Adam was no better than they were, in that respect. He was also a Jew. He couldn't claim his ancestry was any more patriotic. Daria wanted him to know she was aware of that fact. Her mother cringed and later read Daria the riot act. How dare Daria shame her new family in such a brazen manner? Did she want them to send her packing? Did she want to end up no better than before? And after all the labor Mama did to make certain no one could accuse her Daria of being provincial trash! Speaking Yiddish, no less! Daria would be the death of them all!

Daria apologized profusely. Then, when Mama returned home, continued right on doing what she'd been doing. After Adam came to tell Daria Alyssa was playing in front of the building with a dead rat, wrapping it in old newspapers like a baby doll in a blanket, chastising Daria for risking all of them catching the plague, she made sure to thank him and pull a protesting Alyssa away, even as she made it clear the disgust in her voice was targeted not at her daughter's unconventional idea of a plaything, but at him.

She knew it terrified her father-in-law, but Edward took it in stride. "She's merely saying good morning to the *dvornik*, Papa. She's not doing anything wrong. None of us is doing anything wrong, so there is nothing to be afraid of."

Edward believed what he was saying.

Even on the morning when the authorities turned up for them.

Chapter 4

═══

They were no longer called the OGPU, the Joint State Political Directorate. As of 1934, they were the NKVD, the People's Commissariat for Internal Affairs. While the arrival time was familiar—almost four a.m. on the dot—there was no Chaika. Daria and Edward were roused by two officers wearing matching calf-length gray coats with red epaulets at the open collar and parallel golden buttons down the front, and loose pants more appropriate for Russian folk dancing. The coats were belted at the waist, a pistol in a holster over each hip. They advised Daria and Edward that they had fifteen minutes to get dressed, gather their children and whatever belongings they thought they could carry, and meet them outside. The old man was not included in the order. He was to remain inside and not cause any trouble.

"There's been a mistake," Edward began. "We haven't done anything wrong."

Not needing to read off the piece of paper in his hand, the lead officer droned, "Members of the nationalistic Germanic race who pose a threat to the stability and unity of the Soviet are enemies of the people and are to be removed by order of Nikita Khrushchev, Vyacheslav Molotov, and Genrikh Yagoda."

"The Germanic . . . Oh! I see! There's your mistake." Edward smiled, happy to help them identify and rectify this error. "We are not Germans. I'll show you." He hurried to the polished wooden box sitting on the shelf over their bed, where Daria and Edward kept the internal passports they'd reported to be issued as soon as that law was passed at the end of 1932. "There, you see? My passport, my wife's. Look, right here, on the fifth line. Nationality: Jewish. We are Jews, not Germans."

"And loyal citizens!" Edward's father shouted from the room to which he'd been banished. It was February; the front door was open. Isaak was wearing his robe over pajamas. Nonetheless, his frantic shivering was still out of proportion to the temperature.

Their self-described escort barely glanced at the documents. "You have been overheard speaking German."

"To my mother," Daria rushed to explain. "My mother speaks Yiddish—we are Jews." She poked her finger at the passport. "Yiddish sounds similar to German."

"Fifteen minutes," the officer repeated, and stepped outside with his colleague to wait for them.

By this point, the girls had awoken and were sitting in their beds. Well, not beds, exactly. None had been available for purchase over the past several years—a production shortage, they were informed by *Pravda*, caused by saboteurs slowing down their factory work to deprive the Soviet people of basic necessities. So Alyssa and Anya slept on a pair of chairs turned toward each other and covered with a sheet, pillow, and blanket. Edward and Daria agreed it was for the best. Not only did the furniture now serve two purposes—they were being good citizens by not promoting waste or diverting resources from where they were more needed—but it gave them extra room during the day. Beds would have taken up precious space.

"Get up," Daria urged her daughters. Knowing, though she couldn't say how, that the time for appeals had passed. She felt her mother inhabiting her senses, directing her actions, telling Daria their one chance of getting back home was to do what they were told, to deal with each new aspect of the situation as it happened. Anything else would make it worse. Survive now. Figure everything else out later.

Daria hurried to dress her girls in as many layers as she could, the same way she and Mama had first come to Odessa, so they wouldn't have as much to carry. Underpants and undershirts, woolen tights, then their thickest trousers. A long-sleeved turtleneck sweater, warm dresses over that, followed by winter coats she could barely button. She told the children to hold them closed with both hands. Daria pulled heavy socks on over their tights, then stuffed their feet into boots, happy that, on the one day kids' shoes became available in Odessa, she'd been able to get her hands only on pairs two sizes too big. She'd intended for them to grow into the footwear, but this was even better. Alyssa and Anya complained, crying that they were hot, that their toes were squished, that they couldn't move.

"Papa and I will carry you," Daria dismissed, then proceeded to dress herself in the same manner.

Edward stood in the center of the room, looking from her to the girls to his sobbing father, who'd come out to watch them, unsure of what he should be doing to either help or stop the frenzy.

"Here." Daria shoved long underwear, pants, a shirt, a sweater, and a coat at him, along with two pairs of socks and gloves. "Hurry!"

"We should bring money," Edward said as if his metabolism had stalled and it was taking all his concentration just to form a thought, then turn it into words. "Money for bribes. That's always helpful when I travel."

Daria decided now was not the time to advise him that they weren't going traveling. She doubted the accommodations would be up to his usual standards. Why frighten either him or the girls before she had to? Daria could agonize enough for the both of them. And prepare, too.

"Jewelry is better." She went back into the box that once held their passports, grabbing the pearl necklace that had been her late mother-in-law's, the ruby pin in the shape of a rose Edward had brought back from his trip to France the year they were married, and the golden hoop earrings he said made her look like an exotic Gypsy. Whenever Daria wore them, Edward rushed to the piano to sing a rousing chorus of "*Ochi Chernye*," or "Dark Eyes." There were also their wedding rings, their watches. "Jewelry is easier to barter."

Daria looked around, mindful of the ticking clock, trying to think of what else might come in handy wherever they were going, for however long. Medicine? Food? Water? A toy to keep the children entertained? Daria glanced at Edward, hoping he, with his broader experience, might have ideas. She followed his gaze to the object he was staring at with the greatest reluctance to leave.

They were not bringing the piano.

"Let's go," she ordered, lest they exceed their fifteen-minute allotment. Who knew what penalties that could bring? "Goodbye, Isaak Israelevitch. We'll be back as soon as we can. Say goodbye to your grandfather, girls. Say *dosvedanya*." Until our next meeting.

"*Dosvedanya*, Deda," they sang, sleepy and befuddled, but also excited by the unexpected adventure.

"*Proschai*," her father-in-law replied, peering at his granddaughters, at Daria, and finally at Edward. *Proschai* meant farewell. And forgive. It was what people said at funerals.

THEY WERE THE sole family taken out of their building that night. No one else was seen, although Daria knew their neighbors were all awake. None would dare turn on a light and be caught looking. She wondered which ones would attempt to claim their best belongings first, and whether Isaak would have the strength—or if he would feel too cowed—to keep them from robbing him. As a relative of the enemies of the people, anything Isaak owned, by definition, became contraband, and thus fair game for looting.

They were not, however, the sole ones being rounded up as darkness turned into dawn. Which explained the lack of car and the forced march toward the railway station. As they drew closer to their destination, soldiers walking on either side like a perverse honor guard, Daria spied other men, women, and children huddled in uneven groups, whether for warmth, protection, or familiarity. Some German was, in fact, being spoken, but it was mostly Russian, along with a spattering of Yiddish.

Moments after they arrived, the family huddles were broken up, some by a pair of hands and a barked command, others by the long, narrow barrels of rifles wielded by soldiers stationed at key spots along the station to keep the prisoners from escaping. Daria wondered where they thought any runaways could go. The same passports that listed their nationalities as Jewish—though a lot of help that had been—also included Edward and Daria's stamp of marriage and their legally approved residence. Attempting to settle in a different part of town or leave Odessa and blend in elsewhere would lead to criminal charges of relocation without permission.

Lined up side by side, they were ordered to kneel beside the tracks, hands behind their heads, bent at the waist, chins down. Daria was so busy trying to help the overdressed, hard-to-configure Alyssa and Anya into the required positions between her and Edward that she didn't notice the shadowy figure on the other side of her husband, until a quick sweep of a flashlight illuminated his face.

Adam.

"What are you . . ." she blurted out, starting in her normal voice, dropping to a whisper at Adam's murderous expression. This made no sense. "You're the one who turned us in!" Who else had the means and the motive?

"I was turned in," Adam corrected, "for not turning you in. How could there be German nationals living under my own nose, and I not be aware of it?"

Between them, Edward, emboldened by Adam's confirmation that they were here under false pretenses, straightened up and, once again, attempted to get a guard's attention. "Excuse me, Comrade, I believe a mistake has been made—"

Adam's arm swung down from his head like dead weight as he rammed his fist into Edward's stomach. Daria's husband doubled over, gagging. She caught him with both hands beneath his chest before Edward's face hit the ground, struggling to keep him on his knees.

A split second later, a guard came down their row, oscillating the narrow barrel of his Mosin rifle to ensure everyone's head was at the same level. If Adam hadn't knocked Edward down, Daria's husband would have been struck. Instead, the weapon passed over Adam, over Edward, over Daria and the girls, and smashed the skull of a man a few spaces down. Blood streamed from the spot where his eye had been, pooling around his head as it cracked open atop the railroad track. When the rest of them were ordered to stand and commence marching in an orderly fashion toward the waiting cattle cars, he didn't budge. They made a point of pretending not to notice, gingerly stepping over his twitching form, as if he were an inconvenient puddle.

Adam jerked Edward to his feet by the back of his coat and shoved him in the appropriate direction, followed by Daria.

"The wheat that grows tallest," Adam advised them, "gets cut first."

Chapter 5

The children played. As their multiday—multiweek? With so little light, it was impossible to keep track of time passing—journey from the shores of the Black Sea into the depths of Siberia faded into a single, jostling, nauseating ache, the one fact that never failed to startle Daria anew was that the children had played.

There were a handful of them in their cattle car, in addition to Alyssa and Anya. Twenty-five families or more packed in, jostling for a space to sit or, at least, to lean against a wall farthest from the hole cut in the floor that was to serve as a latrine. Frigid air, as well as a sliver of sunlight scraped its way in through slits at the top. Edward, standing on his toes, was able to strain and scrape off a few handfuls of snow that they melted in their hands, then gave to Alyssa and Anya when the girls' polite requests for a drink of water turned into tears. Other parents made do by breaking off the icicles that formed inside and offering them to their children to suck. When the cries of thirst turned to hunger, Daria slipped off Edward's leather belt, soaked it for as long as she could by filling one of her shoes with water, and told Alyssa and Anya to suck on it, along with the ration of bread every passenger received once a day.

The children complained, the children whined, the children

whimpered that they were hungry and cold, that the floor was too hard to sleep on, that being held over rushing train tracks to relieve themselves was scary—what if they slipped out of their parents' hands and fell? They'd be run over by the massive, un-relenting wheels! Daria harbored the same fears, but she insisted on pasting on a smile and setting a good example, hiking up her skirts and yanking down her tights and attempting to remain modest while teetering precariously. Edward stood in front of her to shield his wife from leering or disgusted eyes, but he could do only so much.

And yet the children also played. Patty-cake and twenty ques-tions and, when the adults attempted to clear a little space for them in the middle of the cattle car, goosey, goosey. One child stood at the front and chanted, "Goosey, goosey, ga, ga, ga / Are you hungry? / Yes, you are! / Then fly as you want, but don't get your wings caught! There's a wolf lying in wait!" That child would then turn his back. The rest would attempt to move forward before he pivoted again. Daria wondered if they weren't all playing some kind of perverted, twisted version of the same game.

Every day, she thanked the impulse that had prompted her to bundle them in layers. Many had come unprepared, and their hack-ing, bronchial coughs echoed to disturb the scant minutes of sleep the rest could catch, children curled up on parents' laps, adults taking turns sitting, resting on each other's shoulders, legs tucked underneath, heads bumping against raw wooden walls, precious belongings stuffed behind their backs or buttoned close to their chests to prevent the theft that was already rampant, despite what should have been dozens of witnesses. After the first accusation led to a fistfight, which led to soldiers breaking it up by flinging both men off the train and pumping several bullets into each before they'd even risen to their shaken feet, no one dared risk admitting they'd seen anything.

"This will be over soon," Edward assured Daria and the girls, remaining optimistic after plenty of others had given in to doomed hysterics or helplessness. While they wept or cursed or railed, Edward sang. Long passages from the Gilbert and Sullivan opera *Patience*, translating it from English to Russian. From Italian to Russian, he translated excerpts of *Madame Butterfly*, about her life of patient waiting, and the relevant verses about hope and patience from *Turandot*. Daria spied a theme. She endeavored to hide her annoyance. Matters were rarely as simple in life as they were onstage. But it did keep Alyssa and Anya distracted. Edward assuaged, "Once we get to our destination, I'll speak with the person in charge, and we'll straighten everything out. They'll see they made a mistake. We're not German; we don't belong here." That last part he whispered, lest their neighbors overhear. Edward looked at them with great sympathy. He was a compassionate person. He felt sorry they, too, wouldn't have such an easy out.

At long last, their train creaked into a desolate depot at literally the end of the road. There were no tracks to go any farther. "There, you see, I told you; here we are," Edward announced, acting as if the entire journey had been nothing more than a travel mix-up, which he expected his agent to take care of now that they'd arrived. Soldiers flung open doors, shouting for everyone to rise to their feet. All did as swiftly as they could, pressuring muscles stiffened from the cramped quarters to, once again, serve their purpose. Daria's knees buckled, and she grabbed the wall to steady herself. She raised one arm above her head and haltingly waved it up and down, restoring the blood flow to her fingers. As she did so, she realized there was more room to maneuver than there had been at the start of the journey. In addition to the two men who'd been shot, a trio of elderly women and an infant's corpse had also been disposed of. The mother of the lost baby now needed to be pulled to her feet by her husband. She stumbled getting out of the train and didn't even throw out her hands to break her fall. Her husband picked her up off the ground, her face now bloodied, and dragged her to line up with the rest of them.

How many were there? Raggedy lines of men, women, and

children stretched out in either direction across the otherwise plundered landscape. Daria spotted Adam getting out from a cattle car three over. His height and red hair made him difficult to miss. He glanced Daria's way, noticed Edward, still trying to catch the attention of someone in authority, and shook his head in disgust. Daria would have thought herself capable of feeling only hungry, freezing, and exhausted. Apparently, she still had space left for furious.

En masse, they were marched away from the trains, several kilometers over and toward a wood of pine, cedar, and spruce so dense, there was no room for sunlight between the trees. They followed what must have been a road; the frozen mud beneath their feet was more packed than the mud leading up to the entrances of the lean-tos, shacks, and makeshift cabins on either side that they passed. There were a few traditional houses, too, with glass in the windows and kerosene lamps glowing within. No residents could be seen.

The pretense of a road ended as abruptly as the railroad tracks had. They stood in a clearing between the trees. Wooden barracks, not so different from the cattle cars they'd exited, loomed ahead. Dozens. Yet still not enough for everyone who'd been unloaded.

"Go!" A soldier who'd met them at the station and marched them here, pointed toward the barracks. "Claim your space." The "before someone else does" was implied.

For a moment, no one moved, either not understanding the order or unable to believe it had been issued. Adam was the first to swing into action, pushing aside those in front of him and striding toward the nearest barracks. He flung open the door, poked his head in, then withdrew just as quickly. Daria could see why. It was already packed to the rafters.

Adam moved deeper into the settlement. When, after examining several other options, he didn't exit the last one, Daria grabbed both girls by the hands and pulled them in the same direction, trusting Edward to follow. She barely managed to elbow her way past others who'd come to the same idea. She threw herself down on the first available bunk, the middle of three protruding from the wall, a few meters across from the opposing trio. The room had rows and rows of wooden slats, hardly big enough for one, much less the four of them—Daria noticed Adam managed to claim a single for himself, albeit up top, beneath the rotting boards of the dripping ceiling. Other than that, there was a stove in the corner, a few faint chips of wood glowing and sputtering with every gust of wind, and a bucket that smelled worse than any outhouse Daria had ever known.

"I'm sorry, Mama," Daria couldn't help thinking. "All your hard work, and I'm worse off now than we ever were, just like you warned me!" Because Daria hadn't listened. Because she'd provoked Adam. Daria didn't believe his denial of having been the one who turned them in. Even the fact that Adam had also been ensnared in their dragnet proved little comfort.

The weathered faces of men, women, and disturbingly few children peered out at the new arrivals from the depths of their already occupied bunks. They didn't look curious. They didn't look sympathetic. They didn't look disdainful. They didn't look anything at all.

"Tomorrow," Edward promised the girls as he took off their coats and improvised nests at the foot of the bunk, while he and Daria attempted to wrap around each other at the opposite end. "Everything will be better tomorrow."

It wasn't.

Daria wasn't even sure it was the next day when soldiers came through again, in pairs, grabbing people by the arm, the leg, the neck, and yanking them onto the ground. They wrenched off coats and shoes, stuffing them into burlap sacks, gesturing for them to strip off the rest. Daria was down to her undergarments, when she realized they meant everything. And not just her, the children, too.

"No, please." Daria pulled the shivering girls closer; they clung to her, faces pressed against her thighs. She rubbed their goose-pimpled shoulders with her own frigid hands. "They're so cold."

In response, the guard reached across and yanked down a strap of Daria's brassiere. One breast sprang out and flopped against her rib cage. Edward, who'd been standing stripped beside her, his hand outstretched, clutching their open passports, looked from Daria's nakedness, to the guard, to his wife's stunned face. His arm collapsed, along with his hope. Daria shoved the girls for Edward to hold, freeing her palms to cover herself. But just like she'd once been unable to heed Mama's sensible advice and refrain from baiting Adam, Daria again refused to perform as expected of her. Instead of cowering, she haughtily unhooked her brassiere and dropped the remainder of her clothes into the guard's out-stretched bag.

Edward did the same, though a great deal more meekly. Too late, Daria remembered the jewelry hidden in their pockets. She hadn't thought to remove and hide it . . . where? All they had was their bunk. But she hadn't expected to have their clothes taken away. To think she'd been so proud of her resourcefulness in over-dressing them, and now all the jewelry she'd brought for bribes was gone.

Daria supposed she would have felt more embarrassed to be standing exposed, if everyone around them weren't being equally humiliated. And if it weren't so bitterly cold that it was all she could think about. A second guard maneuvered down the narrow aisle between bunks. His sack was filled with a hodgepodge of army surplus uniforms, prisoner garb, and clothes Daria guessed had been stripped off previous prisoners—or the dead—that no one else wanted. He reached in and distributed indiscriminately, giving Edward a pair of pants too wide at the waist and too short in the legs, while Daria was flung a jacket that barely buttoned across the chest. The girls got men's shirts that brushed the floor. Shoe size wasn't even a consideration.

"Trade." The guard shrugged. "No personal belongings here.

No more bourgeois fashion. You are being granted the privilege of earning your keep. You will no longer be useless persons. Be grateful. Don't make us regret our leniency."

Dressed for their new, productive lives, all the adults were marched outside, the children ordered to stay, no word on whether they'd be taken care of or fed. Alyssa and Anya clung to Daria's legs, then, when she peeled them off, to Edward's. He patted them both reassuringly on the heads but looked to Daria for the next step.

She tugged Alyssa by one arm, Anya by the other, though each kept a hand still glued to Edward's thighs.

"There are rules here," Daria said, "just like at school and at home. If you follow them, everything will be all right."

"I don't want to follow the rules." The frustration Anya had been keeping pent up burst out in a river of tears, with a full-out tantrum not far behind.

Their work details were leaving. Daria glanced desperately over her shoulder, wondering how much time she had to calm Anya down before their guards returned to drag them out.

To her surprise, Alyssa intervened, pulling Anya away from their parents, holding on to both her sister's shoulders. "If you follow the rules," Alyssa repeated sternly, "everything will be all right. Mama said."

Chapter 6

The sun was coming up, though still unable to penetrate the forest. In addition to prisoners and guards, Daria spied men and women she guessed were from the village they'd passed. They were dressed better: sturdier shoes, stockings, hats, scarves, mittens.

"They were once like you," the guard droned on. "Traitors. Parasites. Enemies of the state. This is not a prison." He gestured toward the forest. "There, on the other side, you may see what a true prison is. We are the Siberian settlement of Kyril. We have come to tame the land, to lay roads and cultivate crops, to demonstrate to the world what Soviet labor can produce. We will conquer the tundra even as others say it cannot be done. You are not prisoners. You are pioneers who will prove your worth through honest work. You will build homes to raise your children, you will build schools to educate all children, you will be heroes of the Motherland!"

Daria's teeth chattered. The wind sliced through her chest. Every breath felt colder coming out than going in. Her lungs tightened. The soles of her feet burned. She could no longer bend her fingers. Opening her mouth ripped her stiff cheeks. Daria stole a glance at Edward. He was staring straight ahead, afraid of taking his eyes off their speaker. He breathed in short, nervous gasps. His legs trembled, prompting him to shift his weight from foot to foot.

His arms hung limply, but his fingers twitched, picking out a virtual composition. It had been Edward's calming mechanism since childhood, his father had told Daria. How lucky for him to still have that, she thought.

"You!" The guard zeroed in on Daria's husband.

Edward recoiled. He looked as if he might run, though where? The guard grabbed Edward by the shoulder and tugged him forward, twisting Edward around to face the assembled. Edward stumbled, knees buckling as his ankles rotated beneath him. He was jerked back up onto his feet.

"Confess," the guard ordered.

Edward stared at him dumbly.

"Your crimes," the guard prompted.

"I-I . . ." Edward stammered, looking around helplessly, eyes settling on Daria, beseeching her to explain what was expected of him. "I . . . didn't do anything."

"In that case, you wouldn't be here." The guard shoved Edward down. Edward landed on all fours, his palms breaking through the frozen ground on impact and sinking into the mud up to his wrists, jagged ice slicing his flesh.

The guard pointed at a woman standing next to Daria. She'd been nodding her head the entire time he was speaking. "Please demonstrate for our comrade"—the guard balanced the heel of his boot on Edward's back, forcing Daria's husband to arch his spine under the pressure—"how a righteous Soviet citizen engages in *samokritika*, self-criticism."

She'd been waiting for an opportunity to demonstrate her allegiance and gleefully launched into a prepared litany. "I undermined the work of the Party. I hoarded food. I conspired with foreign elements. I stole from the people. I elevated the individual above the collective. I disseminated anti-Soviet propaganda. I slowed down productivity at my place of employment." This went on for over ten minutes. If she'd been allowed to continue, Daria felt certain the woman would confess to colluding with Leon Trotsky prior to his expulsion—despite being a schoolgirl in 1928.

Her toneless recitation bored even the guard. He kicked her back into line, removing his boot from Edward's back, allowing Daria's husband to painstakingly rise.

"Now, Comrade," the guard repeated. "It is your turn. Confess."

Edward's eyes widened, even as his lips remained all but frozen shut.

Seeing her husband still at a loss, Daria burst forward. "He accompanied the anti-proletariat opera, *Lady Macbeth of Mtsensk*!"

The guard looked at her in confusion. Clearly, he hadn't read *Pravda*'s January attack on Dimitri Shostakovich's music, which prompted Comrade Stalin to walk out of a performance at the Bolshoi and denounce the production as a bourgeois muddle that eschewed simple, accessible musical language for quacks, hoots, pants, and gasps. It was banned immediately. Edward's father went about for days mumbling what a fool Shostakovich was to take such a risk, not just with his professional future but with his life.

The guard, on the other hand, wasn't about to be so foolish. Though he clearly had no idea what Daria was referring to, revealing his ignorance might well prove to be an equally deadly faux pas. How dare anyone not be aware of Comrade Stalin's feelings on the matter? And so he deemed Daria's confession on Edward's behalf an adequate beginning.

"We will now vote," he announced. "Despite your malicious attempts to undermine him, Comrade Stalin still offers a true ruling by the people. Even here. Even for you. A show of hands, to demonstrate who found this criminal's *samokritika* sufficient and sincere?"

The newcomers shifted awkwardly, uncertain what was expected of them. Were they meant to agree that Daria's confession on Edward's part was adequate, since the guard seemed to initially deem it so, or were they meant to judge it insincere since neither had yet to offer remorse, merely acknowledgment? The wrong response could get one of them pulled to the front as another example. Or worse.

They exchanged nervous looks among themselves, unsure of what to do.

"Come now! This is a democracy! Vote! You are Soviet citizens, you know how. Raise your hands to agree!"

That seemed a bit clearer. A smattering of hands went up tentatively. When no punishment proved forthcoming, they were followed by a few more, then a rush not to be the last.

"One hundred percent agreement," the guard praised. "The people have spoken. All voices heard, respected, and honored in the true spirit of Communism."

After that, he lost interest in Edward and Daria and shouted for the prisoners to separate into two groups, men to the left, women to the right.

While the clothing exchange had been a haphazard affair, with more than one item of finer quality that Daria could see disappearing not into the designated sack but into the coat pocket or boot of a guard, job assignments proved brutally efficient. Men were directed deeper into the forest. Daria tried to catch Edward's eye, to smile or wink in spite of her frozen face. She mouthed, "Just follow the rules," the same way she had for the girls.

What had her husband uttered once regarding the arbitrary caprices of history, of life? "It's like music, Papa. You have to let it flow where it wants. You can't force it. All you can do is adjust the key and find your rightful rhythm within it."

Would that be enough to keep him sane here? To keep him safe?

In the meantime, the women were led a kilometer west of the barracks, into an open and iced-over field. They were distributed shovels and seeds, directed to rows. They would be planting cucumbers, carrots, tomatoes, and cabbage. Fresh vegetables! In Siberia! Who but Comrade Stalin would be visionary enough to think up such a progressive plan? They would be self-sufficient, grow the food they needed, reduce their reliance on imports, and free up transportation resources. If there wasn't enough to eat, they'd have no one to blame but themselves—such was the unprecedented social justice of Communism.

Several of the women were farmers. Kulaks, Daria guessed. Landowners from before the Great October Socialist Revolution who'd refused to accept collectivization and thus caused the *Holodomor*, the famines. It was explained in that movie she'd watched with Edward and Mama. As punishment for their treason, Comrade Stalin had millions of kulaks relocated and their land handed over to those who would selflessly grow bread for the USSR. But Comrade Stalin was not a vengeful man. He was a leader who encouraged misguided transgressors to learn the errors of their ways. That's why he was now allowing them to create new, communal lives and ply their trade for the good of all, sharing in the inevitable bounty, despite their earlier intransigence. Except the women were trying to explain to those overseeing the production that this was the wrong season and these were the wrong crops to plant in this sort of land at this depth. Based on how the guard reacted to Daria's plea to keep her underclothes on, when this overseer raised his arm, Daria expected the woman who'd been the most vociferous objector to be slapped in the face. But he merely waved her in the direction of the field with a bored, "Do as you're told."

"Nothing will grow," she protested. "We'll starve." In desperation, she added, "They'll blame you."

"I do what I'm told," he repeated, suggesting, not unkindly, that it was in their best interests to follow his example.

So they dug. And they planted, the skin of their palms cracking from the cold and clogging with mud until the tiny seeds slipped through their numb fingers, falling in haphazard piles along the ground. The uneven gaps in between ensured that even if something did manage, against all odds, to sprout, it would be choked dead before full bloom. As she worked, Daria realized the toil was pointless. Its only purpose was to break her spirit. This was confirmed by one of the women who confided to Daria that, a few weeks earlier, she'd been assigned to dig a ditch "starting from the fence and going until dinnertime."

They weren't allowed to return to the barracks until after sundown. There, Alyssa and Anya came running into their mother's arms, upper lips chapped bright red from the snot they'd kept wiping away with the backs of their wrists.

"I was a good girl, Mama," Alyssa swore. "I watched Anya so she'd be a good girl, too. We followed all the new rules, so can we go home now?" She added the word that she'd been assured all her life possessed magical powers. "Please?"

The men were brought back even later. Daria had trouble picking Edward out of the mass that dragged themselves in, covered in identical rags, faces coated in sweat and grime and frost, until he collapsed on their bunk, curling up in a fetal position, forehead pressed against the wall. The other men around them groaned, cursed, whimpered. Edward did none of those things. Edward hummed.

Daria shooed the horrified girls away, promising she would take care of Papa. She crawled in next to Edward. She stroked his brow, his cheeks vibrating dully beneath her fingers. When he didn't respond to her caress, continuing to lie deathly still, stubbornly humming a tune Daria didn't recognize, she took Edward's hands in hers, tenderly unwrapping the scraps of cloth he'd bound them in. Edward's hands, his mesmerizing, enchanting hands—too valuable to so much as lift her suitcase on the day of their marriage—had been shredded nearly to the bone.

Chapter 7

This was their life now. Rising at dawn, women to the fields, men to logging, the children fending for themselves. Breakfast was a slice of hard bread, supper a watery broth that reminded Daria of what was left after you washed a pot that vegetables had been boiled in. Every morning, a crew came through the barracks to dispose of the dead. Every evening, a few workers failed to return. The children cried that they were hungry, then eventually stopped. The men raged and plotted revenge and threatened escape, then returned to the forest. At night, they drank moonshine that somehow still managed to materialize, even in the depths of the tundra. They played cards and they brawled over the outcomes. They remembered the lives they once had, the men they'd once been and, to hold on to what small vestiges of that they could, they loudly fucked their wives, their girlfriends, any woman they could get their hands on, their groans blending into the moans, the sobs, and the perennially howling winds.

Except for the mandatory work detail, Edward declined to join in their activities. Daria soon wished he would. Even a raging, drunk, brutish Edward would be better than one who shuffled from one narrow end of their barracks to the other. The one who sat on the edge of their bunk, eyes on the ground, humming quietly to himself. Daria attempted to engage him in conversation, if nothing else. Her own days were spent in near silence. Even if Daria weren't too bone-weary to exchange a few words with the women farming alongside her, opening her chapped lips or shifting her cracked cheeks was agony, to be risked only under the most dire of circumstances. She doubted they'd be able to hear her over the wind, anyway.

The surfeit of words congested inside Daria. She arrived back at the barracks each night bursting with them, in a frenzy finally to vomit out everything she'd kept to herself during the day, starved for human contact and connection. Daria tried to make her stories amusing for the girls, turning what had been a bitter incident into a funny one, filtering through the ugly moments to dredge up even a second of beauty, of kindness, of hope. She didn't want to upset Alyssa and Anya any further than they already were, and she didn't want them to worry about her while she was away. So instead of talking about the guard who'd ruined days of their labor by kicking up the rows they'd planted "by accident," Daria focused on the one who, at risk to himself, smuggled in a thermos of lukewarm tea he shared with his workers. When Daria relayed the story to Alyssa and Anya, she made it sound like they'd had themselves a regular tea party!

After they'd gone to sleep, though, Daria yearned to confess the darker aspect of her day to Edward. She wanted to vent. She wanted to complain. She wanted to whine, damn it. Was it too much to desire a modicum of sympathy? Daria would have been happy to do the same for Edward. Unfortunately, all it took was one look at her husband, and the words withered to sawdust in her throat. Every sound prompted Edward to startle. Loud noises made him shudder, and unexpected ones drove him deeper into the darkness of their bunk. Daria imagined if she opened her mouth and let loose with the stream of words she'd pent up for days, weeks, months, it would be akin to pummeling him with a barrage of freshly sharpened arrows.

So Daria kept her thoughts and her feelings to herself, stockpiling them the way she and the other women stockpiled rations for their children. While the men fought loudly—and impotently— the women quietly and efficiently traded clothes among themselves. They stole bones from the once-in-a-blue-moon scraps of dried fish they were accorded and fashioned them into needles they used to unravel a moth-ravaged muffler, repurposing its yarn to knit into socks, a hat. They scavenged for roots and berries, brewing folk remedies for the sick, forcing them down swollen throats, smearing them on wheezing chests.

But when it was Anya's turn to be treated, Daria and Edward's three-year-old remained delirious with fever, her breath coming in painful, desperate gasps after interminable periods of deathly silence. For the first few days of her illness, she'd managed to smile in between the hacking coughs as Edward, rousing himself from his stupor, wrapped their daughter in his arms to rub some warmth into her skin-and-bone limbs. Just like in the cattle car, Edward spent multiple nights distracting Anya with stories of magic flutes and a fiery Spanish temptress torn between a reckless officer and a dashing bullfighter. But soon, even the promise of another exotic tale from Papa wasn't enough to rouse her.

"Pneumonia," a woman from two barracks over diagnosed by putting her ear to Anya's chest and listening to her struggling, fluid-filled lungs. She was a doctor who'd been banished after her husband, a geology professor at a Leningrad university, shared with his class a piece of shale he'd received from a colleague in Australia. Contact with foreign entities was always suspect.

"What can we do?" Daria asked, knowing they had no equipment or medicine. Edward sat next to her, holding Anya.

"Antipneumococcal antiserum." The doctor uttered both words in the same fashion she might have said a fairy-tale goldfish that grants wishes.

Edward raised his head, the shell-shocked, submissive expression he now wore at all times, save when distracting Anya or humming to himself, cracking long enough for him to meekly suggest to his wife, "We could ask . . . Adam."

Though he'd arrived in Kyril the same five months ago, Adam's experience took a sharp turn. He'd been dispatched to the forest along with the rest of the men. Daria had been too preoccupied with Edward, pouring watery gruel down his throat as he gagged, rubbing homemade salve into his hands to stave off frostbite. She'd had no time or interest to gauge how Adam was adjusting. Until she noticed that he was gone. Prisoners—no, sorry, settlers—disappeared for two reasons. They were dead or—

"He's been reassigned," the man who'd slept below Adam, and scurried up to claim the abandoned bunk, told Daria. "Office staff."

A settlement of Kyril's size required massive amounts of paperwork. There were crop and logging output reports sorted by day, month, and season; supply requisitions; payroll for the local staff; and, of course, resource distribution, which included everything from the tiny seeds Daria planted uselessly to the ongoing construction of housing. Prisoners were utilized for administrative tasks, but they had to earn the privilege. Five months seemed a short time for Adam to move up the ranks. A transfer from the fields was merited by good behavior. Most frequently, though, it came about as a result of bribes. It didn't take Daria long to figure out that many of the women she worked with were squirreling seeds in the folds of their ragged clothes in order to trade with those who'd already been liberated from the barracks and allowed to build their own homes, no more than glorified lean-tos, from whatever wood they could scavenge. These families would use the seeds to grow their own secret plots of food. Even some of the highest-ranking Party officials got in on the act. Though they were allowed more sturdy housing—doors, windows, roofs, floors, and other such luxuries—their diets were also limited to what Moscow shipped out to their employees, when they remembered. And when it didn't rot on the way. As a result, their superiors either tried growing their own stash or, failing at it, traded with those who'd somehow succeeded in coaxing a crop from the frozen tundra.

But Adam hadn't been in Kyril long enough to accumulate valuables to trade, had he? Daria wondered, as not only had Adam been excused from the most backbreaking work, he'd been issued one of the largest houses, built with prison labor, which he didn't even have to share.

"Whose mother do you think he turned in this time?" Daria drawled to Edward when they'd first learned the news.

But now, her husband was suggesting maybe their former *dvornik* had somehow procured enough influence to get them the medicine Anya required.

"Write down what I need," Daria urged the doctor. "I will go ask him."

SHE WAS FORCED to wait until total darkness. Although, as they kept being reminded, they were not in prison, they could leave anytime they wished—if they were up for facing the brutal elements that stretched in every direction rather than taking advantage of Comrade Stalin's generosity—unsanctioned movement was always a risk. Especially for women alone. Bored guards, restless townspeople, vengeful fellow exiles . . . anything could happen. It didn't stop some women. Seeds and food weren't the exclusive items traded.

But Daria wasn't ready to be taken for one of those. Yet. She crept around the outskirts of the settlement, hiding in shadow, taking the long way from their barracks to the one-story construction Adam claimed as his own. She spied a sliver of light coming from the inside and quickly, before she could change her mind, knocked on the door. He opened it so briskly, she nearly fell in over the threshold.

They'd all lost weight since arriving. Edward was so skeletal, Daria could see where his hip bones met his legs. Even Adam was thinner. His collarbone was more prominent, his cheeks beneath the ruddy beard a bit more sunken. But the change in proportion made him even more towering. He reminded Daria of the children's book character Stepan Stepanov, a giant nicknamed "Fire Tower" due to his height. Uncle Styopa tromped about the Soviet Union performing charitable deeds. He rescued drowning boys, saved pigeons from a burning building, and joined the navy, as an inspiration to his fellow citizens. Except Uncle Styopa was "all kids' best friend." While Adam was terrifying.

Daria's first impulse was to shrink back, the way Edward now did at everything. But then her past resolve kicked in, and she looked Adam in the eye, needing to crane her neck. Sounding as imperious as if he still worked for her—not that it was ever true—she informed him, "I need to speak with you." She walked in without being invited and closed the door behind them.

Adam's home consisted of three sections, not counting the tiny entry where Daria was now standing. To her left was a sleeping area, housing a bed, the sheets worn and institutional but neatly made. The largest section in the middle held a desk, the legs different colors, suggesting each had been replaced over the years, and, of all things, a piano, its top missing so that the strings, not all of which were present, lay exposed to the elements. Daria guessed this had been the home of an administrator's family, before they'd either moved up, away, or . . . well, no use thinking about any other possibilities—and Adam had inherited the house, furnishings included. It was the room to the right that explained how he'd managed to do it. The room on the right stood bare. Except for the trio of homemade vodka stills chugging away in the center.

"Oh," Daria said. Now everything made perfect sense.

Adam had yet to say anything.

She asked him, "How much are you managing to produce a day?"

"Enough."

"No wonder you're so popular."

"Enough," he repeated.

"You can get anything you want from them. A house, clothes, food."

"What do you want?" Adam emphasized the third word, under no illusion about why Daria was there.

"This." She showed him the scrap of paper with the names and amounts of medication needed.

Adam's brow furrowed. "Are you trying to resuscitate a corpse?"

"My daughter, Anya. The little one. You remember her? The doctor says it's pneumonia. We've tried everything. She thinks this is the thing that might help. Please." Daria took a step closer to him, so close, too close, dangerously close. "Please, help me, Adam Semyonovitch."

Chapter 8

She expected him to ask how. She expected him to ask why he should. She expected him to demand something in return. She was prepared for all of it.

She was not prepared for Adam taking another long look at her list of medications, then folding the paper into quarters and stuffing it in his shirt pocket before escorting Daria to the door, closing it soundly behind her.

SHE DIDN'T KNOW what had happened. She didn't know what they'd agreed upon or what Adam intended to do. All she knew was that the next evening, as Daria and Edward lay in their bunk with Anya between them, trying to keep her warm, watching her struggle so hard for every breath that her face first turned bright red, then a deadly white that faded to near blue before the process started over again, the doctor crept in beside them and showed Daria and Edward the satchel she'd been slipped by . . . she'd rather not say. Comrade Stalin had taught them: *The less you know, the sounder you sleep.* But it was for Anya.

They gave her the first dose immediately. The second at midnight. The five of them were the only ones still awake, Alyssa sitting in the corner, pulling on tufts of hair and sticking the thinning strands in her mouth, chewing and swallowing. No one tried to stop her anymore, not even the doctor who'd initially attempted to explain the dangers, that she could clog up her intestines. But everyone understood how hungry Alyssa was, and if this helped, even for a little while, then long-term consequences be damned.

They tried a third dose during that devil's hour of four a.m. There was enough left for a fourth at dawn, before the guards would come to gather them for work. But Anya was dead by then.

It wasn't dramatic. It was barely noticeable. The intervals between breaths stretched longer and longer, until there simply wasn't another. For a few minutes afterward, Daria and Edward might even have convinced themselves that Anya had turned a corner, that she was no longer struggling, that she was getting some rest.

Glancing through the slats in the walls, Daria glimpsed the sun on its way up. Briskly, she peeled off Anya's clothes and passed them to Alyssa. "Put them on. They can't help her anymore."

The shirt was too small. Alyssa nonetheless forced herself into it, ripping the seams of one sleeve. Anya's hat she pulled over her own head, the socks she used for mittens. They were still warm from her sister's skin.

Daria took off the shawl she'd acquired a week earlier in exchange for a handful of wheat seeds, and began wrapping Anya in it, wrenching her out of Edward's arms to do so. He'd been stroking his daughter's face, closing her eyelids, smoothing back her hair.

"We have to bury her before they come."

"Mama." Alyssa pointed to the shawl. "You'll be cold." She stood in front of Daria in Anya's too small clothes, a reminder that nothing should go to waste.

Daria hesitated. Alyssa was right, even the smallest scraps could be put to some use, and a knitted shawl was nothing to throw away. Still, the idea of putting her naked child in the ground . . .

Avoiding Edward's eyes, Daria undid the knots she'd just made, throwing the shawl back over her shoulders, telling herself that if she fell ill, her husband and the one daughter they had left would be lost for good. Daria stood, cradling the weightless thing that had once been Anya. She headed for the door, hissing to Alyssa, "Bring Papa."

Edward rose and accepted his older daughter's hand, allowing Alyssa to lead him. A few people had woken up and were watching them. There were periodic flickers of sympathy, but most merely looked unsurprised.

One whispered to Daria, "The clearing on the left, by the newer pines. Too small to cut down—they don't look there."

"Thank you," Daria said, but the woman had already scurried away. She'd risked enough.

They buried Anya alongside others whose families couldn't stomach the official mass of graves erected on the other side of the settlement. They wanted their loved ones close by. And they didn't want them spending eternity under the authority of those who'd driven them there.

Daria, Edward, and Alyssa dug with their hands, racing the sun, and the roll call that came with it. Edward was humming again. Alyssa joined him. They started to, of all things, harmonize.

Daria whipped around, about to tell them that this was neither the time nor the place, that they were dawdling, wasting precious energy that could better be spent elsewhere; that they were drawing dangerous attention to themselves, risking their all being caught; that they were driving her mad.

Except that, before the words were out of her mouth, Daria saw Edward and Alyssa, their heads bent together. Her husband was smiling, actually smiling as he looked approvingly at their daughter. Edward told Alyssa, "Yes, remember, the music inside, they cannot take that away from you, not unless you let them."

"I won't let them, Papa," Alyssa promised.

They were back in the barracks in time to report for work.

"SHE'S DEAD," Daria told Adam. For reasons she couldn't explain, not to Edward, not to herself, Daria felt compelled to return and let

Adam know what had happened. "Thank you for getting her the medicine. But it was too late."

"My sympathies," Adam said. Much to Daria's surprise, she felt that he meant it.

"I am grateful to you for trying."

"The medicine." He looked almost embarrassed. "It might not have been any good. They ship it from Moscow, and everyone along the way, they stick their hand in, take a share. By the time it got to us, it might have been no more than sawdust, chalk, and colored water."

"I thank you in any case, Adam Semyonovitch." This time, she didn't wait for him to show her the door. Daria paused, half facing him. She asked, "With the kind of influence you've accrued here, couldn't you get them to send you home?"

"What's for me at home?" Adam mimed sweeping a courtyard. She had one final question. "Why did you help me?"

"Because. You were the only one who ever looked me in the eye."

BY MAY, THE temperatures rose above freezing. In July, it was possible to go without rags stuffed into your shoes or wrapped about your face and head. Everything melted. They attempted to salvage what little food had managed to grow before it was swept away, crushed, or stolen. The women who'd tended the fields weren't allowed to keep any of their meager bounty. All produce was collected for redistribution, with Party members getting first pick, then bureaucrats, then employees, and so on down the line. Exiles were reminded how lucky they were not to be at the utter bottom of the food chain. Those would be the prisoners they never saw but were always in danger of being sent to join.

By August, the thermometer began dipping again and, in October, it was impossible to remember what those few golden weeks of reprieve had been like. Their day-to-day lives didn't change. The single variation came when Daria arrived back at the barracks one evening to find Edward already there, lying on his bunk, eyes blank and staring at the wooden slats above him, fingers twitching. Alyssa, hovering, pointed to Edward's right leg. A huge chunk had been torn from his thigh, then bound in a few rounds of now-blood-soaked gauze.

"Dr. Kholodenko says we were lucky it didn't hit any major arteries or he would have bled to death," Alyssa said. "She put something on to keep it from getting infected."

"What happened?"

Daria asked Edward, but it was Alyssa who answered, repeating what she'd been told. "Batch of logs got loose and rolled free. They yelled for everyone to get out of the way, but Papa didn't move fast enough. He just stood there. Like he wanted to be hit, they said."

"YOU SAID YOU could go home, but you don't want to," Daria challenged Adam, having left Alyssa to watch over her father.

Adam continued tending his stills, adjusting the glass tubes and wooden buckets, wringing every last drop out of the magic elixir *pervach*, meaning *first one*, that made his life of relative comfort possible.

"Does that mean you could get someone else out, instead?"

He didn't stop moving, but Daria thought she detected the shadow of a shrug.

"You could!" She pressed on. "My husband, Edward. He can't live like this. He's not like you."

Adam turned his head in Daria's direction. She thought he might finally say something. But after a look Daria couldn't quite decipher, except to suspect she'd said something catastrophically wrong, Adam returned to his task.

Unable to take back her words or discern how they'd caused offense, Daria tried to drive them from Adam's memory by speaking faster. "You know important people; they owe you favors. We're here because of a mistake. You could get the charges against us dropped. Please. Please, I—I'll do anything." Daria made her offer without any forethought to what it could tangibly mean. But as soon as she heard herself, Daria also felt herself taking a step, tentatively resting her hand on Adam's shoulder.

Her hand. It still shocked Daria every time she saw it. The lily smooth skin her mother had dipped in buttermilk (which she then used for cooking because nobody needed to know) was covered in half-healed, pus-filled abrasions, her nails torn to the flesh, blood clots dotting the cuticles, limp flesh hanging from each joint. If that's what her hand looked like, Daria could only imagine the rest of her. Her hair felt greasy and thinning, and when it fell out in tangled clumps, she spied streaks of gray. Her cheeks had sunk to where it was tricky not to nick the inside of her mouth with her loosened teeth as she perfunctorily worked her jaw to keep her face from freezing. Her lips and nose were always chapped, red, and peeling. She made a point of avoiding her reflection if assigned to work near any clear body of water but still couldn't help catching an unwelcome glimpse here and there. Purple rounded her eyes. *Ochi chernye*, indeed. How in the world could Daria hope to appeal to a man, looking the way she did?

And yet, she had to. Daria ignored what she saw in front of her and what she felt inside and, instead, called up the girl who'd stood by the Odessa Opera House seven years prior. And the mother who'd convinced her she was desirable enough that a single stroll would bait the hook. They would reel in the man of both their dreams by making him work for it. For her.

Daria's impulse was to throw herself at Adam, hideous as she was. To peel off her clothes and stand in front of him, making it clear he could do anything he wanted, any way he wanted, for as long as he wanted—if he would just promise to get her family out of this hell.

But Mama's training ran deep. Daria fought her instincts. The moment Adam turned his head to look at her hand on his shoulder, then trail his gaze up her arm and finally to Daria's face, Adam's eyes expressing an interest she was certain had never, ever been there before, that's when Daria smiled coyly. And took a step back.

Her heart was beating so violently, Daria felt certain Adam could spy her feeble rib cage rattling from the impact. Was she out of her mind? Was she honestly playing hard to get while her family's lives were at stake? Who did she think she was?

Daria kept walking toward the door, away from the room with the still and toward the bedroom. What would she do when she got there? She had no idea. Daria didn't even know if he'd follow her.

He followed her.

Adam rose from his knees, dusted his palms off one against the other, then against the front of his shirt and pants, and he followed Daria. Into his bedroom.

She paused, not by the bed but by the window, looking out onto a street so barren it didn't even warrant a sidewalk or a light, as if it were the most fascinating of sights, her back to Adam, willing him to make the next move and come to her.

He reeked of vodka, the smell growing stronger as he drew closer. She heard his footsteps behind her, his ragged breath engulfing the top of her head. He was pawing her hair with his fingers, then slithering them down to her neck, rough, callused palms scraping her raw, wind-burned flesh. And still, Daria didn't turn around. She wasn't going to make this easy for him.

Mama would be proud.

He stopped. Just when Daria thought he would go further, slide his hand and grab her breast in the same way every guard felt entitled to do to every woman, Adam stopped. And Daria panicked.

She whipped around, convinced she'd played this all wrong. What a fool to think Mama's advice would hold any relevance here! Daria was ready to beg for another chance, to give in, to do anything, just like she'd implied, no more teasing. But Adam was already gone, withdrawn to the farthest corner of the room, the hands he'd used to fondle her hidden behind his back.

"Come back tomorrow," he barked, before Daria had a chance to sort out the implications of his command. "Bring your husband."

Chapter 9

Edward didn't ask why. Which was good, because Daria wouldn't have known how to answer. Twenty-four hours later, she had no more idea why Adam was demanding Edward's presence than she had while leaving his home, confused and humiliated. Daria expected more of that in her future. But for now, she tried to make herself look as presentable as possible. She used her fingers to smooth out the worst of the tangles in her hair, then braided it, starting at the top of her head, pulling up the sides in a style that had once emphasized her delicate bone structure. To disguise her deathly paleness, Daria picked at the half-healed rips in her skin, squeezing out enough blood to smear on her cheeks, giving them what she hoped would be a rosy, healthy glow.

She neatened Edward up, too. While some men still took the trouble to shave, using sharpened rocks or a thread they ran up and down their faces, Edward had allowed his beard to grow in uneven clumps. Daria smoothed it down as best she could. Edward neither objected to her ministrations nor helped. Daria was determined that her husband also look presentable, to give him his dignity, no matter what Adam had planned for the two of them.

"THANK YOU," Edward told Adam. "The medicine for Anya. Thank you very much."

They were the most words Daria had heard Edward utter in weeks. She beamed at him like a proud mother watching her child accept a hard-earned school prize. She couldn't help feeling grateful to Adam for having drawn them out of him.

The three of them stood in Adam's central room. There was the haggard writing desk Daria noticed earlier, a single kerosene lamp whose light didn't quite reach the farthest moldy corners, and the piano, which was where Edward's gaze instantly fixed. Even as he thanked Adam, his eyes stayed steady on the instrument.

"You want to play?" Adam yanked up the lid, revealing a water-stained keyboard with one black and one white key missing. "Play."

Edward approached cautiously, as if it might be a trick or a mirage. He kept checking with Adam, head quivering over his shoulder, expecting permission to be withdrawn at any second, followed by punishment.

Adam stomped over to the desk, grabbed the wooden chair that went with it, and dragged it across the floor to the piano, ramming it against the backs of Edward's knees. Daria's husband collapsed into a sitting position. Adam shoved him closer to the keyboard. "Play!"

"Play . . . what?"

Daria's heart sank. Edward had gotten so used to doing what he was ordered—no more, no less—that her brilliant husband, whose mind once swam with every note to every symphony and opera ever written, now couldn't think of a single option on his own. Or maybe he was too terrified of choosing the wrong one and suffering the consequences.

Daria's first instinct was to urge him to play the tune he hummed endlessly, the one he and Alyssa had harmonized on at Anya's grave. But no, that melody was sacrosanct. She didn't want to ruin it for him.

Adam, for all his belligerent bravado, looked equally stymied.

"Play a . . . a waltz." The answer pried from his brain with great effort and impatient indifference.

Daria hoped Edward wouldn't ask which waltz. Any further exchange seemed beyond them both.

He didn't. Instead, Edward reverently hovered his hands above the keyboard, flexing his battered, stiff, ravaged fingers a ritual three times before lowering them and launching into the first notes of what Daria recognized as *The Blue Danube*.

It was a relatively simple piece. Children performed it at recitals. But as Edward began to play, Daria watched her husband transform. He sat up straighter, loosening his shoulders, straightening his neck, chin up, leaning back, and evening his breath. His brow smoothed, causing Daria to realize how much tension he had been holding in his face.

Adam's hand gripped Daria's elbow. She startled. She'd forgotten he was there.

"Dance with me." It wasn't a request.

Daria whipped her head to check if Edward had heard. But he was lost in his music.

Adam dragged Daria to the center of the room and forced her to face him. He placed one hand on the small of her back and used his other to seize one of hers. His eyes bore down into her. She had no choice but to rest her free palm on his shoulder as, on the next downbeat, he proceeded to whip Daria around to all four corners, sweeping so closely by the piano, Daria's hip brushed against Edward.

When was the last time she'd danced? A New Year's Eve party, most likely. What year had that been? What year was it now? Despite Mama's insisting that Daria learn to waltz properly, there'd been few occasions for her to do so with Edward. He was usually the one playing while everyone else danced, abandoning Daria to be squired by gentlemen too polite to leave her a wallflower. As a result, she'd grown quite skilled at accommodating a variety of partners. Adam moved with unexpected grace for a man of his bulk. What started as Daria's being pulled along quickly turned into his properly leading her. She'd first looked down at his feet, trying not to get trampled, but when Daria realized that Adam, surprisingly, knew what he was doing, she raised her head, staring straight into the broad width of his chest. It was disorienting, having buttons bob in front of her face. When her head spun to the point of collapse, Daria surrendered and assumed proper waltz position. She looked into Adam's eyes.

Adam's eyes blazed.

They noticed, they considered, they appreciated, they wanted . . . they wanted more than just food, more than just warmth. More than just to live through another day.

Adam's eyes wanted her.

Daria still remembered that look.

And she remembered how that look had made her feel.

Beautiful. Powerful. Exultant. Hopeful.

Disloyal.

The next time Adam spun her around, Daria took advantage of the momentum to wrench herself free, letting go and deliberately stumbling into Edward, nearly knocking him off his chair, interrupting him midchord. She clung to her husband, using him as a shield between herself and Adam. Edward stared up at her, as dazed as someone who'd woken up from a nightmare into reality. Or vice versa.

"The piano, it needs tuning. I-I could tune it for you," Edward desperately offered. He'd stood up, one hand remaining on the keyboard, unable to sever the connection.

And for just the tiniest, darkest, split second, Daria hated him. She hated her husband for still having something he loved so much, it could pull him out of this hell from which the rest of them received no reprieve. For believing, like he'd told Alyssa, that no one could take the music out of him, unless he let them. And Daria loved him for, even in hell, somehow managing to cling to a shred of the man he'd once been. While he'd played, he'd become the old

Edward. Even as Daria knew she would never be able to resurrect the girl she'd been.

Adam, however, wasn't looking at Edward. He was looking at Daria, both of them still breathing heavily from the exertion and the dizziness and . . . nothing else whatsoever.

"You want back to Odessa?" Adam growled.

Daria didn't trust her voice. She nodded.

"I can arrange that."

Daria gasped, covering her mouth with her hand. She turned to Edward, wondering if he'd heard, if he'd understood, if he realized what this meant?

"I can get him out," Adam went on. "And the little girl. But you"—Adam was speaking to Daria now, no one else—"you stay. Here. With me."

Chapter 10

Dazed, Daria turned to Edward. He hadn't reacted. Not to Adam's offer, not to his price. It was like that first day, when the guard ripped Daria's brassiere strap, and Edward, not knowing what he should or could do, had done nothing; he'd just let the moment unfurl in slow motion, like the music he claimed you couldn't force but had to allow to flow anywhere it wanted. He looked back at Daria, waiting for her to make the necessary decisions for both of them.

His hand was still on the piano. He was using it for balance. The wound on his thigh had opened again, either from Adam's slamming the chair against Edward's legs or from Daria barreling into him in her attempt to escape Adam's dance hold. Blood seeped through the stopgap bandage, forcing Edward to shift more of his weight to the other foot. He was wobbling, staggering to remain upright. The spark Daria had seen while he'd played was burning so low now, one wrong breath risked extinguishing it forever.

Daria reached for Edward's arm, draping it over her shoulder and propping him up so he could hobble his way to the exit. Edward allowed Daria to lead him, even as his gaze remained longingly pinned to the piano. At the door, she glanced back at Adam, looking him dead in the eye, the way she had all those times previously.

And offering a nearly imperceptible nod of her head.

===

"NO!" ALYSSA SCREAMED, struggling against being hefted onto
the first step of the train once she realized Daria meant what she'd
said about staying behind. "No! Mama come, too," the six-year-
old regressed in language as she kicked her feet and flailed her
arms, refusing to be lifted.

Daria first tried to soothe her with soft words and caresses. Then,
frustrated and pressed for time, she resorted to pinning Alyssa's
elbows to her sides, holding her in a viselike grip until the child
realized her wrestling was ineffective, and finally settled down.

Daria bent at the waist until she and Alyssa were face-to-face.
She cupped her daughter's cheeks between her palms and thought
about how alike her girls had looked, and how, from now on, she
would always use Alyssa as a guide for what Anya might have
grown up to be. That is, if Daria ever saw Alyssa again.

But she had no time to waste on such idle speculation now.

"Allya." Daria used the child's nickname, unable to remember
the last time she'd done so. "I'm counting on you to help me. You
need to take care of Papa."

"But why can't you come, too?" Alyssa pleaded, her already red,
swollen, frostbitten face becoming even more crimson from tears.

"I have to stay here." Daria gave a reason she hoped would make
sense; it was even somewhat true. "With Anya."

Daria sensed the resistance drain out of Alyssa's tiny body. She'd
fretted as it was about her baby sister going into the cold ground
so far away from the rest of them. Alyssa understood that leaving
Anya alone would be unconscionable.

"Look after Papa for me," Daria reiterated, picking Alyssa up
off the ground and setting her down on the train steps, hugging
her as tightly as she could, for as long as she could, until Daria
feared snapping Alyssa's fragile little bones in two.

"Here are your papers." Daria had held on to them until the
last moment, partially from anxiety that they might be rescinded,

partially from concern that Edward would misplace them. But mostly because, as long as Daria still had their papers, she still had Edward and Alyssa.

She put them into Edward's hands, then reconsidered and tucked them into the inside pocket of the coat she'd scrounged by bargaining away all their other possessions. When the woman she was trading with asked what Daria planned to do tomorrow, stripped of everything, Daria told her she didn't give a damn.

"When you get to Odessa, try to find your father. If he's still in the old apartment, you should have no problems. Otherwise, go to the Central Office, show these papers, and you'll be assigned a new place to live. I don't know where, but it has to be better than this, right?"

She attempted a hopeful smile. The smile Edward gave her in return was anything but hopeful.

She cradled his face in much the same way she had Alyssa's earlier, and kissed him, more with affection than passion. His lackluster response confirmed her resolve not to go further.

"You're going to be all right," she promised. "And knowing that you and Alyssa are all right is what's going to make me be all right."

"He'll . . . take care of you?"

"Yes. You know he can. These papers prove how much influence he holds."

"I'm sorry," Edward began. "I'm sorry I couldn't—"

"Take care of Alyssa. Nothing else matters."

"When will you come home?"

"As soon as I can," she swore.

WAS SHE SUPPOSED to go back to the barracks? Daria had wandered away from the train depot, where she'd stood watching Alyssa's and Edward's faces at the window until even the puffs from the smokestack were no longer visible. She had no idea what she was supposed to do next. Her last few days had been focused on making sure Adam kept his promise, and on getting Alyssa and

Edward on board before anyone decided a mistake had been made. She'd given no thought to the moments—and the days and the weeks and the months and the years—after.

Daria began to trudge toward the fields. She stopped. She'd never missed a day of work before, and she had no idea what the consequences for that might be. She found herself wandering, passing guards and other authorities who had every right to demand to know what she thought she was doing, but something about Daria's state inspired them to keep their distance. They thought she was one of the insane. It happened all the time. The woman whose baby died in the cattle car had lasted a few weeks before creeping out of the barracks and into the woods while her husband slept, then beating her head against a tree until she fell unconscious. They found her frozen to death the next morning. She was hardly the first. And now Daria looked like she might be joining them.

Except for two things. Daria had promised Edward and Alyssa she would find her way home to them. And she wouldn't give Adam the satisfaction of making her break that promise.

Daria had tried pretending she was drifting without a direction in mind but was forced to give up the delusion when she found herself in front of Adam's house. The massive lock on the door made entry impossible, and, as it was the middle of the day, Adam wasn't home. Struck by a new sense of purpose, Daria headed for the administrative complex in the center of what passed for town, a collection of wooden shacks built multiple years apart, crumbling at different levels of disrepair. Except these particular shacks had working stoves, lamps, desks, and filing cabinets. Most important, they had men and women who didn't dress in rags, whose skin didn't hang off their skeletons like limp autumn leaves without the color, and who were rationed three meals a day beyond watered-down soup and stale chunks of bread.

Daria entered the bureau where Adam worked, sweeping past his colleagues who demanded to know what someone like her thought she was doing there. She didn't stop moving until she reached the back, where Adam stood holding a ream of papers, surrounded by a dozen crates in the process of being ripped open by a team of men with crowbars. They were inventorying whatever was left from the latest shipment of food or medicine, after it had been pilfered at every stop along the way.

She told him, "They're gone."

He told her, "You have a new job."

Daria awaited further instructions.

"You can read and write?"

Now he thought he could insult her? After the effort Mama had put into getting Daria educated at the Ukrainian school? "Thanks to Comrade Stalin."

"Find Marya Ivanova." Adam mimed huge breasts with both hands, which got knowing snickers out of his crew. "I told her you'd be coming today. She'll assign your work detail."

He'd told this Marya Ivanova that Daria would be coming? How in the world had Adam known? Then again, where else did Daria have to go? His arrogance somehow managed to rankle her in yet a new way. On the other hand, Daria would be an idiot to turn down an indoor position. So for the rest of the afternoon, she followed Marya Ivanova's orders and copied over by hand requisitions for their superiors to sign. Carbon paper never quite managed to reach them this far north, and typewriters were for senior staff. Once upon a time, Daria would have found such mindless work deadly dull. Now, she wanted it never to end.

But of course, it did. Clocks were at a premium, as well, so Daria had no idea how many hours post-sundown it was when Marya Ivanova pronounced their day's work complete and began spitting to extinguish the lamps. Daria had been banished to a desk in the corner that she shared with three other women also transcribing endless documents. The chatty trio flew out the door. Daria was there alone when Adam appeared.

"Let's go," he told her.

HE TOOK HER back to his house, which answered Daria's question about continuing to live in the barracks but not much else. He opened the lock with a single key, making Daria wonder if all her comings and goings would be under his control. Once inside, Adam ditched her for his still. As far as Daria could tell, it percolated all day long. No wonder he needed the heavy-duty lock and the bars on the windows. Otherwise, he'd be inviting endless break-ins. Not that Daria could imagine anyone would be reckless enough to take on Adam in a fistfight. Then again, desperation drove people to all sorts of measures.

Look at her.

Adam wasn't looking at her. He'd discarded her in the entryway, not even bothering to turn on the lights. She did that herself in the main room. Everything was as she remembered. Adam hadn't even closed the piano lid. Daria did that now, imagining she could still feel remnants of Edward's energy radiating from the keys. She remembered how he'd bloomed to life while playing, and it gave Daria the strength to move into the bedroom, where she stripped off her clothes and climbed in.

She sent up a silent apology to Mama. Daria had long passed the point of playing hard to get. She was determined to keep to her bargain, for fear any slight infraction might prompt Adam to void their entire agreement. And then what might he do to punish her, not to mention Edward and Alyssa? It was a risk Daria couldn't afford to take.

And so she waited for Adam to come to her and claim what was his. But he appeared in no hurry, tinkering with his pipes and his cast-iron buckets, pouring the resulting brew into glass jars and tin cans labeled with the names of their designated recipients. It must have been a most time-consuming business, because Daria— lying for the first time in a year in a hay-stuffed bed covered with a thin but nonetheless existent sheet and blanket as well as a pillow filled with horsehair, rather than a bare wooden bunk of ruts and splinters—found herself drifting off to sleep.

She startled awake at the sound of Adam entering the room some time later. It was a habit Daria had picked up from when her children were infants. It came in handy once she was placed in a situation where someone might try to steal her shoes or her sweater or portions of hoarded food while she slept. It was why Daria had pushed Edward and the children toward the wall and had placed herself on the edge, like an ever-alert guard dog.

She braced herself as Adam crawled into bed next to her. In the pitch-dark Daria felt, rather than saw, him lifting the blanket and looking her over, head to toe. Did he realize she was naked? Did he understand that meant she was ready to live up to her part of their agreement? He shifted his weight, and Daria subserviently rolled on her side toward him.

But much to her surprise, Adam turned his back on her, falling asleep before Daria even had the chance to recover from her shock.

Chapter 11

———

The next morning, she was up before him. Despite the comfort, Daria had found it difficult to doze off again. It wasn't Adam's snoring. She'd slept through far worse in the cattle car and barracks, not to mention when she'd shared a single room with her own parents. It was her certainty that Adam would wake up any moment and . . .

Maybe he'd been too worn out the night before? Or maybe it had slipped his mind? Surely, in the morning . . .

She was ready for him. Ready for anything. Except the grunt with which Adam greeted her. He slipped out of bed, dressed in pajamas a bit too close to a prison uniform for Daria's comfort, likely surplus or maybe another case of supplies getting waylaid en route to their designated location. He headed for the outhouse she'd spied and taken advantage of earlier. The next time Daria saw Adam, he was wearing his street clothes, waiting by the door to take Daria to work.

DRESSES APPEARED FOR HER. Undergarments. Wool stockings. Boots. Not new by any means. But clean and more or less her size. She was issued a ration card for the closed-distribution general store and the cafeteria open to select workers. This allowed her to purchase—on credit; Daria had yet to receive wages to go with her new labor assignment, though nobody doubted her ultimate ability to make good—bread, tea, sausage, eggs, butter, and potatoes. When they were available, of course. Beer was also on the list but never in stock. It made Adam's home-brewed vodka even more popular.

"Where did you learn to set up a still?" Daria asked, having learned that any conversation beyond bare necessities would need to be initiated by her. Otherwise, she and Adam could pass days working in the same building, living side by side, sleeping in the same bed, for goodness' sake, and never exchange a word. It was worse than Edward's silence. At least, with Edward, she'd realized he was traumatized. But with Adam, the situation was more confounding. Daria knew other women who'd taken "camp husbands." Attaching themselves to one man with the power to retaliate, they escaped being raped by a succession of guards, supervisors, and fellow prisoners. Or, rather, they preemptively chose their own rapist. Daria thought she'd done the same. Except for one not-so-minor detail. The first few weeks, she'd lived every moment in dread of the inevitable. Now Daria simply lived in dread. She no longer even knew of what.

"My mother," Adam said.

"The one you turned in?" Daria told herself the words had slipped out before she'd had time to think about what she was saying. But she knew that wasn't the case. Adam's taciturnity, coming as it did on the heels of Edward's, had driven her into such an agitated state that Daria could think of nothing more satisfying than breaking through his infuriating reserve, making Adam suffer a bit of the agitation, not to mention the fury, he put her through daily. She couldn't allow herself to be angry with Edward. And even if it were allowed, Daria had no right to express it, not after what she'd done. Daria had no such reservations regarding Adam. And this was the best way she could think of to do it. Her question was no accident. Though, whether it was a mistake was yet to be determined.

"Most people have only one mother," Adam noted.

"Most people don't turn them in to the NKVD." Daria didn't know if that was true. She certainly hoped so.

"My father left when I was a boy. Distilling vodka was how she supported us."

Daria thought of Mama's quest to position Daria for the best. And how her dreams had disintegrated. Mama deserved better than a daughter reduced to prostituting herself. Even if Daria's prostituting wasn't proving successful. That, too, seemed an insult to Mama. She'd given Daria everything she needed. Daria was the one who'd failed them both, in addition to Edward and the girls. Having nowhere else to vent her impotent fury, Daria burst out, "How could you do that to your mother?"

"She wanted me to."

Daria snorted.

"My mother mopped floors at the old Jewish hospital. The doctors, they talked around her like she wasn't a human being with ears. She heard things. She learned things. When doctors told her she was suffering from anemia, she realized they were lying. It was leukemia. She was dying. She had nothing to leave me. No money, no position. So she told me to turn her in. To say that she had been stealing medicine, selling it. She knew I'd be rewarded. It was my mother's legacy to me."

He was telling the truth.

Daria could have gone on asking questions, trying to poke holes in his story, denying it because it was too terrible. But Daria knew Adam was telling the truth. And that she was the only one he had ever told.

What she didn't know was how to react to his confession. Condolences were hardly appropriate under the circumstances. Neither was pretending that what he'd said had no effect on her.

Adam didn't appear to be waiting on any reaction from her. Yet Daria felt it was imperative that she offer him one. For both their sakes. She thought she was reaching out to take his hand, to squeeze it in a gesture of pure mutual humanity. But when she got close enough, to her surprise, she found herself rising up on her toes, which she wouldn't need to do if she were still reaching for his hand.

Daria kissed him.

Adam didn't appear surprised. Then again, Adam rarely appeared surprised by anything. He kissed her back as if his action, and hers, were the most natural in the world, despite their earlier five-minute conversation being, quite possibly, the lengthiest they'd ever exchanged. On the other hand, Daria couldn't help thinking, how long had Edward glimpsed her before he decided she was worth pursuing? Maybe she was more tolerable in small doses?

Except Adam's kiss proved anything but brief. He didn't lay a hand on her. Yet Daria felt herself being pulled toward him, as if he were inhaling her. His lips were warm. After being surrounded by a piercing cold inside and out, this was as much of a jolt as anything else. He didn't push; he pulled. And ultimately, he was the one who stopped.

And then Adam did one more surprising thing. He smiled.

Not menacingly, not condescendingly, not wearily. He simply smiled.

And, after that, everything changed.

NOT ALL AT ONCE, of course.

Adam didn't suddenly become a loquacious conversationalist. But he did start bidding Daria good morning as she wrapped her fingers around a tin mug and hurried to sip her tea before it froze like the rest of their surroundings. On their walk to the administrative offices, he began introducing Daria to citizens they bumped into on the street, residents who'd predated the internment camp and exiles who'd managed to build new lives there. She presumed they were customers of Adam's and so went out of their way to be pleasant. Adam even made Daria laugh, spilling secrets about their former Odessa neighbors, like the couple who were cheating on each other, sometimes at the exact same time and literally next door, while proclaiming themselves the epitome of fidelity and urging the other couple, whom they suspected of carrying on with someone else, to heed their example. The deception got so convoluted that, listening to Adam tell it, Daria laughed until she cried. She hadn't realized she still remembered how to do either.

Daria talked to Adam, too. She apologized for the way she'd treated him in Odessa. He pointed out she'd hardly been the only one. She apologized for the way she'd treated him here. He pointed out they had greater concerns than maintaining good manners. She apologized for what she'd thought about him opportunistically turning in his mother.

Adam said, "She would be happy to know her plan worked."

Daria asked Adam to tell her about his mother. She started by telling him about hers. They agreed the pair wouldn't have gotten along. Daria's mother would have found Adam's common; Adam's mother would have deemed Daria's pretentious.

They talked about her daughters, too. Adam, Daria realized, was one of the few people who was familiar with her girls, the way they'd once been. Adam filled Daria in on instances she hadn't known about, like the time Alyssa, with Anya obediently tagging along, sneaked into the rubbish bins. They'd begged Adam for scraps they could use to play buried treasure. He'd given them an old herring tin and a wedge of a broken plate, which they buried in a shallow hole in the courtyard and swore Adam to secrecy. With memories all she had now, this new one proved as precious to Daria as the booty her daughters once hoarded.

Daria never tired of talking about them. She even invited Adam to Anya's grave. So many of the exiles had buried their loved ones there that it had turned into a de facto formal cemetery. A few of the German speakers had attempted to erect makeshift markers, using two sticks tied with twine to form a cross. Daria certainly hadn't wanted that, yet she was at a loss for what might prove appropriate. It was Adam who'd dredged up a stone wedged into the foundation of his home—he swore he could replace it. Using a sharpened nail, he scratched in Anya's name alongside the years of her truncated life. After a guard, without warning, mowed down the illegal crosses, the rest of the survivors followed suit, etching their own stones, this time with Communist-approved symbols.

"My Anya," Daria had chuckled. "A trendsetter."

The one subject that she and Adam never broached, however, was Edward.

Edward had become, like so many others in the USSR, an un-person. Talking about Alyssa and even Anya brought the girls to some version of life as happy, thriving children whom Daria could pretend were in the next room, giggling and plotting mischief, waiting for their mother. Edward lived in Daria's head. She didn't try to guess his life in Odessa or imagine his growing older, as she did with her girls. The Edward Daria had fallen in love with existed in the past and the present, superseding any other, including the version she'd last spied guiding Alyssa up the departing train's steps. Edward was a chimera. Adam was real.

His presence was everywhere, lingering in the air, not quite a sight, not quite a sound, not quite a smell, but rather a heaviness she breathed in and out whenever Adam left the room. Daria found herself watching him, never head-on, always out of the corner of her eye, hoping to disguise the compulsion. She walked by him more than she needed to. She asked him questions to which she knew the answers. At first, she'd told herself, it was her way of making him acknowledge her, her way of fighting becoming invisible, her way of remembering that, despite the daily humiliations, she was still alive, she still existed, she hadn't been erased like so many others. But eventually, Daria was forced to concede that she was doing it because Adam's ongoing sexual rejection frustrated and confounded her to no end.

Daria was not used to being overlooked. The guard who'd stripped her that first morning—she'd been able to understand his actions then better than Adam's now. Daria remembered Mama schooling her that men were to be tortured by leaving them constantly wanting. She finally understood what that meant. And why it proved so effective. Daria felt like Adam was torturing her daily. Every time he ignored the purportedly accidental brush of Daria's hand along his arm, every time he failed to notice that she was standing as close to him as she had when they'd kissed, every time he climbed into their bed and turned his back on her, Daria boiled with a sensation she refused to call desire, yet one that stirred a hunger even stronger than the endless craving for food or warmth or safety. Perhaps it was because Adam was the nexus of all three. Or perhaps it was something else.

She couldn't wait for him any longer. She couldn't spend another night watching the rise and fall of Adam's back, listening to his breathing, feeling the heat radiating from his body, and continue keeping her distance.

She whispered his name. She'd never done that before. Adam startled fiercely enough for the bed to jolt along with him. But that was the extent of his response. He didn't answer. He didn't budge. She wondered if he'd heard or if his reaction was just a coincidence. There was no way he could not have heard. She wondered if he intended to act as if he hadn't, nonetheless.

Adam slowly rolled over, shifting his weight along the mattress so Daria almost slid into him. They were lying face-to-face in the darkness, Adam's features coming gradually into focus. The shaggy beard first, then the jut of his nose, the ridge of his brows, and, finally, the query in his eyes.

Daria raised her arm and gently stroked Adam's beard with the backs of her fingers. As her hand brushed past Adam's mouth, he fleetingly kissed it, sending a shiver through Daria she couldn't have denied even if she'd wanted to. She didn't want to.

He kissed every one of her fingers, then up Daria's palm, inside her wrist, past the crook of her elbow, and to her neck. She whimpered, and he abruptly halted, terrified he'd hurt her.

Daria rested her free hand on the back of his head, caressing his hair, urging him to go on.

Chapter 12

═══

Their son was born less than a year later, in the spring of 1939. Daria hadn't believed it. The idea that her wasted body was capable of producing life felt as far-fetched as the deception that she'd ever had another existence outside the misery of Kyril—or ever could again. This was Daria's life now. She accepted it would never change. She preferred it that way. The serfs had a saying: *Never ask for a better czar.* The devil Daria knew was preferable to the one she didn't. She'd be content for matters to remain as they were and never to experience another upheaval.

So Daria had ignored the swelling in her abdomen, telling herself that chronic hunger produced a variety of unpredictable changes, and going about her daily routine with near-ritualistic fervor to maintain the status quo. Finally, it was Adam who—over a dinner of stewed bear meat that Daria had managed to tenderize and, she hoped, also purify, by boiling it for several days—tilted his tin bowl and poured half of his allotment into Daria's. He said, "I can hollow out a log for a cradle. Put it on runners, so it rocks. We should keep it in the central room, next to the fire. Warmer, there."

He was looking at her expectantly, so Daria had no choice but to nod in agreement.

Adam visibly relaxed, as if a critical question had been settled.

They continued eating in silence, which was a habit they'd broken over the past few months but now reverted to instinctively. At the end of the meal, Adam was the first to stand. He picked up their bowls and their spoons and carried them toward the hand pump that Daria used to wash dishes. Water had frozen in the basin below. Adam proceeded to crack the surface, using the same knife with which he'd skinned the bear. His back to Daria, Adam said, "I know a child of mine can't replace the one you lost."

"No," Daria agreed.

And yet, a part of her was terrified that it might. Which was why she was so pleased, when the doctor who'd endeavored to help with Anya's illness handed Daria her cleaned-off newborn, first to recognize she held a boy, and second to see that he looked nothing like his lost sisters. Alyssa and Anya had been dark-haired and green-eyed. This child was pale, with pupils as murky as a summer swamp, and a sprinkle of ginger fuzz along his scalp. He was smaller than either of her girls had been. But while their weight had felt ethereal to Daria, as if a light breeze might blow them out of her arms, this baby felt substantial, intractable. Her daughters' bones were filled with seltzer water. Her son's with cement.

Adam waited to see her and the child until after Daria had rested, the air still reeking of blood. He'd provided the doctor with alcohol to sterilize her hands—no medical equipment was available even if she'd wanted to use it—and they'd boiled the sheet Daria labored over, as well as the fresh one they slipped underneath her afterward. Nevertheless, the threat of infection, namely puerperal fever, remained. Adam was loath to get too near either Daria or the baby, lest he endanger them.

So it was Daria who turned his sleeping son toward Adam, hovering above them, and inquired, almost teasing, "Well? What do you think?"

While Adam was often silent, it wasn't the same as being lost for words. This time, he appeared to be the latter. "So . . . small."

"He'll grow," Daria responded with confidence a woman who'd

already buried one child, not to mention seen dozens of others go into the ground beside her, had no right to harbor. Yet the sheer solidity of this infant buoyed a euphoria Daria couldn't recall feeling following either girl's birth.

Adam nodded, unconvinced.

"We should name him." Another vote of confidence. Several babies born in Kyril over the past few months had gone unnamed, their parents waiting to see if they would survive first.

"Yes," Adam agreed. But he declined to offer any suggestions.

Of the babies who had lived to receive names, their cautious parents had chosen the most prudent options, two boys named Vladimir, after Comrade Lenin; a girl named Stalina. One couple wanted to call their son Josef, hoping they'd be safe adopting Comrade Stalin's first name. But when attempting to register it, they were advised it sounded German. They quickly changed it to the more patriotic Ruslan.

"What was your mother's name?" Daria asked Adam.

The question took him by surprise, and the name popped out like a bubble. "Ita."

"Then we should choose a name starting with the same letter." It was the rare Jewish superstition Daria's mother had been able to stomach; both of her girls had been named for Edward's late mother, Ada, and, coincidentally, Daria's father, Abraham.

"Israel," Adam said, and they both laughed. That would be ridiculous for so many reasons. "Ivan," Adam offered next, with less enthusiasm. It was the political choice. No one could claim Ivan wasn't a Russian or Soviet name.

"Like the village idiot?" Daria referenced the Tolstoy children's story. "No."

Adam breathed a sigh of relief.

And then she suggested, "Igor."

Russian enough. *Prince Igor* was the name of an opera by Alexander Borodin. Based on unexpurgated, if vague, historical events, it had yet to be outlawed. On the other hand, the moniker wasn't so Russian that they'd end up raising a son with the name of a Cossack.

"Igor," Adam repeated, and Daria took it as assent.

HE PROVED A HEARTY BABY, making due with the meager breast milk Daria was able to produce and the cow's milk Adam was able to procure. Remembering Anya, Daria lived in terror of his falling ill, but, true to his word, Adam kept the fire by the cradle kindled twenty-four hours a day. Between that, and a fur bunting they had to wrap him in, the infant stayed warm and managed to survive the first year of his life with nothing worse than a handful of colds. Daria and Adam realized that Igor was too adult of an address for such a small baby and, within weeks, he'd become Gosha.

With Gosha around, Adam and Daria now had much more to talk about. They either talked about the baby, or they talked around the baby, using him as a conduit for sentiments otherwise never expressed.

"Give your mama a kiss," Adam would say, lifting the squirming tot to Daria's cheek long before he could have been expected to speak. "Tell her how beautiful she is."

"What a wonderful papa you have," Daria cooed to Gosha after Adam came home with a duck-shaped pull toy. The red paint had chipped off its beak and one of the wheels rattled on its axle, but Gosha, who had never seen anything like it, was mesmerized, laughing and clapping every time he was able to make the duck move across their uneven wooden floor. "The best papa in the world! You must love him so much!"

It was a flicker, but Daria saw it nonetheless, the way Adam flinched. They both knew it was the first time Daria had uttered that word in conjunction with either Adam or Gosha.

She loved her son; of course Daria loved him. But it wasn't the fearless love she'd had with her girls. Daria's love for Gosha was cautious, measured, tempered by the fatalism that she could lose him in the blink of an eye to forces outside her control. As well as by the suspicion that every drop of love she spared his way was a crumb lost from Alyssa and Anya. Daria understood her younger daughter had no more use of it, and her elder had no way of knowing what she was missing. But all the same, each quiver of Daria's heart whenever she looked at her beautiful, healthy, precious boy was followed by a spasm of guilt toward his absent sisters.

It was different with Adam. Adam wasn't like Gosha. Gosha was as much Daria's child as Anya and Alyssa. But Adam wasn't Daria's husband. Edward was her husband. She loved Edward, not Adam; there could never be any confusion over that. She was grateful to Adam. He had saved her family; he had saved her. He treated her kindly, if not always warmly. But her years in Siberia taught Daria that the warmth you drew from a fire or boots was of more value than that which might sporadically eke from a fellow human being. Adam had provided for her and Gosha in that regard. It was what they'd agreed on, no less, and definitely no more.

She shouldn't have said anything about love. She'd been so careful for so long. Weighing every word was second nature to her now. The consequences of uttering the wrong ones were too grave to do otherwise. And yet she'd slipped. Granted, it wasn't as dire as if she'd criticized the Party, or the USSR, or Comrade Stalin. It wasn't as bad as if she'd expressed sympathy for the prisoners quartered in the adjacent gulag, or questioned the wisdom of planting crops unfit for growing in this climate. So why did Daria feel as if it might prove even worse?

It was a flicker, a momentary shadow. Perhaps Daria imagined it. Maybe Adam hadn't even noticed. He didn't say anything afterward. Then again, when did he ever?

Daria told herself it would be fine. There would be no negative consequences from her blunder. She kept telling herself that for several days. Right up until she was summoned to meet with the village administrator.

=

THE ORDER CAME in the middle of the day, while Daria and Adam were at their posts. Daria had returned to work a few days after Gosha's birth to prove that she was a productive citizen and not a parasite living off the labor of others. She arranged for a village woman, a mother of seven, to watch Gosha during the day. Adam's home was larger and warmer than her own, and she was grateful for the opportunity to get her brood out of the cold. Adam was aware that their nanny also helped herself to a bottle or two from his still, but he knew it wasn't to sell—it was for her husband, to keep his temper in check—so Adam looked the other way after each instance.

"The administrator wishes to see you. Come now."

Daria sprang from her desk, then froze, terrified of the implications. She looked around desperately for some clue as to what was about to happen. Surely, someone knew. They processed different papers. Nothing happened in Kyril without proper papers. Yet, of the two-dozen workers packed into this particular office, not a single one dared glance Daria's way. All eyes were fastened on the documents before them. Even their breathing, not to mention the steady hum of ongoing chatter, had stilled.

Adam! Adam would know! Adam dealt with everyone! Adam knew everything!

Daria spun to face him, only to encounter his expression of mystification and dread to match her own. If Adam didn't know . . .

Daria's knees buckled even as she forced herself to lock them and obey the command to report to the administrator's office in the adjoining bungalow. The head of their settlement inhabited a jerry-rigged wooden shack not much different from the one where Daria spent her days, except he and an assistant were the lone occupants. And the view from his window was of the admittedly lovely woods and not the privies the rest of them toiled downwind from. Plus, he had his own Primus stove for warmth, and the teakettle that sat atop it.

Daria deliberately had little contact with the director. Her status as Adam's woman kept her safe from guards who considered grabbing any female—from schoolgirls to grandmothers, knocking them down with the butts of their rifles, and raping them, often in view of their helpless families—as an entitlement due their profession. But a director was different. A director needn't be afraid of Adam, even if he was one of Adam's best customers, as evidenced by the bulging, ruddy veins obscuring his nose and cheeks: a drunk's suntan in the land of no sun.

Planted behind his desk, he looked up at Daria, looked down at a file of papers before him, then back up at her. He said, "You believe you have friends in high places?"

Daria wasn't sure what the right answer might be in this instance. The only thing she was sure of was that, whether or not she managed to produce it, her fate had already been decided.

"Your husband and daughter were sent home, weren't they?"
Daria nodded.

"Would you like to go home?"

Another irrelevant question with no proper answer. "Yes."

"Then you are fortunate." The director stood, rounded his desk, and approached. Daria braced herself, attempting to disguise her disgust and her simultaneous resignation. She remembered yet another of her mother's admonitions: *No matter how bad you think something is, it can always get worse.*

The director smiled and extended his arm, but, instead of lunging for Daria's face, or her breasts, or even for her crotch, as she had expected and had watched him do with others he employed, he stuffed several sheets of paper into Daria's hands and, enjoying her terror and confusion, grandly pronounced, "There has been a change. Your sentence has been commuted. You have been rehabilitated. You may return to Odessa."

Chapter 13

===

"Are these real?" Daria waited until after they'd returned home—doors locked, lights dimmed—before showing Adam the papers she'd been given. She'd left the administrator's office in a daze, forcing her face into an expression of unremarkable neutrality so that when she stepped back into the office, no one might suspect what had just happened. She didn't dare meet anyone's gaze. Which was fine, nobody was dying to meet hers, lest that be enough to implicate them in whatever crime she'd been accused of. Daria wouldn't even look at Adam, afraid she might give something away. He picked up on her reticence and went along with it, the relief of Daria coming back none the worse for wear—never a guarantee—replaced by fear about what had transpired, and what might come next as a consequence of it.

Adam studied the documents Daria spread out in front of him, jiggling Gosha on one knee to keep the toddler from grabbing at them. Daria's hands were shaking so badly, she'd been afraid of dropping the boy if she tried to hold him.

"They look authentic," Adam said.

Daria collapsed into a chair, unsure why confirmation should feel so good and so terrible at the same time.

"How did this happen?" Adam asked.

"My father-in-law." Daria still refused to mention Edward by name. She stuck to a more indirect descriptor. She pointed to the signature of the KGB official who'd authorized her release. "He's a music lover. Isaak Israelevitch used to leave him concert tickets, even for sold-out shows."

Adam could figure out the rest. After all, *po blatu* was how he'd gotten Edward and Alyssa out. It was how the entire Soviet system operated.

"When do you leave?" Adam asked. Not "will you" but "when." Daria didn't blame him for phrasing it that way. Adam was the only person who'd ever expressed a preference for staying in Siberia. Naturally, he expected her to leap at the opportunity. Who wouldn't? Nonetheless, Daria couldn't help feeling a slight disappointment that he appeared so indifferent about it.

"As soon as I can buy a ticket."

He nodded thoughtfully.

Daria wanted to grab him by those broad shoulders, to shake him until his teeth rattled, to scream in his face and demand to know how he could let her go like this after . . . everything?

Staying behind with Adam had been the most painful, debilitating, momentous act of Daria's life, and here Adam was acting like it meant nothing—to him. She supposed it didn't, not like it did to her. If she'd said no two years ago, he'd have carried on as before; he had nothing to lose. She was the one who gave up everything. And now he was expecting her to do it again.

That final, unbidden thought percolated to the edges of Daria's consciousness and, horrified by its implication, she shoved the notion down. The process took less than a second. She didn't hesitate or wonder whether it warranted more careful consideration.

But that instant was also enough time for Adam to say, in the measured, take-it-or-leave-it tone he employed with obdurate customers who believed bargaining might be an option, "Go whenever you like. Gosha stays with me."

===

DARIA HAD SPENT two years watching Adam turn a deaf ear on those who pleaded with him about prices, begging Adam to accept in trade an item he'd already said he had no use for. Now, she found herself in the same position. And on the receiving end of the same response.

She tried to reason with him, she also begged, she even broke down in tears, something she once swore to herself she would never let him see her do, much less drive her to. In desperation, she threatened. Only to get her own back in kind.

Adam reminded, "You've seen the women who had their children taken away, sent to be raised in state orphanages because their mothers can't be trusted to turn them into proper Soviet citizens. I stopped them doing that to us. Take Gosha, and I will make them reconsider."

"You wouldn't risk it," she challenged.

"And once you're declared unfit to raise him, what do you think will happen to your other child? You've already lost one; how many more are you willing to sacrifice?"

"You son of a bitch!" Daria flung her entire body at him, ready to deliver all the blows she'd held back from delivering in the past. "You bastard!"

"Accurate on both counts." Adam grabbed Daria by the shoulders and held her at arm's length.

"You're making me choose!"

"You've chosen. I'm making you admit it."

SHE COULD CALL his bluff. She could stay. Daria's document granted her permission to leave Siberia and resettle in Odessa. It didn't force her to go. But then the door would close permanently, and Daria would never see Edward and Alyssa again. At one point, she had resigned herself to that fact. But that was when she believed she had no other choice. Now that she held it in her hand, how could she turn it down? What would it make her? She'd promised Alyssa she'd come home as soon as she could. Gosha was her child, too, but she'd made no promises to him. And the one she'd made to his father, she'd kept. Daria never promised to stay with Adam forever. It was obvious he had never expected her to.

"Will you tend Anya's grave?" Daria attempted to force at least one, face-saving demand from Adam, but her words came out as a plea.

Adam was in the process of lifting their boy onto his shoulders. "Of course."

"Tell Gosha he has two sisters. One here with him, and one away with his mother."

At this, Adam nodded. Daria had no option but to trust his word.

DARIA UNDERSTOOD THAT PRIDE, and concern for Edward, should have kept her from packing up the clothes and other personal items Adam had procured for her over the years. But she had no idea in what circumstances Edward was now living. She couldn't afford to sacrifice any item that might come in handy. So she packed the spare dress and woolen stockings. She wore her other set along with her coat, hat, gloves, scarf, and boots. And that was it, the extent of her presence in Adam's life. Except, of course, for Gosha.

She said goodbye to him at the house. There was no point in dragging a one-year-old out into the frigid cold. Even if Gosha watched Daria's train pull away, he wouldn't understand what it meant. And he wouldn't remember her, in any case. Daria wished now that she'd had at least one photograph taken. A copy to leave with him; a copy for her to take. There was a camera available. It was designated for official purposes, but a bribe could get you a personal portrait. Daria had never seen the need before to document a life she resisted living.

She had nothing to leave Gosha as a reminder. Nothing she could say that he'd still recall by nightfall, much less into adulthood. So Daria knelt in front of her son, hugged him until he squirmed, tweaked his nose in a way that made him giggle, then returned it to him, which made Gosha laugh even harder.

She had nothing to say to Adam. Or rather, she had much to say, except she had no words with which to say it. He'd saved her life, and now he was crippling it. Daria had no idea why, in either case. She wanted to ask him. But she also didn't want to know. Because she already knew.

Adam escorted her to the door. Daria turned around to take one last look. It didn't appear much different from how Daria first glimpsed it, the night she came to beg for Adam's help with Anya. The house was the same. Daria was the one who was different.

Once, she'd been afraid of Adam. Now, she lifted a hand as if to wave goodbye.

And smacked him across the face with all her might.

He'd barely had time to process what had happened when, in the next breath, Daria stretched up on her toes and brushed her lips against the red mark her palm had left along Adam's cheek.

And then she walked out the door.

DARIA ARRIVED AT the depot early, even though the westward-bound train that passed through every few weeks was inevitably late, sometimes by hours, sometimes by days. It was used to ship oil, coal, and lumber from Siberia, and to bring in the industrial machinery necessary for its excavation.

As Daria waited, she watched the latest cattle car, perhaps the same one she'd arrived on three years earlier, discharge its inhabitants. Mostly men, but some women and children, too. All of them stumbling on shaky, long-unused legs, hugging themselves or pressing together to fight the cold, looking around in confusion, attempting to catch the attention of someone in authority to explain that a terrible mistake had been made. They hadn't done anything wrong.

Daria knew half of them would be dead before the year was out. The rest would somehow find a way to survive. Whichever way they chose, Daria felt no judgment. It would be like judging a person for opting to breathe.

She caught sight of her own train rounding the bend that would bring it into the station. The red star welded on its front declared this yet another product of Comrade Stalin's ingenuity and inspired leadership. It was supposed to be her salvation, but it prompted a spasm of panic. The last time Daria had gotten onto a train, she'd had no idea where she was going and what might be waiting for her there. She felt the same way now.

"Daria!" Adam so rarely called her name—when he did deign to speak, he simply began—that Daria didn't initially recognize his voice. It wasn't until she turned and saw him hurrying up to the depot, Gosha on his back, that she experienced her second moment of panic—mixed with hope.

Adam arrived as the train was pulling in and, not stopping to take a breath, shoved Gosha into Daria's arms. She clutched at the boy, even as she looked up at Adam in confusion. He handed her a small leather bag, frayed, the metal clasp broken and bound together with twine. And then a piece of paper folded in fourths. "His travel documents."

Daria understood and asked, "You, too?"

Adam shook his head. He rifled in the depths of his coat pocket, his hand emerging with a pair of gold hoop earrings. Her *ochi chernye* earrings. Daria briefly speculated how many pairs of hands they'd passed through since the guard took her clothes from her that first day and what they'd been bartered for, inside the camp and out of it, before they landed in Adam's. She wondered how he'd gotten them. She wondered why he was giving them to her now.

"In case you have any trouble," he muttered, "back home. Food, place to live. You can sell them. They belong to you, anyway."

How did he know that? Had he observed her wearing them in Odessa?

Adam stuffed the earrings into Daria's hand. He bent briefly to kiss Gosha. And then, less briefly, Daria. It was, she realized, the first time that Adam had ever reached out to her without cover of darkness to protect them both. And that it would be the last.

Chapter 14

He didn't stay to see them off, though Daria urged Gosha to wave bye-bye to Papa through the train's window. Their designated seat was in the unheated passenger car, the wood benches covered with frayed red velvet, loose springs and stuffing burrowing through the seams. Luckily, the car was sparsely occupied. Daria noted a handful of soldiers either heading home or on leave. An older woman sat knitting in the back, while a man wearing a suit studied blueprints on his lap. At least there would be room to lie down at night. Daria had planned to sleep sitting up if it came to that. What she hadn't planned on was keeping a toddler occupied for multiple days. Or fed. Or clean.

Adam had attempted to help her, packing, along with Gosha's clothes, the toy duck he loved, some tins of condensed milk, a loaf of black bread—half rye, half sawdust, all Kyril—and scraps of dried, salted venison. Daria had brought food along as well, but she'd known in advance it wouldn't be enough. And it certainly wouldn't be enough for two.

Her more immediate concern, however, was the lavatory. Gosha was mostly toilet-trained, but not at night and, if she were honest, not always during the day. If he got distracted by something, or was frightened—as was the case now—he might forget to warn Daria and soil his pants. This had been difficult enough at home, where he'd had only one pair of woolen tights, but where Daria could repurpose old sheets and torn clothes into diapers, and where she had a tub of water to soak them and a fireplace for drying. Here, there was a public toilet at the end of the row of cars, but that proved too long to ask Gosha to hold it. She was forced to remove Gosha's tights, leave him wearing only pants, and cover him with her coat for warmth, while Daria wrung out the tights as best she could by hand and stretched them out on the seat to dry. The man with the blueprints wrinkled his nose at the smell.

Their food, despite careful rationing and two tantrums from Gosha about how hungry he was, ran out on the fourth day. Luckily, the train made a stop to refuel, and passengers were allowed to disembark briefly at the station. There, Daria attempted to buy food, but the locals brushed by her. They knew better than to engage with someone either going to, or even coming from, the East.

Desperate, Daria grabbed Gosha by the hand to keep him from running off and, in the middle of the crowded train station, sank to her knees, crossed herself, and began to pray. She didn't know what she was saying, but she'd heard kulak and German women whispering the words to themselves in the barracks, and she'd memorized enough to give an adequate performance, as long as no one listened closely. That wasn't a problem. Her actions prompted a majority of those rushing by to give Daria an even wider berth. But after a few minutes, an old woman materialized out of the crowd and dropped a carrot as wizened as she was into Daria's skirt, before quickly hobbling away. Some bread appeared. A man slipped Daria a tin can of fish.

The bounty proved enough to feed Daria and Gosha until the next stop. As she prepared to get off and hope long-banned Christian charity lived in this town, as well, one of the soldiers they'd been riding with for over a week sneaked away from his compatriots and guiltily, looking over his shoulder the entire time, forced a pair of hard-boiled eggs into her hands.

"For the boy," he said. Then added, "I'm going home to see my boy. I hope he's big and strong like yours. I have a photograph." He showed Daria a black-and-white snapshot of a child with oval eyes and dark hair whom, in that moment, Daria the non-Christian nonbeliever deemed her patron saint.

Procuring food and rushing Gosha to the toilet, then dealing with the consequences of their arriving too late, took up the majority of Daria's time. Followed by keeping him entertained for the rest of it. There was only so long an active toddler could stare out the grimy window at the barren and dull countryside. Daria and Gosha took endless walks up and down the aisles. She tried to distract him from bothering the other passengers, more and more of whom were getting on now that they'd left the tundra, or from sticking his fingers into every fixture and licking every surface. Exhausted as she was at the end of the day, when Gosha finally fell asleep on Daria's chest, asking for Papa and home, Daria remained wide awake, listening to the jagged syncopation of the rattling train tracks drawing them closer and closer to Odessa, and wondering how in the world she was going to explain Gosha to Edward.

Everything had happened in such a rush, Daria had barely a moment to consider it the first time, when Adam forbade her from leaving with the child. Before Edward had departed, Daria had told him as little as she could get away with about her deal with Adam. She doubted Edward, in his state, had heard or understood half of it. But now that time had passed, Edward must have wondered about Daria's life in Kyril. And Gosha's existence told the whole story. There were women in the camp who'd had no one to protect them, who'd been raped or had prostituted themselves out of hunger and desperation, with resulting children, too. If Daria told Edward the same had happened to her, she had no doubt he would believe her. Daria could even, with certain details left out and others looked at from a different perspective, convince herself that it was true. She was blameless; she'd had no choice. Except

Daria knew that, for some things, she'd had a choice. Adam might never hear what she told her husband about him, but Daria still refused to damn him with the lie.

Their train pulled into the Odessa *voksal* a mere day and a half later than scheduled. Daria had sent Edward a telegram before leaving Kyril, telling him which line she'd be on, but even if the train had arrived on time, she'd departed before he had the time to cable back.

The remaining passengers disembarked. Gosha began jumping with excitement. He grabbed Daria by the fingers, pulling her toward the door. She stumbled after him, attempting to balance her bag and the one Adam had packed for Gosha, without tripping. At the steps, she plopped Gosha on her hip and grabbed the satchels' handles with her other palm.

Stepping onto the platform, legs unsteady from weeks of train travel, Daria was assaulted by a multitude of impressions. First, it was the noise. She'd forgotten what a city sounded like. Kyril had been a muffled world. It wasn't the vast emptiness, or the cushioning of snow. It was that no one dared call attention to themselves. They even breathed more quietly.

Next came the bright light. The sun nearly blinded her. She raised her palm to shield her eyes and winced. Gosha was doing the same, rubbing his lids with both fists, unable to understand what was happening. It was warmer, too. She'd been aware of the train car growing less freezing as they traveled southwest, but the sensation of a wind on her skin that didn't ice on contact startled Daria. She felt a forgotten heat on her face, her neck, the backs of her hands.

And then there was Edward, slowly approaching her across the platform. He looked older, and she realized she'd unreasonably been expecting Odessa not merely to heal the broken husband she'd sent home, but to restore the young musician she'd first met. Edward's once ebony hair was now salted with gray, his skin fluttering loose off the bones of his freshly shaved face. He walked hunched, with short, shuffling steps, hesitating before he set either foot on the ground, as if asking permission. His shoulders swallowed his neck, hands bunched in his pockets, elbows pressed close to his body to avoid jostling anyone. And yet, when he looked up and smiled at her, he was the same man he'd always been. The one who made Daria's heart speed up as she realized that she was, at long last, home.

Much as she wanted to rush into his arms, Daria was weighed down by her baggage. And by Gosha . . . and his inescapable buzz of red hair.

The earrings. That's what Adam had meant. She'd had no time to think about the reasoning behind his odd gesture, until now, when the realization crashed into her. The earrings: she could sell them to buy food or find a place to live . . . in case Edward, upon seeing Gosha, refused to take her back.

Her husband approached them both, still smiling.

Edward took his hands out of his pockets. Daria was relieved to see the open sores and gashes had healed, replaced with scars and calluses. He picked up Daria's bag with one palm, then, just as naturally, reached to take Gosha out of her arms with the other. Relieved of her burden for the first time in weeks, Daria nearly collapsed with exhaustion.

"Let's go home," Edward said, leading the way.

Chapter 15

Though Daria had sent the telegram announcing her arrival to the old Odessa address, she hadn't realized that the Gordons' two-room apartment had been further cut down to only one room now—the smallest, which had been Edward's father's before they left. As they walked through the city from the train station, Edward pointed out recently built sites. He talked to Gosha, too, asking him his name, his toy duck's name, and if he went *quack-quack*. Gosha, clinging to this stranger's neck, would periodically look quizzically at Daria, strolling beside them, but since she seemed comfortable with the man, Gosha was unconcerned. A few blocks from home, the scenery shimmering in and out of focus as Daria's earlier memories of residences and stores wrestled with the subtle changes of present-day peeling paint and chopped-down trees, a horse and wagon passed alongside them, followed by a dozen children taking turns leaping on board, scooping up a handful of colorless mixture from the back, then being shooed off or, if necessary, pried off and flung into the street by the driver. Daria paid them no mind, but Edward paused and, much to Daria's surprise, called out, "Alyssochka!"

A skinny, dark-haired child in a threadbare coat and oversized shoes, whom Daria had taken for just another urchin, looked up from where she'd hit the sidewalk on all fours, skinning her knees yet still clutching her precious booty in one tenacious fist. Daria's stomach opened a chasm as she recognized, between the swinging braids and ancient eyes, vestiges of the little girl who'd once been her daughter.

Edward beckoned her toward them. Alyssa rose, brushed off her legs, and trudged in Edward's direction, glaring from him to Daria and ignoring Gosha altogether. Was she tall for eight? Short? Too thin? Healthy? Daria had no frame of reference.

"Alyssochka," Edward repeated, indicating Daria, presenting her to his daughter like a gift.

Daria's arms twinged to embrace the girl, but Alyssa's skittishness held her back. Instead, Daria reminded, "I came home as soon as I could. I kept my promise."

"So did I," Alyssa said. She looked to Edward. "I took care of Papa."

Scrambling for something to say, Daria indicated Alyssa's hand, and the wagon she'd been chasing. "What's that?"

Alyssa loosened her fist, exposing a gray mash. "Sunflower seeds. From the factory."

"They squeeze them to make oil," Edward explained when Alyssa looked satisfied that she'd done her part in keeping the conversation going. "What's left after goes to make horse feed. But the children, they like to intercept deliveries and grab some for themselves. It's delicious, right, kitten? Sweet. Like candy." He indicated Gosha. "Why don't you share some with your little brother?"

It was the first time he'd made it clear he knew who Gosha was. The shock on Alyssa's face mirrored Daria's. Alyssa dropped a minuscule sample into the tot's palm. She told Daria, "I only have a sister."

EDWARD LED THE WAY, maneuvering through the courtyard, like the rest of the city, now shabbier.

"The new *dvornik*"—Edward shrugged—"isn't as diligent as our previous one." And then he ruffled Gosha's hair.

Isaak Israelevitch had been watching from the window, anticipating their arrival. His initial delight at seeing Daria turned to confusion at the sight of Gosha. He'd come rushing to the front door from the one room the family still had left, eager to greet her. But once he understood that the child in Edward's arms wasn't a mirage, and had such a familiar face—or, rather, head of hair—he pulled back, all but spitting at the ground in disgust. *"Mamzer,"* he hissed.

"Papa . . ." Edward cautioned, the menace in his voice new to Daria's ears.

Her father-in-law turned his back on Daria, heading back to their room. "You should have stayed where you were. We don't need this here."

Judging by Alyssa's expression, Daria's daughter agreed with him.

And yet Daria had no choice but to follow them through the kitchen, where their neighbors, afraid of acknowledging Daria and infecting themselves with trace elements of her disgrace, didn't so much as scootch their chairs a centimeter closer to the table where they were eating and talking, often at the same time, in order to let the Gordon family pass. Daria had to turn sideways to squeeze through, while Edward was forced to hand her Gosha, and lift Daria's satchel over his head to keep from getting stuck. They maneuvered along the hallway jammed with strollers, a bicycle, sleds, and an assortment of dripping boots, before reaching the room that had once been Isaak Israelevitch's alone. Instead of the double bed and chifforobe Daria remembered, there were now two cots shoved against parallel walls, a smaller wardrobe, and a pair of chairs. As well as a noticeable loss.

"Where's the piano?" Daria looked to Edward in confusion.

"No space." He shrugged, as if it were a minor matter.

"No money," his father corrected. "We sold it. Your rehabilitation didn't come cheap."

"Not to worry," Edward soothed. "At the dancing school where I accompany the children's lessons, they let me use their piano whenever classes aren't in session."

"Is that what you do now?" Daria gasped. "That's where you play?"

"It's a good job."

"It's a safe job," his father clarified.

"It's a nice school." Edward appeared to believe what he was saying. "Our Alyssa should take some sessions. For poise, beauty, art. But not our girl. She would rather run in the streets with the boys."

There was no judgment in Edward's voice as he said it, rather a bit of pride. Alyssa had clearly heard it many times before and didn't take offense. Daria, on the other hand, looked at her ragamuffin of a child and imagined what Mama would think about the way Daria's daughter was being raised.

Daria asked Edward, "Have you heard from my mother? How is she?"

Her husband and father-in-law exchanged nervous glances, not unlike the one they'd exchanged all those years ago when Daria urged them to tell Mama she wasn't an embarrassment.

"She's dead, isn't she?" Daria guessed. During her years away, Daria had accepted the possibility that Mama might die before Daria found her way back home.

"We don't know," Edward confessed.

This was the only thing she'd been unprepared for. "How is that possible?"

"Your village," Isaak Israelevitch hedged. "The Ukrainian village next to it was assigned a pipe factory. The Great Leap Forward, you understand. It needed to be built, and it was decided that Valta was the most strategic spot. So all those living there were resettled. We don't know where."

"But how?"

"They were wealthy landowners—their property warranted being returned to the people," Isaak Israelevitch reported dryly.

"But they had nothing. They starved; they froze."

"This wasn't like the kulaks," Edward rushed to reassure. "They weren't arrested. They were resettled."

"Except nobody knows where." Daria's legs gave out, and she sank onto a chair, still clutching a drowsy Gosha.

"You need to rest." Edward directed Alyssa, "Why don't we let your brother have your bed tonight? Tomorrow we can try to scrounge up another pair of chairs."

Her daughter was still sleeping on two chairs, Daria realized. And she was sitting on one of them. But Alyssa was so much bigger now, how could she fit? The answer became obvious when Daria saw her dragging over a solid wooden slat from the corner, to put on top of the chairs. Daria recognized it as the leaf to their old table. Not wanting to take the child's bed on top of the other upheaval she'd rammed into her life, Daria quickly stood and protested, "No need for that. Gosha can sleep with me. He did it for the entire trip here. Anything else would scare him."

"All right," Edward agreed, as he had to everything. "Papa to your bed, Alyssa to yours. Daria and Gosha can take mine. I'll make myself comfortable on the floor."

His bed. Of course Edward had expected her to sleep in his bed. She was his wife. And now she had taken it for herself and another man's child.

He saw the worry on her face and reassured, "Sleep now. We will have plenty of time to settle everything in the morning."

"I'm so sorry," she whispered. "For everything."

He kissed her lightly, almost as if it were the first time, and they were still the people they'd once been. Younger than anyone had a right to be. "Welcome home, my Daria."

THEY WERE ALL gone by the time Daria woke up the next morning. To work, to school. Gosha sat quietly, waiting for Daria to stir. As soon as she did, however, he jumped on top of her.

"Papa?" Gosha wondered.

Daria sat up, already rolling to get out of bed. Prison ingrained productive habits. "Papa isn't here. Time to get up, wash, and find out who is."

The answer to her question was: the same neighbors who'd ignored her last night. Spending the day with women who'd looked down on Daria as common and provincial even before her political disgrace made venturing out seem less intimidating. Daria took Gosha by the hand and offered him an encouraging smile to prove that Mama wasn't afraid, so no reason for him to be. In the courtyard, wrenching her eyes from the spot Adam had described Alyssa and Anya burying their treasure, and torturing herself with the thought that some remnant of her Anya might still be there, Daria instead fixed her gaze on the garbage dumped out yesterday, now more sodden, more spread out, and more putrid. The *dvornik* was making a token effort at poking through it with his broom, as if it were an animal that might be coaxed into fleeing of its own accord. He was a scrawny man, perhaps half Adam's height and width, with a bald head that he attempted to cover by looping a single lock of hair from ear to ear. He moved so slowly, he might have been treading through tar. Daria wondered who in the world had decreed such a man a fit replacement for Adam. But then she remembered that competence was not the most important part of the job description.

He glared up at Daria, making it clear he knew who she was and where she'd been. And then he sent the sloppy pile of refuse he'd been pretending to contain straight at Daria's feet. The goal was to intimidate her, to remind her of her place. But he wasn't her first *dvornik*. Daria bent to pick up the scraps of day-old newspaper wrapped around her ankle. Did he really think petty tyrants like him still had the power to frighten her?

"You defaced the image of Comrade Stalin!" Daria pointed to the front-page photo, smeared with mud. The *dvornik* turned pale and scurried away.

Arrests had been made for much less.

Since she was already holding the discarded *Pravda* in her hand, Daria gave it a glance. Comrade Stalin was pictured with the Austrian Daria recalled ruling Germany, alongside a new face, a Romanian military man called Antonescu, who'd deposed the royal family. Comrade Stalin was praising the end of King Carol's rule, even as he welcomed the crown's generous ceding of the Bessarabian territory to its rightful owners, the Soviets, following the wishes of its people, who'd been so cruelly conquered by Romanians following the Great War.

News took a long time to reach Kyril, and as Daria read, she learned for the first time of a non-aggression pact between the USSR and Germany, their joint purging of saboteurs in Poland, complete with parades to commemorate their success and the establishment of free elections in the Baltic States, which resulted in a triumph of Communism that led to a petition to join the USSR. Daria read that an unjust, imperialist war had been going on for two years now, between Germany and the capitalists of England and France. Comrade Molotov was quoted as saying that Germany had a legitimate interest in regaining its position as a great power, and the Allies had started an aggressive war in order to maintain the Versailles system. They were using the pretext of defending democracy as a way of exterminating any political position with which they did not agree.

Just reading this nonsense left Daria exhausted. In Kyril, life had been simpler. You did what you were told. No thinking was required. In fact, it was actively discouraged. Just do what everybody else did, agree with what everybody else agreed. Unlike the *dvornik*, Daria neatly folded the newspaper before depositing it in the trash, in case anyone was watching. She took Gosha by the hand and turned back to wait for Edward, his father, and Alyssa to return for their midday meal.

Daria had considered cooking something, but she didn't know which food in the communal kitchen might be theirs and didn't dare risk an accusation of thievery. Back home, Edward told her they didn't keep their food in the kitchen. Others weren't as concerned as Daria about taking their neighbors' supplies. Instead, the Gordons kept their things hidden in corners of their room. A loaf of bread buried at the bottom of a drawer, a tin of sardines atop the chifforobe, a bottle of milk on the cool windowsill, a packet of tea squeezed between the covers of a book. They rarely had enough to sequester. They depended on whatever they could pick up that day. While Alyssa went to school and Edward worked, his father spent every morning moving from food line to food line, an *avoska* woven of string in his pocket, gathering whatever was available.

"I can do that from now on," Daria offered, wanting to prove herself useful.

"No," her father-in-law snapped. "You stay home, watch . . . him." A nod toward Gosha's direction. "I'll take care of my family."

It was clear he wished to pretend that Daria had never returned. He refused to let her help with the meal, and when he passed the soup pot, it was in the opposite direction of Daria. He spoke to Edward, and he spoke to Alyssa. And that was all. Alyssa had yet to address Daria, either.

Daria resolved to give the child time to get used to her return. And, in an attempt to work her way back into Isaak Israelevitch's favor or, at the very least, lessen the silent tension simmering around them, Daria brought up what had previously been one of her father-in-law's favorite topics to expound on. Remembering what she'd read in *Pravda*, Daria asked about the situation with Germany and the other countries split between Communist and Fascist powers.

"God willing the Germans should come to Odessa," the older man prayed. "Free us all."

"I saw in the newspaper that it won't happen. Molotov-Ribbentrop Pact."

"Germans signed a pact with England. France, too. Look at them now. We should be so fortunate. No one else has the power to save us."

"So you think there will be war?" Daria noticed Edward had been keeping his eyes down the entire time his father prognosticated.

Her husband now shrugged. "I don't worry about things I can't control."

Chapter 16

===

"I don't worry about things I can't control," Daria soon learned, was her husband's response to everything. Resigned, stoical, passive, compliant. Her playful, opinionated, teasing, passionate Edward was gone. Not merely in public for fear of censure, or even in private, where he knew the walls still had ears, but also in moments where it was just the two of them. After a few nights of sleeping with her, Daria had evicted Gosha from the bed, tucking him into a two-chair setup like Alyssa's. She'd feared he'd fuss, but Gosha was thrilled to be like his sister—even as she refused to give him the time of day. Daria wondered if Alyssa remembered when it had been her and Anya's beds set up in identical fashion. Daria didn't know whether acknowledging it would show that she was sympathetic to Alyssa's loss, or whether it would open up old wounds and push her daughter further away. So Daria kept silent. The first night Gosha was squared away, Daria indicated that Edward should be the one in bed with his wife. Edward climbed in dutifully, which was no less than Daria expected. But when she reached for him once she was certain the rest of their household was asleep, Daria had to admit she did expect something of the old Edward to show itself. Surely, when it was just the two of them, like this, he would no longer feel compelled to keep up his facade—he could feel safe, he could feel free . . .

But as in all else, Edward did what was required of him, no more, no less.

No passion.

No heart.

No life.

For the first few weeks, Daria racked her brain, convinced there must be some magic word she could say, some magic act she could perform that would break Edward out of his stupor; perhaps a kiss that, in an ironic role reversal, would awaken the handsome prince from his sleeping spell and set the kingdom right. Her first instinct was to ask him to play the piano for her. His deft, limber fingers were what had made Daria fall in love with him. She hoped to re-ignite that spark. But then Daria remembered the last time she'd heard Edward play. *The Blue Danube*. For her and Adam. Surely, Edward remembered it, too.

Besides, they no longer had a piano in the house.

Daria tried asking Edward about his work, but his monosyllabic answers made her think he was ashamed of how far he'd come down in the world. From packed concert halls and ecstatic fans throwing flowers to background music for oafish little girls. Even his daughter wanted no part of it.

Then again, Daria wondered what Alyssa did wish to be a part of. Certainly not becoming reacquainted with her mother. While Daria's repeated overtures to Edward were met with a vague politeness, Alyssa's answers to Daria's questions were equally monosyllabic— and a great deal more hostile. She didn't speak, she hissed. And she responded to any request from Daria by making it clear she was performing under duress. If Edward was in the room, he ignored her behavior. If Isaak Israelevitch was present, he actively encour-aged it.

Mama would have never tolerated such disrespect. Daria was

willing to accept it as her due. But Daria's tolerance failed to extend to the way Alyssa treated Gosha.

The toddler adored his big sister. Gosha eagerly followed Alyssa around, tripping over his unsteady feet to keep up, only to be left behind in the courtyard as Alyssa dashed off with her gang of friends, or to receive a door slammed in his face. He'd dangle from the knob with both palms, too short to turn it, plaintively calling out, "Issa! Issa!" Then he would pull up a tiny chair and sit patiently, waiting for her to return.

It broke Daria's heart to see the little boy who'd stopped asking for Papa, having realized that he'd never get an answer, now face such additional rejection on a daily basis. Daria might not have been able to break through to either Edward or Alyssa on her own behalf, but she'd be damned if she allowed her son to suffer.

Daria told Alyssa, "I'm going to the store. You need to watch Gosha." It wasn't a request; it was a command. It was the way Mama would have done it.

Up to this point, Daria had been tiptoeing around Alyssa. Couching all communication in a soft, subservient voice. "Would you please, Allysochka," and "If you wouldn't mind, Allysochka." The change in tone shocked her daughter to where she didn't argue as Daria hurried out the door.

Daria realized she was taking a risk. For all she knew, Alyssa would abandon Gosha to his own devices. Or she might stuff him into a corner and forbid him to come out. Pinch and taunt him as a way to get back at Daria.

And yet, Daria retained faith that the little girl who'd taken care of Anya while her parents were dragged into the forest, the one who'd stopped fighting and given in when Daria explained she had to return to Odessa so she could take care of Papa, the one who'd shared her precious allotment of sunflower seeds, no matter how grudgingly, would do no such thing.

Daria didn't go far. She lurked just outside their door. If Alyssa and Gosha ventured outside, she could pretend to be returning from her shopping trip. Daria didn't bother actually purchasing an item to make her cover story plausible. Nobody would find it odd if she came back with an empty *avoska*.

Shamelessly eavesdropping, Daria first heard Gosha's muffled voice entreating Alyssa to play with him. Her initial answers were brusque, but Gosha refused to give up. After fifteen minutes, Daria heard Alyssa responding in a more pleasant tone. And then she heard giggles. Followed by music. Alyssa was singing, urging Gosha to join in. The tune was familiar.

It was the tune Alyssa and Edward had hummed as they buried Anya.

Daria staggered away from the door as if singed. But then an equal burning force propelled Daria forward. She burst through the door, unsure of what she expected to find.

What she found was Alyssa giddily spinning, Gosha perched on her hip, holding his hand in hers, both their arms outstretched.

"Waltz!" her son proclaimed happily, cheeks flushed with excitement, curls whipping into his face. "Issa, Gosha waltz!"

Alyssa appeared caught in the act, looking guilty when, as far as Daria could see, there was nothing to feel guilty about. And then Daria realized that her daughter wasn't feeling guilty before Daria. She was feeling guilty before her grandfather. And her sister.

Attempting to defuse the situation, Daria swallowed the question she'd truly wanted to ask, the one about the tune Alyssa had been singing, and, instead, pivoted to a more harmless one. She adopted a jolly tone when she teased Alyssa. "Papa is right, you're a natural dancer. You should be taking classes at his school."

Daria had been aiming for a light remark that wouldn't upset her daughter. But instead of laughing or simply dismissing Daria's suggestion, Alyssa's expression darkened. She let go of Gosha. He slid down her leg, hitting the floor on his bottom with a thump, looking quizzically up at Alyssa, wondering what he'd done wrong.

Daria was wondering the same thing.

"I'll never go there," Alyssa snarled.

Daria couldn't understand what had provoked such an extreme reaction.

"You said everything would be all right"—Alyssa tried to cling to her anger, but it wasn't powerful enough to hold back a sob—"as long as we followed the rules."

Yes, Daria had said that. She'd even believed it once.

"Papa followed the rules." Alyssa angrily wiped the tears from her cheek with one palm. "You lied."

DARIA STOOD OUTSIDE the door to the studio where Edward played piano at the Lenin School of Dance. Not wanting to upset Alyssa further, she'd intended to bring Gosha with her. But, much to Daria's surprise, a still sniffling Alyssa had taken his hand and, attempting to sound nonchalant, offered, "He can stay with me. If he wants."

Of course Gosha wanted. And it made it easier for Daria to stand to the side and remain unobserved as she watched the proceedings through the tiny window in the door.

A dozen little girls, no more than eight years old, all dressed identically in black leotards with white tights and ballet slippers, their only individuality expressed in how big and how many hair bows their mothers had managed to affix atop their heads, stood in solemn rows, facing a bony, angular woman, her gray hair swept in a bun, a ruler in her hand long enough to reach even the farthest child. The piano was off to the side, by the window, meaning that Edward was little more than a shadow. He sat patiently, waiting for the minuscule nod from Madame that indicated he should begin playing.

When he did, she barely let him get past the first few bars before the ruler whipped out to thwack the top of the piano, missing Edward's face by centimeters. Unlike back at the camp, when any noise made him cower, Edward had gotten so used to the abuse that, now, he didn't flinch.

"No! Imbecile! Too fast!"

Edward obligingly began again.

"Too slow! Did they not teach you meter at that prestigious music school of yours?"

Another try. This time, Madame allowed him to finish the exercise before asking the girls, "Did you hear this? This is what happens when *zhidy* force their internationalist playing into good Soviet spaces. Absolute butchery of our great Tchaikovsky." She commanded Edward, "Again! In rhythm this time, perhaps?"

Edward played. Madame stopped him. It went on like this for the duration of the forty-minute class. He was playing the wrong piece. He was playing the right piece badly. He was off tempo, he was off pitch, he was clearly doing it on purpose, he was obviously too incompetent to be capable of sabotage.

By the end, Daria was shaking with rage. Edward just kept playing. He sped up when told to speed up; he slowed down when told to slow down. He never blamed the piano, which even Daria could tell was out of tune, or the conflicting instructions. He just played. At the end of the lesson, as the girls curtsied to their teacher, he sat on the bench, hands on his lap, waiting for the next class to begin. A few of the girls, presumably out of habit from previous instruction, also bowed their heads in thanks to Edward. At that, he offered a smile in return.

But Madame cut them off. "No," she barked, pounding the floor with her ruler. "In this class, we don't salute enemies of the state."

The door opened to let them out and the next batch of ballerinas in. Daria ducked out of the way, lest Edward see her. She told herself that what she felt for Edward was pity. She didn't want to humiliate him any more than he obviously was already each day. But the self-deception could last only so long. What Daria was really feeling toward Edward was anger.

How could he just sit there and take this abuse? Edward, who'd once held gigantic concert halls in thrall, was allowing some skeletal nobody barely good enough to instruct clumsy children in a dingy ballet studio to criticize his playing. He was letting her call him names and even forbidding him from receiving the piddling accolades to which he was rightly entitled. Why didn't he speak up? Why didn't he play something so wonderful, it would crack that ruler of hers straight in half? Why was he being such a . . . such a . . . coward?

Just thinking the word snapped Daria back to reality like the most frigid of Siberian winds. She had no right to do this. She had no right to judge Edward. It wasn't her husband's fault that his early life had been too easy, too privileged, too genteel. Unlike her, he'd been conditioned to expect special treatment, to be feted like a prince, to be allowed to forget what his true place should have been, if not for all that prodigious talent. No wonder he broke in Kyril. There was no place for a man like him there. And if a man couldn't be a man, then he became a machine, doing what he was told without complaint or resistance. A cowering animal fearing the lash.

Daria was to blame for making him this way. She'd said if they followed the rules, they'd be all right. So Edward had done as she'd said. He'd buried their child as she'd said; he'd accompanied her to Adam's as she'd said. And he'd left Kyril. As she'd said. It wasn't Siberia that destroyed her husband's spirit.

It was Daria herself.

THIS TIME, THERE was a Chaika limousine. But it came right after dusk, not just before dawn. Every building surrounding their courtyard held its breath, wondering for whom they were there. A lone officer mounted the steps to their apartment, as all those he'd passed by exhaled in relief. He knocked on their door. He asked to speak with Isaak Israelevitch Gordon.

Their communal neighbors scurried out of sight as Daria's father-in-law trembled down the hall, his legs giving out so that Edward had to grab him under the elbow, and half carry him the rest of the way. Daria rushed to follow, telling the children to stay in their room. Neither listened.

"You are acquainted with KGB officer Roman Anatolyevitch Luria?" asked the KGB officer who did not feel the need to share his own name.

Was it a trick question? How could it not be?

Daria's father-in-law opened his mouth to speak but managed only a dry gargle. A single twitch of the chin constituted a nod. Roman Anatolyevitch Luria had signed Daria's release papers.

"He has been arrested," they were informed. Naming the charge was irrelevant. The charge was irrelevant. "We are investigating known associates."

"Concerts," Isaak Israelevitch croaked. "He would come to my son's concerts. Many years ago. Before."

"We would leave him tickets," Edward said.

Was that delight in the officer's eyes? "Bribes?"

"Tokens of respect," Daria interjected.

Why wasn't Edward doing anything? Couldn't he see what was going on, the danger they were all in? Adam would have done something. He would have sized up the situation, understood what the officer was really after, and found a way to give it to him. Adam would have known how to save them. But Edward just stood there, as accepting as always, braced for whatever happened, instead of making something happen.

Was it up to Daria now? She took stock. The officer had arrived alone. That was unusual. They usually traveled in pairs, sometimes more, in case the prisoners caused trouble. And so they could keep an eye on each other. He came in uniform and in an official car, but not at the traditional time. It was too late for daytime working hours, and too early for the morning assault.

So that was it . . . of course . . .

Daria whipped around, rushing past Alyssa and Gosha to their room. She squeezed beneath the bed and dragged out the traveling case she'd brought from Kyril. Ripping at the lining, Daria found the hoop earrings she'd hidden there and hightailed it back into the hallway. Isaak was still in the process of trying to assemble a coherent sentence, while Edward stood by, watching.

"Would you be kind enough to do me a favor?" Daria dredged up a flirtatious demeanor she hadn't seen fit to unleash since . . . she'd gone begging to Adam. She held out her earrings to the officer. "These belong to Roman Anatolyevitch's wife. I borrowed them. Would you please see that they are returned?"

Did Roman Anatolyevitch have a wife? Daria had no idea.

The officer accepted her jewelry in the spirit in which it had been given. He studied them closely. He held them up to the light; he jiggled them and listened to the sound they made. He did everything but bite them to test the karats.

He slipped them into his pocket and bowed his head slightly in Daria's direction. "I will make certain they end up in the right hands."

And he was out the door, his "Thank you for your cooperation, Comrade" echoing in the stairway as a lesson for eavesdropping others.

Isaak slumped against the wall, teeth chattering, the nails of one hand scraping the flesh of the other until it bled. Daria hadn't exactly been expecting thanks, but she had been looking for some sort of acknowledgment of what she'd done. If not from Isaak, then at least from Edward. Did he recognize the earrings? Did he remember how she'd lost them? Was he curious about how she'd gotten them back, or why she'd been hiding them?

Her husband took his father's elbow again, gingerly escorting Isaak back to the bedroom. He did smile at her over his shoulder. "You always looked so beautiful in those, my Daria."

DARIA THOUGHT THAT Edward was asleep. If she hadn't thought he was asleep next to her, she never would have allowed herself the indulgence of tears. Daria sobbed soundlessly, clenching her teeth together and concentrating on taking long, even breaths through her nose, even as her cheeks grew wetter. She buried her face in the pillow to muffle any remaining sound and locked her body stiff as a tree branch, lest shaking give her away.

Still, it wasn't enough. She felt Edward roll toward her, pressing against Daria, one arm sliding around her waist as he stroked her hair with the other.

"Don't grieve. They were only things."

Through sheer force of will and well-practiced habit, Daria raised her head from the pillow, offering Edward a heartened smile to show that she agreed, of course they were just things, things were meaningless, and she was grateful for his comfort. All the while keeping to herself what she was truly grieving.

AND SO THEY lived in such a manner for close to a year, saying all the correct things publicly, even to each other, while holding their own protective counsel. It felt unnatural and uncomfortable and stifling. And then it grew impossible to recall that there had ever been any other way. What you said was for others. What you thought was for yourself. So it couldn't be used against you. Until one day toward the end of June, when Daria opened the door to find Adam on the other side of it.

She could only gape, waving her hands behind her back, as if the flurry of meaningless action might keep Edward, his father, Alyssa, and Gosha from seeing what Daria was seeing. "What— What are you doing here?" she managed to say.

"He sent for me," Adam said. And pointed at Daria's husband.

Chapter 17

He didn't seem real. It was impossible that Adam was now standing in front of Daria. He looked too big for the doorway, too big for their tiny room. Daria was embarrassed at how small her life was. He sucked the air out of her lungs. Gosha looked at Adam curiously, then went back to his play. He still had the duckie pull toy.

Edward stretched his hand for Adam to shake, drew him in, and closed the door. "Thank you for coming."

Adam ignored the formality, eyes shifting from Gosha to Daria, but when Adam spoke, it was to Edward. "You wrote they were in danger."

Daria wasn't sure which shocked her more, the fact that her husband had told such a blatant lie, or that he'd taken the initiative to do so. "Why would you tell him that, Edward?"

Edward didn't take his own eyes off Adam. "The Germans, they'll be here any day now. By end of summer, most likely."

"No!" Daria objected. "I was listening to the radio. They said it's only Poland and the other territories. Hitler would never be so foolish as to attack the USSR. The pact—"

"Let them come!" Isaak Israelevitch interrupted. "The Germans are civilized people. Not like these Cossack barbarians. We'll greet them as liberators."

"You weren't there, Papa." The words came tumbling out of Edward. Daria was reminded of how Anya had nearly thrown a tantrum after weeks of being good and keeping it all penned up, and of how frequently Daria herself had ached to blurt out the forbidden. She'd never imagined it might also be true of her now taciturn Edward. But, then again, why wouldn't it be? Why should he be different from the rest of them? Why couldn't Edward be suppressing his authentic voice just as strenuously, and for the same reasons? "You didn't see. I was in Germany. In 1933, in 1936. I saw. There's an evil there. It's festering, it's growing. They're coming for us next."

Daria didn't understand. "The Germans aren't bad people. We lived with so many of them, in the camp. Those families were as falsely accused as we were; they didn't do anything wrong."

"Those are not the Germans who are coming," Edward said. "You don't know what they're doing to Jews in Germany. I saw their leaflets, I watched them burn synagogues, ransack stores, attack old men in the streets."

"Ridiculous," Isaak Israelevitch spoke up. "You didn't see this. You've been listening to capitalist propaganda. That's all this is, like during the Great War. The West claimed German soldiers were bayoneting babies, drinking their blood! No such atrocities happened—we know that now. It was deliberate disinformation to convince us the Germans were our enemies and the Soviets our saviors. I tell you, compared to what we're enduring under their rule—"

"The Germans," Edward hissed, "will make the Communists appear like benign occupiers. Adam, you must get them out of here. Daria and Gosha, Alyssa, too. Take them east. The Germans will never advance that far. The cold will stop them, like it did Napoleon. Daria and the children will be safe. Please." His voice broke and, for a moment, Daria thought Edward would sink to his knees. *"Please."*

"No." Daria piped up before Adam had a chance to answer. "We're not going anywhere."

"You must." Daria would have said she was seeing glimpses of the old Edward, except he had never been this forceful, this decisive before. "You'll die if you stay here. We'll all die."

"Then we'll leave together." The decision seemed simple to Daria.

"We can't just ask for permission to leave. No one will grant us that. We don't have the political capital. Besides, you need someone who can take care of you and the children, someone who can protect you no matter which side is in power."

Edward knew that person could never be him.

And thanks to her afternoon spent lurking at the ballet academy's door, Daria knew who had made him feel that way. Just because it was true didn't mean she wasn't to blame.

"You're my husband," Daria said, although that didn't address Edward's argument. She could never leave him. Precisely because what he'd said was true.

"I'll take them," Adam cut in brusquely. The strength holding Edward upright left him as he all but collapsed in gratitude. Except then Adam said, "If Daria wants me to."

If Daria wants me to . . . The words swam in her brain. What the hell did Daria's wants have to do with anything? Daria's wants and actions were what had brought about this situation. Daria's wants were of no relevance. As Comrade Stalin loved to distort Tolstoy and remind his citizens, "You have no rights, only obligations."

"Thank you," Daria told Adam, letting a fraction of the emotion that she felt for him come spilling out, even as she was already pulling herself back together. "You were kind to come. But this is where I belong."

"At least take the boy." Edward swung Gosha up off the floor and thrust him into Adam's arms. "He's your son; you can take him—you have the right. Then Daria will have to come, too." He looked at her desperately. "She'd never choose me over him."

Gosha looked questioningly at Edward before turning his attentions to Adam. Or rather, to the sole gold button of Adam's coat.

He twisted it curiously in both directions, paying no attention to the man staring longingly at him. Daria waited for Adam to contradict Edward, to reveal that Daria had already chosen her husband over her son once before. That should be enough to convince Edward. It should be enough to send Adam on his way. Before Daria's resolve began to waver.

"No." Adam peered over Gosha's head at Daria. "I'm afraid I cannot do that."

"Let me talk to her," Edward pleaded. "Reason with her. Give me until tomorrow morning."

"I won't change my mind," Daria said, as much to herself as to either of the men. "I won't leave you."

"I'll come back in the morning," Adam said.

EDWARD BEGGED, EDWARD CAJOLED, Edward wept. The latter disgusted his father, terrified Alyssa, and prompted Gosha to toddle over and pat Edward on the head, the way Edward did when Gosha hurt himself. It was that last move that solidified the resolve Daria earlier feared shattering. After everything she'd put Edward through, after the way he'd taken her back and accepted Gosha, treating the boy like his own no matter how cruel the derision from Isaak, Daria couldn't abandon Edward—not for anything, not for anyone, and that included her children. She'd done it once before. Staying with Edward now would be her penance for that betrayal.

Daria tried to convince him they would be fine. Their families had weathered the previous German occupation and, as his father kept insisting, even thrived! They would manage whatever came next. Daria possessed skills now. She couldn't imagine a future she couldn't handle, one that would prove more cataclysmic than her recent past.

But Edward kept talking. He talked through most of the evening and, after everyone else had gone to bed, he whispered. He embraced Daria; he shook her. She kept expecting him to grow weary, but the more she resisted, the more fervent he became.

Daria found it impossible to keep wrangling, especially when she was determined to keep her true argument hidden from him at all costs. Finally, Daria collapsed into an exhausted sleep, Edward's words still buzzing in her ears.

She thought she woke because he'd at long last stopped, and it was the silence that roused her. Edward had, at some point, collapsed on the bed beside her, twitching and mumbling with his eyes closed. Yet what she'd actually heard were Adam's footsteps outside their room. She could still pick them out, even while asleep. Daria slipped out of bed and hurried to the door, opening it and darting outside before Adam could knock. It was dark, barely dawn. Daria hadn't realized that when Adam said he'd be back in the morning, he'd meant at first light.

"I wanted to get you alone." Had he anticipated her hearing him and dashing out before anyone else? Did he know her that well?

"I haven't changed my mind," she said.

Adam sighed. "We can take him with us. Your husband. His father, too. I can try to arrange the papers. It may take a while."

"And what would happen to me?" Daria demanded.

"Whatever you want."

"I want to stay with my husband," she declared, then wavered. "I need to stay with my husband."

"And he needs to know you and your children are safe."

"Gosha," Daria prompted, as if Adam needed reminding. "He's been so good to him." Her next thought may not have made sense coming directly after to Adam, but it did to Daria. "I can't leave Edward."

"He wants you to."

"He doesn't know what he wants. He needs me to look after him."

"And you need to play martyr. Again."

She knew what he meant. That didn't mean she had to like it. "Go to hell."

"I plan to. It's still frozen over."

Despite herself, Daria smiled.

"I missed you," she confessed, locking her hands behind her back again, to keep herself from rushing to him. This conversation couldn't be happening. How could this conversation be happening? How could Adam be standing in front of her, close enough to touch? Close enough that he shouldn't, under any circumstances, be touched?

Adam followed her lead, keeping his distance, though Daria had no way of knowing if it was for the same reason. Was he feeling it, too, this irresistible pull? This unacceptable pull? She understood no more about what Adam was thinking or feeling now than she ever had.

Voice devoid of judgment, he observed, "When you're with him, you miss me. When you were with me, you missed him."

What was there to say to that but . . . "Yes."

"And I'm the one who should go to hell?" Was that amusement or fury Daria was seeing? "You've reserved yourself the main room!"

She sighed. "Good thing we're so used to living in crowded quarters."

To hell with distance, to hell with following her lead. Adam grabbed Daria and kissed her. It felt so much like the first time, the urgency, the unrestrained passion, the need, and the release. But Daria also knew it was the last time for them both. So she didn't rush. Yes, they could be seen; yes, they could be caught; yes, they could be reported. But once again, Daria couldn't find it within herself to be scared of anything that might happen in preference over what currently was. She raised her arms to wrap around his neck, then slid her palms until they were cradling his cheeks. Adam's hands went around her waist as he lifted her off the ground. He broke his mouth away from hers and buried his lips in her neck, moving around to the crest of her throat, then up to her chin, her jaw, and back to her lips, her tongue, anything and everything, greedy and demanding and giving, remembering and memorizing her at the same time.

They couldn't have stood as they were that long, because it was still barely day outside when they heard Alyssa's frantic screaming from the other side of the door.

Adam and Daria broke apart. She tore back into their room, where Daria encountered a hysterical Alyssa, Isaak Israelevitch beside her, Gosha right behind, tugging frantically at what it took Daria a stupefied moment to comprehend were Edward's legs, hanging limply from the ceiling.

Chapter 18

═══

Daria's first thought was how quiet Edward had to have been, making sure no one woke up while he was methodically stringing his belt over the water pipe, tightening it around his neck, and, especially, during the last of his death throes. What self-control it must have taken, how determined he must have been.

Adam sprang into action, cutting Edward down with a single swipe of his knife. Edward's body collapsed to the floor. Adam stretched Edward out on his back, sending the chairs in his way crashing in all directions and dropping to his knees. He slapped Edward across the cheeks, he pounded his chest, he opened his mouth and breathed into it. But Daria realized it was too late. Edward's face was a Kandinsky of blue and red blotches, his tongue swollen and slack. She'd seen too much death not to recognize when it was irrevocable.

Gosha ran crying, terrified, into Daria's arms. Alyssa hovered over Edward and Adam, gazing at them with a hope Daria also knew too well. She'd seen it on Alyssa's face even as she'd hurried to bury Anya. Isaak Israelevitch was pummeling Adam's shoulders, trying to pull him off Edward, screaming that Adam was murdering him, calling him names in Russian, in Ukrainian, in Yiddish, cursing him, accusing him, entreating him. It was only when Adam sat back on his haunches, spent, hands by his sides, surrendering to the inevitable, that Daria's father-in-law turned his curses toward her. He called Daria a whore, a wretch, a home-wrecker, a killer. She let his words hit her like waves, like arrows, welcoming them, embracing them as the very least she deserved.

With Daria's help, Adam moved Edward's body off the floor and onto the bed. He volunteered to see if he could round up an undertaker. Daria nodded. She couldn't take her eyes off Edward, couldn't stop smoothing the matted hair across his forehead or stroking his still warm cheek, the way she remembered his doing to Anya. She linked her fingers through his; she massaged his palm with her thumb, the way he'd once playfully done to hers. Behind her, Daria could hear Alyssa's hysterics settling into breathless, ragged sobs, while Gosha sniffled alongside her. Isaak Israelevitch had gone silent, sagging onto a chair, head in his hands. She knew she should turn around and address them, comfort them, at least remove the children from the room so their last memory of Edward wouldn't be this horror. But Daria had no strength left for any of it.

Instead, she remained as she was until Adam returned with word that the undertaker said it would be a few days—a week, at most. They should wrap the body in a shroud—bedsheets would do; as if they had a set to spare—and wait for notification regarding when they'd be allowed to bury him.

"No!" She was shocked by her own scream. Alyssa and Gosha jumped in terror, though Isaak Israelevitch didn't so much as budge. "I can't leave him."

"You will." The words came, muffled, from behind Isaak's palms. So faint, Daria at first thought she'd misheard. But then he raised his head and repeated, "You will get out of my house, and take your goddamn bastard with you."

Daria looked toward Gosha, but, as he had no idea what the expression meant, or that it was directed at him, her son remained unaffected. Adam also declined to respond to the old man's taunt.

Then again, Adam never minded when she'd used it against him. It was a factual term, he said.

A moment earlier, Daria had been determined to stay as she was, where she was, to stay by Edward's side forever, like she'd promised that breathless day back at the ZAGS. She knew her father-in-law's threat was empty. Daria's *propiska* had her assigned to this space. Even with Edward dead, Isaak Israelevitch couldn't evict Daria or Gosha. Relocation was up to the regional leadership, not personal preference. The old man couldn't do anything to Daria. And yet, this was what Daria deserved. She deserved punishment; she deserved disgrace, abuse, banishment; she deserved it all.

"All right," Daria said. "I'll go."

Her father-in-law looked triumphant, but also aware that it was a hollow, pointless victory.

"What about Alyssa?" Daria wondered if she'd be losing another child in another well-earned penance.

"She stays with us." Isaak, sensing Daria's surrender and the chance to hold on to at least some part of his beloved Edward, moved in for the kill. He cajoled, "You would like to stay here with me, wouldn't you, Allysochka?"

The child hesitated, looking from Edward's body to her mother. "Are you going back to Anya?"

"Yes."

Her daughter thought it over, the push-pull of dual loyalties written across her face even as she apologetically told her grandfather, "I'll go with her."

"You can come, too, Isaak Israelevitch." Adam's generosity stunned Daria. "I can arrange travel papers. It may take a few days—"

"Damn your days! Damn all of you for what you've done! Get out of my house! Leave us alone!"

"Edward . . ." Daria began.

"I'll bury my son on my own. Just like you buried my granddaughter."

"Please," Daria entreated, sounding as desperate as Edward had when he was begging her to go, begging Adam to make her go. "Please, he's my husband. Please, let me—"

"You killed him." Isaak Israelevich indicated Adam. "Listen to this savage of yours, and at least do the last thing my son asked of you. Go!"

DARIA HURRIEDLY PACKED UP her and the children's few things, leaving Alyssa to say goodbye to her grandfather while Daria, Adam, and Gosha waited in the courtyard, ignoring the curious and mercenary looks of their neighbors, not to mention the *dvornik*, who eyed Adam warily, as if afraid of being picked up by his collar and tossed into the street, a pretender to the throne.

"I can't do this," Daria whispered. "I have no right."

"He's dead." Adam's voice was matter-of-fact. Daria knew better than most that energy was to be expended on the living. "He wanted me to take you away from Odessa."

"I wanted that, too," Daria confessed, horrified to hear words that previously had only echoed inside her head bursting like icicles into the otherwise moderate June day. "I had dreams, over and over, once, sometimes twice a week, of you coming for me. Not Gosha, me."

"Edward was grateful you came back to him. He wrote me."

Stunned to hear that, Daria faltered. "What—What else did he say?"

"That Gosha was a good boy." That part visibly touched Adam most. "And that none of you were safe in Odessa."

"It's my fault he didn't trust himself to take care of us. I made him feel that way,"

Adam pointed to the room where Edward's body still lay. "He did take care of you."

"I loved Edward," Daria said. "And I loved you, too."

The word had never passed between them. They'd pretended not to notice, but its absence was perennially there. They'd felt it, more even than the lack of food or heat. For two years, Daria and Adam had lived alongside a sensation they didn't dare name, because, like in Brothers Grimm, where saying a creature's name robbed it of its power, so would giving voice to their feeling risk instantly shattering it.

Adam nodded slowly, thoughtfully. For a minute, Daria thought they'd been transported back to their early days, when she could go weeks without hearing him speak.

But then Adam said, "Edward understood that."

"Do you love me?" Daria challenged, realizing that, so far, the sentiment had been hers alone.

"From the first moment I saw you." He turned toward the court-yard's tunnel. "Over there."

"That silly girl is long gone."

"Good," Adam said, tentatively reaching for Daria's hand, as if his mouth hadn't been crushing hers only a few hours earlier. As if their son weren't standing between them, indifferent to their conversation. "Because I love this one more."

AT THE TRAIN STATION, Daria sat on a wooden bench pressed against the wall, Gosha on her lap, Alyssa with her head on Daria's shoulder, watching Adam negotiate four tickets east for them. She couldn't quite believe what was happening, that she was returning to Kyril. At Edward's request. That Edward was dead. That he had died because of her. And for her. She'd loved him, but she hadn't known him. She'd thought him weak, but he'd proven stronger than she was.

"It's like music, Papa," Edward had tried to explain when this all began, and the first edict came, banning him from traveling outside the country. He'd gone along, uncomplaining. "You can't force it. All you can do is adjust the key and find your rightful rhythm within it."

It's what he'd done in Kyril. Daria had judged his passivity as surrender, but in reality it had been the opposite. Edward gave up everything without so much as a token protest—except that which was actually important to him. While the rest of them wasted energy battering their heads against walls that were never going to break, Edward had conserved his for what really mattered.

"The music inside, they cannot take that away from you," he'd told Alyssa, "not unless you let them."

So he'd hummed. With his last exhausted breath, he never let them take his music. He'd fought in his own way, in a way Daria wasn't used to, in a way she didn't recognize. He couldn't force Daria to do as he begged, so he'd adjusted the key and altered the circumstances until she had no other options. *It's like music, Papa . . .*

It was nearly midnight when they boarded the train, Adam carrying a dozing Gosha, Daria propping up an exhausted Alyssa. Adam had secured them a private cabin with four berths. He lifted the children onto the upper bunks, while he and Daria sat across from each other on the bottom two, talking into the night, filling each other in on the months they'd been apart, making tentative plans for the days ahead.

Plans that grew a great deal more critical as, in the distance, they heard the first muffled explosions from the bombs incoming planes boasting swastikas on their tails were starting to drop with great precision straight into the heart of Odessa.

Book II

Natasha

1970–1991

Chapter 19

═══

In the spring of 1970, Natasha Crystal received two lessons regarding the infamous Jewish problems. Those that were about math, and those that were about men.

Natasha stood with her back to the wall of an Odessa University hallway, Boris sitting on the floor by her side. Twelve years from now, Natasha's daughter would introduce her to what Americans thought when they heard the names Boris and Natasha. They thought of secret agents out to capture Moose and Squirrel! Her daughter would observe that neither Natasha nor Boris fit the stereotype. She would be half right.

For now, Natasha and Boris were waiting to take the oral part of their university entrance exams. Natasha had already taken her written test a few days earlier, as had Boris. They'd walked into the auditorium together, hoping to be placed in the same row so they might write their essays on the same theme. But the proctor had separated them. Natasha was assigned to expound about the USSR's right to mass along the Sino-Soviet border, and why the proper name for the contested area was Damansky Island, not Zhenbao. Boris wrote about why dual-use civilian and military space stations such as those developed in the USSR were a greater contribution to science and mankind than America's recent moon landing.

Their scores had been posted that morning. Boris received a 4, while Natasha got a 5, the highest possible score. She wasn't surprised. Until last month, she'd been expecting to graduate with a gold medal, indicating she'd earned 5s in all her classes and, as such, could skip her exams and head straight for an interview with the university admissions committee. Except, at the final marking period, her history of the Communist Party teacher shocked Natasha by asking her to stand up in front of the class and explain why sexual contact between Young Communist League members was a crime against socialism. All a blushing Natasha could get out was the official line, "Good *Komsomolniki* don't engage in such activities."

Afterward, Boris attempted to comfort Natasha, telling her that it wasn't her fault, the teacher had been trying to trip her up. Natasha refused to let him conjure up excuses or to appeal the grade. She didn't want to worsen the situation and make other teachers think she was a troublemaker. So Natasha was issued a silver medal, testifying to her 5s—and one glaring 4. Which meant she had to write the composition and take an exam in her chosen field of study, math. Boris was also applying for the mathematics department.

Remembering his attempt to buck her up after the sex and socialism fiasco, Natasha now tried to do the same for Boris, disheartened by his 4 in composition.

"It doesn't matter." Natasha faked a confidence she couldn't back up with facts. "As long as you ace the math exam, nobody will care about your writing. It's not as if you're applying to study Russian literature or humanities."

Boris smiled wanly. A Jewish boy applying to study Russian literature, that really would be something laughable.

Every forty minutes, a handful of students were escorted inside a classroom. As they exited, they already knew how they'd done, and whether they'd accumulated enough points to be granted access to the major and university of their choice.

"Natalia Crystal!" A voice echoed down the hall. The proctor jerked her head to indicate Natasha should follow her into the classroom, where a panel of three teachers—two men and one woman—sat behind a table. In front of them were five rows of seven white cards, facedown.

Natasha stepped forward, ostentatiously confident in a way her mother insisted would get them all arrested one day. Was it Natasha's fault math had always come easily, numbers lining up, one after another, so all she had to do was follow their logical procession to the answer? Natasha's eyes swept over the cards. She reached forward and snatched the one at the left edge. Mental statistics in the hallway had convinced her it was the card least likely to be selected. As soon as she touched the paper, though, with its still damp fingerprints of previous geniuses who thought they had the system figured out, she realized her miscalculation. Natasha had assumed the cards in the middle and toward the right would be the most-frequently selected. She gambled the testers would place their difficult equations there, with the easier ones hovering along the top and edges.

Natasha glanced at which equations she'd drawn. There were three of them. One was on the sums of the lengths of pairs in a tetrahedron, one was finding a point within an ABC triangle, and the last asked her to construct a quadrilateral using a ruler and a compass.

The panel gave Natasha thirty minutes at the rear of the classroom to work on her answers, while they dealt with other students. Natasha only needed twenty-nine, and that included checking her work. She stood before the trio and went through her solutions. Each of the teachers took an opportunity to stop her and ask follow-up questions. She had answers for all of them.

She watched the head tester pick up his pen in order to record her result. It was going to be a 5. It had to be. She hadn't missed so much as a parenthesis.

"One moment," the man sitting behind where her card had been, spoke up. "Miss Crystal?" The emphasis he put on Natasha's name made it clear what he was asking. The only Crystals in Odessa were inevitably Jewish. In America, Natasha would claim the comic Billy Crystal, whose grandparents came from Odessa, had to be a relative.

So Natasha gave the expected answer. "Yes, Crystal. Natalia Nahumovna." Now that they had Papa's ethnically identifiable first name, too, that should settle any doubts. But just in case there remained a question regarding her loyalty to the USSR, Natasha added, "My father is a decorated veteran of the Great Patriotic War. He gave his eye for the cause." The grandparents who'd been deported to Siberia as enemies of the state, Natasha opted to keep to herself. That information was likely in her file, already.

"Natalia Nahumovna," he repeated, grateful for her help identifying Natasha as another Jew who thought she was so much smarter than everyone else. "We have one more problem for you."

Natasha flipped over her card. "No. I finished them all."

"One more," he insisted.

The other teachers shifted in their seats. The woman stared past Natasha, out the window. The man put down his pen and waited obediently. He may have been the head of the examination panel, but his colleague was the Party member.

Natasha was handed a second card. One that had never been on the table. It came out of the tester's pocket.

Natasha told herself she had nothing to worry about. She'd already faced the worst they could do, and she'd beaten them. No reason she couldn't do it again.

Her final problem read: *Find all real functions of real variable $F(x)$ such that for any x and y the following inequality holds: $F(x) - F(y) \leq (x - y)^2$.* It looked like something she'd solved a thousand times in preparation. It looked like something she should be able to solve.

But it was different. She'd already used up twenty-nine minutes. Did they expect her to tackle this in sixty seconds?

They weren't even willing to offer that much.

"Your answer, Natalia Nahumovna?"

"I—I'm not sure."

The tester leaned over the chairman, picked up his pen, and wrote down her final grade.

"THREE," BORIS SAID. Natasha wondered how he could already know her result. Then she realized he was talking about his own score. Boris had been called into a different classroom right after her. In his case, they didn't even bother with the charade of letting Boris pick a card. They handed him three problems, none of them, as far as Boris could see, solvable.

"Me, too," Natasha admitted. They stood there, looking helplessly at each other—Natasha trying not to cry and draw attention to herself, Boris trying not to reach out and hug her because that would do the same.

"Jewish problems," a voice behind them said.

Natasha, sniffling, turned around to tell whoever was offering his unsolicited two *kopeiki* to get lost; she wasn't in the mood for anti-Semitic gloating. She found herself nearly nose to nose with a stocky young man, maybe a year or two older than she was, barely taller, but much broader. Natasha was used to boys her height being thin and sickly, with bronchial coughs from endless colds and allergies. But this one's shoulders and arms were so muscular that his shirt looked a size too small. A pair of glasses sat on his nose, giving him the appearance of a scholarly boxer. She'd never seen anyone quite like him before. The dichotomy intrigued Natasha in spite of herself.

He stretched out his hand. "Bruen, Dimitri. Dima."

If he was an anti-Semite, he was a Jewish one. Not that there weren't plenty of those, too.

Looking from Dima to Boris, Natasha had a fleeting image of

the pair sculpted from identical pieces of plastiline, Boris stretched to skinny capacity, while Dima was pounded into a hard, tough block.

"Jewish problems are a myth," Boris dismissed, attempting to turn his back on Dima and usher Natasha away.

But the stranger had gotten her attention, in more ways than one. "What Jewish problems?"

"Ones they came up with, special," Dima explained, amused she didn't know. "They can't be solved; to keep Jews out of universities."

"Why would they need to do that? They already have quotas."

"Some people think they're too high. This makes it easier. We failed, so no university placement for us."

"You didn't get in, either?" Natasha couldn't imagine this confident, charismatic young man, with his fine, light brown hair and pure azure eyes, failing at anything.

"My name wasn't on the list of students to accept no matter what answers they gave."

That list wasn't a myth. Those on it felt no shame about boasting. But, like Dima, Natasha wasn't in competition with those privileged souls. Her rivals were other Jewish girls who wanted to study math. Quotas dictated a set number of spaces for applicants who fit that description. They were competing against each other, not against unrelated nationalities, or the children of Party members and other politically connected candidates.

Dima said, "This is my third year applying. I graduated with a gold medal."

Natasha was about to say she had as well, then remembered that wasn't the case.

"I felt confident the first time. Applied to Moscow University, wanted to be a doctor."

"That's just foolish," Boris snorted. "Everyone knows Jews can't—"

"They told me I couldn't go to medical school because I wore glasses. The doctor on the panel, the one who told me? He wore glasses. What a joke! But my parents didn't have the going 20,000 rubles for a bribe."

Natasha gasped. Her own parents barely earned 1,200 rubles a year. Is that what it would cost to get her a university place now that her exams had gone so badly?

"I thought I'd try again, get a different group of testers, some-one my family could ask a favor of. I thought I could scrape out a good enough score to at least get into the night school. That didn't work, either. So I decided to come to Odessa. More Jews here than anywhere in the USSR, right? I gambled they'd be friendlier to us. Plus, I've finished my two years as a worker. They're supposed to give preference if you've worked for two years. But I miscal-culated. More Jews in Odessa doesn't mean they're more gener-ous here, it means there are more Jews fighting for the same quota spots. So that's it, no university education for me. I'm done. And my *propiska* is for while I take the exams only."

"You're not staying in town?" Natasha's heart sank.

"If I had my way, I wouldn't even stay in the USSR."

As quickly as her heart had sunk a moment earlier, now it did a complete one-eighty in Natasha's chest, Dima's words hitting her as forcefully as seeing that 3 on her results sheet had earlier. Did Dima just say it was possible to leave the USSR?

Years later, Natasha would look back on that moment and mar-vel at how anyone could have been that naive. Had it honestly never crossed her mind that there was a world outside her homeland? One that she might someday see? One that she might someday opt for? She knew how Baba Daria had left Odessa with Mama. The first time they'd been forced to; the second time they'd had to. But the family had stayed inside the Soviet Union's borders. The possibility of not being so constrained had never been so much as broached at their house.

"Quiet!" Boris, who shared Natasha's house and appeared equally discombobulated by Dima's pronouncement, hushed him. Even when they were children, playing Fascists versus Red Army soldiers in the courtyard—Natasha made Boris be the Fascist so she was guaranteed victory, and so Mama wouldn't catch Natasha pretending to speak German—he only dared whisper his threats of Nazi world domination, lest anyone overhear and accuse Boris of genuinely holding such views.

"There's three of us congregating," Dima mocked, "so we must be plotting political mischief. Is that what you're afraid of being charged with?"

"Not three. There's us two"—Boris reached for Natasha's hand as she continued staring at Dima, trying to process what he'd said, the world he'd opened up for her—"and there's you. We don't even know you," Boris pronounced loudly, and not for Dima's benefit.

"Is your boyfriend always such a coward?" Dima asked Natasha.

"He's not my boyfriend," she quickly corrected. "We live in the same *kommunalka*, that's all."

"Just because you have no future, Bruen," Boris spat, "is no excuse to ruin it for us."

And there it was. The inferred reason why Natasha had never so much as daydreamed about the possibility of leaving the Soviet Union and going somewhere else. Because, up until this afternoon, all of Natasha's daydreams had centered on the life she strove to achieve here, the one that everyone had assured her was possible, just as long as Natasha did as she was told, followed the rules, did not make any waves, accepted the price of everything—and expressed gratitude for what she'd already been given.

"What future?" Dima pulled down his lips with two index fingers in, Natasha had to admit, an uncanny impression of Boris's disappointed face—and Natasha's equally crushed spirit. "Weren't you just crying over your three?"

Boris refused to take the bait. Mustering as much dignity as possible while being teased, he defended, "They told me, at the examination, there is room this year at the technical institute."

"Nursing? Cooking?" Dima sang in imitation of a little girl.

"Economics?" Natasha leaped on the possibility, wondering if a fragment of her daydream might yet be salvaged. Some years, those with an interest in mathematics who didn't do well on their university examinations could talk their way into a night course at the economics technical institute. And by talk, Natasha meant a bribe to the right person, hopefully for less than 20,000 rubles. If there was room for Boris, maybe she could apply, as well.

"The Polytechnic," Boris said. "To study computers."

"Computers?" As far as Natasha could glean from dribs and drabs heard around the math department, computers were machines designed to do calculations in more time and with less precision than an adept human. They were dull instruments for even duller people.

"I know there's little future in it"—Boris straightened to full height, still refusing to be cowed into embarrassment, even with the latest revelation—"but they said they might be able to find me a spot, maybe even to attend during the day."

"Will you apply?" Natasha asked.

"As soon as I get my papers back from here." It was illegal to make copies of documents, which slowed down the admissions process for those who failed to get into their first choice.

Dima challenged, "Are you going to let them keep treating us like this?"

He'd mentioned three distinct groups. You, them, and us. Natasha knew she wasn't Them. She was definitely You. And yet, she would have given anything in that instant to be Us.

Because You had just realized she'd be permanently deprived of the privileges accorded Them. But that Us might have access You had never previously known existed.

"No, of course not." For the first time in her life, it was no honor to be the one with the answers. For the first time, Natasha was the one with the questions.

Dima patted Natasha on the shoulder. "When you're ready to put actions behind those words, you come find me." He raised his eyebrows in Boris's direction, somehow managing to look down on a man several heads taller. "If your guard dog lets you."

Chapter 20

===

"How can I do that?" Natasha whined as she and Boris meandered along Primorsky Boulevard, surrounded by mothers pushing baby carriages and old people strolling, arm in arm, beneath the blooming trees. "He didn't say where he was going!"

"Siberia, that's where he's going." Boris appeared eager to change the subject.

"He can say hello to my Baba Daria," Natasha snapped, tired of Boris whipping out the threat of Siberia whenever he needed to win an argument.

Boris maneuvered Natasha toward the statue of Alexander Pushkin. The great man's bust stood surrounded by three small fountains shooting streams from its base. When Natasha and Boris played there as children, they'd splashed and called it Pushkin's pee-pee. Now, Boris was hoping for the water to muffle the sounds of Natasha's criminal dissent.

"Spoiled brat," Boris mumbled. "Doesn't get his way, and it's the whole system that's to blame, not him. How do we even know the story he told was true? Maybe he didn't study, failed his exams, and is using anti-Semitism as an excuse. It's not as if there are no Jewish doctors in the USSR, so someone must get accepted. Maybe he just wasn't good enough."

"Those people have connections. We don't. I didn't deserve a three, and neither did you."

"They can't take everyone who applies. Only as many candidates as there are jobs planned. What would happen if everyone was allowed to study whatever they wanted? If everyone wanted to be a . . . an actor, for instance. There aren't enough theaters or films. Or a writer. They can't publish everyone. Sure, every city has its own newspaper, but they all run the same stories from Moscow, and we already have plenty of books. They graduate, and then what? Unemployment, like in the West. You can't have one hundred percent employment if people are left to pick their own positions. Can you imagine what that kind of capitalist competition would lead to? If you don't assign people jobs, how can you ensure that everybody has one?"

A week ago, a day, heck, earlier that morning, Natasha would've parroted identical rhetoric. But that was when she'd believed her years of study, dedication, and good behavior would lead to being accepted at the university, garnering more academic excellence, rising to the top of her profession, getting showered with accolades, and dying in glory—as long as she followed the rules. Now that Natasha understood it had all been out of reach for her from the start, the idea of keeping her head down and doing what she was told suddenly seemed asinine. If she could see it—if she could, thanks to Dima, suddenly see beyond the borders they'd been raised with, why couldn't Boris? He'd been right there. He'd heard what Dima said. They didn't have to settle. "So you're just going to keep believing and doing whatever they tell you?"

"When you have a better idea . . ." Now it was Boris's turn to make fun of Dima. He rocked from leg to leg and hiked his clenched fists to his waist, an ungainly bear stomping around without concern for what he destroyed, performing as apt a mockery of Dima as Dima had earlier of him. Boris patted Natasha's shoulder condescendingly. "You come find me."

═══

"WHY DIDN'T YOU TELL ME?" Having found Boris an unenthu-
siastic audience for her distress, Natasha shifted to her parents. And
Boris's. Their families had split a *kommunalka* since Natasha was
four, becoming best friends out of necessity and proximity. Because
the Rozengurts were there first, they claimed the main bedroom, and
the tiny room off it. Boris's room was filled with his bed. His clothes
hung from hangers off a metal pipe overhead. Beneath it were makeshift bookshelves nailed into the wall. It was a palace compared to
the living room, into which Natasha and her parents were crammed.
All six of them shared the kitchen and sole bathroom.

"About the Jewish problems?" Natasha grilled. "Did you know
about them?"

Natasha's parents exchanged looks. Boris's parents exchanged
looks. Even Boris looked guiltily down at the floor. Realizing he'd
known all along, Natasha demanded, "Why didn't any of you warn
me? And why did you claim they were a myth, earlier?"

"I didn't want to discourage you from reapplying next year,"
Boris said. "Some Jews are allowed to pass eventually."

"We wanted you to study hard," her mother said.

"Even though it didn't matter? My grade was decided before I
went in."

"No," her father insisted. "If you had done horribly on all the
problems, you would have failed unequivocally."

"Not everyone fails," Boris's mother echoed her son. "We wanted
to give you both the best chance. We didn't want you approaching
your studies already defeated. If you thought there was no hope,
why would you try?"

"An excellent question," Natasha said, stomping off into their
room and slamming the door behind her.

MAMA LET NATASHA stew for exactly an hour. She couldn't let
it go more than that because there were items in their room she

needed. Mama ordered Natasha to hand over the documents testifying to her grade. She told Natasha to wash her hands, put on an apron, and start dinner: they were having Olivier salad. There were potatoes cooking on the stove. Natasha could cool them; peel them; slice them; mix them in with the eggs her mother had hardboiled earlier; add some canned peas, pickles, and onions; and set the whole thing in sour cream. Mama would be back by the time it was ready.

Meanwhile, Mama had roused Natasha's father to review the list of men he'd served with. She was unafraid to use Papa's lost eye to guilt men who'd gotten through unscathed. Mama then had him go through the list of men he drank with. Between the two groups—there was overlap—they came up with three solid prospects who, after Natasha's parents explained the situation, were able to use their assorted influence to get Natasha a spot in college.

"A teachers' college?" Natasha all but spat. Her parents had waited until supper before springing the news on her. They thought she might be happier over a small plate of cookies they'd set out to "celebrate" the occasion.

"Mathematics," Papa said, handing Natasha a cookie to keep her from crushing the teacup she was holding. "You will be teaching mathematics."

"But I don't want to be a teacher."

"You would rather work in a factory?" Mama removed the cup and cookie from Natasha's hands. If her daughter wasn't going to be pleasant, she wouldn't eat. Stalin had taught them that. "Or maybe a butcher shop, sweeping bloodied scraps? I know! You would prefer to wash public toilets rather than take advantage of this opportunity Papa and I slaved to provide you."

"You brought a bottle of vodka to one of his friends."

"Three bottles of vodka," her father corrected. "You did not come cheap, my kitten."

———

SEPTEMBER 1. FIRST-TIME first graders hurried down the streets bearing bouquets of flowers—the boys in brown slacks and crisply ironed white shirts, the girls in brown dresses covered with white aprons decorated in as much lace as their grandmothers could beg and bargain, the ribbons in their hair dwarfing the size of their heads.

The same day, Natasha began her own first year of teachers' college.

Two weeks later, she was pulled out of school so its students could be shipped out to the countryside for their patriotic *kolkhoz* duty. For one month, they would be helping harvest corn alongside the glorious workers.

When Natasha asked Mama why they didn't hire locals to help until the season was over, her mother said dismissively, "No locals want to—they get paid so little. Students are free labor."

No one cared that Natasha disliked the outside, prone as she was to sunburn in summer, frostbite in winter, and allergies in spring and fall. She expected Boris would be equally reluctant. His idea of a good time was to stay indoors and read, or for other people to play soccer outdoors while he cheered from the safer side of the radio. Yet Boris acted happy to be going.

That, Natasha ventured, was because Boris didn't need to worry about a menstrual period hitting him, with no place to buy the cotton balls and gauze necessary to roll sanitary napkins. Natasha was forced to bring her own, and to find a place to hide her indecent supplies among the clothes she was bringing, which included workpants, shirts, shoes, and hats, as well as one pretty sundress. Because a girl never knew whom she might run into.

The *kolkhoz* sent a fleet of open-backed trucks to drive them to Krasnoznamensk. There were more than one hundred students gathered at the meeting spot. Natasha looked through them. She always looked through crowds now. Though she wasn't admitting to herself what—or whom—she was looking for. Boris was so used to her ritual that he waited, hands on his hips, for Natasha to complete her overview, followed by the sigh of disappointment she could not quite suppress.

"Done?" Boris asked. "Can we get on now?"

He gestured toward the truck back, indicating Natasha should climb in first and he'd follow. But instead of hefting herself into the spot he'd picked, Natasha walked away, wandering between the available vehicles parked on the street and the gaggle of exuberant youth who were throwing their duffels onto the truck backs, positioning the bags as seats, jostling for position, and waving good-bye to anxious parents. Natasha spied an empty space next to a boy with hair so light, it might have been white, already unwrapping the butter-and-sausage sandwich his mother had packed for him. He took a huge bite, ripping the bread with his teeth. Crumbs flew every which way, and pink bologna flapped like a bird's tongue.

He caught sight of Natasha, swallowed, then grinned, wiping his mouth with the back of his hand. "Why wait to enjoy yourself, right?"

"Right," Natasha affirmed the new life philosophy she hadn't been aware of until right this minute, and sat down next to him, leaving no room for Boris.

Chapter 21

Three trucks in their nine-truck convoy broke down. The two-hour ride to Krasnoznamensk ended up taking five hours. A personal best, their teachers assured. Soviet technological expertise was progressing in leaps and bounds, wasn't it, boys and girls? Furthermore, the waits while their drivers fiddled with engines and traded spare parts in the spirit of Communism gave them a chance to appreciate the roads laid, the electrical lines strung, and the pipes run, thanks to the local soviet, bringing modern conveniences to formerly oppressed serfs. Wasn't it lucky the pipes and wires stopped before reaching the town, so they could see the work in progress? And the cracks and pits in the road? Did they notice the cracks and pits? Proof how desperately this road was needed, as evidenced by the traffic it received! People came miles out of their way, in cars, on carts, even on horseback, to use this road. Their own villages had yet to be so blessed. Did they realize how lucky they were to be seeing such beneficence in action?

Luck was again invoked when they arrived at their destination—parched, their eyes, ears, mouths, noses, and hair full of dust—and saw the lean-tos in which they'd be sleeping. Wooden barracks, with bunk beds, three to a wall. Natasha heard Mama asking, "For this I left Siberia?" At least these barracks had mattresses, sheets,

even pillows stuffed with protruding chicken feathers. Did they realize that other *kolkhozniki* had no more than canvas tents to sleep
in? Tents they had to pitch into the hard ground themselves? This
group was so lucky! They must know some powerful people!

At least here came the food. Fresh chicken not trucked for days.
Milk straight from the cow, still warm and foamy. Carrots not
cut into the shape of metal cans, and potatoes and onions without
rotten brown spots or budding eyes that made a spud look like a
matron with pin curlers. Suddenly, Natasha could see the attrac-
tion of *kolkhoz* service. Even if they had to work for it. Especially
once she realized the work wasn't that bad. They weren't picking
the corn. That was done by men with machines who shook their
heads when they looked at the soft city dwellers imported to help
them. The students were merely sorting corn into burlap sacks.
And nobody cared how fast—or how well—they did it. By the
second week, there was more gossiping and flirting than farming.
The boys tossed ears of corn back and forth, ganging up to pelt the
day's arbitrarily chosen victim. The girls egged them on, taking
breaks to run behind the lean-tos and apply lipstick, or the latest
mascara, spread with a tiny brush, which solidified so quickly into
a gelatinous lump that you had to spit in it before every application.

"Enough," announced Natasha's sandwich-chomping seatmate
halfway through their tour. Seryozha flung down the ear he'd been
holding and smashed it with his heel until kernels popped like a
sunburst. "Let's go."

"Where?" Natasha asked.

"The village. Have some fun."

"What kind of fun do you expect to find?" Boris continued sliding stalks into their sacks.

"The kind that doesn't involve corn." Seryozha bopped Boris
on his sweaty black curls, though without enthusiasm. Ever since
he'd grasped Boris's unflappable nature, the fun had gone out of
teasing this target. There were plenty of better sports willing to get

indignant and demand a fistfight. Boris somehow managed to keep his dignity, even while being provoked.

"We're not supposed to leave until after dinner," Boris reminded.

"Do you always do what you're supposed to?" Seryozha sang in a schoolmarmish voice that made Natasha wince, even as she admitted that her childhood friend attracted such queries at above-average rates.

"Yes," Boris replied, as if it had been a legitimate question.

"I'll go with you!" Natasha piped up, only partially to draw attention from Boris. From the moment she'd ditched him and climbed into Seryozha's truck, Natasha had steeled herself to be the kind of girl who did these kinds of things. While in the country, she planned to go along with whatever was suggested, even—especially—if her instinct was to reject it out of caution. If no one else was going to follow the rules, Natasha didn't see why she should. What had that ever gotten her? Taking chances would make her a more interesting person. She'd steeled herself to believe that, too. And if it backfired, well, then at least Boris would be the only one who knew. Natasha expected Boris to forgive her anything. And to keep her secrets.

"Me! I'll go!" A dozen others chimed in, making Natasha feel like she was finally the trendsetter she'd always intended to be, instead of just another follower, the way she feared she was. Even if the sensible side of her remained aware she was courting danger in the safest way possible.

Seryozha sneaked a token look around, though most of their supervisors had already taken off for the afternoon. The one who hadn't was asleep under a tree. Seryozha grinned and gestured with his arm for everyone to follow. About half the group did, Natasha among them. She even sped up her pace and elbowed her way to the front.

Of course, once she got there, she had no idea where they were going. And, once they'd been walking for over a half hour, Natasha realized there was nowhere for them to go. They'd left the fields behind, but it was tough to tell where farmland stopped and village began. Ramshackle houses popped up, along with cows grazing in pastures, chickens fenced in by wires, rabbit hutches, and small plots of vegetables. Women in dresses so faded it was impossible to tell what the original pattern or color had been, kerchiefs on their heads tied behind their necks, trudged from place to place, some carrying buckets of milk, others tubs of steaming water brimming with laundry. Their towheaded children ran underfoot, boys and girls wearing nothing but underpants.

Natasha asked Seryozha, "Where are we going?"

"Don't worry"—he winked—"I know a guy."

The guy in question turned out to be one of their absent field supervisors.

"We pretend to work; they pretend to pay us!" the supervisor pronounced, leading the group down a steep flight of rickety stairs into pitch darkness beneath the house he shared with his parents.

Natasha heard the strike of a match. A kerosene lamp illuminated the tiny room. Besides the burlap sacks scattered in lieu of furniture, hay protruding through ripped seams, the only other object was a haphazard monstrosity of three wooden buckets, rusty pipes running through each, and smelling so strongly Natasha was amazed it hadn't blown up the second a match was lit.

"*Samogon!*" came a triumphant cry. "Still!" Natasha watched as rubles changed hands and her companions charged forward, despite the lack of cups, dipping their hands right into the *pervach*.

"What's the matter, afraid of germs?" Seryozha teased, noticing Natasha hanging back.

Natasha wasn't germaphobic. She had no problem stopping by a public drinking kiosk, throwing in one *kopeika* for a cup of seltzer water or, feeling flush, a three-*kopeika* coin to add a splash of syrup. There was one glass for everybody (chained to keep from being stolen). Natasha didn't hesitate to drink from it. Besides, thanks to family lore, she knew that *pervach* was the initial step of the distillation process, so strong it would kill even the germs of a dozen youth sticking their grubby hands in it.

Except Papa had regaled Natasha with stories of how, during the war, his unit had stumbled on a peasant with a still. In spite of the 100 grams of vodka rationed per Soviet soldier per day ("How do you think we kept warm at the front while Germans froze?"), the soldiers fell on the still, sucking up every drop, despite the peasant's warning. They assumed he was hoarding and shot him. Except the alcohol had been mixed with methanol. A third of the unit died from poisoning. Another half was blinded. Natasha's father escaped. Having been young—too young to join up, but no one was checking passports when the fate of the Motherland was at stake—he didn't drink much. Then. Since that day, Papa stayed away from moonshine. If he wanted to get drunk, he either drank at home or, when Mama chased him out, scraped up two compatriots to share a three-ruble bottle of vodka in an alley, using a matchstick to make certain not a drop remained. Papa was a good drunk, a happy drunk. He never hit either Natasha or Mama. He simply started speaking too loudly. Which terrified Natasha's mother. She couldn't predict what he might say. Or who was going to hear it. She'd wait an hour or so. If Papa fell asleep, she'd drag him to bed, cover him with a blanket, and consider it another crisis averted. But if he went on and on, growing louder and louder, moving from talking about how much he loved her and Natasha and the entire human race that he'd saved from fascism, and started ranting about the government and how they treated veterans and what they'd promised ("Housing, they promised! For those who served! As a reward! Where is it, I ask you? Where's the housing they promised us?"), then Mama would shove him out the door to get lost in the throng of drunks weaving through the streets and into random courtyards. If they were making too much noise, a housewife might fling open her curtains and threaten to douse them with boiling water. The *dvorniki* shooed them away perfunctorily, out of respect for their service. "Go home, Uncle, sleep it off." It was too dark to tell one drunk from another. Mama gambled that if Papa did utter treasonous sentiments, eavesdroppers wouldn't know whom to report.

Mama didn't blame Papa for drinking. All who returned from the war drank. Considering what they'd seen and—it was implied; no one asked—done, it was the least they deserved to help them forget. Still, Natasha's mother warned her, not everyone became a drunk like Papa. Some managed to drink heavily only on special occasions, holidays, birthdays, and when someone else was paying. They stayed sober the rest of the time. Papa couldn't. That meant Natasha had bad genetics. She should stay away from alcohol altogether.

Mama had been talking about social drinking. Not a home-brewed concoction that might be 80 proof.

But then again, there was Seryozha. He was looking at Natasha now like he'd looked at Boris bagging the corn. Seryozha was looking at Natasha like the person she was, not the one she'd intended to be on this excursion. So despite her better instincts—remember, she'd made a vow to ignore those—Natasha stuck her hands in and drank. It tasted like rubbing alcohol smelled, with an undercurrent of rusty metal. A few hours into their renegade outing, barely anyone could stand. They lolled, instead, on hay-stuffed sacks, boys and girls in piles of arms, legs, breasts, and lips, several of them committing precisely those criminal acts against socialism forbidden to good young *komsomolniki*.

Natasha had no aversion to said criminal acts. Her aversion was to their consequences. Condoms were impossible to get. Sometimes a med student would have access to one they'd stolen from the hospital. But that meant washing and reusing it every time, which risked tears, not to mention abrasions. Granted, abrasions were nothing compared to the pain of an abortion. Sure, they were legal and free. Did Natasha know there were places where abortion was illegal and also where it had to be paid for? Can you imagine paying for medical care? Those people were savages! Wasn't she lucky to be living in the USSR?

Not if she needed an abortion, she wasn't. They might have been legal, and they might have been free, but they were also done without anesthesia. If you wanted anesthesia, you had to bribe the doctor.

So despite the earlier vow to go along with whatever was suggested, Natasha opted to pick and choose her rebellion. She'd play hooky from work. But she wasn't going to drink (much), and she wasn't going to offend socialism.

At some point, a guitar appeared—it was missing a string, but they could drown out the dissonance by singing louder. A girl Natasha had said barely six words to began strumming tunes by Vladimir Vysotsky. The raspy-voiced bard's socially critical, politically charged music and general existence had been dubbed "scandalously recognizable." Singing his underground hit, "Capricious Horses," with a fatalistic narrator begging his unruly animals not to speed so quickly toward self-destruction, managed to sober up even Seryozha. They warbled along, a small collective act of defiance. That each sincerely hoped nobody else heard.

Or planned to report.

NATASHA WAS AMONG the first to wake up the next morning, though she had only her watch to confirm it was daytime. Their basement distillery, now reeking not just of moonshine but also of sweat, vomit, and other bodily fluids, was as dark as ever. Natasha stumbled up the stairs toward the light. She wondered why she'd originally thought this was a good idea. Sure, she'd wanted to create a new persona, one a boy like Seryozha and his followers could respect. But judging by his current state, Seryozha was unlikely even to remember she'd been there the previous night, much less what a grand rebellious figure she'd cut.

Next, Natasha wondered how she'd find her way back to the *kolkhoz* when her compatriots were having trouble assuming an upright posture. If she intended to get back in time for her shift, she was on her own. No one was coming to rescue her. Natasha recalled a children's story about a rosy-cheeked brother and sister who'd gone out in the hot sun looking for a well from which to drink and, by the end, the brother had somehow turned into a goat. Natasha couldn't conjure up what the moral of that story had been. It might have been *Don't make the bad decision of stumbling lost around the Russian countryside in the sweltering summer.* Which was what she was about to do.

Natasha sighed, blinked, then rubbed her eyes with the palms of both hands to get rid of the crud that had gathered overnight. She bit the bullet and pushed open the front door, heading for the porch. Even squinting, it was as if the sunlight were shoving her back in. Natasha's eyes were still growing accustomed to the brilliant assault, when she thought she saw Boris standing at the corner, leaning against the remnants of a fence, reading a book.

It was the rescue Natasha had been hoping for. But it wasn't the man Natasha had been hoping for. Boris could never be the man Natasha was hoping for.

He caught sight of her wavering on the porch and stuck the paperback in the front pocket of his shirt. Boris approached Natasha, gazing up the steps at her while shading his eyes with a flat hand to his forehead.

"Did you have a nice rebellion?" he asked.

When Natasha merely grunted in lieu of an answer, Boris added, "You know you don't have to pretend to be someone you're not to impress these idiots."

Natasha knew that. But, as she grudgingly allowed Boris to show her the way back to the *kolkhoz*, she also knew that, despite the earlier pep talks to herself, these idiots weren't the ones—one—she'd been trying to impress.

If Dima were here, he'd understand. If Dima were here, everything would be different.

If Dima were here, Natasha wouldn't have to be.

Chapter 22

One *kolkhoz* down, then three more, and finally Natasha found herself graduating from teachers' college, feeling no more enthusiastic about the profession than she had upon first being forced into it. Natasha requested assignment to a school with advanced tenth-grade math students. She knew there was an opening at the program from which she'd graduated, and when she spoke with the principal there, the woman who'd once been Natasha's teacher expressed interest in having her.

Yet when placements were announced, Natasha learned her request had been denied. The official reason was that Natasha had once shirked her *kolkhoz* duty, going into town to get drunk. She'd been written up by her supervisor. It was the first Natasha had heard of the reprimand.

Instead, she was assigned to teach sixth and seventh graders algebra and geometry. The school was an average one. Which meant its students were as interested in math as the average child. On her first day, Natasha followed the principal down the hall, counting her steps, calculating when she was one-fourth of the way there, one-half, three-fourths. If this were Zeno's paradox and every distance was cut in half, she would never get there.

"Children, this is Natalia Nikolayevna," the principal intoned.

"Give her your complete attention." He scurried off so quickly that Natasha didn't have a chance to tell him he'd made a mistake with her name.

"It's Nahumovna, not Nikolayevna," Natasha corrected at the end of the day. Getting her name right felt like the sole bit of control she might exercise over her life.

"Your students are young," the principal responded, avoiding calling her anything. "It's distracting to them."

"My name is distracting?"

"They're not familiar with cosmopolitan patronymics. It's best not to confuse their study of mathematics with irrelevance."

Natasha was about to point out his non sequitur, then figured that he might not be familiar with cosmopolitan expressions, and that she'd be confusing him with irrelevance.

So she went back to the classroom and remained Natalia Nikolayevna. It proved the least of her irritations. Behind students who refused to crack a book or do their homework, forcing Natasha to stay after school and redo every problem with them, because she was the teacher, and students' passing was her responsibility, no matter how much of her own time she had to sacrifice. It made Natasha long for the days right after the Revolution when, according to Baba Daria, USSR universities were so eager to prove that, unlike the czars, they would educate everyone, even peasants, that they formed groups where one proficient student was tethered to a handful of unprepared ones, many of whom were attending school for the first time and could barely read. All worked together, and all received the mandatory passing grade. Not only were they able to graduate five times the number of engineers, doctors, and academics in this manner, the communal learning process was praised as uniquely Soviet.

But Natasha's dim, lazy students didn't irritate her as much as the overeager ones. The ones who sat straight as sentries—as the Young Pioneers motto promised, "Always ready!"—arms folded, fingers touching elbows atop their desks. Natasha would barely finish asking a question before the top arm would spring up, as if jerked by an invisible string reaching to the ceiling. They were always polite, always prepared, always ready with the answer. Their uniforms, the crimson scarves tied around their necks, were spotless and ironed. But Natasha knew they didn't give a damn about the beauty of math. All they cared about was getting their 5s, their gold medals. It made Natasha sympathize with the instructor Boris once asserted was deliberately gunning for her. She realized now why that teacher felt compelled to ruin Natasha's perfect record, giving her that solitary 4, in order to wipe the expression of smugness—the one she now saw reflected in her most unbearable students—not from Natasha's face but from her soul. Never again would Natasha feel as confident that she knew who she was, what she was doing, and where she was headed as she had back when she was the one with her hand perennially in the air.

Boris was the first to recognize Natasha's melancholia. He gallantly attempted to buck her up, reminding her there was more to life than work. Boris, for instance, was struggling to learn a programming language called Ratfor so he could coax a computer into not sending him repeated error messages. Did Natasha believe he found that enjoyable? He didn't! He focused, instead, on the part of his day that he did enjoy. Family, friends, other emotional entanglements . . .

Boris didn't need to elaborate. Natasha knew he meant her.

She'd known for a while, since they were in school and he'd brought her presents, like wildflowers picked from an empty lot, or chestnuts he'd knocked out of trees by hurling a stick at the branches, or a tiny square of pink chewing gum his mother, who worked at the port, got from a visiting sailor. They'd been ten years old and determined to make the gum last. Every day for two solid weeks, they'd each dug a fingernail into the mass known as Bazooka Joe and chewed the tiny sliver they'd plucked out. But now they were past squashed chestnuts and rationed gum. Boris had moved on to writing her long, poetic letters, littered with quotes by Pushkin and Balzac. Natasha kept pointing out it was silly—they lived in the same apartment, and she didn't even have her own room where he could slip his letters under the door. The first time he'd tried, Papa found it, read it, and passed it to Natasha, saying, "For you. I hope."

She told Boris she was flattered. She told Boris he was sweet. She told Boris to think about this logically. What would happen if they did attempt a relationship, it didn't work out . . . and they were still living in the same apartment? They knew couples who'd married, divorced, and then, because one or the other couldn't get an alternate *propiska*, were forced to continue sharing a home, a room, a bed, even. Did he want to risk that?

Boris said he did.

Natasha said she didn't.

Boris, in an uncharacteristic fit of temper, accused her of comparing every man with whom she came into contact to a guy she'd barely brushed by almost four years ago. How could any flesh-and-blood mortal hope to compete with a fevered fantasy?

Natasha said she had papers to grade.

What she didn't say was anything about the postcards.

The first one was waiting for Natasha when she returned from her freshman-year *kolkhoz*. The handwriting was unfamiliar, there was no return address, and no message on the back. All Natasha had to work with, to figure out who'd sent it and why, was the garishly colored image on the front. It was the children's book character Dr. AiBolit (Ow, It Hurts), a jolly old fellow with a bald head; a gray, Trotsky-like mustache and goatee; and glasses. Someone had circled that last detail with a pen, though you had to look closely; it could have been mistaken for a mere postmark. And then Natasha knew.

She wondered how he'd gotten her address. She wondered what it meant. She wondered when she'd hear from him again.

The next card arrived before the New Year. It featured a red-sketch outline of the Kremlin, the hammer and sickle wrapped in a green wreath beneath a red, five-point star hovering over it like a protective satellite, and a generic New Year's greeting. But it also trumpeted, in big block letters, GLORY TO THE UNION OF SOVIET REPUBLICS! There was nothing improper or incriminating about it, unless you were clever, like Natasha, and picked up on the irony. Glory, indeed.

The postcards kept arriving. There was no pattern Natasha could detect, though she spent hours trying. She spent even more time decoding the subversive messages embedded in each one. There was the New Year's card with Santa sitting atop an airplane . . . heading west: an immigration metaphor. There was the snowman holding an open mailbag: a reminder that their communication was being monitored and must remain cryptic. There was the Hedgehog in the Fog, just another generic cartoon character to those not in the know, to signify how lost they all were, followed by three little pigs (three!), and Crocodile Gena playing the accordion, his famous lament about what a shame it was birthdays came but once a year. This was clearly Dima's way of telling Natasha what a shame it was they could communicate so rarely, and in such a roundabout fashion. Postmarks indicated he was reaching out from across the country, Alma-Ata in Kazakhstan, Yekaterinburg in Omsk Oblast, Kishinov in Moldova. Natasha wondered how he'd gotten permission to travel. She fantasized he'd done it without permission. Dima was defying the authorities, living as a free spirit . . . and pining for Natasha to join him.

Why else would Dima be taking the risk of contacting her, if Natasha weren't on his mind as frequently as he was on hers? She'd made an impression; they'd made a connection. Dima had all but promised Natasha a way out of the life she could no longer have and into one they could both share. Boris was wrong. Natasha wasn't comparing every man she met to a guy she'd barely brushed by almost four years ago. She was comparing every man she met to someone with whom she'd been having a four-year-and-counting conversation, one in which Dima had bared his soul, his hopes, and his dreams. Even if Natasha had no way of writing back with hers. The fact that Dima kept reaching out to her, in spite of the one-way nature of their communication, proved that he wanted Natasha to continue being privy to his thoughts . . . so that they might be pondering the same great questions of life at the same time, so that when they met again, they would still be as in sync as they'd been that first afternoon in the halls of Odessa University.

Was it Natasha's fault the flesh-and-blood men she went out with these days fell into one of two categories? Either obsequious rule followers who were terrified of doing, saying, or thinking anything that might be construed disloyal or original. They were exactly who she'd once been. Or they were of Seryozha's ilk, louts who proclaimed their defiant independence and lack of fear of retribution . . . while doing nothing beyond drinking, swearing, and stealing as much as they could from their employers. They were what Natasha feared becoming. One candidate boasted about how, at the fruit juice factory where he worked, he'd threaded a separate tube from the main pipeline so he could fill his own bottles, then sell them on the black market. Another, a doctor who'd managed to evade the big-city ethnic quota by traveling so far north for medical school the village he'd stayed in barely knew what a Jew was, much less considered them a threat, sought to impress Natasha with tales of how, working as a health inspector, he forced restaurants to bribe him with choice cuts of meat and fresh fruit in exchange for a good report. Those without profitable graft stories were left to demonstrate their refusal to kowtow to authorities via the playing of illegal records. One told Natasha about painstakingly transcribing lyrics to Western rock-and-roll songs to learn English; did she happen to know what the word *wanna*, as in "I Wanna Hold Your Hand," meant? He couldn't find it in the dictionary. At the very least, they listened to Voice of America on a shortwave radio using coat hangers for better reception. Natasha felt sorry for them. They believed they were striking a blow for freedom, while they were really nothing more than useless blowhards.

And so Natasha continued accepting invites to movies and cafés, then conjuring up excuses to avoid second dates—in case her lack of enthusiasm failed to get the point across on the first. She wasn't playing hard to get the way Baba Daria recalled she'd attracted her world-renowned piano-playing husband. In Natasha's mind, she was already taken.

Her days blended one into the next, with Monday proving no different than Friday, Tuesday the same as Saturday, since it was also a school day.

Until Dima returned.

SHE RECOGNIZED HIM immediately.

Natasha was crossing Soviet Army Street, not looking where she was going—getting hit by a car would at least break up the monotony—when, in her peripheral vision, she registered a truck idling at a red light. A ZiL model with a green front cabin and a rusty, gray flatbed in the back, covered by a flapping tarp held down by ropes. It had four large wheels that elevated it above the majority of the traffic, save for buses. And Dima sat behind the wheel, sunburned elbow resting on the bottom of the rolled-down driver's-side window, a cigarette dangling from his fingers and dripping ash onto the sidewalk.

First, Natasha thought she was imagining him. Her second, more fanciful assumption was that she'd conjured Dima out of her fervent, unceasing desire, but that he was just an illusion, destined to go up in smoke. Her third was that Dima had finally come for her. Now Natasha's life, which had effectively ended the day they'd met, when she'd received her cursed 3, could finally begin. And, this time, she'd get it right.

Natasha rushed into the street, ducking honking cars and their epithet-spewing drivers in her fevered rush to get to him before the light changed.

Dima paid no notice to the ruckus. He continued staring ahead, languidly lifting the cigarette to his mouth for another puff. Natasha took a desperate leap onto the step below the driver's-side door in order to pull herself up to his eye level, nearly falling out of her left sandal in the process. If he'd decided at that moment to lurch forward, she would have been run over.

Natasha clutched the open window, fingertips slipping on heated metal. Dima blinked in her direction. He smiled lazily. "Well, well. Look who it is."

He remembered her! Well, of course he remembered her. They hadn't stopped talking!

"Figured out what to do with your life yet?"

He definitely remembered her!

"I got your postcards."

The briefest of nods.

"Why—Why did you send them?" It was a question Natasha had never dared ask herself, terrified that even contemplating such a treasonous thing would somehow cosmically make them stop. But now that Dima was here, now that he was finally back . . .

"I wanted to make you think."

So she'd been right after all! Dima had wanted to make sure they remained connected, even while separated by the injustice of time and space. This was the time for Natasha to say something clever, to indicate how she'd been able to decipher his covert message for each and every one. But the only thing she could think of, the solitary fact her overwhelmed mind had just now managed to piece together, in spite of the evidence that had been there all along, including the cards that arrived from across the USSR, was, "You're . . . a truck driver?"

That couldn't be right. A poet, a philosopher, an academic, a revolutionary, yes. But a truck driver. A driver . . . of trucks? Natasha struggled to hide her confusion and her disappointment. She failed. Dima didn't look offended.

"Come see me tonight." He rattled off an address in the Moldavanka district. "Ten o'clock."

The light changed. Dima maneuvered Natasha off his door, plopping her back onto the street next to his discarded cigarette ash.

NATASHA DID NOT, as a rule, dress up to go to Moldavanka. Natasha, as a rule, tried to avoid it. By the 1970s, it may have been much less Jewish than it had been when Baba Daria shared an unheated room with her own mother. But it was still poor, even by Soviet standards. And crime-ridden, though, officially, there was no crime in the USSR; everyone had everything they needed so why would anyone need to commit a crime?

Moldavanka was a neighborhood a well-brought-up, respectable young lady of any ethnicity was not advised to venture into alone. Especially after dark.

The address Dima gave her on Myasoidivska Street was not a café or a music club, as Natasha had assumed it would be for their first date. It was a two-story home with no lights on in any of the windows. It looked like it predated the Great October Socialist Revolution, barely managing to remain standing throughout the subsequent Romanian occupation during the Great Patriotic War.

Natasha wondered if she'd misheard.

Natasha wondered if he'd been playing a joke on her. Natasha wondered if the decision to ignore her better instincts had been that smart of an idea, after all. Natasha felt like an idiot.

That's when a woman her own age opened the door and beckoned Natasha inside, as if she'd been waiting for her.

A party, Natasha decided. He'd invited her to a party, one with lots of people. Not a private, romantic date at all.

Well, it was better than a joke. She'd make the best of it. Maybe they'd still get a chance to talk, and Natasha would dazzle Dima with . . . something. She'd play it by ear.

The girl, who introduced herself as Ludmilla, led Natasha down a flight of stairs to the basement. Why, Natasha wondered, did her entire social life consist of basements?

Then she saw Dima.

He was sitting in the windowless room, at the head of a wobbling, scratched wooden table also occupied by a half dozen others. Ludmilla pulled up a chair from the far corner and dragged it so that she was sitting next to Dima's right hand.

Subtle.

A bare-bulb lamp illuminated everybody. Natasha saw only Dima. The way his silken hair shimmered, the way his translucent azure eyes glowed—Natasha finally understood why Russian needed a separate word to differentiate it from the more commonplace *blue*; the way Dima stood up when she entered the room, as if Natasha were whom he'd been waiting for. "You came."

"I—Of course."

"Welcome."

"Thank you." Natasha looked around. Everyone was watching her, wondering what Dima saw in her, what made her so special. Maybe he'd tell them. Maybe he'd tell her. "Where—What is this?"

"This"—Dima gestured grandly to his right and to his left, Natasha imagining him smoothly shoving the pushy Ludmilla from the intimate circle—"is our way out."

Chapter 23

===

Out of where? was Natasha's instinctive first thought.

She refrained from saying it out loud. See, ignoring her instincts was starting to pay off!

Instead, Natasha smiled in the vague, noncommittal way she'd perfected for staff meetings.

"This is Natasha," Dima introduced her to the rest of his cronies. "I told you about her."

He'd told them about her!

"I think she might be exactly whom we've been looking for."

She was exactly whom they'd been looking for!

"I sent her postcards from the road, checking to see if she could be trusted."

It was a test! Had she passed?

"She didn't turn me in. I covered my ass, made sure I could explain away every single one, if it came to that—love-starved suitor, the usual nonsense."

Did Dima just say something about love?

"Sit down, Natasha," Dima said. And then he continued talking, no longer about her, now about their group, who they were, what they wanted, what they'd accomplished so far, growing more animated as he went along, cheeks glowing pinker, saliva moistening his lips, making them fuller, more luscious, more tantalizing. Others around the table joined in, tossing out horror stories like gambling chips. One-upmanship tales of Jews forbidden from leaving the USSR because the government claimed they were in possession of state secrets, but it was just an excuse to harass them. They talked about how those who'd dared request an exit visa were persecuted. This one lost her job; that one was evicted from his *kommunalka*. One woman was publicly shamed; a man was stripped of the medals he'd earned during the Great Patriotic War.

"We're so glad you're here with us." Dima beamed.

"I'm so glad to be here with you," Natasha enthused, making sure to put special emphasis on the last word.

"We need your help," Ludmilla said, even though Natasha had not meant her.

"How can I help you?" Natasha stammered. "I-I'm not political." A childhood spent exiled in Siberia had made Mama quite clear on the subject.

"That's why we need you," Dima said. Suddenly, Natasha was reconsidering her position. "We're known dissidents. We've applied to leave and were turned down. They call us agitators. We're being watched. You're not."

"You can do things we can't," Ludmilla elbowed in.

"Do you know what this is?" Dima slid a book across the table.

Though the publisher, Éditions du Seuil, appeared to be French, the title and author were in Russian. *"Arkhipelag GuLag,"* Natasha read out loud. *The Gulag Archipelago.*

"By Aleksandr Solzhenitsyn. Of course you've never heard of it or him. Owning a copy is grounds for a prison sentence. Solzhenitsyn couldn't work on it all at once. He stashed sections at friends' houses around Moscow. It had to be smuggled out on microfilm and published in France. He's been deported. They were too scared to imprison him again. Can you imagine?"

"It's vital that every citizen of the USSR read this book," Ludmilla said. No, it was the other woman at the table, the one plucking her cuticles with her thumbs and pinching her tongue between her lips. Natasha found both females equally immaterial.

"We"—Dima indicated his group, Natasha not included—"are being stopped on the street and harassed. They search our homes. We can't risk being caught with the book."

"But you," said a man who wasn't Dima, "are not under suspicion."

"We need you to take it, copy it—you don't have to type, longhand is fine," Dima assured. As if that were the biggest inconvenience. "So we can distribute it. Expose how the Soviet system brutalizes its people, not just for political crimes, real and imagined, but also for trivial offenses."

Natasha wondered why Dima thought it was a good idea to use the word *brutalize* while trying to convince her to commit one of those trivial offenses—which carried the penalty of a political crime.

She asked, "And after I copy the pages, do I bring them back to you?"

"Yes."

"All right."

WALKING HOME AFTER dark, Natasha feared an attack, a senseless drunk, a punk boy snatching her purse, a sexual assault. But with the forbidden book in her bag pulsating like an untreated burn, Natasha almost wished to be robbed. At least then it would be someone else's problem.

Then again, a savvy thief might run her purse straight to a *militsia* station in exchange for amnesty. She'd be even worse off. The nightmare scenario jogged Natasha's memory of a story Baba Daria told. About her second husband, not the one for whom she'd played hard to get in front of the opera house but the one who'd engineered their lifesaving escape to Siberia, turning in his mother to set himself up better in life. For a moment, Natasha even considered doing the same to Dima; it's what Mama would want Natasha to do.

"No!" she blurted out, then, despite there being nobody to overhear, promptly covered her mouth with her palm, conditioned as she was to express only the most sanctioned of thoughts.

The anger that flooded through her took Natasha by surprise. She wasn't certain at whom she was angry. Mama, for lying to Natasha all her life about what she could expect and turning her into someone too afraid to demand anything different? Dima and his ridiculously blue eyes, for putting Natasha in this dangerous situation? Herself, for so much as momentarily entertaining the notion of a self-serving betrayal?

The system, Natasha decided. That's what she was angry with. The entire political system of the USSR. It was to blame for her current discomfort. It was to blame for Mama's terrible child rearing, and for Natasha's earlier disenchantment and depression, and even for her moment of cowardice just now. After all, if it weren't for the USSR, Natasha would have never needed to fear the consequences of her work with Dima in the first place!

It made sense now. Natasha finally understood what Dima had been trying to tell her, why his revolution was so important and why she was destined to play a critical part in it. His cause was her cause now. Nothing would stand between them! She didn't even mind the danger. Or at least, she resolved not to think about it. Not the most heroic of approaches, Natasha was self-aware enough to realize. She also knew herself well enough to comprehend it was necessary, for the time being, to keep her from changing her mind.

Natasha crept into the apartment after everyone was asleep; she imagined Boris's door closing seconds before she entered. Natasha tiptoed past her parents' bed and climbed into her own, slipping the book under her pillow, her mind—and her heart—made up. She was in!

WHEN SHE'D FIRST accepted the novel, Natasha had given scant thought to where she planned to fulfill her clandestine task. A public place such as a café, park, or library was out of the question. She might be able to spirit a few blank notebooks from school to write in, but she couldn't risk bringing the actual book to work. She'd be ratted out before end of day by the red-scarved brownnosers always looking to cause trouble under the guise of patriotic duty. Meanwhile, every room in her apartment was communal. The only one who had a private door he could close was . . . Boris.

She sneaked in for the first time when she knew he was working late. Natasha told her parents she was going out, then closed the door to their room and let herself into Boris's. She stayed for half an hour. Pressing her ear to the door to make sure no one was in the hallway when she reemerged, she slammed the front door to make it sound like she'd returned.

The second time, Natasha found an hour when Boris went to a football tournament with friends, his parents had departed for the movies, and Natasha's mother was in the kitchen, baking a cake after the miracle acquisition of butter, for which she set Natasha's father on a stool next to her, cracking a mountain of walnuts.

After a few weeks, Natasha had painstakingly tracked everyone's schedules to the point that she could predict when Boris's room would be available, and nobody would catch her coming in or out. It was a shame she couldn't pass her work to Dima directly, as she'd expected. He said it would be too dangerous for them to be seen together. Swallowing her disappointment, along with the urge to remind Dima he'd promised she'd be handing the materials over to him, not some go-between, Natasha suggested meeting at Pushkin's fountain, pretending to be young lovers walking hand in hand, exchanging deliberately distracting kisses, using the rushing water to cover up their renegade talk. Dima said no. He said it was even too risky for Natasha to be seen openly with Ludmilla, the go-between she'd been trying to avoid, as Ludmilla was under surveillance, too.

Instead, on Saturday afternoon, during its busiest time, Natasha lined up with dozens of other Odessa residents waiting to use the public *banya*. When Natasha was younger and their apartment had no indoor plumbing, she and her parents used to come regularly. Then, when Natasha was in her teens, Papa bribed a workman installing bathrooms in the compound next door to divert some of his equipment and build them a functioning toilet in a lean-to adjacent to the kitchen. Once that was done, Papa threaded the pipe that ran under the sink toward the ceiling. He took a metal basin, drilled a hole in the bottom, and attached a shower nozzle. The basin went on rods that he screwed into the wall. Redirecting water from under the sink filled the basin. When you loosened the nozzle, water rained down. To keep the basin from overflowing, Papa got a piece of cork and stuck a tiny flag into it. When the flag appeared above the edge of the basin, it was full. The flag was red. No one could say they weren't patriots!

Thanks to Papa, Natasha hadn't needed to use the public bath in years. She didn't miss the four-hour waits, though it had been handy for getting homework done. Natasha had a different agenda now. She waited in line, and Ludmilla waited a handful of folks behind her. They didn't speak. They didn't even make eye contact.

When Natasha's turn finally came, she purchased her ticket and moved to the women's side of the *banya*, while the men crossed to their side. When Dima first proposed this plan, Natasha had the fleeting notion they might rent the more expensive bathrooms that were designated for families. But singles weren't allowed to share. So Natasha stepped into the changing room and handed her ticket to the attendant, knowing odds were fifty-fifty it would be pocketed and resold several more times by the end of the day. Natasha followed the grim-eyed woman to the lockers, each with a deadbolt on the inside opened via a hook slipped through a tiny hole by the matron. Natasha undressed, folded her clothes, and left her bag in the locker . . . the bag holding the precious pages. She grabbed her soap and proceeded to the main washroom, picking up the wooden *shayka* bucket and dragging it to the faucets in the wall, one hot, one cold. Natasha mixed the water, then squeezed in between two other women sitting on the stone benches, slowly proceeding to wash herself, biding her time until she saw Ludmilla enter. Natasha stretched as if working out cramps in her shoulders and hands, but, in reality, she was flashing Ludmilla her locker number with her fingers. Ludmilla did the same.

Natasha dumped her soapy water down the drain in the center of the room and returned to the changing area, telling the matron Ludmilla's locker number and gambling that, at rush hour, the woman wouldn't notice the switch.

Natasha dried herself off with Ludmilla's towel, then reached for the clothes Ludmilla had worn, putting them on quickly and telling herself not to be squeamish about sharing undergarments—for the cause! A few minutes later, Ludmilla would do the same with Natasha's locker, towel, clothes . . . and bag.

They met the following week to pass on more papers and to switch back. After that, they decided not to use the *banya* anymore. The official reason was Natasha and Ludmilla didn't want their faces to become too familiar. But there was the more immediate concern that Natasha couldn't let anyone see her in Ludmilla's clothes. Her parents and the Rózengurts were way too acquainted with Natasha's meager wardrobe. They'd notice a whole new outfit.

The next time, they performed the handover in another madhouse, a pediatric medical clinic congested with hysterical mothers and hyperactive children waiting hours for their appointments. It was elementary for Natasha to switch her bag with Ludmilla's while Ludmilla distracted the nurse at admissions with woes of her baby spitting up milk after nursing—he must be allergic to it.

"Impossible," the nurse insisted. "It's impossible for a child to be allergic to dairy."

Ludmilla proceeded to scream obscenities, making sure all attention was on her rather than Natasha. Ludmilla ended up being placated with a prescription for yogurt, which she was told the clinic was out of—come back next month. Ludmilla stomped out in a huff, grabbing Natasha's bag as she went.

Each operation went off without a hitch, swelling Natasha's confidence about her usefulness to the group, and to Dima. Confidence that lasted up until the evening she and Boris were alone in the kitchen, cleaning up their respective families' plates after supper, and he, again using water to keep from being overheard—in this case, it was the trickling sink—asked Natasha, "What were you doing in my room earlier today?"

Natasha managed to catch the glass she'd been holding before it hit the ground. "Why—Why would you think—"

"I could smell you," Boris said, which shocked Natasha by its intimacy, before she realized they'd gone through puberty together in a cluster of rooms that rarely got a breeze. Of course he knew what she smelled like. Natasha bet she could pick Boris out in a crowd, too, even on a bus stuffed to the rafters with commuters returning from work on a summer day, arms raised, pits at nose level, no soap or perfume to speak of.

Nonetheless, she went with denial. "I wasn't in your room."

"Do you have a boyfriend?" Clearly her repudiation had been less than convincing.

"Yes!" Natasha leaped on the out he'd given her, then lowered her voice to sound guiltier. "Don't tell Mama and Papa." She lowered it even further. "He's not Jewish." There was nothing more sinful than that. Except . . . "He's Romanian! Black. A Gypsy."

"Doesn't he have his own home?"

She went with what easily could have been the truth. "He shares a room with his parents." And since locals were forbidden to check into hotels, which were for out-of-town visitors, "We have nowhere we can go to be alone."

"So you chose my room?"

"I'm sorry. I wish I could have thought of something else."

"Was it worth it?" From anyone else, the question would have sounded prurient. But there was an innocence to Boris that made Natasha opt to be honest with him. Up to a point.

"You and I," Natasha began, "were raised to do what we were told, follow the rules, be good. Sure, it was the way to survive, but it also came with the promise of reward. Except we were lied to. Our parents said it was to protect us, but they were still lies. I'm a teacher, you're a . . . what do they call it? Computer programmer. You rearrange ones and zeros. That's not what we wanted. That's not what we earned. That's not what we deserved. Doesn't it make you angry? Doesn't it make you want to do something? Break a rule? Fight back?"

Boris looked unconvinced. Which Natasha found disappointing. She'd had no intention of telling him about her recent activities. Yet a part of her had been craving his tacit agreement. She'd wanted Boris to validate her choices even if he didn't know the truth about them. What else was a childhood friend who'd been in love with you for years for? It bothered Natasha that Boris's good opinion of her still mattered.

Realizing she wasn't going to get what she wanted, Natasha flipped from aching sincerity to joke mode. "From each according to his ability, to each according to his needs. I needed your room more than you did. You can't deny me; it would be anti-Marxist! I'd report you!"

"Would you?" There went that innocent curiosity of his again. Natasha found it completely disarming.

She'd made a similar joke multiple times when they were kids and Boris wouldn't share the floppy, azure flexible disc he'd cut out from a magazine and spun on his child-sized record player. But was he honestly asking her now whether she meant her threat? Did that mean he considered it a genuine possibility?

Horrified, she rested her fingers on Boris's arm and reassured, "I'm kidding. I would never do that. You know me."

"I know you," Boris agreed, even as he continued looking unconvinced.

Which unexpectedly disappointed Natasha even more.

Chapter 24

━━

"You were there, weren't you, Papa?" Natasha waited until her father was drunk enough to be gregarious, but not so drunk that his testimony couldn't be trusted. "At the Twentieth Party Congress? When Khrushchev exposed Stalin?"

Papa was in their room, smelling of acetone, weaving as he pawed through the chifforobe looking for his coat. "No, kitten. Your papa wasn't important enough to be at the congress. That's for higher-ups. I was at work. They called us Party members together. This was before the congress. Weeks before. They told us what Comrade Khrushchev was going to say. So we'd be prepared. So we would support him. I was one of the trusted. I was among the first to know!"

"You knew Khrushchev was going to denounce Stalin? Expose the Gulags?"

"Expose Stalin's cult of personality, yes." Her father straightened up, saluted, and began to warble, "Long live beloved Stalin, long live dear Stalin." Then he switched to a different song, somehow still managing to retain the melody, "The people sing a beautiful song of Stalin, wise and dear . . ."

"Sha!" Natasha's mother materialized abruptly, slamming shut the door.

Papa explained, "Natashenka was asking me about our great Comrade Stalin."

"She should read a book, the official story."

"Which one?" Natasha demanded. "There's a new one every few years!"

"Whichever one it is now—that's the one you should read."

"It's all lies. Even Khrushchev's speech, he blamed everything— mass arrests, torture, forced confessions, deportations, Gulags— on Stalin, when it was Lenin, Lenin who started it; they were his decrees. It's what the USSR was based on!"

"*Zatkniz!* Shut up," Mama growled, shoving her daughter's shoulder hard enough so Natasha stumbled backward, plopping onto her bed, Mama towering above her. "You don't know anything."

"But you do." With Mama this uncharacteristically angry, Natasha saw an opening to pry out some truths—and lay some truths on her, in return. "This happened in your time. How could you not have known? The Great Purge, the Doctors' Plot, the millions deported to camps. You had to be aware of what was happening. People were disappearing right and left! And you still pinned that Lenin red star on my school uniform, and you made me stand on a chair and recite those ludicrous poems. Even the one by that idiot American, Langston Hughes. I didn't know what I was saying!" Natasha assumed a little girl voice to chant in English, *"Lenin walks around the world / Frontiers cannot bar him / Neither barracks nor barricades impede / Nor does barbed wire scar him."* She resumed a normal tone. "Lenin was to blame for how many barracks? How much barbed wire? You were there, you saw them, you tell me! He imprisoned his own people for disagreeing with him. I dare you to tell me I'm wrong!"

"You're more than wrong. You're foolish. Ignorant. Naive." If Natasha thought fury would make Mama lose control, she'd miscalculated. Instead of flaming, Mama's anger froze. "Do you not recognize how fortunate you are, with a name like Natalia Nahumovna Crystal, to be allowed to live in civilized Odessa instead of banished to die of pneumonia in some frozen shithole, no proper burial even?"

Natasha startled. She'd never heard Mama use such language before. Maybe she had gotten to her, after all.

"You talk about barracks and barbed wire as if you know anything. You know nothing. Yes, I pinned on the Lenin star. Yes, I taught you the poem. And I sat in the auditorium, listening to you recite, proud that the star and the poem and Papa's war record were keeping you safe. I made certain my family was beyond reproach. No one was going to accuse us of impropriety. I made sure we said the right things to the right people. No one would have anything to use against us, ever."

"So you selfishly kept silent, and your silence underpinned a genocidal regime. I know all about it. Baba Daria told me."

"What," Mama's voice grew even icier, "did my mother tell you?"

"How none of you did anything wrong, but you were still arrested. How your neighbors watched you get taken away, but nobody objected. How she had to make a choice, and she chose to sacrifice herself."

"Is that how she characterized it?" Mama's tone hinted that she and Baba Daria held divergent interpretations of the same event.

"Well, no." Natasha didn't want to get her grandmother in trouble and, truth was, this was Natasha's take, not Baba Daria's. "But she didn't give in. She fought."

"And did she tell you how that worked out? Her noble, selfless choice. For all of us?"

"It saved you from the war."

"That," Mama corrected, "was not *her* sacrifice."

"At least Baba was honest with me." Natasha understood when she'd gone too far and changed the subject. "You and Papa told me lie after lie, and now you want me to keep lying!"

"What difference does it make?" Unlike her mother, Natasha's father insisted on remaining jolly. "When we marched off to fight in the Great Patriotic War, you know what we said? We said: *If I die, consider me a Communist, and if not, then not!* Wrong, right, Communist, capitalist, fascist, even—who cares? A bullet doesn't care. Frostbite doesn't care. Only difference is, survivors of Communist Party members got better widows' and orphans' pensions."

"You're no wiser than she is." Mama couldn't decide which of them to gag first. "Maybe the pair of you could deign to care about who might be overhearing this nonsense of yours?"

"Don't be ridiculous, Mama. The only ones who could overhear us are the Rozengurts. I don't think Boris and his parents are salivating to turn us in so they can colonize our room."

"How can you be so certain?" Natasha's mother inquired matter-of-factly, her tone strangely reminiscent of Boris's when he'd asked Natasha more or less the same question.

"Are you serious?" Natasha felt like she was answering them both. "You've known the Rozengurts for how long? Twenty years? They're your best friends."

"And what makes you think that, to save themselves, they wouldn't turn us in for the things we've said? If they don't, and someone else does, they'll share our fate. Did Baba Daria not tell you that?"

"I can't believe you'd say that about them."

"Why not? It's what I would do."

Natasha stood there, dumbfounded and shaking. Her father chuckled, having located the coat for which he'd been searching. As he pulled it on and headed for the door, he observed, "You know what they say, in every group of two, one is an informer. If it's not you, then it must be me!"

NATASHA NEEDED TO speak to Dima, to share with him her horror over what had happened, how her mother had all but confessed to being an agent of the state, an informer—or had that been Papa's virtual confession? Except there was no way to do it. Neither the Crystals nor the Rozengurts had a phone. Papa said it was too expensive, and what was the point when you could achieve the same result by going to someone's home and tossing pebbles at their window until they answered or you realized they weren't in? And Dima had warned Natasha against using a public booth, for security reasons.

If she couldn't be with him, Natasha could cling to something that reminded her of him. Even though it was risky, she ducked under the bed and crawled toward her hiding place, behind the nylon-stored, decomposing onions and potatoes, for her contraband book.

Only to find it missing.

WHEN WOULD THEY come for her? Natasha wondered. They came for Baba Daria during the predawn hour of four a.m. Natasha lay awake all night, stomach contracting each time she heard the wheels of a car or the shuffle of footsteps. Maybe they would come for her at school. Make an example of her in front of the children. She could barely get through the day's lessons for worrying, stammering at the chalkboard, losing her place in the algorithmic sequence, making silly arithmetic mistakes that prompted the know-it-all girls to roll their eyes and twirl their fingers next to their foreheads. Natasha considered not going home, running away. But where could she go? Unless she planned to live in the forest like the partisans, she lacked the paperwork to switch apartments, much less cities or republics. Suicide was her only option. She'd go out a martyr for the cause of freedom. But would it count as martyrdom if no one knew of her sacrifice?

Unable to think of anything better, Natasha returned home. The minute she entered, Boris grabbed her arm, pulling her into his room, closing the door, and whispering urgently, "I burned it."

Fury overwhelmed any urge to defend—or deny. "How dare you go into my things?"

"You think the KGB would have made the distinction between your things and ours? They'd have arrested us all!"

Not if Boris had reported her first. And yet he hadn't. After their earlier conversation, that made Natasha even angrier. Was Boris trying to prove he was better than her? Wasn't that what he was always trying to prove, going back to his unsolicited *kolkhoz* rescue? Natasha wasn't about to let him get away with it. "So now you're helping the KGB keep the truth from our people?"

"I'm helping you not end up in front of a firing squad."

"I'm not afraid," said the woman who'd spent the past twenty-four hours nearly vomiting whenever a man in uniform entered her field of vision. Natasha wished Dima could hear how brave she was being. "Don't you understand that by not resisting, you're helping perpetuate a murderous regime?"

"So the solution is to get murdered yourself? How will that help anything?"

"At least I'm doing something! If you're not part of the solution, you're part of the problem!"

"We had a problem," Boris agreed. "I found a solution."

NATASHA SHOOK FROM anger at Boris, but mostly from fear at having to tell Dima that his precious copy of *The Gulag Archipelago* had gone up in smoke. He'd trusted her with the most critical task. If Natasha didn't copy out the book's text, others wouldn't be able to distribute it. She was the rate-determining step, the linchpin of the entire operation. And she'd let him down.

Yet, to Natasha's surprise, the next time their group met under cover of darkness and she gathered her courage to confess, Dima barely allowed her to finish before dismissing it as of no consequence.

"We've been talking," he said, indicating the others. Without her? Had Dima found out about her failure? Could this be her expulsion? Was it a done deal?

Natasha bet this was Ludmilla's doing. Ludmilla had long been looking for a slip that wasn't even Natasha's fault that she could use against her. Ludmilla saw how Dima ignored her whenever Natasha was around. She'd decided to eliminate the competition.

"We've decided there's something more important you could be doing for us," Dima said.

"I'd do anything for you," Natasha swore.

"We need to get word of our activities west. Mail is out of the question. The KGB intercepts our letters. Getting a telephone connection is impossible. What we need is someone to speak for us in the United States. Natasha, we need you to apply to emigrate."

Chapter 25

═══

"You want me . . . gone?"

"No one knows you're with us; you're more likely to get permission to leave."

Leave? Leave her family, her home? Leave finally finding something to believe in again after years of feeling adrift and directionless and cruelly let down, even if all that came with risks Natasha allowed herself to dwell on only late at night, confident the fears would have dissipated by morning? Leave Dima?

"But I want to stay here. With you." Fearing not getting her desired response, Natasha pivoted from the specific to the general. "I can't go and leave you, my comrades, behind."

"You'd be our flag bearer in the West. It's a critical position, Natashenka. You're the only one who can do this for us." Fearing not getting his desired response, Dima pivoted from the general to the specific. "For me."

THE FIRST THING Natasha needed was a *visov* from a relative abroad. Because nobody could want to leave the USSR for economic, religious, ethnic, or civic reasons, sole grounds for receiving permission to emigrate were for family reunification. Natasha lamented she didn't have anyone outside the country to invite her. Dima showed her a document from a woman living in Israel for whom they'd forged papers to prove she was Natasha's second cousin, and who would sponsor her exit.

Natasha struggled to wrap her head around the setup. "I'm asking for permission to leave my parents in order to reunite with a second cousin? Someone I never met? That's crazy!"

"That's the rule." Ludmilla shrugged, looking much too pleased about their plan.

"Take this to OVIR," the Otdel Viz I Registracii, the Interior Ministry's Office of Visas and Registration, Dima said. "They'll give you the rest of your paperwork. The most important thing is that no one knows you're connected to us. That's why you're so valuable." He curled his palm over the back of Natasha's hand.

"I won't let you down," she swore, fortifying herself with the conviction that "flag bearer to the West" meant she'd be blazing the trail. The sooner Natasha left the Soviet Union, the sooner Dima would be free to join her.

NATASHA USED TO wonder why Mama hardly ever spoke of her family's banishment, or denounced the forces that sent them there. Now that Natasha was about to take a massive risk, she understood. Mama was desperate to protect her privilege. If Mama had her way, Natasha would be following in her traitorous footsteps. Mama had Natasha's life planned out, and Natasha had gone along, expecting to attend university, get a job, marry an apolitical Jewish boy, produce a single child—so family resources could be focused exclusively on him/her—and, most important, never rock the boat. Even when Natasha's dreams of studying math imploded, Mama acted as if nothing had changed. Everything had changed. Natasha didn't want the leftover crumbs of the life that had been promised her. If she couldn't have all of it, then she wanted none. Natasha wanted something different now. She wanted the kind of life only Dima could provide. She wanted to be by Dima's side when he made his speeches, while he was storming the barricades or launching sneak attacks from underground catacombs, his blood-spattered hand wrenched out of hers as he was dragged off by the police. She wanted to stand vigil outside his prison and demand his release and be talked about in hushed, awed whispers as Dimitri Bruen's muse, the woman who inspired him to keep going when all seemed lost, as the one without whom none of their great achievements would have been possible. Natasha understood the danger. Not just to herself but to her family. They would see, Mama and the rest. She was doing this for them. They would be grateful, in the end.

Today, however, Natasha's revolutionary agenda consisted of ducking out early from work. The students weren't heartbroken to see her go. Natasha consoled herself imagining how shocked they'd be once they learned about the secret life their boring spinster teacher had been living right under their noses. And here the brats thought they were so smart!

Natasha reported to OVIR as directed, stepping in line behind a motley cohort of academics seeking permission to attend overseas conferences, laborers hoping to vacation somewhere exotic like Bulgaria, and other aspiring emigrants. You couldn't tell who was who merely by looking. The uncertainty helped Natasha feel less anxious. With Dima by her side, she could execrate the entire corrupt system, storming barricades and all. Sans him, she preferred to get through the application process without drawing attention to herself.

In line before Natasha was a young woman around the same age, her straight, ebony hair and bedroom eyes suggesting Eastern ancestry. The third time she looked at her watch, then peered around to check how many aspirants were still ahead of them, she told Natasha, "I was here yesterday. They shut the window right in my face. I hope I can get the application today."

"Are you going for school?" Natasha asked out of politeness and boredom.

"My honeymoon." The girl giggled, flashing an as-yet-untarnished wedding ring.

"Congratulations," Natasha said.

"How about you? Where are you trying to go?"

Spurred by the woman's oblivious happiness, Natasha felt compelled to top it. "I'm going to emigrate. My boyfriend and I are. Together." Much more romantic than some ordinary honeymoon.

"Oh!" Her line companion looked impressed. "Are you Jewish?" Natasha nodded.

"I heard you people were being allowed to leave." The girl sighed, envious. "Like always, my papa says, Jews get the best luck . . ."

"NATALIA NIKOLAYEVNA." The OVIR official looked over Natasha's documents. He tapped her forged invitation with his pen and observed, "That doesn't sound Jewish."

"It's Nahumovna," she defended. "The principal at my school, he changed it because—"

"You're going to need to prove that. Also"—he handed Natasha her application—"bring your passport, birth certificate, work authorization—you married?"

"No." She blushed, as any single girl her age was required to do.

"Children?"

"No."

"If you're leaving kids behind, support has to be paid up in advance till they're eighteen."

"I'm not married, and I don't have any children."

"Parents? Going to need their permission. Also grandparents."

"Three of them are dead and one lives in Siberia."

"Death certificates, then. We can't have you leaving any dependents behind."

"My parents aren't dependents. They're working adults."

"Still your responsibility. Need their signed affidavits that you're not abandoning them."

Natasha felt an urge to clarify if that wasn't the point of a socialist state to take care of those who needed it whether or not they also had relatives to do the job?

"Oh, and one final thing—higher education? University?"

"Of course."

"You'll need to reimburse us the cost of that. Diploma Tax. Twelve thousand two hundred rubles." What an oddly specific amount. "Payable upfront."

THE NEXT MORNING, Natasha was headed for her classroom when she was waylaid by the principal, who insisted on seeing her in his office.

"Is this about yesterday?" Natasha asked as she followed his scurrying figure down the hallway. "I felt ill; I got another teacher to cover for me."

He shuttled Natasha into his office and yanked the door shut, whipping around to face her, seething, "You could have quit!"

"It was one afternoon."

"The others of you people—they were considerate enough to quit before they filed! Do you know how badly it reflects on me that someone in my employ is betraying the Motherland? They're going to wonder what I did to encourage you. What if others decide to follow your example? What if they think there's subversive activity going on right under my roof?"

"I requested an application. I haven't even—"

"Get out. I don't need trouble. As of this morning—no, as of yesterday—you don't work here."

"WHAT HAVE YOU DONE?" Mama demanded the moment Natasha stepped through the door that evening. Despite being newly unemployed, she'd put off telling her parents, wandering around the park for most of the day. Natasha didn't come home for supper, either, choosing to slink in when Mama would be getting ready for bed and Papa would already be happily inebriated. But as it turned out, they were sitting in the kitchen, waiting for her, the

Rozengurts out of sight. Mama still had her work clothes on. Papa was acting sober.

Mama raged, "You couldn't have given us a warning? A chance to prepare ourselves?"

"What happened?" Natasha looked from one to the other.

"Nothing important," her father dismissed with a wave of the hand that had been resting against his cheek, not even bothering to make a joke. Which is when Natasha knew it had to be heinous.

"They called him in," Mama contradicted. "Party meeting at the factory. Important officials, his supervisors, his coworkers. They put him in front of the room and they let him have it."

"Wasn't so bad." Papa acted more interested in calming Mama than in rehashing his shame. "Not the other fellows' fault. They were ordered to be there, told what to say. I've done it myself against others. No choice."

"The names they called him! A traitor! A turncoat! Because of you!"

Natasha winced as she pictured all the men and women from Papa's factory, the ones who'd treated her like an honored guest when she'd visited as a little girl, letting her pretend to turn the big mechanical cranks and try on the heavy aprons, the ones who'd taken sandwiches out of their lunch pails, broken off pieces, and offered them to her, telling Natasha she was too skinny, the ones who'd slipped her sucking candies because she'd been so good and well behaved. And now these people were hurling invectives at Papa. Just like he'd done at them on different occasions. The image brought tears to Natasha's eyes.

"Mama, I'm sorry. I didn't think—"

"About us, no, you most certainly did not think."

"That the word would get out so quickly. I was fired today. Papa, did you—"

"Not yet," Mama steamed. "But tell her what they did do. Tell her!"

"A symbolic gesture, that's all."

"They stripped him of his medals. Every last one of them. They said a man who raised a child capable of such high treason doesn't deserve to be called a Hero of the Soviet Union."

"Oh, Papa, no . . ."

"Medals? Feh. What use are medals? You can't eat medals."

"And that's another thing. How do you plan for us to get by without your salary and, God forbid, if Papa and I are removed from our jobs?"

This, Natasha suspected, was another inopportune time to make a crack about the socialist state taking care of its citizens regardless of circumstances.

"I'm sorry it's come to this. But once I'm in the West, I could send—"

"You're not going anywhere." Mama crossed her arms in a defense even their Hero of the Soviet Union couldn't breach. "Because Papa and I will not sign papers granting you permission."

IN HER INFAMOUS history of the Communist Party class, Natasha learned that socialism led not only to sexual emancipation and greater freedom for women (which was why the USSR had no need for a women's liberation movement, unlike the United States) but higher sexual satisfaction as well. In 1952, at a conference in Czechoslovakia, it was unanimously resolved that, due to the equality between women and men in the Eastern Bloc, socialists enjoyed more fulfilling sex lives than capitalists. Natasha wondered where this alleged satisfying and fulfilling sex was taking place. Everyone she knew shared either an apartment or, like her, a room with their parents or, worse, their in-laws. Trying to squeeze in stolen-moment sex while your family was out or pretending to be asleep a few inches away, behind a flimsy curtain, was, she inferred, less than satisfying. And those were her state-sanctioned married friends. If you were single, borrowing a room was about the best you could hope for.

Which was why, the first time Natasha and Dima got to be truly alone together, it was in the dorm room of Dima's acquaintance at Odessa University. Floor matrons were known to look away from girls being sneaked in—for the right price. Nonetheless, Natasha and Dima entered separately, playing it safe.

There was nothing romantic about the room, or its cot, writing desk, chair, and coatrack, from which hung the official resident's spare set of pants and shirt.

Natasha gushed, "It's beautiful!"

Dima turned quizzically in place, wondering if he'd missed something.

"I've never done anything like this before," Natasha confessed. "I knew other people did, but not girls like me." She fumbled finding the words to explain how giddily releasing it felt to, for the first time, not be surrounded by a throng of censorious passersby or by intimates who'd known everything about her since the cradle. To be alone, to be anonymous, to be . . . free.

"This is our way out," Dima had told her in Moldavanka. He'd meant from the oppression of the USSR. Natasha thrilled at his words. When Dima spoke of his cause, Natasha saw the poetry mathematics used to hold for her, the promise of a brilliant life glittering tantalizingly in the distance. A chance for her to stand out, to be special, to be somebody. She imagined them hand in hand, fighting for his noble cause, no longer at the mercy of people telling her what she could or could not do. Natasha embraced her vision and flung herself into the arms of the man she'd been unable to stop thinking about for nearly half a decade, kissing him as if she didn't need anyone's permission. Not even his.

An only slightly startled Dima returned Natasha's kiss, then moved to unbutton her blouse. Her hands reached for his shirt. It would be effortless to keep going, to forget what she'd come to tell him. But it would be dishonorable, and Dima deserved the very best of her.

Reluctantly, Natasha withdrew, leaving him to stare at her, puzzled and breathing heavily.

She told him, "My parents said they wouldn't give me permission to emigrate."

He looked relieved the problem wasn't something he'd done. "They will."

Dima wrapped his arms around Natasha's waist, his face buried in her neck, his lips tracing a trail from her shoulder to her chin.

Natasha moaned. And then she said, "There's another problem. The Diploma Tax. I could never raise twelve thousand rubles."

"You won't have to," he murmured. "It hasn't been enforced since 1973, though the OVIR drudges are still instructed to act as if it is. Americans have this amendment"—he was kissing her cheek—"Jackson-Vanik. It ties trade to human rights." Her brow. "The U.S. objected to the Diploma Tax. A group of their Nobel laureates protested against it. So while it remains on the books, the Politburo decided not to enforce it, to keep the Americans trading with them." The last thing Dima said before catching her upper lip with his teeth was, "You're in the clear."

"Oh." Natasha wasn't as thrilled as she knew she was expected to be. She'd been hoping to use it as an excuse not to have to go against her parents, and to remain with Dima—through no fault of her own.

"Once you receive permission"—Dima began unbuttoning his shirt—"we'll hand you a list of others looking to emigrate, so you can arrange *visovy* for them, like we did for you."

"Isn't that dangerous?" Natasha followed suit, undressing, while her mind skittered in multiple directions. "Can't you be arrested for that?"

"You won't be carrying the information openly." Off came Dima's pants. "You can try to memorize it—that's the best way." He sat on the bed and beckoned Natasha to join him. "Or we could hide it on you." Natasha's clothes were now off, as Dima embarked on a thorough investigation of potential hiding places. "The courier for the list with your name on it, he took out the elastic of his underwear, wrote the pertinent details on it, then slipped it back in.

They stripped him at the border, even stuck a speculum up his ass, but they never found our index."

It wasn't the most romantic sentence Dima could have uttered at the moment, Natasha noted. But it was also, for the first time since they'd met, the first moment when Dima's attention, his passion, his concern was focused exclusively on her, and nothing else.

It would have to do for now.

Chapter 26

Natasha didn't expect everything to change immediately, but she did expect something to change eventually. The first time their group assembled after Natasha and Dima spent the afternoon together, Dima sat at the head of the table, as always. Natasha hadn't expected him to save her a seat next to him—this wasn't grade school. But it did feel odd that Ludmilla still occupied that right-hand place of honor. Natasha ended up in her usual spot, three spaces down, one ahead of the cuticle-chewing Marina who, a few months earlier, had decided to turn religious, change her name to Miriam, and start covering her hair with a scarf. She hardly ever said anything, so it was easy to forget she was there. A fate Natasha was determined not to share.

She was heartened when the first item on Dima's agenda was the announcement that Natasha had begun her emigration process. He beamed at her, and she basked in the glow.

Sadly, the remainder of the meeting consisted of items that didn't require beaming. Dima updated them on the efforts of counterparts overseas, the peaceful rallies staged in the United States by the Student Struggle for Soviet Jewry, and the more militant sit-ins of the Jewish Defense League, as well as the underground efforts of Israel's Nativ, who suspected they were being spied on by the

KGB, making smuggling out information about refuseniks even more difficult. When Dima brought up that last point, Natasha attempted to catch his eye, so they could share a furtive smile about the last time they'd discussed the matter. He shook his head and looked away.

And so it went, Dima covering their ongoing *samizdat* distribution of not only handwritten copies of *Archipelago* but also a Russian translation of Leon Uris's *Exodus*, as well as the poems of Joseph Brodsky. The latter weren't political, but since they'd been judged anti-Soviet and their author locked up in a mental institution as a parasite who failed to contribute to the good of the Motherland, Dima felt they owed the brave rebel their support.

At the end of the meeting, however, outside of everyone's hearing, Dima sidled by Natasha and casually let her know that his acquaintance at Odessa University would be taking a long exam tomorrow afternoon. Natasha smiled.

She was the favorite now.

THERE WAS A different floor matron patrolling the hall, a crone who barely reached Natasha's shoulder yet sat so regally, she managed to look down her nose while looking up from beneath an ill-fitting wig the color of rancid beets. Natasha presumed she and Dima would enter separately. But at the sight of this Oracle of Delphi, Dima assured, "It's all right," and grasped Natasha's hand to lead her inside.

"Youdifa Solomonovna," Dima greeted her. "You're looking wonderful!"

"That's because I live a wonderful life," she repeated by rote, and discreetly tucked the rubles Dima slipped her into a pocket already bulging with similar bills.

"Aren't you afraid she'll report us?" Natasha asked as soon as the door closed behind them and Dima set immediately to removing his clothes. What had his admonitions about their never being seen together been for all these months, if he felt free to disregard the precaution on a whim?

"Youdifa Solomonovna is one of us. She teaches Hebrew to our group of refuseniks every Tuesday and Thursday night."

A group Natasha wasn't invited to, allegedly for the same reason she and Dima couldn't be seen together in public. She told herself it was further proof of just how valuable she was to the group— and to Dima. She told herself she wasn't jealous of the extra time women like Ludmilla and Miriam got to spend with Dima. She told herself those women had to share that time with assorted others and spend it reading children's books written in a sequence of squibbles. She told herself the time she and Dima spent together was their own. And a lot more fun.

"She was in Leningrad during the siege. That's how she lost her hair, typhus. When there was no food or drinking water to be had, she was one of the women you hear about, still scrubbing revolutionary monuments for the glory of Stalin. She survived all nine hundred days. Decorated a Hero of the Soviet Union! Then, last year, she applied to emigrate to Israel. She was fired from her job as university librarian and sent here, instead. But she's a tough one. She'll outlast us all."

An inspirational and courageous story, yes, the sort of story that, one day, Natasha expected wide-eyed acolytes to be telling about her. But that was in the future. At the moment, all Natasha could focus on, even as her skirt slipped to the floor and she unbuttoned her blouse, was, "I feel like there's so much I'm missing. So much more help I could be to you, if you'd just let me participate. Like Ludmilla and Miriam."

It may have sounded as if Natasha were being petty. She sounded that way to herself. But the reality was, Natasha yearned to open her soul to Dima, to tell him how much the previous months had meant to her. She ached to explain how she'd grown resigned to relegating her dreams of becoming someone of note to the dustbin of childish fantasy. She'd accepted being ordinary, no different from anyone else, the Soviet ideal. But then Dima had returned, and her ambitions were reawakened, flipped on their heads yet suddenly again within her grasp. Whenever Natasha attempted to turn feelings into concrete words, she ended up sounding greedy or shallow or, yes, petty, when that wasn't how she saw herself at all.

So Natasha stumbled on, trying to sound like the woman she believed herself to be, instead of the one she secretly feared she was, cajoling Dima, "I know I'm doing my part by applying to emigrate. I don't want to sound ungrateful about the huge trust you've placed in me. But I feel like I'm just on the fringes of our work. I want to be in the heart of it."

Dima had crawled into bed, naked except for his watch, which he'd already checked twice to calculate how much time they had left. Seeing precious seconds ticking away, he decided now was not the time to get into a philosophical argument. If Natasha were honest with herself, she'd admit that was precisely why she'd chosen this moment to bring the subject up. But that would make her sound devious and cynical. And that wasn't how Natasha saw herself, either. Especially when it came to the man she loved.

"Tomorrow, we have a planned demonstration," Dima said. "You can't stand with us. But if you find a hidden spot far enough away, you can watch."

"Just watch?" Natasha struggled to keep the disappointment from her voice.

Dima consulted his timepiece again, raising the blanket, gesticulating for Natasha to join him. "And you can take notes, keep the record about how we're treated, so you can report on it once you're free in the West."

It wasn't what Natasha had been hoping for. But it was more than she'd honestly expected. If it meant playing even the smallest part in their plans, if it meant spending even a few minutes more in Dima's presence, it, too, would have to do.

Natasha had passed the majority of her life delaying gratification while focusing on a long-term goal. She stood well versed in how to bide her time and keep her eyes on the prize. Natasha's only hope—one that she pushed to the back of her mind, for even thinking it was disloyal—was that this bout of sacrifice wouldn't disappoint her.

Like the last had.

WHEN DIMA CALLED it a demonstration, Natasha expected something along the lines of what she was used to for May Day or Victory Day or Veterans' Day; thousands of citizens packing the streets, bouquets of flowers everywhere, placards with pictures of Lenin and Brezhnev, a forest of giant red flags. As a child, Natasha had loved the holidays, putting on her school uniform with the white, special-occasion pinafore and marching with her class. Afterward, she'd beg Papa, his chest overflowing with medals, to let her hold one of the flags he'd been given to heft onto his shoulder.

Natasha hadn't been expecting flags and placards of their leaders at this demonstration. But she had been expecting something more than the Odessa University matron and her equally short, albeit wigless, husband standing on their apartment building's balcony, her holding a sign that read I WANT TO EMIGRATE TO ISRAEL, his proclaiming LET MY PEOPLE GO. On the street below, Dima, along with Ludmilla and Miriam and a half dozen men who weren't Dima, formed a line of similar protesters. And that was it.

How could that be it? Surely, something that played such a dominant role in every waking moment of Natasha's life—and in her dreams, as well—was worthy of a larger manifestation in the outside world? How could something so all-encompassing to her be so negligible to everyone else?

"Remember, keep your distance" was the last thing Dima said as he left Natasha lurking behind a lamppost almost a full block away and jogged to join the others. First, she felt abandoned. Then, she felt bored.

It was a silent protest. The only noise came from the handful of passersby heckling them, but even that was low-key. Schoolboys threw rocks and pinecones and called them "dirty *ƶhidy*," but most adults scurried by, averting their eyes lest their even acknowledging the event put them at risk of being misconstrued as endorsing or, God forbid, participating in it. Natasha's favorite critic was the one who shouted, "Go back to where you came from!" As if that weren't exactly what they were trying to achieve.

The *militsia* arrived within ten minutes. Which was faster than when Natasha's neighbor had called an ambulance for her convulsing husband. That took six hours.

Natasha should have expected the police, and she had—intellectually. Of course a protest by someone as significant as she believed Dima to be would court censure. But she hadn't expected it on a visceral level. Nor had she expected what proved to be her response to the sight of Dima being repeatedly punched in the stomach and face, until he finally stumbled and sank to his knees, still clutching his sign, demanding FREEDOM FOR ALL!

Before the attack began, Natasha had expected she'd want to drop her notebook and pencil—red on one side/blue on the other, filched from the children's art room at school the day she was let go as yet another act of rebellion—and rush to Dima, no matter what he'd told her about staying out of sight. She'd expected to want to throw her body between his and the blizzard of blows, to absorb them herself and spare him, to cradle his bloodied head in her lap, and to dab at the worst of it with a strip of cloth she'd torn from her sleeve, refusing to be dragged away in a feat of passive resistance rivaling the Mahatma himself.

But while it was happening, what Natasha most wanted to do was drop the notebook and pencil—and run in the other direction. She wanted to close her eyes and plug her ears and pretend that none of this was happening. It was too horrible. It was too real. It was just like that 3 she'd received on her exams, the sense that she'd miscalculated and any attempt to rectify the error would only make matters worse. Then, she'd been helpless and uninformed;

she couldn't be blamed for her inaction because it was before she'd become enlightened. Now that Natasha knew better, she must simply be spineless and unwilling.

No, Natasha chastised herself, that wasn't it. The only reason she wasn't running to Dima was that she was following his orders. Keep your distance, take notes, report it all later, and raise awareness of their cause . . . Once she was safe in the West. That's what Dima wanted Natasha to do. That's what he'd ordered her to do. Natasha was a good soldier. Natasha was brave.

Natasha watched Dima and the rest, including the elderly couple on the balcony, being dragged, barely conscious, into the backs of *militsia* trucks pulling away in a cloud of exhaust.

Natasha wrote down what she'd seen. And then she went home.

Chapter 27

═══

For almost a week, Natasha didn't hear of or from Dima. There was obviously no mention of what had happened in the local edition of *Pravda*—that would be preposterous—but Natasha had expected to hear whispers from among her own and her parents' Jewish friends. Surely, somebody had to have heard something. Where were those braggarts who wanted to impress her with their illicit shortwave radios souped up with coat hangers now? Dima's story must have made it to Voice of America. But there was nothing. Natasha did overhear one of Papa's drinking buddies blathering on about "hooligans making it tougher for the rest of us." She chose to think he was referencing Dima and took preemptive offense.

Natasha wondered whether she should risk showing up at the group's meeting spot on the usual time and day. What if one of them had broken during interrogation and told the authorities about it? Natasha wouldn't put it past Ludmilla, to pretend to have slipped due to sleep deprivation and torture but, in reality, to have done it on purpose, to incriminate Natasha. Even when she knew such an act would go directly against Dima's wishes. Though, to be fair, Natasha doubted she herself would last more than one sleepless night under inquisition. Or, God forbid, a beating.

Natasha told herself she wouldn't let Ludmilla cow her like that. Dima would want Natasha to do her duty, no matter the danger. If Dima were still being detained, he had every right to expect Natasha to pick up the baton he'd been forced to drop and unite whatever ragged survivors were left to continue fighting in his name. He was counting on Natasha. She wouldn't let him down.

So Natasha went to Moldavanka. Well, technically, she crept there, scurrying from shadow to shadow, staying out of sight the way Dima would want her to. She lurked outside the abandoned house where they met until she saw a flicker of curtains. Someone was there. That someone could be a KGB officer lying in wait. Natasha told herself she wasn't afraid and went in.

She almost wept with relief when her gamble paid off. No KGB officer. (Well, none she knew of; as Dima and Papa pointed out, in any group, one is inevitably an informer.) Only Dima, Ludmilla, Miriam, and the rest. They were all accounted for!

The right side of Dima's face was a swollen sickly yellow crisscrossed with broken blood vessels, while the left side was a more freshly bruised purple. Ludmilla's left eye was swollen shut. A slash ran from the side of her mouth up her cheek. Miriam's flowing auburn hair showed signs of having been ripped out in clumps, as if grabbed to pull back her head. The other men were equally marked, knuckles scraped raw where they'd tried to fight back.

And yet, none of them were acting as if anything was different. The meeting proceeded as if nothing out of the ordinary had happened. Their demeanor reminded Natasha of friends who'd had abortions. They'd been through a terrible, excruciating, brutal experience. But it needed to be done. They just never wanted to talk about or reference it again. Natasha obeyed their wishes. She didn't gasp or fuss over Dima's injuries. She didn't tell Ludmilla or Miriam how genuinely awed she'd been by their stoic bravery (and how much she was presently regretting some of her previous, less-than-charitable thoughts about them). She didn't gush over how inspirational she found them all. For months, it had been all talk and no action. Now that Natasha had seen action up close, she realized how inadequate talk would be.

So Natasha simply took her seat and joined them in pretending everything was normal. All the while knowing that, finally, everything had truly changed.

"DID YOU GIVE one minute of thought regarding what you were doing to your parents?" Boris, who'd gone about for weeks pretending he had no idea about the latest developments in Natasha's life, took advantage of an afternoon when the two of them were home alone to pull her into his room and, despite the closed door and lack of windows, still only allow himself to whisper.

"They're going to be fine." Mama and Papa had yet to sign her permission papers. Having seen what Dima and the rest were put through, Natasha had ceased pushing them. Yet, for Boris, Natasha answered the way she knew Dima would expect her to. "I had to do it. I have no future here. Neither do you. They made that clear the day we took our math exams."

Natasha had never understood why, while she couldn't help thinking about it every day, Boris appeared to have put the travesty behind him. He never mused about what might have been, never lamented the life he'd lost. It forced Natasha to wonder if she wasn't making too big a fuss. Boris acted like he wasn't the first person ever forced to let go of a dream, and he wouldn't be the last, so he moved on and found something new to occupy his time, something he was confident would make him equally happy. It was most infuriating.

Boris crossed his arms and leaned against the wall. When they were kids, he'd given in to Natasha's arguments without a fight. The most he'd put up in token protest was, "I don't care what you say, as long as I know I'm right." Since Natasha met Dima, however, it seemed as if Boris were intentionally overriding his innate tranquility for Natasha's sake. It wasn't that he cared about being right, it was that he felt terrified of what would happen if Natasha were wrong.

She rolled her eyes as he gravely intoned, "October 1941, the Romanian headquarters of the occupying army in Odessa was blown up. In retaliation, hundreds of Jews were hanged."

"Every schoolkid knows that story." Except the official version had it that hundreds of loyal Soviet martyrs were hanged. The fact that they were Jews was information passed around surreptitiously.

"The same thing happened in Kiev. After the Nazi headquarters was blown up, how many tens of thousands of Jews were slaughtered at Babi Yar?" The monument over the mass graves there read CITIZENS OF KIEV AND PRISONERS OF WAR. Natasha refused to listen to what Boris was saying, even as she heard his message loud and clear. "You selfishly run away, and the people you leave behind pay the price. Like our first *kolkhoz*."

"Quit complaining. You didn't suffer any consequences."

She watched the debate in his head flare up briefly before Boris confessed, "I didn't report you for leaving. So I got reported."

"I-I didn't know that," Natasha stammered, shocked not just that it happened, but that he was only telling her now.

"I was up for a promotion at work a few months ago. Manager said he'd been planning to give it to me. Showed me the already filled-out papers. There'd have been a raise. Then he said he reviewed my disciplinary file and found out about my offense. He ripped up the papers in front of my face. 'Better luck next time, Rozengurt.'"

Guilt sucker-punched Natasha's chest and stomach. She pushed back against it, the way you fought the urge to vomit by swallowing hard and thinking of something else.

How dare Boris do this to her? Attempt to make Natasha question the righteousness of Dima's cause by bringing up his trifling setbacks? Didn't he realize the fate of millions was at stake? What was Boris's piddling promotion compared to the bruises on Dima's face? Compared to the elderly couple who, unlike their group, hadn't been perfunctorily tortured and released? They never returned to the apartment where they staged their protest. Nobody knew where these Heroes of the Soviet Union currently were.

"You're only worried about how what I've done might affect you," Natasha accused.

Boris let it pass with a look that suggested her blow wasn't low so much as it was beneath her. "You should have warned your parents. They were blindsided. If you'd warned them and your principal, they'd have warned their higher-ups, and the higher-ups wouldn't have reacted so aggressively. If you give people what *they* need, they're more likely to give you what *you* want. When are you going to understand that?"

"SPOKEN LIKE A true collaborator," Dima sniffed. They were getting dressed after another hurried assignation, Natasha ignoring the marks on Dima's body the way she'd pretended not to notice the ones on his face. Yet while they were making love, she'd brushed her fingers along the worst of them, hoping Dima wouldn't notice. She needed, in this small way, to feel a part of what had happened. She hoped some of the bravery manifested in those marks might rub off on her.

Dima stuck his head through the top of his sweater, smoothed his hair with both hands, and announced, "It's people like that who make life difficult for people like us."

They were finally an *us*. Natasha liked the sound of that.

"The ones who fight us, I can handle," Dima went on. "It's the namby-pamby appeasers I can't stand. They keep accommodating and accommodating, no matter how bad things get. They never want to rock the boat."

"I think he's concerned about me and my family." Natasha hated contradicting Dima, but remnants of childhood loyalty didn't want Dima thinking Boris was looking out only for himself. Or expressing any concerns Natasha hadn't at least entertained. "Is he right?

Am I being selfish? What will happen to my parents if—when—I leave?"

"Nothing. As long as they stop being a part of the system and actively resist it."

Natasha thought of the missing floor matron and her husband. "If Mama and Papa are fired from their jobs, could they end up like Brodsky? Imprisoned for being parasites?"

"Brodsky's biographer wrote that, after the suffering of the trial and the mental hospital, the months Brodsky spent in exile in the Arctic were the best times of his life."

Natasha noted that the biographer had said that, not Brodsky. Probably because the biographer hadn't spent months in exile in the Arctic. Natasha imagined Mama banished to a frozen waste-land for the third time, not because of her mother, now, but because of her daughter. All Mama's efforts to keep them safe, and she'd end up even worse than she started.

"And then Brodsky got deported to Vienna!" Dima playfully waved his fist at the window. "I hope they punish me like that!"

"Brodsky had Jean-Paul Sartre lobbying for him. I don't think Sartre is acquainted with my parents." Papa had already lost his medals, been called names, censured. To be banished as an enemy of the state after everything he'd given to the USSR would destroy him along with Mama.

"In the Warsaw Ghetto, there were politicians who thought if they went along with what the Nazis wanted, they'd spare the Jews."

Oh, good, another World War II metaphor.

"Imbeciles like your Boris go way back in our history. Tell me, when was the only time the world ever respected Jewish might?"

Was this a trick question?

"Nineteen sixty-seven," Dima enlightened. "The Six-Day War. You'd be walking down the street and Russian thugs who'd sooner spit at you than give you the right of way would get in your face and they'd say, "Damn, you people! Look at what you pulled off!""

In 1967, Natasha was more concerned with earning her gold

medal than with foreign affairs, especially of a nation that, she'd been taught, had rejected the USSR's magnanimous offer of friendship to ally itself with the capitalist West and join them in oppressing native people from the Congo to Vietnam. She'd had no time or compulsion to think of anything outside of herself. She thought she'd changed since then. What if she hadn't? Is that what Dima was trying to tell her? That Natasha was still the self-centered girl she'd been then? The one she'd been trying so hard to leave in the past?

Dima reminded for the umpteenth time, "The only way we'll ever get out of this prison country is by decisive action. Let cowards like your Boris—"

"He's not my—"

"Let cowards like them play nice. It's your choice which side you prefer."

THE GRIM LOOK on Mama's face when Natasha came home triggered her to fear the worst. She imagined both parents losing their jobs. She imagined exile to the Arctic—without a troupe of international poets clamoring for their release. She thought of Papa, not only forced to give up his hard-won medals but forbidden from marching in the Victory Parade every May 9. Papa pretended it was just another duty to fulfill, but Natasha saw how his eye filled with tears as the children ran up to him, handing him bouquets of flowers and thanking him for his service.

Natasha was prepared for anything. Except Mama offering Natasha her papers, signed by Mama, Papa, and even by Baba Daria.

"What changed your mind?" Natasha managed to choke out, a maelstrom of conflicting feelings clogging her throat.

Mama held up a crumpled envelope, the address on the front inscribed in an elegant, if shaky, hand, its flap sealed and resealed several times by censors. "Baba wrote that what you need should take precedence over what we want."

Chapter 28

===

Natasha knew she should be ecstatic. Finally, her file was complete. She turned it in to OVIR. There was nothing to do but wait.

Her days fell into a routine. Mornings were spent with Dima making love. Afternoons were for OVIR, reading a book, waiting for the lists to be posted of those who'd been given permission and those who'd been denied. Some cooled their heels for years. Most waited months. With a mere few weeks under her belt, Natasha barely gave the results a perfunctory glance. Until she caught sight of her own name.

Under those who'd been refused.

SLAVA BOGU. THANK GOD.

The words flashed through Natasha's mind before she had the chance to censor herself and recall that she was disappointed. Crushed, really, by the latest turn of events.

"What reason did they give?" Dima demanded.

"My association with you." Natasha secretly crowed at the notion that even the government was blessing their relationship—in its own way.

"Damn it! And we were so careful, too."

Natasha thought now might be a good time to bring up another issue about which they thought they'd been so careful. Except Dima was in no mood to hear it.

"At least we don't have to sneak around anymore," Natasha said, offering what she hoped would be a silver lining. "It might be for the best. Now I can be free to help you in all sorts of ways."

Dima nodded absently, prompting Natasha to wonder if what she was saying was actually what he was hearing. Dima pinched the bridge of his nose, squinted his eyes, and mumbled, more to himself than to her. "We'll have to change strategies, add another person."

Was Natasha supposed to know what he was talking about?

"Do you trust me?"

"Always," Natasha swore, happy finally to be telling the truth, especially to herself.

"Good. Because what we've got planned, we can't risk a single detail going wrong."

"ARE YOU GOING to tell your parents?" Boris sneaked up on Natasha when she thought she was home alone.

"Tell them what?" It had been a week since Natasha had received her refusal, and she had yet to fill her parents in. It should have been good news for them, yet Natasha couldn't shake the suspicion they'd be disappointed. Once they'd committed to their sacrifice, they'd be expecting her to make it worth their while.

Boris blushed and waved his hand in the direction of Natasha's waist. "The baby."

It was the last thing she'd expected him to say. Natasha was operating on the premise that as long as she refused to acknowledge reality, it wouldn't manifest as a concept identifiable by others. It wasn't denial or wishful thinking. It was quantum mechanical thinking. The USSR was famous for erasing individuals and events from existence. She was being a patriotic citizen.

"How did you know?"

The blush acquired a second, even redder layer. Boris's arm jerked upward in the vague vicinity of her chest. "You're . . . um . . . bigger."

"You've been tracking?" she asked, incredulous.

"Since I was twelve." Did he seem proud of himself? Natasha's stomach churned as she recalled all the opportunities he would've had, starting from when they were still young enough to go to the beach only in their underpants and ending with how often Boris still saw her laundry drying on the clothesline. She would have never guessed he had it in him.

"It's none of your business."

"Were you hoping to emigrate before your parents figured it out?"

Natasha hadn't been thinking that far ahead. Not that it mattered now. "I got rejected."

"You don't seem too upset about it."

First her breasts, now her emotional state? What else did Boris think he knew about her?

"You seem relieved," he added.

Natasha did her best to snort derisively. "About being trapped here for the rest of my life?"

"With Dima?"

When had Boris become so perceptive? And when had he become so assertive?

"How do you know I'm with Dima?" Natasha challenged. And stalled.

Boris's derisive snort proved much more successful. "Every word out of your mouth the past few months has been a diluted echo of his. Who else would you be so happy about staying for?"

"You think I'm happy about a future where the two of us are constantly watched, unable to trust anyone but each other, exiled someplace so remote we might go days without seeing another soul? Does that sound romantic?" Natasha hoped she injected enough sarcasm into her words to keep Boris from suspecting she might be sincere.

"Plus, it lets you off the hook," he said.

"What's that supposed to mean?" The only hook Natasha had been thinking about was the one the abortionist used.

"It means you don't have to try. The last thing you tried was getting into university. When that didn't work out, you gave up. On everything. You're certainly not trying to be a good teacher."

"When those brats try to be good students, I'll try to be a good teacher."

"You haven't tried to get another position, one you'd like more."

"Like you? Tell me again how writing strings of numbers to make machines buzz is math."

"You didn't even try that hard to emigrate."

"I got refused," Natasha reminded, then added proudly, "due to my subversive activities."

"You could reapply, but you won't. Because then you'd have to live up to other people's expectations. Your parents', Dima's. You'd have to justify their faith in you. This way, you can keep criticizing how other people live without having to do anything yourself."

"You think it's easy to get permission to emigrate?"

"Not if you self-sabotage."

"You don't know what you're talking about. I filed every document they asked for. I paid the official fees, and the unofficial bribes."

"While hanging around a group of known troublemakers, playing at being rebels."

"What qualifies you to judge? You've never broken a rule in your life," Natasha taunted, even as she knew it wasn't true.

"Maybe that's why I got permission to emigrate." Boris reached into his shirt pocket and pulled out a folded piece of paper, presenting it to Natasha for inspection.

She accepted it gingerly, convinced he was lying, tricking her to make a point. But the papers looked exactly the way Natasha had imagined her own papers would look. The ones she hoped to bring triumphantly to Dima. The ones she was terrified of bringing triumphantly to Dima.

"I didn't know you'd even applied." Her head was spinning. How could Boris have pulled this off? Natasha thought she knew everything about him. That she could predict everything about him. It was the reason she dismissed Boris as being dull and reactionary. He wasn't capable of surprising her, of exciting her. Yet here he was, revealing facets of himself she'd never imagined. How could Boris have succeeded where she—and Dima—had failed? "This can't be legitimate. You didn't lose your job . . ."

"I went to my boss, told him about it beforehand so he wouldn't get caught unawares. I offered to quit. He asked me, 'What? You don't need money anymore?' He said he'll keep me on until the day I leave, if I want."

"You have a departure date already?"

"Not yet. Mama and Papa have a few loose ends they need to tie up first."

"They're going?" Amazing how many secrets six people could keep in four rooms.

"I couldn't leave them behind to fend for themselves." Like Natasha was planning to? "I can take you, too," Boris added, though it came out as a question.

"How?" The prospect was so preposterous, Natasha was sure he was teasing.

"If we were married." Now he had to be kidding. "It would solve several problems at once."

"For whom?"

"Well, you," Boris offered. Then, seeing that rationale wasn't picking up much traction, he switched tactics. "And your parents. We can apply for them, too. Your father has already been publicly shamed. He doesn't have much left to lose." Facts not in evidence. In Natasha's experience, matters could always get worse. "As soon as we're married," Boris added, which created a confusing synergy between the two sentences.

"Dima," she began.

Boris cut her off. Which was good, as Natasha had no plans for any words after that.

"What you said before, about being constantly watched and possibly exiled. Is that the kind of life you want?"

She'd been imagining the romance of her and Dima allied together against the world. Like Lenin and his wife, the formidable Krupskaya. Napoleon and his beautiful Josephine. Franklin Delano and his homely but progressive Eleanor. There'd been no child in the picture. No boiling of dirty diapers, no scrounging for milk, no being left behind to rock a cradle while Dima continued his battle for freedom. Suddenly, instead of Krupskaya, Josephine, and Eleanor, Natasha considered Jenny von Westphalen, Karl Marx's wife, who bore him seven babies and lived in filth and poverty while her husband wrote about the workers' struggle and why his own work should be limited to thinking.

"It won't be like that," Natasha said, responding more to the clash in her head than to the question Boris actually asked.

"Not if you marry me," he confirmed.

Chapter 29

—

"There might be another way," Natasha told Dima, "for me to leave the country."

It wasn't her imagination. Since learning of Natasha's refusal, Dima had taken less of an interest in her. Not in the sex. He was still interested in the sex. But before, pillow talk consisted of Dima's plans for Natasha in the West. Now he lay on his back, arm over his face, and sermonized about the growing Free Soviet Jewry movement, the protests outside Lenin Library, the Belgian and French scientists demanding a reversal of sexologist Michael Stern's hard labor conviction (had he pushed back on the socialism-leads-to-better-sex concept?). Dima talked about a Passover service broken up at Moscow Synagogue, about hunger strikes and the international Day of Solidarity with Soviet Jews on April 28, 1974, where 125,000 allies turned out to protest in New York City alone. Natasha figured if her lying there naked couldn't compete with the daily news, maybe her latest bulletin would.

It did manage to capture Dima's attention. He rolled onto his side, propping his head up with his palm while he rested his elbow on the pillow. "How's that?"

"Boris received permission to emigrate."

"Of course," Dima snorted. "The authorities know he'll cause them no trouble overseas. Instead of advocating for the rest of us, he'll keep his head down, make his money, get fat, and give no thought to those who struggled to make his easy life possible."

Natasha tried to imagine telephone-pole Boris fat—but that image was overwritten by the Boris who'd confronted her in their kitchen, the Boris who was confident and imperturbable and in a much better political position than either of them. "If I were to marry Boris—"

"Marry him!" Dima yelped, the first show of interest he'd directed Natasha's way in ages. It made Natasha's heart spin in her chest, only to skid to a grinding halt when Dima added, "How in the world would you get that ninny to do it?"

"Well," rather than confess he'd already asked, she played it coy. "I could seduce him."

"How long do you think it would take?"

Less time than with you, Natasha thought, then chastised herself for thinking Boris could be superior to Dima. The reason Boris was quicker to recognize Natasha's pregnancy was that Boris's head was filled with commonplace thoughts, while Dima's was generating subversive ideas. He had more important things than Natasha's breasts to mull over.

"Not too long."

Dima thought for a moment, then shook his head. "We can't risk it."

Natasha exhaled. Dima didn't want her sleeping with another man. Dima wanted Natasha all to himself.

"There isn't enough time," he explained. "Remember when I told you we were planning a major act of resistance? We're going to hijack a plane. Take it to Israel."

Her eyes widened. "You can't do that!"

"We can," Dima reassured, as though Natasha was questioning the logistics rather than the suicidal lunacy of it. "I was hoping to wait until you were in the West to disseminate the news, but there's no time for that now. You'll have to come with us."

He'd said she had to. That meant he couldn't live without her. Except, if Dima went through with this, he likely wouldn't have a life left to live.

"I can't. I want to. I want to be with you—no one else—for always. Don't worry, you've convinced me. I won't marry Boris. I won't put you through that heartache. But you can't take such a huge risk, either. I—I'm going to have a baby. Our baby. Your baby."

"That's wonderful," Dima finally said, prompting Natasha's heart to resume its spinning. Wonderful! He'd said her pregnancy was wonderful! "The Western press will love you!" Natasha had been hoping for a different pronoun. "A young family fleeing totalitarianism! They'll eat it up!"

All Natasha could hear was he'd called them a family. All she could see was the two of them escaping the USSR together, exiting, hand in hand, into a barrage of press flashbulbs. They'd be the most famous couple in the world!

Of course, there were risks. Not just for Natasha, for her family, too.

Then again, didn't true love always come with risks? No matter who? No matter where? It was par for the course. Natasha couldn't—shouldn't—think of those now. She should focus on the reward. The reward she'd waited too long for. The reward that should have been hers all along.

"So you're in." It wasn't exactly a question.

Which was why Natasha's only possible answer could be, "Yes."

THE PLAN WAS to buy out the tickets of a fifteen-seater plane, claiming they were traveling to Alm-Ata in Kazakhstan for a wedding. Considering all of them were refuseniks, it wasn't a simple matter of walking into any tourism office and laying down enough bills to cover the cost of the tickets and bribes. The task would require finesse, quick thinking, and nerves of steel.

"You should do it," Dima told Natasha. "You're still the least compromised of us all."

"How? What do I say if they ask questions?"

"Tell them a good story," Dima urged. "Convince them. You're a pretty girl. It shouldn't be hard."

Natasha, flattered, agreed.

THE MORNING NATASHA walked into the Travel Bureau, there were two clerks on duty. One was an elderly woman with eyes narrowed from a lifetime of squinting at imbeciles who dared think they deserved a chance to leave the city. The other was a middle-aged man who, while filling out papers for a dowdy couple clutching the bag of apples they'd brought him as a thank-you, looked up when Natasha walked in and gave her a smile. It was a smile similar to the look he gave the apples. It gave her hope. So of course, Natasha was assigned to the beady-eyed old lady.

"Alma-Ata," she repeated Natasha's destination as if she didn't believe the place existed.

"For a wedding." Natasha stuck to her script, heart hammering so madly, she was surprised no one else could hear it. Or see her chest bouncing as if a kitten were trying to claw its way out of her dress. Boris would have.

"You have the money to purchase all the seats on a single plane?"

"Yes." Natasha laid the prepared stack of rubles on the table.

The woman pawed the bills, licking her thumb each time. Natasha had given her enough to cover fifteen tickets. And an extra 100 rubles on top of that. Natasha wasn't expecting change.

"This is very last minute. You should have made the request months ago."

"The wedding was very last minute," Natasha improvised, the kitten turning into a cougar.

"Your friends should have planned better."

"I'm sure they wish they had." Natasha burst into unexpected tears. "If they had more time, they could have planned a better wedding, something not so last minute. Or maybe they would've tired of each other and broken up. But it's too late now; they don't have any choices left. They have to get married quickly. That's why we have to be there. What if the groom changes his mind and leaves her high and dry? What's she going to do? Her life will be ruined. She'll have nothing left. She'll be stuck because she made an error in judgment. It could happen to anyone, but she'll be the one paying for it until she dies, while he gets to walk away scot-free!"

Natasha's words tumbled over one another. She couldn't be sure if they made sense or if it—she—was a mishmash of worst-case-scenario anxiety. Natasha was crying, wiping her cheeks with the backs of both hands, her nose running, her mascara smearing. The travel agent who'd smiled at Natasha earlier was now sneaking disgusted peeks and looking relieved to have dodged this bullet.

The older woman, however, offered Natasha a handkerchief. It smelled of cloves and was embroidered with a lace border.

"When is the baby due?" she asked.

"Seven months," Natasha sniffled, telling the truth.

"And your friend, she's afraid the father might not step up to his responsibility?"

Natasha nodded miserably. "He's a very important person. He has so much on his mind, so many other priorities. If this isn't nailed down immediately, who knows what might happen?"

The agent turned her back so her colleague couldn't see. She reached into the lowest drawer of her desk and pulled out a stack of papers, sliding them toward Natasha, whispering, "These are for Party members. Last-minute tickets. I'm supposed to hold on to them, in case of an emergency." She patted Natasha's hand. "If your friend's situation isn't an emergency, I don't know what is."

"Thank you." Natasha swallowed, relieved she hadn't failed in her endeavor. Terrified about what her lack of failure meant.

"Good luck." The old lady almost cracked a smile.

She didn't, however, return the extra 100 rubles.

"YOU'RE MARVELOUS!" Dima swept Natasha into a hug. "Look at what she did!" He flapped the tickets at their comrades. "Party member passes! No one would dare question us with these!"

"Wonderful work," Ludmilla chimed in. Less than enthusiastically, Natasha thought.

"Yes, wonderful," Miriam echoed.

Natasha accepted their kudos magnanimously, stressing how she was just doing her part. But while her head may have swiveled to acknowledge everyone singing her praises, Natasha kept her eyes peeled on Dima.

"You're our heroine," Dima said and, right there, in front of everyone, kissed Natasha on the lips. "I don't know what we'd do without you."

NOW THAT THEY had tickets, step two involved practicing how they would tie up and eject the pilots, and what would happen next. One of their number had flown in the army. He would be in charge. Just in case, the rest of them read smuggled books about how to fly a small aircraft. They simulated a cockpit out of discarded household items, broken clock faces for the dials, a gutted television set for the window. They composed manifestos to overseas news outlets that they planned to drop in the mail the morning of their escape. They didn't fear them being opened by authorities because, by that point, they'd either be in the air (assuming the course they plotted from stolen maps proved accurate) . . . or under arrest. If Natasha's parents wondered where their unemployed daughter was disappearing to daily, they kept the questions to themselves. *The less you know, the sounder you sleep.* Even Boris was keeping his distance. Following their initial conversation, he never again brought up emigration or marriage or the baby Natasha had yet to confess to anyone else. He merely kept a stealthy watch on Natasha, like those paintings in which the figure isn't moving but its eyes seem to be following you.

Under different circumstances, Natasha would have been annoyed. Under different circumstances, she would have barked for him to cut it out. But these were exceptional days, and Natasha's giddy happiness at finally being a full-fledged member of Dima's inner circle, at finally doing something more productive and exciting than sweatily switching satchels, at finally having Dima publicly acknowledge just how much she meant to him, extended not only to Dima and his cause but to everyone who so much as brushed up against his aura. Instead of feeling exasperated by Boris, Natasha gazed upon him affectionately, as something that, in the past, held sentimental value to her; something that, in the near future, she would never see again.

As the day of reckoning drew closer, Natasha realized she would soon be waving farewell to everything and everyone. Mama and Papa, her friends from school, Boris. Natasha couldn't risk saying goodbye out loud, even as she walked about doing it mentally toward every tree, every edifice, every café and statue in Odessa. Goodbye, Duc de Richelieu with his outstretched hand; goodbye, peeing Pushkin; goodbye, flower-strewn Tomb of the Unknown Sailor.

As part of Natasha's *dosvedanya* tour, she found even the most mundane exchanges rife with meaning. Her last morning at home, when she had to act as if it were just another day—some of the others told their families they were taking a holiday, but Natasha feared even a casual goodbye would break her—she accepted the cup of tea Mama proffered her with shaking hands, breathing in the aroma to imprint the smell. She ran her hand against the frayed plastic tablecloth. She stared out the window at the courtyard and mourned that the next time the dandelions went to seed, she would be gone. Who cared that, in the past, she'd raged against their fluff getting caught in her hair, sticking on her clothes, and clogging her nostrils?

She stirred her *mannaya kasha* listlessly, as if Natasha's dawdling might keep Papa from inhaling his portion of semolina before rushing off to work. Papa was making small talk about the workday ahead, dabbing at his sticky lips with a handkerchief and using the back of the same to wipe up drips of porridge his spoon left on the table. He had no idea that, before the day was out, he'd be called before another committee. Last time they'd excoriated him and taken away his medals. What punishment was in store this time? Natasha struggled to keep from imagining Papa and Mama fired, the Rozengurts stripped of their permission to leave. Both couples tossed out on the street. The shaking in Natasha's hands migrated the length of her body.

"Are you coming down with a fever?" Mama pressed her palm against Natasha's forehead. "You've been looking haggard for weeks. Maybe you should spend today in bed. Resting."

She'd uttered the sentiment dozens of times throughout Natasha's childhood. Illness was about the only thing that could make Natasha's usually stoic Mama tremble. She lived in terror of every cough, every sneeze, every sniffle turning into pneumonia. Was it Natasha's hypersensitive state that was prompting her to imagine Mama putting particular emphasis on the word *today*? And what about her saying Natasha was looking haggard? Had Mama, like Boris, put two and two together and come up with an almost-four-month-old secret? What was Mama trying to tell her when she suggested Natasha spend today—today specifically—in bed?

"I don't know," Natasha began, standing up on equally shaky legs, moving for the door.

"I think it would be for the best," Mama said firmly.

The pair locked eyes. In her peripheral vision, Natasha saw Papa. He'd stopped eating. He was watching them. While Natasha was watching Mama, whose body stood angled in such a way that she could as easily stop Natasha from heading for the door as she could let her go. Did Mama even know she had such a momentous decision to make?

Natasha's head moved independently of her will. It took a moment before she realized she was nodding.

Chapter 30

Mama and Papa left for work. So did the Rozengurts. Natasha was home alone, tucked under the duvet smelling of home-brewed lye soap, a plate of bland soft-boiled eggs mixed with scraps of bread—a favorite from childhood sick days—on a chair next to her. Natasha lacked an appetite. That would help with her illness excuse. Because that's what this was, an excuse. Had Natasha been looking for one from the moment she awoke? Had she never planned to meet Dima and the others? If it hadn't been Mama's suggestion that she stay home, would Natasha have loitered until something equally acceptable turned up?

She watched the clock. They'd worked their strategy out to the last detail. Natasha knew when everything was supposed to happen. The question was, would it happen? And then, did it happen? She turned on the radio, though she knew there'd be no news. If the hijacking succeeded, authorities would ensure no word of it ever trickled down to the public. And if it failed, the notion that anyone might be so desperate to leave the USSR would still be an international embarrassment.

Still, whether TASS was authorized to announce or not, there was always gossip. Like *samizdat* copies of forbidden books passing hand to hand, rumors traveled mouth to mouth. It's how they knew about the Lenin Library protest, the Passover service, and the worldwide rallies. Or about Solomon Mikhoels, artistic director and star of the Moscow State Jewish Theater. He met everyone from scientist Albert Einstein to singer Paul Robeson while traveling across the United States to gain America's support in the fight against German fascism. But then Stalin had decreed that contact with citizens of non-Communist countries was bourgeois, and he'd had Mikhoels murdered. The official cause of death was a hit-and-run, but everyone Natasha knew was convinced the reason their icon had a closed-coffin state funeral was to hide evidence of the torture he'd endured prior to being dumped on the side of the road and crushed by a truck. They laughed at Mikhoels's self-proclaimed friend, Robeson, accepting the Stalin Peace Prize from the man himself, telling the international press regarding Stalin's war against the Jews, "I heard no word about it." Maybe he hadn't. They all had.

Mikhoels had been judged too famous and beloved for a public show trial. But Dima and his cohorts wouldn't be. Odds are, something would eventually appear on the official news if they were caught. And yet, for days, nothing did.

Natasha once again vacillated from a feeling of terror—that every knock on the door, every squeal of a tire in the middle of the night, was the KGB coming for her; if they'd been caught, that meant they'd been watched, and if they'd been watched, they had to know Natasha was part of the group—to a sinking realization that the others must have gotten away with it.

And that Natasha had given up her chance to make history.

She imagined the heroes' welcome Dima and the rest must have received after they landed in the West. They'd be celebrities, feted by prime ministers and presidents, having their photos taken, granting interviews where they told and retold their thrilling tale of escape. There would be ballads written about them, books, perhaps even a film made. Natasha fantasized that Dima would send for her. He wouldn't abandon the woman he loved or permit his child to grow up trapped in the USSR. But as days passed without a representative from the U.S. embassy showing up on Natasha's doorstep with a visa and a one-way ticket to New York, she told herself Dima wouldn't risk her safety in such a manner. He would keep her name out of it, for fear of reprisals.

She could have gone with him. She could have been a hero, too. She could be in America right now, living in a mansion where they had closets so big they needed their own lightbulbs, wearing a silver mink coat to drive her gold Cadillac to a restaurant where you didn't even have to go in, they brought the food straight out to you! No waiting in line!

She and Dima would be married. He'd want a religious ceremony. Natasha wasn't sure what that entailed. It wasn't as if she could ask. There were short stories Sholom Aleichem had published in Russian available at the public library, but anything that referred to religion had been exorcised in order that, according to the introduction, they could better focus on the writer's love of Russian culture and its progressive ideals in the face of international moneybags. They were no help.

Still, Natasha was able to glean something about the bride and groom standing beneath a canopy, a smashed glass, and a wedding contract you were supposed to frame. She imagined the rest, popping herself and Dima into the scene. She visualized their wedding pictures in the newspapers, and, when their baby was born, it would be on the cover of one of those glossy French magazines, like European royal families. But most important, they would have made a significant political statement and advanced the cause of Soviet Jewry worldwide.

Except now all that would happen without Natasha.

Her baby would be born in Odessa, where she would have to bribe the anesthesiologist for medication and give birth in full view of any hospital personnel who happened to wander through, including the janitor. She'd spend a week in the maternity ward, lying side by side with other new mothers in a row of identical cots. Then she would bring the baby home—to the same crowded room she already shared with Mama and Papa—and proceed to drown in a cascade of cloth diapers to be hand-washed, starched, and ironed; bottles to be sterilized; and screams to be hushed. She wondered if she'd be allowed to go back to work, if her child would still be eligible for a place in a public nursery and if her political pariah situation would be permanent. Like her misery. And her regret. And her stupidity. She'd been given a once-in-a-lifetime opportunity. And she'd been too cowardly to run with it.

Natasha's remorse grew so severe, she would be walking down Primorsky Boulevard by day, yet seeing before her Times Square lit up at night. Instead of the white Potemkin Steps rolling down, she saw the gray Empire State Building towering up, and instead of the Monument to Catherine the Great, she saw the Statue of Liberty. In each location, Natasha walked hand in hand with Dima. Sometimes she was pushing a fancy American stroller. Once in a while, she allowed some of Dima's comrades to flank them on either side, like an honor guard.

So habituated was Natasha to her parallel existence that, when she spotted Miriam crossing the street, it took Natasha a moment to recognize the woman was actually here, rather than a chimera like the others.

In a half dozen brisk strides Natasha caught up to Miriam and tapped her on the shoulder. The girl whipped around as if struck by an arrow, the terror on her face a replica of how Natasha had felt during those first days before realizing Dima and the rest had succeeded in their escape. Natasha expected Miriam to relax once she realized it was just her, but Miriam, if anything, looked more panicked. She whispered, "Follow a couple steps behind me," as she about-faced and began walking in the opposite direction. Confused, Natasha did as she was told. She kept a half block's distance between them for over a kilometer, running out of breath as her newfound queasy exhaustion made its regular afternoon debut.

Finally, Miriam ducked into an alley that smelled of rancid soup and backed-up sewage and made Natasha gag.

"Morning sickness?" Miriam clucked, still whispering.

"How did you know?" Natasha sputtered, forcing down the bile that didn't so much rise in her throat as take up residence there—a sour, immobile clump of mucus.

"Dima told me. Before he left."

Natasha supposed she could take offense at Dima's sharing their private business. Despite the public kiss, they'd kept every other aspect of the relationship to themselves. But Natasha was proud that Dima appeared so excited about the baby he couldn't keep the news to himself.

"I thought you were supposed to go with them." Natasha took heart in not being the only coward. And she didn't even have God's benevolent protection to hide behind. The way Natasha looked at it, that made her less of a coward than Miriam.

"After he realized you weren't coming, Dima told me to stay behind, to watch out for you."

Natasha instantly forgave Dima for all the trysts she, in her weaker moments, imagined him having with Western floozies who threw themselves at heroic celebrities. Dima had been worried enough about Natasha and the baby to leave behind his most trusted lieutenant (Natasha promoted Miriam from the farthest end of the table) to ensure their safety. What a sacrifice!

"Dima needed to know you wouldn't inform on us."

And just like that, Natasha's faith crumbled. The stopper of phlegm in her throat barely kept Natasha's stomach contents from joining the overall stench.

"Dima thought I might betray you?"

"He didn't want to take any chances. He sent me to your house. I saw you were in bed, sick. The baby." Miriam offered Natasha a way out, though she didn't sound as if she believed it. "You didn't want to slow them down."

Natasha nodded weakly, confirming the assessment. "I would never betray him."

"Not that it mattered in the end. They were still caught. Ambushed right on the tarmac. They're in Lubyanka. It's only a matter of time before they come for us, too."

Natasha's bladder clenched as if she were peering down from a great height. "I thought they got away. When there was nothing in the news—"

"I heard it on Voice of America. The KGB intercepted them as soon as they got to the airfield."

"And we're next?" Natasha suspected she should be more worried about Dima. The stories she'd heard about Lubyanka's treatment of political prisoners—sleep deprivation with bright lights, beatings, starvation, isolation, naked dissidents getting hosed down with either freezing or scalding water—suggested Dima deserved her horror and concern. But all Natasha could think was, "Then why haven't they come for us already?"

"They're watching. They want to see who we contact so they can arrest even more of us." Which explained why they were having this conversation in secret. But not why Miriam followed up with, "We need you to go public."

"What?" Natasha all but shrieked, her head not so much spinning as throbbing.

"We've been talking about this, those of us who are left. Ludmilla's husband is trying to secure her release on humanitarian grounds, her being the mother of a small child, but he thinks—"

Ludmilla had a husband? A child? Why hadn't Natasha known this? She'd suspected Ludmilla saw her as a threat. But was the truth that Ludmilla had never taken Natasha seriously? That she thought Natasha was simply playacting at being a radical, just like Boris accused?

Miriam was still talking. "People in the West, they need specifics; names, faces, stories. Look at the support for Begun or Sharansky. Americans prefer to fight for a person rather than a cause. They're good people, but they're simple."

"Dima is a person. Why aren't they fighting for him?"

"He doesn't have as good of a story yet. Begun was arrested while the American president Nixon was visiting, and Sharansky is a translator for the dissident Sakharov. Felix Kandel is a famous cartoonist—you know *Nu Pogodi*? And Ida Nudel is a woman!" That last one seemed to be the only category in which Natasha could compete. But Miriam had something more ambitious in mind. "Nobody, though, has a pregnant girlfriend they left behind. That's even better than Ludmilla's husband and little boy."

Natasha suspected that delight at still being called Dima's girlfriend should not have been her first emotion. It was followed by dread as Natasha made the realization. "You want me to be Dima's face for the Americans?"

"Yes! They'll love it! And even the KGB wouldn't dare arrest an internationally renowned pregnant woman!"

Natasha liked the sound of *internationally renowned*. She could see it now, her and the baby on posters and placards held by marching students in New York City, Paris, London, Rome. She would give rousing speeches in front of cheering crowds, grant interviews to magazines, and have her picture taken. Then, thanks to her tireless advocacy and heroic sacrifices, she and Dima would be triumphantly reunited, their first embrace and the tearful moment when Dima finally laid eyes on his strong, healthy son (or would a precious daughter dressed in pink be more stirring?) broadcast around the world. Dima would be physically—though never mentally—broken from his time in captivity. Natasha's love would nurse him back to health, and they would marry in a lavish Jewish ceremony, attended by those generous Westerners who'd supported them. This was even better than her original fantasy. But then there was the inconvenient fact that the KGB never had any moral qualms about arresting pregnant women, or young children. Just ask Mama or Baba Daria.

"You want me to publicly confess my connection to Dima?" Soviet citizens didn't confess to anything publicly, unless as part of a show trial where the defendants confessed to what they were told to confess. In order to facilitate the process, confessions were written out in advance, sometimes in a language the criminal didn't speak.

"Yes!" Miriam glowed. "We can smuggle out your statement with a photo. It's the best way to draw attention to Dima's cause. Men like him are sentenced to ten, twenty years' hard labor in Siberia. The authorities will want to make an example of him. Show what happens to those who try to leave. The only way to shorten his sentence is to exert international pressure. Once they hear about you, the Americans will demand Dima be released so he can see his child. At the very least, they'll ask for his sentence to be reduced to internal exile so you can go be with him. That, honestly, is the best Ludmilla's husband is hoping for."

Was it just a few weeks ago when Natasha had been romanticizing Dima and herself as political allies à la Lenin and Krupskaya and she had been brought down to reality by the fate of Mrs. Karl Marx? At least Mrs. Marx got to be miserable and exploited in Brussels, London, and Paris. Natasha wouldn't be that lucky.

"The KGB will come after me." Natasha balked, which wasn't exactly an answer.

"We'll make sure the world knows of it," Miriam said, halting Natasha's objection, which wasn't exactly a denial.

Chapter 31

"I will marry you," Natasha informed Boris. After a night of *samokritika*-level struggle, Natasha had come to the depressing conclusion that she had no option in the matter. She could either believe Miriam was conveying Dima's true wishes—and how could Natasha be certain of that, it could be a setup by the KGB—and risk the ax coming down to chop her head off like the tallest wheat in Baba Daria's parable, or she could marry Boris and get herself, her parents, and Dima's child to America before the truth of her insurgence came out. Natasha owed it to her innocent family to give up her well-earned glory in order to keep them safe.

Natasha's intended had been sitting at the kitchen table, slurping a bowl of noodles cooked in milk. He looked up, popping in one more spoonful, his expression curious, though not surprised. He was that confident she'd agree? It made Natasha want to take her words back.

"You have to take my parents to America with us, too. We can go to ZAGS tomorrow."

Never had Natasha pondered how apt it was that one of the Russian words for getting married was *razpesaleese*. It meant "to sign." Because that was all she intended to do, sign her name in order to get the emigration paperwork started.

Boris reached for a napkin, wiped his lips, and returned his spoon to his bowl. He half rose from the wooden stool he'd been sitting on and stood face-to-face with Natasha. She braced herself for Boris to ask why she'd changed her mind, what was the rush, and how was she expecting him to deal with the presence of Dima's child?

But all Boris did was lean in and peck Natasha on the lips. She responded politely, startled to note Boris's kisses didn't feel that different from Dima's. Then again, a mouth was a mouth—how much variation could there ultimately be? She wondered if the same would apply to all aspects of married life. Natasha was equally startled to realize the thought of it didn't fill her with the expected dread and revulsion.

Just a low-key indifference.

And that, pretty much, was the state she remained in for the next several months, as if the passion she'd expended working with Dima had exhausted Natasha's lifetime supply.

There were papers to be filled out and bribes to be distributed to make certain those papers went through. The Crystals and Rozengurts sold as many things as they could and gave away the rest to friends, rather than leaving them for the neighbors to loot. They packed wooden cartons to ship ahead of them, via the United States embassy. Papa managed to get (no one asked how, so *get* was the verb they went with) four discarded shipping containers off the docks. They reeked of herring that had overstayed its welcome. Boris's mother procured plastic garment bags from a department-store clerk who was willing to smuggle out a dozen, one at a time, in her purse, which they used to wrap their belongings and pretend the smell wouldn't permeate during the multimonth journey.

They left in the heat of July, pushing their way through the stinking armpits and dripping necks congregated on the sizzling steel platform, wading toward a train that didn't fully stop, only slowed to a crawl, prompting a mad, trampling rush to climb on. Each of the six adults had been allowed one travel case, but Boris was so scared someone would get left behind that he shoved Natasha and their parents on board, then proceeded to run up and down the platform, picking up their abandoned suitcases and sliding them in through doors and even windows, alongside parents who were doing the same with their young children. The two fathers reached out their hands to pull Boris in just as the train picked up speed in preparation for exiting the station, and he collapsed into the cabin, soaked with sweat and out of breath.

They were processed in Chop, the last border town before leaving the USSR. The guards not only unpacked all their luggage, confiscating—and slipping into their pockets—such vital-to-national-security-interest items as six silver-plated spoons that belonged to Boris's grandmother; Mama's gold hoop earrings, which had been a wedding gift from Baba Daria to replace a family heirloom lost years earlier; and Papa's camera. They also ordered Boris to drop his pants and Natasha to lift up her dress to verify they weren't smuggling anything else of value.

Once, Natasha had imagined this scene with herself as the fearless heroine, clandestine intel sewn into her undergarments, glaring defiantly at her oppressors as she struck a triumphant blow for freedom and dignity. Now, she waited passively for a teen border patrol agent with razor burn along his jaw to finish jabbing her bloated stomach, as if a strategic poke might release a jackpot of contraband. She thought of Dima, enduring much worse treatment at the hands of much less apathetic guards. And then she thought how nice it would be to take a nap.

Natasha napped through the remainder of their journey to Vienna, Austria. Everyone else gaped at the historic sights—Imperial Palace! Ringstrasse! Albertina!—they'd never dreamed they'd get to see in person. Natasha gorged herself on local delicacies of the dessert variety—Buchteln! Strudel! Bohemian plum cake! What was so great about America? she wondered. As far as Natasha was concerned, they could settle down right here.

Except that, of course, they couldn't. Austria didn't want them staying any longer than they had to, when terrorist groups like Black September were being arrested for plots to blow up centers housing Jewish refugees. So within a few days, they were loaded onto buses headed for Italy, each clutching a one-day tourist visa— with instructions not to come back.

In Rome, Natasha continued eating—Cannoli! Panna cotta! Zabaglione! Did pasta count as a dessert?—and avoiding questions from her mother. She'd been doing it since before the wedding, ducking Mama's attempts at girl talk, where she prodded about when Natasha began finding Boris attractive, how did they fall in love so quickly, and why in the world would they have hidden it from their parents, who were obviously delighted at the match?

Natasha told Mama the truth. She'd known Boris all her life, but it was only recently she'd realized how much she needed him, how perfect he was for her, and how foolish she'd been for ignoring what was right under her nose. It was so perfect, she'd wanted to keep the wonderful news a secret for a while, lest it tempt the evil eye into ruining their great fortune.

"A husband, a baby," Mama said. "This is what you need. It will be good for you. Take your mind off unimportant things. There will be no more nonsense, yes, Natashenka?"

"Nonsense?" Natasha trod carefully. Afraid of what Mama might say, yet unable to squelch her curiosity. "What nonsense?"

"The kind that can make a girl sick. Girls get caught up worrying about the wrong things; you do not even realize how it is hurting you. Do you remember that morning, before we received our permission to emigrate, when you were looking so out of sorts? It took my pointing it out for you to realize that all was not well, that you should rest until the feeling passed."

"I remember . . ."

"I'm happy you listened to your mother." Mama attempted to sound jovial, but there was no mistaking the steel undercurrent behind each word. "I listened to my mother. Your Baba Daria told me it's more important to get the things you need than the things you think you want. The things you want, they do not always come in the ways that you want them. But now everything is fine, yes? Better, in fact."

"Everything is fine," Natasha repeated, wondering if Mama had just told her what Natasha thought she'd told her. Wondering if Mama had known all along what was going on with her and Dima? If she'd known exactly what she was doing that morning, advising her daughter to spend the day in bed? "Better, in fact."

Mama wanted Natasha to believe that. Natasha wanted to believe it, too. She'd done the right thing. For her parents, for Boris, for the baby. It proved surprisingly easy to convince herself. Much easier, in fact, than it had been convincing herself to go along with all of Dima's plans.

"Everything is fine. Better, in fact," Natasha told anyone who asked.

Even her baby's delivery. This wasn't a Soviet hospital, where you were lucky if the medication you required hadn't been stolen and having access to sterilized instruments was asking for too much. In Brighton Beach, everything was not only free—"Tell them you're poor," they'd been advised upon arrival. "The poor get everything here, and no one checks if you're telling the truth! Americans are so stupid!"—you didn't need to bring gifts for the anesthesiologist or bribe a nurse to change soiled bedding. Though there had been some confusion the first day, when an orderly came for the sheets and Natasha thought he was spiriting them away for good because her family hadn't paid up, which resulted in a brief Russian-Spanish obscenity-laden tug-of-war match.

Natasha allowed Boris to name the baby. He selected Julia, after the month in which they'd emigrated, which was fine by Natasha. Anything to make the semi-opaque infant—her eyes were like mirrors, brows and eyelashes so faint they appeared invisible—more connected to the swarthy Boris and the rest of his clan.

Thanks to America, taking care of Julia was not the all-consuming nightmare Natasha had dreaded. There were disposable diapers, and a washing machine for everything else. There was formula she paid pennies for, thanks to the Women, Infants, and Children welfare program they'd also been advised to sign up for. The first thing that went through Natasha's mind when Boris announced he'd found a computer-programming job was whether it would cost them their benefits. She was furious when she found out it would, and even more angry when she learned that Boris's new boss had offered to pay him under the table so they could keep on receiving welfare, but Boris had refused.

She tried reasoning with him, reminding Boris, "In Odessa, the rules were set up to work against us. Here, we can make the rules work for us."

"Not by lying."

"If they didn't want us to lie, why would they make it so easy? They're just testing to see who is smart enough to take advantage."

"Oh, my Natasha, be careful you don't outsmart yourself," Boris said, which made no sense whatsoever, but before Natasha could ask what in the world he was talking about, Boris turned his attention to Julia.

He found the child's every grimace fascinating. He read to her and played with her—Julia dropping things and Boris picking them up. He bought her whatever she wanted, and even items she expressed no interest in, in case she might want them later. He might have spoiled her. Except that, like Boris, Julia seemed incapable of provocative behavior of any kind, good or bad.

To think that Natasha had been terrified of anyone noticing how unlike Boris and his family her straw-haired, pale, broad-shouldered and square-hipped daughter was, when Julia proved to be exactly like Boris. Woe be to those who broke any rule, including beginning to eat before everyone else was gathered at the table or going swimming in the ocean as the lifeguards were approaching their stations, rather than having ascended to their designated seats. Not that Julia threw tantrums. She merely plopped on her bottom, burying her face in her knees, silent tears dripping down her cheeks.

Boris always commiserated with her, no matter how stupid or trifling were Julia's complaints. When she came home bawling because classmates had teased her about having parents named Boris and Natasha, or accused Julia of being a Communist and ordered her to go back to Russia, did Boris back up Natasha's rejoinder that those children were idiots? If the Rozengurts were Communists, they would have stayed in the USSR, not emigrated to the United States! Did those first graders understand nothing of geopolitical realities? As for the Boris-and-Natasha thing, Julia had no inkling of what true suffering was! She was like all American children, convinced that no one in history had ever suffered the way they were now suffering. Natasha saw this on television and read it in magazines constantly. Julia should better listen to her parents and grandparents recall what they'd so recently escaped, instead of making excessive drama out of insignificant matters.

Boris merely smiled at Natasha, rather infuriatingly, if she did say so herself. He gently advised, "If it is dramatic to her, then we must respect and take it seriously, to demonstrate that we respect and take her seriously."

But who, save Boris, possessed that level of indulgence? Julia was, as far as Natasha could tell, afraid of everything. The dark, loud noises, pigeons. She was afraid of strangers, but also afraid of being chastised for rudeness, so she interacted when commanded, but without meeting their eyes or raising her voice. Most of all, Julia was afraid of doing the wrong thing. That part was all Boris.

When they first arrived in the United States, Natasha, Boris, and eventually Julia had shared an apartment with her parents, as well as his. It was funded by the same organization that sponsored their immigration. But that was only for a few months. Then they were expected to start supporting themselves. Boris did as told, with a salary he continued reporting honestly. As a result, unlike their parents, both sets of whom qualified for subsidized Section 8 housing, Natasha and Boris were forced to move into a different apartment, for which they paid, much to Natasha's outrage, market price. It wasn't the money. It was the principle. If fools were giving free goods away, it was your duty to take advantage and grab as much as you could carry—then return under a different name for more. Anything else branded you the fool. Natasha had no doubt their neighbors, who lived in the exact same configuration of rooms—sometimes literally next door—but paid one-fifth the rent, were laughing at them. As were the women in fur coats who pulled out their food stamps at the supermarket, while Boris handed over hard-earned cash.

She tried reasoning with him yet again. Didn't Boris see that this was their chance to avenge the way they'd been treated in the USSR? Yes, yes, America was a different country, but a government was a government, and just because this one had yet to mistreat them didn't mean it wouldn't in the future. They might as well get ahead of the game, just in case, and get their revenge before the authorities got them.

Her husband refused to budge. There was a right way to do things and a wrong way, and Boris would always choose the right, even if it was to his own detriment. Watching television during every U.S. election, Natasha would hear dumbfounded talking heads asking in despair, "Why would people vote against their own interests?" She thought they ought to meet her husband.

For more than fifteen years, a grudging Natasha lived with Boris and Julia on one side, herself on the other. Until, in 1991, the world as everyone knew it turned permanently on its axis.

Chapter 32

===

For most, it was the sudden and unexpected collapse of the Soviet Union.

Natasha's and Boris's parents sat glued to the television, watching the images from Russia, the crowds at the Kremlin, Yeltsin on the tank, Gorbachev resigning. The republics, some of which had been connected for five hundred years, falling away like crumbs.

"I don't believe it," Papa kept mumbling. "I can't believe it. I know history. I know all empires end. But I never expected to see it. What did we do it for?" Papa's confusion turned to anger. He pointed to his sightless eye. "What were we fighting for?"

Natasha understood their bafflement. It had been difficult enough as Gorbachev's glasnost spewed out revelations about crimes committed by the Soviets. Her parents had known it was bad; there were always stories, always rumors. But they hadn't known just how bad. The final straw for Papa was confirmation from the Katyn Forest where, in 1940, fifteen thousand Polish nationals had been executed and buried in mass graves by the NKVD. They were supposed to be allies, but Stalin saw them as threats. When the Red Cross investigated, Stalin severed relations, insisting the murders had been committed by Germans, not Soviets. Now Gorbachev was admitting complicity.

"Not our boys," Papa moaned. "Not our soldiers. They were good boys. We were defending our Motherland. We were heroes."

Natasha sympathized with his heartbreak.

Because she was in the throes of her own. Along with glasnost and the dawn of a new political age came the release of political prisoners.

Dima, among them.

It was in all the local Russian language newspapers. The American ones, too. Everyone was buzzing about these freedom fighters, now being showered with Congressional Medals of Honor, Medals of Freedom, book contracts, and invitations to tell their stories in the United States.

Dimitri Bruen, Natasha read in *Novey Amerikanetz*, would be speaking at the YM-YWHA in Bensonhurst about his life as a prisoner of conscience. Accompanying him would be his wife.

Miriam.

The ex-Marina had spent the sixteen years since Dima's capture championing his cause, at home and abroad. She'd been placed under house arrest, she'd been exiled, and, as a reward, she'd been among the first released by Gorbachev under pressure from President Reagan. Miriam moved to Israel, where she and Dima were married by an Orthodox rabbi in absentia. Not the way Natasha had imagined it but close enough for her to feel robbed. Now that Dima was free, he and Miriam went everywhere together. At each venue, Dima swore that half his medals and accolades belonged to her. She'd done the hard work of keeping his memory alive and mobilizing the masses to fight for him. He'd still be in Siberia if it weren't for his Miriam.

That could have been Natasha.

That should have been Natasha.

Just because she wasn't the hero of the hour didn't mean Natasha hadn't worked just as hard as Miriam. Natasha had taken just as many risks, put her life on the line in the exact same way, even if the media didn't know about it. Natasha realized, now that she'd had over a decade to think about it, that she hadn't been a coward. She'd simply been brave in a different way. She'd chosen to obey Dima's wishes and put the safety of their daughter ahead of personal goals. Miriam hadn't been compelled to make such a difficult decision. Miriam was free to continue flitting about the globe, untethered and irresponsible. She didn't understand a mother's sacrifice.

Natasha checked the date and time of Dima's appearance at the Y. It was scheduled for a weekday morning. Boris would be at work. Julia would be at school.

Natasha told her daughter there'd been a change of plans. They were going to hear a great man speak. It would be much more educational than any classes she'd be missing.

"No," Julia wailed. "You don't understand, Mama. This could lower my grade!"

"You're coming," Natasha informed her daughter, gambling that Julia would be too cowed to push back. And one more thing. "Don't tell Papa about it. Don't tell anybody."

NATASHA STOOD AT the back of the auditorium, Julia by her side, watching the crowd fill in for Dima's lecture with the elderly and the unemployed. Who else had free time on a Wednesday morning? Julia had her nose buried in a textbook, whimpering about the science class she was missing.

Natasha asked, "Did you tell Papa we were coming here today?"

"You told me not to."

Natasha recognized the conflict trembling through her daughter's body as she struggled to decide which was worse, disobeying an order from her mother, or keeping a secret from her father. Which was the right thing to do and which was the wrong thing?

Natasha considered telling Julia that was why she'd majored in math. In math, there was always a correct answer you could prove. Well, unless you'd been assigned a Jewish problem. Which, of course, made Natasha think of Dima.

Not that she'd managed to think about much else since news broke of his release. Natasha scoured each television interview and newspaper article, looking for a message meant for her, a private signal that Dima's priority upon being set free was to track down his child—and her mother.

Miriam must have told him about Natasha's immigration to America. Surely, that had been among Dima's first questions. Miriam would have tried to twist Natasha's motives, make her look bad, suggest she had fled in fright, first from the hijacking attempt and then from the scrutiny that followed. Miriam would make it sound like Natasha broke from the KGB questioning and from being tailed night and day. But Dima would know better. He wouldn't say anything to Miriam. She wouldn't understand. She wasn't a parent like they were.

The auditorium grew hotter, a mass of bodies that, despite living in America, hadn't caught on to the deodorant trend in tipping-point numbers. The women sat fanning their dripping necks and cleavage with folded programs. The men rolled up their shirt-sleeves and loosened their top buttons, revealing tumbleweeds of graying hair at odds with their bald heads. It smelled like everyone had brought a snack. Natasha could make out cans of sardines, a jar of herring, sliced sausage on rye bread, pickled tomatoes, an uncut hunk of Swiss cheese, and a small orchard of seasonal fruit.

A cohort sitting in front of them noticed the hardworking Julia leafing through her book and wiping at the sweat beneath her nose with an index finger. The woman thrust a handful of green grapes at her, urging, "Eat, eat, little one. They'll cool you off." When Julia hesitated, looking to Natasha for permission, the woman pressed on, "You're too skinny. You need to eat."

Natasha shrugged, indifferent, and Julia accepted the grapes, thanking her in Russian. The woman beamed. "Such a well-brought-up girl." Then, as an aside to Natasha, she harkened, "In USSR, fruits so shriveled, so ugly. In America, it is like all food wears makeup, no?"

Natasha smiled wanly, hoping that would terminate the conversation. She wished to avoid drawing undue attention to Julia, fearful that everyone would spot her resemblance to Dima the moment he ascended the stage. This was a private matter. Natasha refused to be the subject of gossip.

A smattering of applause starting at the front and spreading outward like a nuclear blast cued Natasha to Dima's arrival. He sauntered onstage behind the center's director, Miriam a step behind. She looked no different than Natasha remembered. But that could have been because all Natasha remembered were Miriam's shapeless, long-sleeved dresses that fell below the knee, and a scarf tied beneath her left ear.

Dima, on the other hand, now lived trapped underneath the casing of an older, pudgier man. She'd expected him to be thinner. More than a decade in Siberia suggested drastic weight loss would be on the menu. Instead, he had rounded out, the vast shoulders hunched over a paunch, his forearms and palms downright beefy, his thighs brushing against each other. Natasha guessed that, since his release, Dima had been overindulging in the delicacies of the West.

His hair was speckled with gray, though the original silk-stalk color made it difficult to tell. Natasha sneaked a peek at Julia, wondering if her daughter would also be able to hide her aging in such a manner. While Natasha was looking at Julia, she searched the teen's face, wondering if Julia sensed something, anything? The girl was focusing on Dima, having dutifully put her textbook away.

"What do you think?" Natasha couldn't stop herself from asking.

"He's a brave man," Julia responded, like the gold-medal student that she was.

Natasha sighed.

Chapter 33

====

The brave man commenced speaking about his bravery. And Natasha wondered if she'd misunderstood. Dima claimed he was talking about his years of activism in Odessa. But the existence he was describing, of loneliness, of isolation, of never knowing whom he could trust and not being able to expose his real self with anyone, that had to be about his time in the Gulag. He talked about the boredom and drudgery of day-to-day resistance, how much of it was futile. What good, Dima asked, did the longhand copying of forbidden books do anyone in the end? Or furtive meetings where wannabes talked much and did little? No—Dima raised his voice in rehearsed passion—action was the only thing that mattered. Bold action, drastic action, committed action. It's not enough, he exhorted the crowd, to cluck in sympathy and shake your head about how awful things are. Change can come only through action. And the only action that brings about change is the kind that brings with it great personal risk—and great group reward.

The audience erupted into applause. Julia had to elbow Natasha to prompt her into raising her palms and bringing them together, out of sync with the rest.

Dima went on talking. He talked about the horrors of prison, interrogations that went on for weeks, questioners changing in shifts, while Dima passed out from lack of sleep and was revived with hoses spraying ice water. He talked about his hunger strikes and his forced feedings, tubes jammed down his throat while he lay strapped onto a metal table. He talked of sharing cells with rats and body lice, of the untreated infections that erupted over his body. And he talked about the woman who'd allowed him to survive it all.

Natasha's heart plummeted into her stomach. Surely, now . . .

But no, of course, it was Miriam. Miriam who stood by him; Miriam who never gave up on him; Miriam who, Dima was thrilled to announce, was pregnant with Dima's first child.

They were both excited. They had waited so long to become parents.

The crowd applauded again. Some shouted, "Mazel tov."

Natasha clutched Julia's wrist, uncertain whether it was to stop her from clapping or to reassure herself that the girl was real.

"Anyone can have a baby," Natasha told Julia, in response to her questioning look. "It's not an achievement worth applauding."

THERE WAS A meet-and-greet after the formal talk. Fans queued up to shake Dima's hand, ask him questions, slap him heartily on the shoulder. Natasha lined up, waiting her turn.

"Hello, Dima," she would say.

"Natashenka!" he would gasp.

"I live in America now," she would say.

"I didn't know," he would say.

Natasha would smile forgivingly at Miriam. She would keep her secret and not tell Dima that his wife knew. Natasha understood Miriam's desperation to hold on to him, to let Dima think she would be giving him his first child.

"This is my daughter, Julia," she would say, nudging the girl forward. "She's fifteen years old."

They would need to go somewhere private to talk after that.

The line stretched on. You'd think they were selling opening-day movie tickets—the only thing, Natasha and her family had been shocked to realize, for which Americans were prepared to stand in line. That's what Natasha got for hiding in the back. She should have grabbed a seat, front and center. Everything would have gone differently if Dima had spotted her right away.

And then he did. Like the song promised, Dima looked across a crowded room, and he saw her. But did he fly to her side? Did her make her his own?

No.

Because that happened only in Rodgers and Hammerstein musicals.

Though, to be fair, like the tune promised, Dima did gaze across a crowded room. And what he saw there was . . . a stranger.

There was no recognition. No recognition of Natasha, no recognition of Julia. How could he not recognize Julia? She was the spitting image of him! How could Dima not recognize his own child? More important, how could he not recognize the physical manifestation of everything he and Natasha had shared? It was that last part that shattered her the most. There they were, Dima and Natasha, alive in one body. And it meant absolutely nothing to Dima.

Had Natasha truly aged so much? Or had she ultimately meant so little to him? They'd spent nearly every day together for months. Natasha still recalled the faces of colleagues she'd worked with then, even of some of her students. They would run into each other on the Brighton boardwalk, and there was always a flash of recognition, no matter how much time had passed.

Yet Dima had overlooked Natasha without a blink.

"AM I LOOKING OLD?" Natasha demanded of a startled Boris the moment he walked in the door after work. She'd passed the afternoon studying herself in the mirror, pulling on her skin to see if that made the wrinkles smooth, plucking gray hairs, and smacking the bottom of her chin with the back of her palm, commanding the wattle to stay in place. Yet, no matter from which angle Natasha scrutinized herself, she still recognized the brave young woman who'd made the resistance possible. They wouldn't have been able to do it without her. Dima had said so himself, hadn't he? The day she procured their tickets. He'd said it in front of everyone.

"You're looking beautiful," Boris answered, not even waiting to remove his shoes before rushing to appease her. The most shocking part was that he appeared to mean it. Boris honestly didn't see the wrinkles, the gray hair, the teetering chin.

Natasha said, "You knew I'd been in your room because you could smell me. You knew I was pregnant just by looking at me."

He cocked his head, wondering why the dive into ancient history. They hadn't discussed or even alluded to these incidents since they happened.

"You'd know me anywhere," Natasha said.

"Where are you, my light, Natasha?" Still standing in their apartment entryway—among the shoes on their shelf, the umbrellas in their stand, and the jackets hanging on their hooks—Boris launched into Pushkin's poem. *"No one's seen you—I lament."* He went through the whole thing, line by line, ending with, *"And at home, depressed and dazed / I'll recall Natasha's grace."*

"Papa!" Julia came bursting through the door to her bedroom, and, for a moment, Natasha feared she'd be unmasked.

But their daughter wanted only to report some triumph from math class, a complicated problem she'd been the sole student to untangle.

"Sha!" Natasha raised her hand, holding the child at bay. "Let Papa catch his breath. He works so hard for us, he doesn't need to be jumped on the moment he walks through the door!"

Julia ground to a halt. Not due to being reprimanded—she was used to Natasha reprimanding her—but over the reprimand's context and content. Boris froze in his tracks, as well. Both peered at Natasha in confusion.

"Sit down," Natasha ordered Boris. "It's sweltering. You must be dying from waiting on the subway platform. I will get you some ice cream." Before he could remind her, she added, "Warmed up a little in the microwave, so it doesn't hurt your teeth. Julia, run and get the fan from our bedroom; set it up so Papa can have some air."

As the girl scurried off, and Boris moved hesitantly toward his La-Z-Boy, peering curiously at Natasha over his shoulder, she went on, addressing their daughter, "Do you ever think about the sacrifices Papa made for us? He had a good job in the USSR. He was an important man. He gave it up to come to a place where he didn't speak the language, where he didn't know if he'd be able to find such important work again, where he might have been forced to sweep the streets, like some *dvornik*. He did it for us, so we could have a better life."

"I know that, Mama." If Julia had been a different child, the words might have come out defiantly. But Julia was merely meekly agreeable.

"Your mama made sacrifices, too." Boris sat down, startled when Natasha reached over to yank the handle that would put his legs up. "She is a marvelous mathematician, much stronger than me. She could have had a successful career in America, but she chose to dedicate her time to you, instead of to the money she could have made."

"We did not need the money," Natasha said. "Papa took care of us. He promised he would, and he did. I never had to worry, not like some others. I knew Papa would keep his promises. He wouldn't forget." Natasha stroked the top of Boris's head, smoothing down the strands of damp hair that grew thinner every year. "Thank you, my Boris."

He tentatively raised his arm, squeezed her wrist between his thumb and forefinger, brought it nervously to his mouth and pecked the back of Natasha's hand, then quickly released it, reluctant to press his luck.

Natasha bent over and, much to the shock of all three of them, kissed her husband fully and deeply on the lips. Then she went to pop his ice cream into the microwave.

Boris sat glued to his chair, stunned. Julia first turned away, embarrassed, then turned back to check if the unprecedented public display of affection was over. She waited to see if any more odd things would happen. When they didn't, when Natasha handed Boris his tepid ice cream, smoothed down his hair yet again, and bustled off, Julia figured it would be okay to start telling Papa about the math problem. It would help both pretend everything was normal.

Natasha watched them from the side. How could two people who looked so little alike . . . also look so much alike? It wasn't their physical characteristics. It was their gestures. The way they cocked their heads in consternation, the way they furrowed their brows in disapproval. What did Americans call it? Two peas in a pod? That's what Boris and Julia were.

And, oh, how Natasha had resented her daughter for it.

All these years, Natasha told herself she was angry over how much Julia took after Boris instead of Dima. But in reality, what she really hated was seeing so much of herself in the girl.

Dima was a hero, a risk taker. Which meant Julia's cowardice had to have come from her mother. The one who'd stood and watched while her comrades were beaten, bloodied, and dragged off. The one who'd faked illness rather than show up at the designated airfield. The one who'd been afraid, for over fifteen years, to admit that the real hero in their home was Boris. Boris had been the one who'd risked everything for her. He'd been the one who'd risked loving her.

Even the heroic Dima hadn't been able to do that.

Book III

Zoe

Chapter 34

══

"Love is not a potato," Zoe's great-grandmother Alyssa has been telling her since before Zoe was old enough to know for certain what either word meant.

"What Balissa means"—Mama's lips flatten and purse—"is there's nothing more important than choosing the right person to spend your life with."

"She is right." Zoe's Baba Natasha has never encountered a topic on which she doesn't have a strong opinion. This one's a favorite. Ironic, considering that, as the family struggles to plan her and Deda's forty-fifth-anniversary party, Baba is giving every indication of having done anything but.

Zoe waves goodbye and grabs her bag off the peg near the door. Mama asks, "Are you taking the long way home?"

Zoe knows what she means. Zoe knows what she's asking. Zoe nods.

Mama reaches for her sun hat, which is hanging next to Zoe's bag, and affixes it atop her head. "I'll come with."

THERE'S ONLY ABOUT a two-mile distance between the Brighton Beach and the Manhattan Beach bus stops. The aesthetic difference, though, is enormous. Brighton is a combination of housing

projects, private apartment buildings of varying heights and varying degrees of maintenance, and old-age homes that Baba refers to
as "old-people prisons"—as in, "Don't you dare think of locking
me up in one of those old-people prisons." Shadowy, exhaust-filled
streets run crammed beneath elevated subway lines; the streets are
jam-packed with produce displays spilling out of crowded mini-
markets that smell of fruit a few days past peak ripeness. Gold-
toothed vendors sit atop wooden crates hawking garishly colored
plastic toys, beach paraphernalia, and bootleg Russian-language
DVDs.

Manhattan Beach, on the other hand, once you make your final
right turn onto Oriental Boulevard, is suburban heaven.

"Like the difference between Moldavanka filth and our chic opera house," Baba says. Zoe has seen pictures of both in colorful
coffee-table books and grainy black-and-white family snapshots,
but she's never been. Even after the USSR collapsed and refugees
were allowed to return for a visit, or to stay—Russia's President
Putin made a speech welcoming those who'd fled any Soviet re-
public to come "home" (along with their American money)—
Baba refused. The chance to show off for old friends and the jealous
anti-Semitic teacher wasn't enough to convince her. "There is no
one for me in Odessa," Baba pronounced. "I have nothing left to
look forward to, save death."

Balissa went. To Siberia. To tend to her family's graves.

"I will be the first one buried in America," she said upon her
return.

Cheery!

Zoe suspects their dour attitudes stem from living in Brighton,
not Manhattan Beach, with its fecund trees, tidy cul-de-sacs, and
ocean breezes blowing in off the water, cutting the humidity. Plus
the McMansions. So many McMansions. This one has roaring lions sitting before a gold-plated gate decorated with an explosion of
curlicues. That one looks like it has three battleship turrets rising

from the roof. Another has no windows, like a terra-cotta Egyptian pyramid.

But when Mama asks Zoe if she's taking the long way home, she knows that's not the house Zoe is detouring to see. The one Zoe's been stalking since middle school is a unique monstrosity. Its first level boasts more columns than *Gone with the Wind*'s Tara. Its second level looks like someone swooped up Hansel and Gretel's gingerbread cottage and positioned it on top. But Zoe doesn't come visiting due to its dubious aesthetic value. She comes because it's her father's house.

It would be unfair to say Zoe never laid eyes on the man. She's seen the posters he plasters across Brighton, advertising his medical practice. She's watched, like the coward she is, from behind a lamppost, as he comes and goes in his Porsche Panamera or Honda Odyssey minivan.

When Zoe was growing up, Mama would say only that she and Eugene had married too young, too quickly. She didn't get the chance to know him adequately, and it didn't work out. On the rare occasion the subject came up, Deda would inevitably add that Mama did the right thing; she stayed true to herself. Baba would then observe that it must be nice, going through life thinking solely of yourself; such a shame some people never have the option.

At twelve, Zoe looked up her dad's name on the Internet and got his address—it was that easy. She blew off her high-school-entrance-exam prep course at the Shorefront Y, and walked over to take a look for herself.

She didn't know what she expected to find. Which was good, because she didn't find anything. But she kept on coming. It became such a regular thing that, one day, she found Mama there, waiting for her.

Mama didn't look mad. She didn't look curious. She looked like she knew exactly why Zoe was there. Which put her one step ahead of Zoe, who still has no idea.

"Did you love him?" Zoe asks Mama for the first time now. Watching Baba and Deda go through the motions of planning an unwanted anniversary party has made her curious about relationships in a way she's never been before.

"Oh yes," Mama says without hesitation. "I thought he was wonderful. A doctor, already! I couldn't imagine what he saw in an eighteen-year-old baby like me!"

"You must have been a heck of a bookkeeper," Zoe teases.

"Yes, I was good at my job . . . I was not so good at other things, unfortunately. All my life, I tried to be a courteous girl, to do what everyone wanted of me, to not upset anybody. Did you know I got into Cornell for university? An Ivy League!"

"Baba told me." Multiple times.

"Of course she did." Mama laughs. "She was so angry when I turned it down for Brooklyn College. I thought it was important to stay close to home, save money. I didn't want them going into debt for me."

Zoe tells herself that wasn't a dig at her own choice to take out student loans to pay for NYU. Her family teases her about being so American, moving out when she had a perfectly fine room at home. "If I had apartment this size, I never would have left USSR," Balissa chortles. Baba rolls her eyes when she hears Zoe is diligently paying those loans back. True Americans, Baba claims, welsh without a second thought!

Something else that makes Zoe's grandmother roll her eyes is reading how stressed and anxious modern college students are, the most stressed and anxious ever!

"Ha!" Baba mocks. "How hard their life is! Place to live, three meals a day—plus snacks! A little homework and written exam at the end, maybe with open book! Try sharing room with parents and grandparents, standing in line for food and to take bath; then oral exams, with special questions for Jews. Some do it with husband, maybe pregnant, maybe with baby. But Americans, they say, university tuition is free in USSR, how lucky you are, how easy it was for you. One American, he say this to me, you immigrants, you luckier than poor us, you come already with college degree, no debt. We worse off than you! Your mama, she finish school divorced, with little Zoya to take care of alone. When she complain, I tell her, at least you are not in Soviet Union. Having babies in America is like vacation!"

"You didn't quit college to get married, like some people do," Zoe offers to Mama. "That must've made Baba happy."

"Your baba liked Eugene. She thought he was smart, dynamic, ambitious. I believed I would make her happy by marrying him, yes. But, you know your baba, no one has any idea what makes her happy!"

This is true. It's easier to predict what might make her unhappy. That would be everything.

"Then, when we didn't work out, I thought, well, my divorcing him will make her happy." No word about how or why that divorce came about, and in less than two years yet. "But wouldn't you know it, that somehow made her even angrier! I can never win with her." Mama sounds so sad when she says that, so confused.

"But you keep trying." That's the most amazing thing about Zoe's mom. Responsible little Julia is still trying to please. Zoe finds it both admirable and frustrating. She wishes she were less like her. "Why do you keep trying, Mama?"

"Baba is an unhappy person," Natasha and Boris's daughter sighs, avoiding the question. "Life disappointed her early on."

Yes, yes, Zoe knows about the gold medal and the Jewish problems, the forced labor in the countryside and the dead-end job teaching brain-dead children. "That's still no excuse for her to take it out on you!" And Deda, Zoe doesn't add.

Mama smiles, part in gratitude, part in condemnation, part in resignation. "I've disappointed her." Mama strokes Zoe's hair. "I've disappointed you, as well." She makes a vague gesture in the direction of Dr. Venakovsky's McMansion. "But you, my Zoyenka, you will not disappoint your baba. You will never disappoint any of us.

Your expensive school, your important career, and soon, a nice boy, yes? A nice Jewish boy, even from Brighton, maybe, who understands Russian so it isn't too difficult for us. Who is successful and smart. The right man to spend your life with. You will be the one to achieve all of Baba's dreams that she left the Soviet Union for. You will make her happy, this I am sure of."

Mama has been drilling this into Zoe since the day Julia realized she was never going to get the job done herself. Though it's not the reason Zoe took out those loans for her expensive school or embarked on her questionably important career. How pathetic would it be if every decision Zoe made in the present was somehow connected to a past that isn't even hers?

To drive that point home, she corrects, "It's not Zoya, Mama, it's Zoe."

"Yes, yes," Mama laughs guiltily. "I remember. Zoe. My perfect American."

TO ADVANCE HER important career, Mama's perfect American has a new project. Her biggest yet. Zoe should be thrilled. Except she's certain the reason her boss picked her for it was not her stellar work up to this point, but because the founder and CEO of Nuance Translation Software for the Multicultural Century is one Alex Zagarodny. Alex Zagarodny was born in Brighton Beach to Russian-speaking parents who emigrated from the USSR in the 1970s. Zoe's boss assumes that makes Alex and Zoe twinsies.

It would be futile to tell him how much time Zoe devotes to making sure no one can tell that by looking at her. She doesn't have an accent. She doesn't dye her hair neon blond or a shade of red not found in nature. She owns no leopard-print clothing. She's not collecting welfare while earning cash under the table. In other words, Zoe is doing everything she can to distance herself from the Little Odessa ghetto, while her boss—an Upper East Sider whose sons wear tiny blue blazers and ties to first grade, for Pete's sake—is shoving Zoe back in like those snakes in fake peanut cans her deda thinks are so funny.

As far as Zoe is concerned, Alex Zagarodny may headquarter his company in Silicon Alley, but he's Brighton Beach all the way. Software development? All the guys Zoe grew up with who were not smart enough for business or law school, and too squeamish for med school, are learning to code and promising their worshipful *mamachkas* they're going to be the next Bill Gates or, better yet, Mark Zuckerberg. (At least he's Jewish, despite the unfortunate shiksa wife, but, as per Baba, if that flat-chested Oriental was clever enough to snag the billionaire first, America's Jewish spinsters have no one to blame but themselves.) Every bum in Brooklyn who ever downloaded App Developer onto his smartphone thinks he's hatching the next Big Thing. Alex Zagarodny claims his software won't just translate words between languages, it will "equate idioms, decipher tone, and incorporate cultural nuance in order to facilitate better business and personal conversation around the globe."™ All he needs is a couple million dollars to make it happen.

That's where Zoe comes in. Not that she has a couple million dollars to give anyone. Her important career is researching businesses in which her boss might want to invest his couple million dollars. Assignments are supposed to be distributed randomly. Zoe refuses to believe there was anything random about her drawing this one. They might as well have sent her to assess an artisanal *balalaika* boutique while wearing a headscarf.

"Zoya?" Alex is waiting at the glass doors to his office suite when she arrives.

"It's Zoe," she corrects.

"Zoe," he instantly agrees. "Welcome to Nuance Translation!"

Alex Zagarodny looks the way Zoe expected. Brown hair, moist eyes to match, a nose their Long Island brethren might have taken to a plastic surgeon, plus a smattering of freckles not just across his face but also along his forearms, suggesting he began life as a redhead—a gift to Eastern European Jews from long-ago Vikings. He's a head taller than Zoe, standing sentry straight, which keeps you from realizing how short he actually is. He offers a strong, executive handshake. He looks you in the eye when he talks. Although he doesn't talk the way Zoe expected. No Russian accent, no Brooklyn accent, not even a New York City twang. Just that flat, mid-Atlantic inflection newscasters use to recount horrible catastrophes. He sounds like somebody who made an effort to teach himself to speak as generically as the folks on TV. *It takes one to know one.*

"I'll show you around." Alex guides Zoe past the glass doors into an open floor space. Above cubicle dividers, she sees the tops of heads slouched over screens and keyboards. She counts a dozen employees, and an equal number of whiteboards covered in foreign phrases, along with their English translations, literal and idiomatic. Some are circled; some are crossed out. Some have smiley faces. Some have devil horns.

"We're not just another translation start-up," Alex extols while they weave through a maze of cubicles as if he's the solitary rat who knows where the good cheese is hidden. "Our software takes into account the regional, cultural, religious, and geopolitical implications of each word and phrase before offering a conversion."

He rests his elbow atop a divider. The woman working inside has been trained not to notice, though she does slip on a pair of headphones. "You know how your grandmother calls you a *mamzer?*"

Zoe isn't sure how he knows her grandmother or what Baba calls her, but, well, "Yes."

"Technically, it means bastard. If you go with the biblical definition, it means the child of a married woman and a man not her husband. But that's not what your grandmother means. She's using it as a term of affection."

"Some of the time."

"There are millions of colloquialisms like that, in every language and dialect. Imagine what a disaster it is when they are translated literally, especially in a business negotiation." Alex declines to give Zoe the time to imagine anything as he pivots and escorts her by the elbow into the cubicle of an African American fellow about Alex's age. "Gideon, my good man!"

If Gideon is startled by the interruption, he, like the woman with the headphones, gives no sign of it. Blinking, he looks up from his keyboard, reaching to remove his glasses and revealing two wrists wrapped in black nylon braces to prevent carpal tunnel.

"Gideon Johnson," Alex announces with all the drama of *And the winner is . . .* "My chief engineer. Also my former tutor. Gideon pulled me through Caltech, like the Russians say, by the ears. He's doing the same here. I couldn't make any of this happen without him."

"Nice to meet—" Zoe begins, but there's no time for introductions during a sales pitch.

Alex continues his earlier thought. "Imagine what our app could do for diplomacy! Avoiding riots! Ending civil strife! Preventing nuclear war!"

Zoe wonders if said app comes with built-in exclamation points to match its developer's speaking style. Yet, even as sarcasm runs through her head, Zoe can't help feeling impressed. With many of the Brighton contingent, the bravado is fake: little dogs yapping the loudest to cover up fearing they're about to be smacked down. Insecurity, the knowledge that they'll never belong, oozes from the pores of nearly everyone Zoe knows. They scurry, heads down, shoulders hunched, practically groveling along the ground. They can barely look you in the eye. Once again, it takes one to know one.

But that's not the case with Alex. The vibe Zoe gets is that his bluster is sincere. He really believes what he's saying. He really believes he's as great as he claims.

Zoe tells Alex, "I'd like to see more."

Chapter 35

The tour ends in Alex's office, the cubicle in the farthest corner. Start-up workstations are typically disaster areas: electronic devices piled atop jumbles of printouts and fast-food containers, all covered in a light dusting of Post-its. Alex's counter is clear, save for a desktop computer, a laptop zipped into a padded case, and several brands of cell phones on which to test his app. There's no obvious way for him to keep an eye on his employees unless he makes a deliberate point of standing and walking several yards toward the main area.

"I like the quiet," Alex explains. "People think raising your voice conveys power. It's the opposite."

That may be the most un-Russian thing anyone has ever said. Zoe wonders if Alex meant for it to sound as hot as she finds it.

"That's something else my app is going to do."

Evaluate phrases for hotness? Zoe most definitely doesn't say.

"Send a warning when you're pissing someone off. The Japanese smile when they're angry, get more polite, but Westerners might not realize it, so they keep doing what they're doing. My app is going to pick up on changes of mood and let the user know before he does any more damage. It's a way to let you in on what other people are thinking without their needing to come right out and tell you. They keep their pride—and their secrets, but you get what you need, too. Win-win."

The possibility is music to Zoe's ears. Forget world peace and business meetings, think of what it could do for her own family! As Baba would say, that means it's too good to be true. Zoe hears Baba's voice coming out of her mouth as she says, "There are so many cultural norms, though, even within the same culture. It's going to be a massive task to compile that data, much less tweak your code to recognize such a fine level of nuance and convey it instantaneously."

"Go big or go home, right? You know the Billy Joel song 'Movin' Out'?" Alex hums the catchy chorus. "I used to think that when he's singing 'Is that all you get for your money?' he meant, is that all you're going to settle for, when there's so much more available? Here's this song about a guy jumping out of the rat race, and I thought it meant, if you just work harder, you can have so much more than a house out in Hackensack or the fender of a Cadillac to polish! Middle-class banality isn't truly moving up, that's why he's moving out."

"I used to think 'you won't fool the children of the Revolution' meant the survivors who had their lives destroyed know revolution is a horrible thing, and you won't fool them into supporting another one." It's one of Zoe's most embarrassing memories. She's never shared it with anyone. "My best friend from high school, Lacy, I said it to her mom when we were talking about music. I was trying to sound hip about the old stuff. It was mortifying. Luckily, she already thought I was a poor, unfortunate immigrant. Lacy's mom calls herself the last of the red diaper babies. When she found out my family was from the USSR, she was dying to meet them, hear about their authentic experience. She wanted to trade stories about how her grandparents from the Lower East Side were also warriors for socialism. Can you imagine if I'd let that happen?"

"Americans are adorable, aren't they? They're the ones who

truly believe in international brotherhood. Remember how they sang about Russians loving their children, too?"

"Knowing Lacy's mom got me prepared for NYU. Whenever I'd say something negative about Communism, I'd get smacked down with how somebody as privileged as me could never understand the experiences of the oppressed, and my passing judgment was culturally insensitive. The professor said I had to apologize for making my classmates uncomfortable before her lecture could continue. At least I had enough sense not to tell my grandmother when it happened. She'd have given me a different smackdown about my privilege and made me apologize again!"

Alex looks sympathetic, shocking Zoe with the realization of how desperately she'd been waiting for someone—anyone—to understand how odd it was to be American, feel American, look American on the outside—and yet somehow still be so foreign on the inside.

"That's the nice thing about going to a glorified trade school like Caltech. No engineer would talk up a theoretical idea that hadn't been field-tested. Or one that failed every time it's been tried. We're not like those hippie pure-math guys."

"Ooh, nerd burn!"

"Hey, I'm speaking as a reformed sinner." Alex mea culpas his chest with a fist. "I thought I was going to be a math major myself. Till I got to Caltech and found out that, compared to those guys, I couldn't do math at all. Thank God for Gideon showing me the light—and his notes—and guiding me into something practical."

At the mention of his friend's name, Alex briefly pivots in the direction of Gideon's work space. Zoe can see the top of Gideon's head, like black sheep's wool. She feels an urge to run her palm against it. Now that, she understands, actually is culturally insensitive. A microaggression.

Back to his sales pitch, Alex says, "Gideon calls me Icarus, flying too close to the sun. He's ridiculously well read. Private school all the way. Classic literature is a huge help in translating. Latin, too. All that metaphor, instead of saying what you mean. It's a master class in beating around the bush, not to mention covering your ass by leaving everything open to interpretation and plausible deniability. How totally Communist is that?"

"I wish I were better at it," Zoe confesses, shocked, once again, by the unexpected catharsis of saying what she'd only thought—and even then, hesitantly—before.

Alex doesn't appear to notice the soul baring going on. Why should he? These are colossal moments for Zoe. For Alex, it's just another pitch meeting.

"I'll take the Icarus comparison with pride," he says. "Why would the sun be there, if we're not supposed to reach for it?"

"I'd like to get hot with you," Zoe blurts out, still on a candor high. Then she hears herself.

Alex doesn't look taken aback. Maybe it's still just another pitch meeting. Maybe he hears things like that all the time. Self-confidence is scary-sexy in a guy. And Alex reeks of it, like he's been attacked by an army of department-store salesgirls pushing Eau de I'm Great.

Zoe stumbles to recover. "What I meant was, I'd like to hear details regarding how you expect to blast your company off into the stars, as it were. And how my company might help you achieve your objectives." That is *not* what she'd meant.

"I have a proposal for you."

Zoe nods, ready to agree with anything he's about to say.

"Go out with me."

Except that.

THIS CALLS FOR reinforcements. Zoe asks Lacy to meet her after work at a bar that serves alcohol alongside Rice Krispies treats and ironic, retro board games like Battleship, Operation, and Connect 4. Lacy instantly agrees. Because she is Lacy.

Lacy is Zoe's most American friend. Out of all of Zoe's friends, she's the only one who believes everything will always turn out fine. Her last name is Freeman. Her grandfather took out the *d* to make a point. She's Jewish, like Zoe, except Lacy doesn't believe in the evil eye. She doesn't believe in not telling people your good news because they will be jealous and curse you. She doesn't believe in never relaxing enough to enjoy the present because even the best of situations will go wrong.

"Of course not," Zoe's grandmother snorted when she heard this about Lacy. "It's easy to believe the world is good when nothing bad has ever happened to you."

It's not that bad things have never happened to Lacy. It's that she refuses to see them that way. Lacy's parents are divorced, like Zoe's. Lacy insists it's great. "My mom and dad were miserable together. Now they can be happy apart! It's best for them, and it's best for me, too."

Of course, unlike Zoe, Lacy spends time with her dad. He's a dancer turned stuntman turned performance artist. Lacy has taken Zoe to a bunch of his shows, held in sketchy clubs in even sketchier neighborhoods that Zoe most definitely didn't tell her family she was going to. Zoe was freaked out every minute they were there, but Lacy acted like the old drunk guy chatting her up was just being friendly, and the five frat bros who surrounded them and pushed the girls to do shots were something Zoe and Lacy could disentangle themselves from as soon as they felt like it. And, because she was Lacy, she was right.

Which is why Zoe loves Lacy.

Which is why Zoe needs to speak with Lacy, ASAP.

Zoe needs someone to tell her that everything will be fine.

"Everything will be fine," Lacy says the moment she slides into the booth next to Zoe. Lacy doesn't even know what the emergency is, but she knows it's what Zoe needs to hear.

Zoe tells her about Alex. The work part, and the part where he asked Zoe out.

"This is great," Lacy squeals. "He sounds perfect for you."

Let the record show that Lacy says this about everyone.

It just so happens that, this time, Zoe might agree with her.

"I don't date guys from Brighton," Zoe reminds her, as if Lacy hasn't heard her singing this song for exactly a decade now.

"But this one's different—you said so yourself."

"I said he seems different."

"He's ambitious."

"He is."

"He's cute."

It's entirely possible that Zoe may have shown Lacy Alex's photo off his website.

"Your family will love him!"

"Is that really a good thing?"

Lacy laughs. Let the record also show that Lacy's family loves everything she does. After dropping a quarter of a million dollars on her college education, Lacy's family thinks it's thrilling that she's working a combination of TaskRabbit and waitressing jobs, since connecting with a wide variety of people is vital for an artist!

Zoe would love Lacy's family, too. Except they confuse Zoe so.

Lacy's mother, who was dying to talk politics with Baba— she had Lacy in her forties, so she and Baba are practically the same age—lives in a classic-six apartment on Manhattan's Riverside Drive. She inherited it from her parents. It's decorated with framed posters from famous protest marches, including one that proclaims all property is theft. It would be so easy to make fun of her. Except Lacy's mom is so darn nice. To everybody. The only time Zoe let Baba and Lacy's mom exchange words was at Lacy and Zoe's high-school graduation, when Lacy's mom gushed about the Rozengurt family's inspirational courage in fleeing the USSR and Baba magnanimously let her. Baba thinks Lacy and her mom's perennially upbeat air is, at best, naive, and, at worst, an act so they can lord it over everyone else. She doesn't understand that they honestly think people are good at heart. They have that Anne Frank quote up in their classic six, too.

This time, it was Balissa who took umbrage. "The Frank girl wrote this before Auschwitz, yes? Did anyone ask her after? No. Because she was dead."

When Lacy predicts Zoe's family will love Alex, she isn't being naive or condescending. She's just being Lacy. Which is why Zoe called her in the first place.

Because this whole Alex thing is making Zoe very, very nervous. Her day wasn't supposed to go like this. Her day was supposed to go like every other day. Work, meeting, work, meeting, work, text from Mama, work, text from Mama asking why Zoe hadn't replied to her earlier text, work, meeting, call Mama back, argue about minutiae for Baba and Deda's anniversary party, run errand to fetch last-minute item for said anniversary party, home, microwave meal, sleep, rinse, repeat. At no point did her schedule include: meet the most potentially perfect guy ever, get asked out by him, freak out.

If Zoe wrote down her requirements for the ideal man and her family did the same, there would be a tiny Venn diagram overlap. Alex Zagarodny was it. He had all the qualities Zoe was looking for, as well as enough of what Mama had been listing just the other day. He seemed too good to be true (thanks, Baba). And if he was as ideal as he seemed, what would someone like Alex want with someone like Zoe? Better temper her expectations. Baba always encourages Zoe to imagine and prepare for the very worst outcome, then she's less likely to be disappointed. And Baba can say, "I told you so."

So Zoe hedges, "There's still the conflict of interest with my job . . ."

Maybe if she hedges enough, the evil eye will become bored and look elsewhere, thus not screwing up what had the potential to be a really great thing—pu, pu, pu, knock wood, we should only live so long.

Then again, who needed the evil eye? Zoe could screw up any potentially great thing all by herself. Just look at her now, conjuring up excuses to avoid so much as giving Alex a shot.

"Oh, that'll work out, don't worry." Lacy gets the look she first assumed when she decided, back in high school, she was going to make Zoe her fixer-upper project, *Wicked*-style. "Cut it out." Even when Lacy gets exasperated, she remains buoyant. "Quit making excuses for why this won't work before you've given it a chance." Does Zoe get any credit for at least thinking that? "Why not take a leap of faith and assume Alex is the perfect guy for you, you're happy, your family is happy, Alex gets his investment, the company is a huge success, I get to wear a hot bridesmaid dress, and absolutely nothing goes wrong ever?"

Lacy bites into her Rice Krispies treat and washes it down with a shot of tequila.

Zoe wants to be Lacy when she grows up. She wishes she'd grown up as Lacy.

However, at this point in time, she is still, unfortunately, Zoe. Who grew up with Mama and Baba and all the self-doubting self-sabotage therein.

Lacy knows this. Which is why she makes Zoe take out her phone and text Alex.

Now.

Chapter 36

—

Lacy holds her hand over Zoe's and makes her text, Yes.

Alex responds barely a second later.

"You see?" Lacy beams. "He was waiting for you!"

Zoe manages to be both thrilled and terrified. At least, if he'd ghosted her, she could say she'd tried. And the failure was absolutely not her fault. She'd have taken that as a win.

Alex writes, Cool.

"Write him back," Lacy commands.

"Balissa says you should make men wait. So they want you more."

"That is so last century," Lacy groans. "Since when are you a *Rules* girl?"

Zoe declines to clarify that the rules she's been raised on go back to the century before the bestselling book. And involve standing in front of the Odessa Opera House in a tight white dress. "What should I write?"

"Something clever. But not too serious. Sincere. But no pressure." Zoe notes Lacy doesn't actually offer any examples.

Zoe types, Don't you want to know: yes, what?

Alex responds, Surprise me.

And then a date, time, and place.

═══

ZOE DUTIFULLY RETURNS to Brooklyn on Saturday. This is the anniversary party that will not die. At least, one Mama refuses to put out of its misery.

"Why are we doing this?" Zoe demands during a tour through Brighton's 99-cent stores, on the hunt for decorations that don't look cheap—but are. "Baba has said, over and over, she doesn't want a party."

"That's what she says," Mama dismisses, picking up off a shelf a Japanese spinning lantern made of tinsel. She checks the bottom for a price. She makes a face and sets it back down, as though the tchotchke tricked her into giving it a second glance. "It's what she's supposed to say."

It's what all properly raised people are supposed to say. Zoe was taught it's bad manners to accept something the first time it's offered. When you're visiting someone's home and they ask if you'd like something to eat or drink, you're supposed to decline. They then spend fifteen minutes cajoling you—"Not even a tiny slice sausage? I bought it fresh"—then guilting you—"Such shame to waste, I went especially looking for it, I heard it was your favorite"—then threatening—"Since I can't serve the main meal until after you've had the appetizer, I suppose we'll all just go hungry." The ritual ensures a good time being had by all, while proving you are a classy person. It wasn't until Zoe visited American friends' homes, was offered a snack, refused it, and then went hungry for the rest of the afternoon that she learned the ritual wasn't like that everywhere else.

"What's the point of saying what you don't mean?"

Mama moves to examine dented on-sale stacked boxes of candy. She considers buying the lot, tossing the boxes, stacking the candy on a festive plate and, there you go, problem solved, with no one being the wiser. Except all the guests who do the same at their houses. "Baba can't say she wants this party. It would sound greedy and selfish."

Mama keeps moving. The store aisles are so narrow, the pair of them can't walk side by side. Zoe ends up ducking other customers and addressing Mama's neck. "But just this one time, how can you be sure Baba doesn't mean what she says?"

"Because she never does this," Mama tosses over a shoulder. "It wouldn't cross her mind."

"It wouldn't cross her mind to tell the truth?"

Mama stops, sighs, and turns around, exasperated. "What is this American fascination with truth? Do you swear to tell the truth, the whole truth, and nothing but the truth, so help you God? Can you not see truth is different, depending on who is saying what to who and why? God, I am sure, can see this."

Zoe echoes Lacy. "That's so Soviet!"

"Not just Soviet." Mama shakes her finger in Zoe's face, forcing a pair of children to duck beneath her elbow. "American, too. American schools. You don't remember?"

"Of course I remember."

"So who was right, you or me?"

In eleventh grade, Zoe's teacher assigned an essay analyzing *The Catcher in the Rye*'s Holden Caulfield. Zoe had been shocked by how Holden bad-mouthed adults, how little respect he showed, how he presumed to know better than them despite lacking life experience, how everyone indulged his hissy fits instead of telling him to pull himself together or matching his stories of imaginary suffering with real suffering, like exile, physical labor, starvation! The teacher gave Zoe a D. Poor Holden, she explained, was alienated. We should pity him and his traumatic, tragic life. No, Zoe countered, Holden was spoiled. We should send him to a Soviet work farm. Because Zoe had such an outstanding record up to that point, the teacher offered to let her rewrite the paper, this time with the correct opinion.

Mama told Zoe to do it. "Your teacher knows what is right."

Baba told Zoe to do it. "Do what she says and get the grade you deserve. Why risk your average for something so unimportant?"

Balissa told Zoe to do it. "Write how she wants it and she will leave you alone. You do not want to get a reputation for trouble-making."

Deda said, "Let our poor girl be. She is intelligent; she will decide for herself." Though later, he did whisper, slipping Zoe a piece of candy, "Why not do this one little thing to make everyone happy and bring peace to the house? For your old deda?"

Zoe couldn't do it. Not for him, not for herself. She refused to rewrite the paper and ended up with a B for the course. Which kept her out of Advanced Placement English the following year. Baba was, naturally, quite disappointed.

"Who won in that case?" Mama taunts now. "And who suffered? And all because you wrote the wrong truth."

Zoe follows Mama out of the store, into the street. Mama lowers her voice. Though if she thinks they're less likely to be overheard here, she's delusional. The sidewalk is as packed as the shop was. There are people rushing by in all directions, reckless children on scooters, women swinging their massive, knockoff designer purses. Mama returns to her original point. "When Baba was young, she learned you say proper things in public because you are always being listened to, and you think your own thoughts in private. Nobody intelligent expects the words coming out of your mouth to match what is going on in your head."

"But we're not in the USSR. Nobody is listening to us." Except the NSA. When news of their spying came out, nobody was more vindicated than Balissa. "You see? Even here they do this! Why you should always be careful!" Zoe presses on. "Nobody cares what we say. Why do we have to keep lying to each other?"

"Because your thoughts are the only things that are yours. If others know what you think and how you feel, they can use those thoughts and feelings against you. They can hurt you. Why take such a risk? What you think is private; what you say is for others."

"How can anyone live like this? It's insane! How can you love a person you'll never truly get to know? And they'll never get to know the real you, either!"

"The real you is so wonderful?" Mama challenges. "When you go out on date—the rare time you go out on date—you are completely honest? Or are you a little bit"—she holds up her thumb and forefinger, first close together, then stretching them out until they are longer than her palm—"better? Nicer, friendlier, politer, prettier?"

"Well, yes. But that's just in the beginning, while we are getting to know each other."

"How will you get to know each other if you are not, as you say, yourself?"

She has a point. Which is why, rather than concede it, Zoe tells Mama that, as a matter of fact, she has a date tonight. With a Brighton-born boy, no less.

"And you will be completely honest with him immediately?"

"Of course."

Mama sighs. "This is big mistake, my Zoyenka."

ZOE HELPS MAMA carry her purchases home. She plans to dump the bags on the kitchen counter and make a quick getaway. Instead, Mama calls Baba and Deda in from the balcony, where they are "taking sun." No matter how many public-service ads Zoe's grandparents watch about the dangers of skin cancer, neither can shake their Old World conviction that the way to absorb vitamin D is to fry until your skin peels. That means it's working and leaching down into your bones. A bit of folk wisdom handed down from Balissa's childhood in Siberia.

"Our Zoya has a date tonight," Mama announces loudly enough not just for Baba and Deda but for half of Brighton to hear. The news brings Balissa from her bedroom. She proceeds to riffle through the bags while listening keenly. Mama's tone grows grim. "She intends to be herself with him!"

"No, Zoyenka," Baba advises, her nose and cheeks brimming that healthy red. "This is not wise. Men, they are to be tortured. Men do not want what they can easily have. You must to make it difficult for them, or they will lose interest."

Zoe thinks about what Mama said, about how the public face you show has nothing to do with the private person you are. Zoe wonders if the family she's certain she knows is, in fact, completely different from what she's assumed. Zoe looks at her churlish Baba and, like an X-ray, imagines catching a glimpse of the southern belle trapped inside. (Zoe defaults to southern belle because she's thinking Scarlett O'Hara at the barbecue and can't summon up an equally Russian example—Anna Karenina at the . . . Borscht Belt?)

Deda assures Zoe, "You are a lovely girl. Do not worry about this. If something is meant to be, it will happen; you do not need to manipulate. You must be patient and wait. Your moment of opportunity will come. And you will to take advantage of it."

Patiently waiting then taking advantage of an opportunity the moment it comes up? Like a sniper? Isn't that what they do? Sit for hours, days, weeks, then, when a split-second chance opens, they blow their enemy's head off? Deda is the most tenderhearted, gentle soul Zoe knows. He feels bad for contestants voted off *American Idol.* "They tried so hard!" But could something darker be lurking underneath?

Balissa is the next to chime in. "Being yourself not always best idea. There is much that can then be used against you."

Balissa is always on guard against being exposed. Zoe chalked it up to good ol' Soviet conditioning. But what if she has her reasons? Balissa makes no secret of what her life in the USSR was like, neighbors spying on each other, turning people in for off-hand remarks or ill-advised jokes. When Zoe kidded that it was the original political correctness, Balissa didn't laugh. Could Zoe's quiet, inoffensive great-grandmother have been an opportunistic informer? Could that be why she's on guard all the time? Balissa never explained exactly how her stepfather got Balissa and her father out of Siberia. Or how he brought Balissa and her mother back. What crimes were committed on her behalf? How might Balissa have repaid her family's debts?

Mama confirms. "I told Zoya it is better to first listen to what person wants, then to give it."

"What good advice," Baba says to Mama, adding, "only twenty-five years too late."

Seeing her opportunity, just like Deda advised, Zoe leaps in. "Then why aren't we listening to Baba? She said she doesn't want an anniversary party, yet here"—Zoe indicates the bags of paraphernalia—"we are!"

Cheap trick. But it works to divert their attention.

They're still arguing, Baba grandstanding, Mama cajoling, Deda trying to calm them both, and Balissa, impervious, putting away the purchases into their appropriate cabinets, as Zoe steps out the door—and to her date with Alex.

Chapter 37

═══

Alex told Zoe to surprise him. He ends up surprising her. What Zoe presumed was a date turns out to be a Young Entrepreneur Mix, Mingle, & Pitch Session, according to the sign hanging above the check-in table.

Disappointment mingles with a trace amount of relief. Zoe had been stressing about what she and Alex would talk about. She'd rough-drafted a dozen different options. The fact that theirs wouldn't be an intimate tête-à-tête was disheartening. Baba always instructed Zoe, "If man to avoid being alone with you, if it is habitually party or, how you say this, a group hang? He is not serious in feelings for you. You are merely way for him to get what he truly wants."

On the other hand, making conversation should be easier if they're surrounded by people eager to talk about themselves. Which is what events like this inevitably are.

Zoe peers into the main room. Over a hundred Young Entrepreneurs in casual business attire are gathered in loose circles, balancing paper plates of shrimp and grits on edible spoons, fried mac and cheese lollipops, and mini tacos. They wield plastic cups of something colorful and alcoholic, and wear earnest facial expressions.

Alex materializes from the crowd like toothpaste squeezed from a tube, pecking Zoe on the cheek and drawing her inside, like he had a few days earlier for his office tour.

Before any other conversation can take place, Zoe expects him to ask whether her company had decided to fund his. Instead, Alex, seemingly without a care in the world, proceeds to introduce Zoe to one new face after another, urging each to expound on their own projects, in case she might be interested in funding them. One woman talks about developing ebooks that gauge reader interest by measuring eye speed, respiration, heart rate, and perspiration, then customizing the story to their tastes. Somebody from the bio-tech industry is working on harnessing the HIV virus so its camouflaging properties can be used to burrow in and treat cancer at the cellular level. Another is testing cheap, lightweight desalination plants that can be shipped to parched areas. A fourth is modifying nanotechnology so parents can track their missing children.

"My great-grandmother would buy one of those for every member of our family," Zoe jokes. To cover up how inadequate she feels.

Alex subtly nudges Zoe with his elbow to join the conversation as more than a listener. He seems disappointed every time she merely smiles and nods to cover up not knowing what to say. She wishes she could make him understand.

No matter how alike they might seem superficially, she isn't like him.

Alex transforms into whatever an occasion calls for. Hard-selling entrepreneur at the office; cheerleading team player here. Zoe, however, possesses great faith in her ability to say absolutely the wrong thing at absolutely the worst time. To cover up that deficit, she's watched lots of TV. She's learned how to mimic a reasonable facsimile of acting correctly. Which means saying the appropriate things, looking like she fits in, being wholly American. Except what comes naturally to everyone else is practiced panto-mime for Zoe, like speaking English without an accent. It's not that she speaks it flawlessly, it's that she knows which words she can't pronounce—anything where a V and a W come too close together is a dead giveaway. It's why she never waves at a Volkswagen or microwaves vodka. She'd suspected as much before, now Zoe feels certain: Alex isn't faking his self-confidence. He really does move effortlessly from group to group, not forcing his way into the conversation but gliding. No one is surprised to see him—it's like he's been there from the start—and no one is offended when he peels off. That's what real aplomb looks like, not whatever it is Zoe's been doing. Real self-assurance isn't bluster, where you make such an ostentatious showing of how in control you are that it's obvious you're anything but. Alex isn't trying to prove he belongs. Alex knows it. Which makes everyone around him know it, too.

If Zoe found Alex attractive when she thought he was merely better at faking than she was, that's nothing compared to how hot he seems now that she realizes he's the real deal.

Of course, the obvious question that comes up is—and Zoe's already wondered as much—what could someone like him possibly see in someone like her?

In a move Zoe tells herself has absolutely nothing to do with that particular concern, she pulls Alex into a quiet corner and tells him, "We're going to fund your company."

Alex grins, but not in an obnoxious way. He's like Lacy. He assumed everything would be fine. So it was. He looks at Zoe expectantly. She's not sure what he's expecting. She'd planned out a dozen conversations they might have. She'd never planned for this. Which, in retrospect, was a mistake. She'd always intended to give Alex the good news. She just figured he'd take the lead on what came next.

Luckily, Zoe has her years of TV watching to fall back on.

On TV, moments like this always lead up to a kiss.

So she closes her eyes. And she hears bells ring.

It's Alex's cell phone.

Zoe opens her eyes in time to see Alex answering it. When he says his name, it's like a challenge to the person on the other end to justify their interruption.

"Sorry," he says as he hangs up. "Gotta run. American ambassador to Argentina is in town and she wants to see a demo of the app. This could be huge for us. You don't mind, right?"

Zoe smiles and nods and recalls what Mama said about not admitting what you really feel. Zoe sends Mama a mental text making it clear this isn't at all the same thing.

"Rain check?" Alex wonders.

"Sure."

"You're the best." It wasn't the most romantic sentence Alex could have uttered at the moment. But it was also, for the first time since they'd met, the first moment when Alex's attention was focused exclusively on Zoe and nothing else. It feels only a little manipulative, considering he'd just been doing the same with everyone else. "I couldn't have done any of this without you."

"HE'S THE MALE version of you!" Zoe calls Lacy the minute she's out the door.

"He sounds perfect," Lacy cheers.

Zoe pauses at the entrance to the subway, loath to hang up before she's gotten the answer she specifically called for. "You know how, when I date American guys, I feel like I don't fit in with them, and when I date Russian guys, I feel like they don't fit in with me?"

"I believe you've mentioned that once or twice." Just because Lacy is the nicest person ever doesn't mean she's immune to a periodic sarcastic interlude.

"I thought Alex would be the perfect intersect."

"He's not?"

"He's better."

"That's great!"

"He's also worse."

"Of course."

"I'm not just being negative, like usual."

"You are." Lacy isn't so much judgmental as wishing to set the record straight. "Even if you don't actually say the words *evil eye*—"

"No. I'm being negative in a whole new way."

Lacy laughs. "Okay, let's hear it."

Zoe takes a deep breath, pushing out words one after the other, hoping they'll make sense when rearranged into some semblance of order later. "When Alex looks at me, he sees the person I wish I was. When I'm with him, I kind of feel like I'm on my way to becoming her. I like it. But it also makes me nervous. Because when he finds out that's not who I really am, he's going to be disappointed. And I'm going to be disappointed. For disappointing him, and for losing my chance to become the person I really want to be."

"Yeah, that's a new one," Lacy concedes.

"What should I do?"

"Risk it."

How American of her.

And how exactly what Zoe needed to hear.

ALEX BARELY WAITS a day before cashing his rain check. He takes Zoe to the Museum of Arts and Design at Columbus Circle. He says it inspires him. He kisses Zoe as they're exiting. Right across from the towering statue of Columbus. How symbolic.

Alex asks her out again for the following day. Zoe knows she's supposed to say no, play hard to get. She says yes. Alex wonders if she'd mind meeting him at the office; they can head out from there. Zoe tells him she doesn't mind. Zoe tells herself she believes that. Zoe doesn't tell Baba or Mama anything. Not even that she's about to have a third date with a boy whose parents still live in Brighton. No sense in their getting too excited. No sense in her getting too excited.

It's a sensible precaution since, when she arrives to meet Alex at the office, he isn't there.

Gideon swivels in his chair and pops his head out of his cubicle to fill Zoe in. "He's in a meeting. Doesn't want to text, disrespectful. He asked me to tell you to wait, if you don't mind."

"I don't mind," Zoe lies again, wondering where she's supposed to not mind waiting.

Gideon says, "You can hang out here, if you want."

His space is smaller than Alex's and, unlike Alex's minimalist decorating style, Gideon's cubicle is stuffed full of books.

"Sorry for the mess." He clears a stack off a chair, adding it to another one on the floor.

"Got much free time for reading?" The tech guys Zoe knows live, breathe, eat, and groom tech. That's another way Alex is different. He's so well put together. He smells nice, too.

Gideon fits somewhere in between. His clothes are washed but wrinkled. His shirt has hanger bumps on the shoulders where he hung it up to dry but didn't iron it. "I make the time."

"You'd rather read than dedicate your every waking moment to the pursuit of Internet fame and fortune? How in the world did you end up working with Alex?"

Zoe settles into the chair Gideon offers, craning her neck to peruse the titles he moved. It's an eclectic mix of technical manuals, *PHP Cookbook*, JavaScript, C++, MySQL, Perl; classic sci-fi like Robert Heinlein and *Dune*, along with books on metacognition, the physics of superheroes, a history of Chinese sailing ships, and a tome on sustainable salmon fishing. Gideon reads like an alcoholic who'll chug anything. His openness about his habit makes Zoe smile. When Zoe still lived in Brighton, Baba frowned on her buying books. She pointed out they were free at the library, so why waste the money?

"But what if I want to keep something I really love?" Zoe asked.

"Copy it out longhand," Baba snapped. "See how much you love it then."

Now that Zoe lives alone, she could, theoretically, buy all the books she wants. But old habits die hard. She hoards them on her phone, instead. And Zoe never lets Baba know how much she paid for a book that "isn't even real."

"If it weren't for Alex"—Gideon sits across from Zoe, swaying side to side in his chair—"I'd be hanging out at home, working on programming puzzles that interest me, giving my code away free for the thrill of watching what others do with it. Alex is the one who insists on my being paid for my work."

"You're not interested in making money?"

"Not as much as I should be, according to my grandma. She likes to remind me how much they spent on my education. And it wasn't so that I could, quote, sit around playing with my crazy toys all day, end quote."

Zoe wonders what Gideon's grandmother thinks of his wasting money on books. Especially ones that don't apply to his chosen career or other moneymaking endeavors.

"Alex said you went to private school," Zoe recalls. She can guess how much his family spent. And why they expect a return on their investment.

"Yeah, only kid in my neighborhood. Every morning, I got to stand alone at the bus stop in my khaki pants and blue blazer, people staring at me like I came down from Mars. You should have heard me complaining. And you should have heard my grandma telling me to talk to the hand. You know how, when you're a kid, all you want to do is fit in?"

"Yes," Zoe says. "Good thing we all outgrow that."

She wonders if Gideon will realize she's joking. She wonders if he'll get the joke. She wonders if the joke's on her.

"Well, my grandma wasn't playing. It's our family tradition, she said, not going down the same path as everyone else. My grandma was a Black Panther—can you believe it? She remembers when gun control was another tool to keep the black man down. Now, she's got her NRA card and she flashes it every chance she gets. You can imagine how popular that makes her."

"Your grandma is brave."

"My grandma is something." Gideon grins. "Not sure if *brave* is the right word for it."

"My grandma is something, too," Zoe echoes. "Not a fan of do-ing what's asked of her, either, especially if it's the government asking. Brave isn't the word I'd use, though. Spiteful, maybe?"

Zoe feels a twinge of guilt at not only sounding like she's criticizing Baba, but for blabbing family secrets. Baba hates anyone
knowing their business. She says she refuses to be the subject of
gossip. But then Zoe decides she and Gideon are engaging in a
fair and equitable exchange of goods and/or services. Information
is the ultimate twenty-first-century good, according to the people
who decide these things. So Zoe is being a proper capitalist. Baba
can't object to that!

"My grandma marched, protested, and got arrested"—Gideon
equitably spills his own family tea—"so my dad could become a
lawyer who could send his son to private school. They sacrificed
so I could become the man I wanted to be, no matter what anybody
else, including the government, thought. If the man I want to be
is a guy who doesn't care if he sets the world on fire, who wants to
play with his code and read books and enjoy himself, that's still a
victory for what they fought for. That I even have that choice to
make." Gideon qualifies, "That's what I keep telling my grandma.
She's not exactly on board."

"I wouldn't dare try that argument. My family didn't come
to America so I could disappoint them. Though they constantly
make me feel like, no matter what I do, I have." Zoe isn't sure why
she's telling Gideon this. Except maybe his expressing opinions she
didn't know people were allowed to have is giving her the confidence to express opinions she knew she had but understood she
wasn't allowed to express.

"What about Alex? Does your family not like Alex? Everybody
likes Alex."

"Yeah, Alex is the bright spot. He's exactly the kind of guy I
should be dating."

"Should," Gideon muses. "What a romantic word."

If he only knew for how many generations of Zoe's family *should*
was the operative romantic word.

Her phone buzzes.

It's Alex. He's sorry, he's being held up.

"Rain check?" Gideon guesses.

"Yup," Zoe confirms, sighing as she hangs up. She'd made an effort, put on makeup and everything. A whole face wasted.

Gideon picks up on her disappointment. He asks, "Want to catch a movie instead?"

Chapter 38

Based on the collection of books in Gideon's office, Zoe is thinking: comic-book blockbuster. She's sort of right. Gideon does take her to see a sci-fi flick. A double feature of *Little Shop of Horrors*, the original black-and-white Roger Corman cheapie from the 1960s and the movie musical from the 1980s, being screened in the back of a Village comic-book shop. About fifty people are packed into a space meant to hold, at best, thirty. Based on the number who wave or nod their heads in his direction, Gideon is a regular.

Zoe and Gideon arrived too late to snag a folding chair, so, after raising a hand in greeting to some of the other audience members, Gideon drags in an empty packing crate from the storage room. He links his fingers and drops his arms, indicating Zoe should step on his conjoined palms, and he'll give her a boost up. It's a bit of chivalry Balissa never mentioned in her litany of things men should do, or Baba in her litany of ways to make them suffer, which Zoe finds touching.

The first movie starts. So does the conversation. Barely a line is uttered in either film that doesn't provoke a response from the audience, especially when a ridiculously young Jack Nicholson appears as a dental patient who gets off on pain. There are cries of "Here's

Johnny," "You can't handle the truth," and even something about holding a chicken between your knees. Zoe wants to join in. Zoe always wants to join in. Primarily so she doesn't stick out. But she's not certain what the correct response is in this situation. Lacy once dragged her to a midnight screening of *The Rocky Horror Picture Show*. Zoe recalls that audience interaction is extremely regimented. Saying the wrong thing at the wrong time can get one banished to hipster Siberia.

Zoe whispers to Gideon, "What am I supposed to say?"

He looks at her queerly. "Whatever you want."

His confidence in Zoe calls to mind Alex. And puts Zoe under the same amount of pressure. After she left the Mix & Mingle, Zoe would confess only to Lacy how Alex's inherent trust made her feel unworthy. She wouldn't dare express the same thought to Alex. Yet, with Gideon, Zoe doesn't hesitate to sheepishly admit, "I don't want to embarrass you. If I say something stupid, you'll look stupid for bringing me. And if I don't say anything, they'll think I'm stupid. Or that I think I'm above all this, like I'm too good for it."

"Just be yourself, Zoe," Gideon says, vocalizing the exact opposite of what her family would say. It's exactly what Zoe must have known he'd say. Why else would she have trusted him with the confession in the first place? Gideon indicates the crowd in all their geeky glory. "Does it look like anybody here came to judge?"

GIDEON IS RIGHT. Nobody at the comic-book shop cares what Zoe does or says. Even Gideon watches the movies, not her. The exception is, when Zoe laughs, he turns and grins, pleased to see her enjoying herself. When she gathers the courage to sing along with the onscreen bouncing ball, he joins in. After Zoe comments how Seymour and Mr. Mushnik are stereotypical Jews who'll do anything for a buck, including sacrificing human beings to a carnivorous plant, and wonders whether *Little Shop* could be a Muppets version of the *Protocols of the Elders of Zion* libel about Jews killing Christian children to make matzo with their blood, he does not look at her like she's out of her mind.

"That's the spirit!" Gideon says.

This not-being-judged thing is intoxicating. Zoe wonders if this is how Lacy and her fellow Americans feel all the time. She wonders if this is how Alex feels most of the time. She wonders how he does it. She wonders if he'll teach her. She wonders if maybe Gideon already has.

AFTER THE MOVIES, Gideon and Zoe say goodbye in front of the comic-book store. It feels like they've been through some momentous experience together, two soldiers returning home from war. Or something more intimate.

"That was fun. See you later, Zoe."

Funny story: When her family first came to the United States, the American volunteer assigned to help them get settled took her leave from them that first night by saying, "See you later." They thought she'd meant later, as in later that night. So they stayed up until one a.m., waiting for her to come back.

Zoe is tempted to blurt out this personally embarrassing tale to Gideon, to keep things from getting awkward. And to keep the evening going just a little while longer.

But Gideon doesn't do awkward. After saying it was fun, he gives Zoe a hug. That lingers sweetly after he's disappeared down the block.

"WHY DIDN'T YOU tell me the boy who's courting you is Alex Zagarodny?" Mama and Zoe are shopping for Baba's party again, this time on the hunt for a T.J. Maxx dress that doesn't look like it came from T.J. Maxx.

"I'm sorry, Mama." There's a Russian saying: *Beat a child every day. If you don't know what they've done to deserve it, they will.* Zoe's philosophy is the inverse: *Apologize every day. If you don't know what for, your family will.* "How do you know about Alex?"

"Alex's mother's neighbor is the sister of your great-uncle's nurse."

"In Israel?" Zoe's love life is now a matter of international importance?

Having failed to find a non–T.J. Maxx–looking dress at T.J. Maxx, they exit in an offended huff. A car whizzes by on the street, all four windows open, rap music blasting loudly enough for Zoe's stomach to clench in synch with its rhythm.

Mama clutches her purse closer to her body, even though the car is now half a block away. "Those hooligans . . . They think they can do whatever they want with no consequences. No manners, those people, no respect."

If Zoe knew what hackles were, and if she felt certain she had some, they would now be on the rise. "You can't say that, Mama. You can't generalize about all black people like that. How would you feel if you heard someone say all Soviet immigrants are welfare frauds and . . . and . . ." Zoe can't think of anything equally bad that also isn't a synonym, and so completes her righteous indignation with, "and . . . computer programmers."

Mama's stride doesn't break. "Spare me your internationalism." She spits it like the dirty word it is at their house. "You went to your school for smart children in Manhattan—Baba and I saw to that. You didn't have to walk the halls of public school in Brooklyn every day, getting called a nasty-ass Communist who should go back to where you came from, or a stuck-up bitch who thinks she's better than everyone because you study hard and answer the teacher's questions."

Mama is right. But her experience doesn't complement the narrative Zoe has decided on, so she ignores it, pushing down her guilt at having escaped the same fate, in the service of a greater, universal good. "I'm sorry that's how you remember it, but fear-mongering stories don't make it okay to tar everybody with the same brush." After the topsy-turviness of the past few days, it feels soothing to articulate finally what Zoe has been drilled is the correct thing. To feel confident that she is right and Mama is wrong.

"Who is tarring? I am not tarring. Where do you see me tarring? You are the one who is tarring. You are like the people on the television, and the Facebook. Somebody says one thing about one person, and you act like she has said many things about many people. Just like in USSR. First they make you confess, does not matter if you did this thing or not, you must feel guilty and confess. Then they force you to beg forgiveness, explain how you know better now—self-criticism, it is called. Still they say no forgiveness for you. Because you confess to this once, you are guilty for always, there is no sorry, no changing your mind. Anything you say can and will be used against you forever; it is the law here today in America, too, that is what I think."

"What about Baba and Deda? And their friends?" If the suspect won't immediately confess to your satisfaction, go after their family and known associates. "Don't tell me they don't stereotype all black people as hooligans."

Mama laughs. She laughs harder than Zoe's heard in a while. "Do you know what your baba said when I cried about being bullied? She said, in the USSR, there were African students at the university, brought over so they could see how wonderful Communism is. But they were all so serious, so hardworking, the other students complained that they were no fun, that all they cared about was their grades! And your deda, he chimes in, the Vietnamese students, they were the ones who only wanted to have fun; they so lazy, they hardly showed up for class, and they didn't care for studying at all!"

There's too much for Zoe to unpack, including the blasphemous notion that there could be different stereotypes about the same people in different cultures. She, once again, ignores anything that doesn't conform and sticks to her initial point. "Baba and Deda aren't in the USSR anymore. I've heard how their friends feel about the African Americans here. The words they use. Sure, they say *negr*," Zoe whispers, "which means Negro in Russian. But they've lived in the U.S. long enough to know what it sounds like to other people. I can tell what they really believe."

"Have you ever seen your baba go along with what everyone else believes?"

"Well, no . . ." She'd told Gideon that only the other night.

"And does your deda treat everyone as an individual, regardless of the people they come from?"

"Well, yes . . ."

"So you see, you are the one who is tarring all of us. I know there are many fine blacks"—Mama hesitates, then confesses—"but I do not like Oprah. Always telling me how I should live my life. I do not need this."

True. Mama and Zoe have Baba for this. Unlike Baba, though, Oprah doesn't designate twenty minutes after they depart any social gathering to reciting an inventory of the things they did wrong there. The first time Lacy invited Zoe to a party, Zoe felt so peculiar afterward. It took her several occasions before she understood it was because Lacy didn't harangue Zoe as soon as they'd left. When Alex seemed a little disappointed in Zoe during the Mix & Mingle, she'd felt more in her element than after seeing the movies with Gideon, when he'd acted like she'd done nothing indecorous. Where was the closure?

"Alex's business partner is black," Zoe blurts out, not sure to what purpose.

Mama nods as if she expected nothing less. "He is a nice boy? Smart?"

"Very nice. Very smart." Zoe feels bummed Mama deprived her of the chance to enumerate Gideon's sterling qualities as part of a soul-stirring defense in the face of her unrepentant racism.

"I am sure your Alex only works with very nice, very smart people." Mama changes the subject, though, in her mind, she's done no such thing. "You must invite Alex for supper. Do it quickly, Zoyenka. Before he loses interest in you."

"I thought men were to be tortured," Zoe teases.

"You are enough," Mama reassures her, in what passes for a compliment at their house.

Chapter 39

"Our Zoya is ashamed of us," Mama announces over the supper their Zoe has agreed to share with her, Baba, Deda, and Balissa, in exchange for Mama calling a cease-fire in the argument to get Alex to do the same. Mama collects the empty soup plates while Baba brings out the roast chicken and potatoes powdered with dill, clucking as usual. "I do not understand this, in Odessa, we buy one chicken, it lasts a week. Here, one chicken, one meal and it is gone!"

"I'm not ashamed of you." Zoe sighs.

"Then why will you not invite your young man to visit with us?" Mama persists. "We can help you, Zoyenka, to evaluate if he is appropriate person. We have much life experience. Better to make decisions than you youngsters."

"Did Baba and Deda think my father was the appropriate person?" Mama pretty much told Zoe the answer to this while they stood in front of her father's house. But Zoe's goal here is not to get information. It's to deflect attention.

Baba opens her mouth. Deda cuts her off. "I did not."

It's the most definitive thing he's ever said on the subject.

"Why not?" Zoe asks, stunned.

Baba interrupts, "What difference does it make now? What happened is what happened, no going back for anyone. What's the point of combing through the past? That's not the direction time moves in. My mama and papa loved," Baba puts heavy emphasis on the next word, "*this* one." She flaps her hand in Deda's direction. "I had no choice but to marry him."

"Because I am so wonderful," Deda chortles.

Baba ignores him. "So that is that, too."

While they've been talking, Balissa has been nibbling, ladylike, at her chicken wing. Once she's done, she dabs at her lips with a napkin, sets the napkin down next to her plate, and lifts the now licked clean bone, snapping it in half and gracefully inserting the jagged ends into her mouth. She is sucking out the marrow.

When Zoe was little, any ill table manners were greeted with the query, "Would you eat in front of the Queen of England like that?"

Zoe suspects Her Majesty frowns on marrow sucking. But just like they insist sunburns lead to good health, Balissa can't surrender her Soviet conviction that marrow sucking is the prime way to get iron.

"Sometimes"—she slides the cracked bone out of her mouth—"no choice is the best choice."

INSTEAD OF A family supper, which Zoe doesn't mention, for their next date, Alex escorts her to the Guggenheim Museum for a reception honoring New York City's most dynamic 30 Under 30. Is it supposed to inspire her, or make Zoe feel guilty for not being among them? On the one hand, Alex makes her feel like she could be. On the other, he seems to be chastising her for not doing enough to make it happen. Just like at home!

Everywhere Zoe looks, they're surrounded by tuxedos and cocktail dresses; outside, a red carpet with photographers, and inside, towering art that nobody understands but everyone pretends to. She whispers to Alex as they breeze by the indifferent-to-them paparazzi, "Will Oz the Great and Powerful rear up in flames and throw me out for being Dorothy the Small and Meek?"

Her reference is to the movie, though Zoe first came to the story via a Russian translation of the book, where the heroine's name is Ella, and her slippers aren't ruby but gold.

Alex squeezes Zoe's hand reassuringly. "You belong here."

That should have answered Zoe's earlier question.

It leaves her feeling only more confused.

Alex is so confident, Zoe suspects now wouldn't be a good time to reveal she's never been to the Guggenheim before. Not that her family is uncultured. They've hit the symphony, the ballet, the opera. But they prefer that culture come to them. Operas, ballets, and symphonies tour. Museums stay put. Baba does remember visiting the Vatican while they were emigrating. Seeing Catholic splendor, on the heels of Soviet deprivations, made such an impression that now, when the Pope makes declarations regarding the evils of capitalism, conspicuous consumption, and how we should do more for the needy, Baba informs the TV, "When the Holy See sells off their mansions and their paintings and their helicopters, and hands over their profits to the poor, then I will listen to what he has to say about me giving away my things."

Zoe tried to fill in the gaps of her New York City cultural education. She's been to the Met, MoMA, the Whitney. But the Guggenheim never appealed to her. Maybe because it looks like an upside-down planter. Maybe because there's usually a line to get in. As Balissa says about any line, "That's not what we came to America for."

Or maybe it's because, as Zoe promptly learns, the place is petrifying. Not the art. That's just confusing. The layout. The interior is a huge spiral, a giant's DNA strand. The barriers come up only as far as her elbow. She gets vertigo whenever she looks down. She tries to fight it by looking straight ahead, but then she sees taller people, and on them the barrier comes up only to their hips. She imagines them tumbling over, which prompts her stomach to roil like a plummeting elevator. She clutches Alex's arm even tighter until they're back on solid land.

Alex pats Zoe's hand reassuringly, if distractedly, looks around, and spots one of the 30 Under 30 honorees, a man who, according to the program Zoe skimmed, runs a nonprofit that opposes child labor, or one that creates jobs for at-risk youth.

"Harris!" Alex greets him as if they were friends. By the man's confusion, it would appear they are not. Nonetheless, when Alex proffers his name along with an outstretched hand, it's in the form of a subtle memory jog. "Alex Zagarodny. Good to see you again!"

"You, too," Harris says politely, then smiles at Zoe, wondering if she's also about to claim familiarity.

"This is Zoe Venakovsky."

"Nice to meet you," Zoe says, and Harris relaxes at not having to pretend to know her, too. He shakes Alex's hand, then crosses his arms and eyes them warily. When you have a last name for a first name, you're used to being accosted by strangers.

Alex asks Harris, "You're an Old Boy, aren't you? Zoe works for Derek Webber. His sons go to St. Bernard's, too."

School of tiny blue blazers? Zoe remains confused, until she realizes that mentioning it has spurred Harris into believing he and Alex are friends, after all. He uncrosses his arms and sticks his hands casually in his pockets. He and Alex commence chattering away about people they know; who is summering where; and, yes, it is a travesty the Community Board keeps refusing permission to build a helicopter landing pad on the Upper East Side. It would make the Hamptons commute so much more convenient. If only Amazon hadn't given up on Long Island City . . .

Zoe gazes at Alex in awe. Here he is, a curly-haired, big-nosed, skinny guy who comes up to this titan's waist, a Brooklyn kid who most certainly did not wear a blue blazer to school or take a helicopter to get there, and he's talking to Upper East Side money (in the form of a person; like how a corporation is legally a person) as if they're equals. Zoe wonders what the WASP word is for *chutzpah*.

As the conversation goes on, Zoe hears Alex's speech begin to mimic Harris's cadence and vocabulary. She watches him mirror the taller man's body language, hands also in his pockets, rocking back on his heels, head cocked to his side. It's mesmerizing and inspirational.

It's also, after ten indistinguishable minutes, rather boring. Zoe never knew the three sensations could occupy the same space at the same time, but physics be damned!

A quarter of an hour in, Gideon shows up. Zoe hadn't realized she'd been waiting for him. How could she? She didn't know he was coming. And yet, the moment she saw him, Zoe realized she'd been waiting for him. To rescue her from all this. It's the way she feels when Baba and Mama argue with each other and take a break from criticizing Zoe. It's the way she hopes to feel when she triumphantly presents them with Alex. Like a problem has been permanently fixed.

Gideon crosses the room and exchanges words with the bartender in the corner, who laughs and hands him a drink.

"Excuse me, please," Zoe says to Alex and Harris, both of whom bob their heads like the gentlemen they are and/or are pretending to be, before resuming talking business.

Zoe walks over to Gideon. "Hey."

"Yo" is his response. He takes a sip of his drink, compliments the bartender, then indicates Zoe's date. "Alex being Alex?"

"To the Alexest degree."

Gideon marvels, "Like watching an artist at work."

"This is the place for it." Ha. Museum humor.

"I'm supposed to be networking," Gideon says, making no move to do any such thing.

Zoe isn't sure what she's supposed to be doing. Which makes it as good of a time as any to ask Gideon, "Do you ever get the feeling that, when Alex looks at you, he's seeing the person he wants you to be, not the person you actually are?"

"Twenty-four seven," Gideon confirms.

That's good. At least she's not going crazy. But it's also not good. "So would you say Alex is dating me, or dating the Zoe he's conjured up in his head?"

"Which one do you want it to be?"

"Oh, definitely the one in his head. She's a much better model."

Gideon grins. "I know the feeling."

He does? Based on what Zoe saw at the comic-book store, Gideon is as comfortable in his skin as Alex is in his. It never crossed her mind that he might be feigning it the same way she is. Or, in Zoe's case, trying to. She'd have expected the realization to disappoint her. Instead, it makes her respect Gideon more. It's one thing to be born confident. It's another to fake it so convincingly. If Gideon can do it, there's hope for Zoe the Impostor yet!

"You're not afraid of not living up to Alex's expectations of you?" she double-checks.

"What goes on in Alex's head is Alex's business," Gideon says. "I don't worry about things I can't control."

"You're not even a little bit Jewish, are you?"

Gideon laughs. "I grew up in New York and I'm an engineer. Does it get any more Jewish than that?"

There's a circumcision joke in there somewhere, but that would be classless. Thinking it, though, makes Zoe blush.

Gideon picks up on her discomfort and gallantly moves to defuse the situation.

"Come on." He downs his drink, returns the glass to the bar alongside a generous tip, then gestures with his head toward the canvases and sculptures on the horizon. "Alex is doing his thing. Let's go look at art."

Looking at art requires getting back on the spiral walkway. Gideon positions his body so Zoe is on the inside, making it easier for her not to peer down and freak out. He runs commentary on the pieces they pass, like what happened during the movie, forcing Zoe to look up, rather than down. That one, he says, looks like a broken kaleidoscope; this one is the napkin Jackson Pollock used to wipe up his breakfast. In the Impressionist room, they muse that since a musical based on Seurat's painting was called *Sunday in the Park with George*, they should expect Picasso's *Lobster and Cat* as a children's show, and Manet's *Before the Mirror* as a reality beauty pageant.

They stop in front of Maurizio Cattelan's eighteen-karat-gold toilet, installed in a public bathroom and open for visitor use. A docent lurking at the door explains that it requires steam cleaning and special wipes to keep it pristine, and that it was created in order to give patrons a unique, personal, and up-close experience with a work of art. It symbolizes equal opportunity and the American dream.

Zoe thinks of Baba using a community toilet in her courtyard and washing once a week at a public bathhouse. She thinks of Balissa shivering in a cattle car with no bathroom facilities beyond a hole in the floor. And Balissa's mother squatting over a fetid chamber pot in the same room where they cooked and ate, cleaning it out by hand every morning and every evening.

All previous wisecracks suddenly feel woefully inadequate.

"God bless America," Zoe says at long last.

"THERE YOU GUYS ARE!" Alex catches up with Zoe and Gideon on the ground floor, when the other guests are on their way out. "I was looking all over for you." He slips one arm around Zoe's waist in a move that might be romantic, possessive, or merely practical, Alex's way of not losing track of her again. To nudge it toward the former, Zoe leans into him, resting her head against his shoulder. He doesn't need to worry about losing track of her. She's right here. He's got her. She's not going anywhere with anyone else.

Alex startles, but goes with the flow. "What've you two been up to?"

"We saw a golden toilet," Zoe says, because she still can't get over it.

"Great. Perfect place to scope out prospects. Everyone's got to go eventually. Why I always ask for a seat at the back of the plane, where the bathrooms are. Gives me access to everybody by the time the flight is over."

There's something you don't learn in an MBA program. Alex could teach a course in doing your business while . . . doing your business.

"Listen, Alex, speaking of something everyone's got to do"— Zoe leaps on the closest thing to a smooth transition she can think of on the fly, straightening up to face him—"I've got to go see my family this weekend. They've invited you, too."

"Aw, Zoe, no. I haven't got time to schlep out to my own parents', much less get interrogated by someone else's."

"You don't have time not to go," Gideon corrects before Zoe can concede Alex's point, a touch relieved by the opportunity to put off the judgment from her family's first contact with Alex. Even if, as far as Zoe can tell, he's everything they've ever dreamed of, Baba will find something to nitpick.

"If you don't let Zoe's family give you the third degree, they'll keep calling her, texting her, *distracting* her. We're ironing out long-term funding. You want nonsense getting in the way of a check getting cut?"

"That won't happen," Alex says, but he doesn't sound quite as self-assured now. He knows the power of Repeated Calls from Brooklyn. And Gideon is one of the few people he listens to.

"Not if you break bread with these people and satisfy their curiosity. Give 'em the Awesome Alex Premier Condensed Package, and they'll get off Zoe's back."

"I don't have time to go to Brooklyn," Alex repeats.

Zoe shoots Gideon a grateful look for trying, especially since this isn't his fight.

"But if your family wants to come to Manhattan . . ." Wait, what's this? "I don't have time for dinner, either," Alex rushes to clarify before Zoe gets too excited. "I know how important this is to them, and how they can get if we don't give them something to talk about, let them get their shots in." Alex says the words, but he sounds confident he can deflect anything they throw his way. "Your family can come by the office. How's that?"

Zoe exhales in disbelief—and relief of a different kind. She won't be compelled to keep having this conversation with Mama and Baba. She can rip off the Band-Aid and get it over with. Zoe shudders at the thought of what's to come, yet pastes on a smile. "Thank you."

She's speaking to Gideon. Alex assumes she's speaking to him.

He's so busy accepting accolades for his massive sacrifice that he doesn't even notice Zoe is looking at Gideon.

Or that his friend is mouthing, "You're welcome."

With a wink.

That manages to both reassure Zoe . . . and throw her off balance.

Chapter 40

Zoe invites her family to stop by Alex's office at lunchtime. Dinnertime by Russian standards, though Mama assures it's no trouble, she'll adjust their schedule—they'll eat first, they don't expect to be fed. They opt not to take the subway, and a cab is too expensive. Baba knows a guy who drives for a limo service who's happy to pick up money on the side, charging less as long as you pay in cash.

They arrive, as Zoe predicted, twenty minutes ahead of schedule. Deda's phobia of being late, triggered by the scramble to catch their trains while emigrating, prompts him to factor in way too much buffer for any journey. Zoe watches them through the security camera as they enter the lobby and head for the elevator—Mama and Baba propping Balissa up by the elbows, Deda bringing up the rear with his cane. Balissa is in her eighties but walks so regally that, despite needing help getting around and barely being able to see beyond her arm, it still appears as if she's leading the pack. Balissa's mother taught her that. Always stand tall. Always look everyone in the eye.

There's not much of a dress code at Alex's. He's wearing jeans and a red T-shirt with a blazer thrown over it. Gideon's in khakis and a black tee that reads WORLD'S #0 PROGRAMMER. Mama, on the other hand, is wearing a navy dress Zoe knows is new—she can see the creases on the sleeves and skirt. Baba is in a teal jacket with 1980s shoulder pads. She says it gives her the illusion of a waist. Why should she forgo such a figure-flattering style merely because a faceless authority deemed it over? Deda has on a white dress shirt buttoned up to his chin. Balissa is in a flower-print dress cut surprisingly low in the cleavage, with a gold brooch pinned to the lapel.

Zoe presumed she'd need to drag Alex to greet them at the elevator, but he beats her to it. When the doors open, there he suddenly is. Zoe's family startles. As does Zoe.

"Welcome!" Alex effuses. In Russian. Zoe has never heard him speak Russian before. He's got a bit of an accent. As he shakes everybody's hand and leads them toward the office, Zoe realizes that his vocabulary is limited, like that of a child. But his charm isn't.

Alex directs the bulk of his tour at Balissa; he understands that being gracious to her will trickle down. He shows Balissa the break room, with its abundance of free food and drinks for the staff. He offers her a cup of tea, which she politely declines. He asks again. She declines again. He makes her one anyway. "Just in case, for later." Everybody beams.

He takes them to the conference room, with its whiteboards covered in equations and code, and proceeds to explain what he's working on. Mama asks questions about the algorithms in a quiet voice, sorry to be troubling him. Alex answers, making clear it's no trouble. Baba isn't as sheepish. She wonders how much money this is costing, where he got it, and how he plans to make it back.

Alex explains about investors and angels, first- and second-round financing, IPOs. He doesn't know the Russian words for those terms, so toggles back and forth while everyone nods thoughtfully.

"Zoe's been an incredible help," he says, "getting her company to fund our beta launch."

For normal people, this would trigger concerns about conflicts of interest. But to the Brighton contingent, who else would one do business with, strangers?

Next up is a stroll through the cubicles. Alex takes the route with maximum Russian-speaking programmers. He introduces Zoe's family, asks the coders to explain what they're working on. Some are recent arrivals. Their language skills are far above Alex's. Deda is interested in what they're saying, but Balissa is overwhelmed by the jargon. Alex moves the tour along, for her sake. Deda looks longingly at the computer monitors, then dutifully hustles with his cane after the rest.

The final stop is Alex's office, where he's set up chairs for everyone. There's one for Deda, but, when Zoe looks around, he's hanging back, studying a snippet of code that's hanging from a strip of paper thumbtacked to the outside of a cubicle wall. Zoe is about to go get him when she sees Gideon move in and ask her grandfather something. Deda nods, waving his arms enthusiastically. Gideon points in the direction of his own cubicle and takes Deda's arm to help him navigate. He catches Zoe's eye over her grandfather's head, and mouths, "I got this."

Deda so often gets overlooked at home. Sweet how Gideon singled him out for personalized attention. How many times is it now that Gideon's come to Zoe's rescue? And each time, before she figured out she needed it. Zoe isn't certain how she feels about that. Heck, Zoe still isn't sure how she feels about Gideon's wink the other day. So like with all feelings she can't understand, she chooses to ignore them.

She catches up to her family.

No one else has noticed Deda is gone.

Granted, Mama, Baba, and Balissa are engaged in the more pressing task of cross-examining Alex. Baba is doing the majority of the talking. Mama is holding back, afraid of saying something that might ruin Zoe's matrimonial chances. Balissa prefers to sit back and watch. She believes in letting people hang themselves. Though it's also a turn of phrase she hates. The Russian expression *In a home where someone hanged himself, don't bring up rope* isn't a metaphor for Balissa.

Baba wants to know if Alex ever goes back to Brighton.

"Of course," he says. "To visit my parents."

What a nice boy.

Will he ever move back there?

"Maybe. When I have children."

What a sensible boy!

Where did he go to university?

"Caltech."

"In California? Why so far away from home?"

"I wanted the best opportunity to make something of myself."

What an enterprising boy!

Where does Alex live now?

"Battery Park City."

"Own or rent?"

"Rent. I'm more flexible that way. I can relocate wherever I need to."

Ready to flee at a moment's notice? That's a feature, not a bug.

"What do your parents do?"

"They're engineers."

Of course they are.

"How do they like our Zoya?"

"They love everything I've told them about her."

"So you're meeting us before they're meeting her?"

"Naturally," Alex says.

It goes on in this vein for another twenty minutes. Alex never loses patience, even when the questions begin repeating themselves, checking for inconsistencies à la the KGB. Zoe is the one who finally can't take it. She tells her family Alex needs to get back to work. Alex says they're welcome to stay as long as they like. To be polite, the family then insists that no, really, they must be leaving.

They lasso Deda from Gideon's cubicle on the way out. He is standing, delighted, in front of a screen. He pokes a finger at the monitor and claims, "This language, this C you are using, it is like the Ratfor language. I learn little in USSR, before I get married.

Ratfor is like the Fortran with C syntax, yes?" He turns to Gideon for confirmation.

"Yes," Gideon says. "That's exactly what it is."

"I learn it, too." Deda grins proudly. He asks Alex, "I come work for you?"

"Anytime." Alex half bows. "It would be an honor." But he isn't looking at Deda as he says it. Zoe hopes her grandfather doesn't notice. When his smile falters, it's obvious he does. Zoe feels a flare-up of anger, followed immediately by guilt. How dare she nitpick like this after everything Alex has done for her this afternoon? Zoe is getting as bad as Baba! Will nothing ever be good enough for her? That, Mama would say, is why Zoe is alone. That is why Zoe is dying to prove them all wrong.

"We are to be leaving." Her grandmother waves the backs of her hands in the direction of the elevator. "*Kish*. Alex and Zoya are busy."

"Goodbye, Gideon." Deda pronounces it Gee-Dee-One.

"Goodbye, sir. It was a pleasure meeting you."

"Much pleasure for me, too." Deda only nods in Alex's direction. And Zoe feels strangely vindicated. Followed by more guilt.

Alex offers his own goodbyes in Russian. Balissa reaches into her bag and hands him a plastic container of *zephyrs*, whipped strawberry puree mixed with sugar, egg whites, and gelatin, then stiffened into flower shapes.

"My favorite!" Alex says.

There is more handshaking and beaming all around.

And the elevator doors finally close.

Zoe sags like all the water has been drained from her body. She is nothing but packed dry sand. Any move will cause the edifice to crumble.

Alex suffers no such exhaustion. He got to be the center of attention, receive waves of positive feedback—he obviously missed Deda's diss—plus earn Zoe's goodwill in the process. What's not to like? Certainly not how calculated it felt.

Alex opens the box of *zephyrs* and pops one in his mouth. He chews, swallows, then decrees, "They still taste the same."

"Are they really your favorite?"

"They're fine," he dismisses. "It made your babushka happy."

"You were fantastic."

"No big deal. I knew what they wanted; I gave it to them."

"I really appreciate it."

"All in a day's work." Alex leans in and gives Zoe a quick peck on the lips, the rest of his body already turning toward his cubicle. "I'll see you later."

Unlike her family when they first immigrated, Zoe knows that means no time soon.

ZOE STOPS BY Gideon's cubicle on her way out. It's in the opposite direction of her way out, but it would be rude to leave without saying goodbye and thanking him for indulging Deda.

"No big deal," Gideon echoes Alex, offering Zoe insight on why they work so well together. What others would consider a major effort or, at the very least, a generous concession, they take in stride. Nothing is difficult for either of them, because they refuse to see it that way.

"I love talking to old computer guys," Gideon says. "Hearing about the early days, how they had to stick wires into circuit boards or punch holes into cards, then sit around waiting overnight to see if they got it right. God help anybody who dropped their box of cards and got them mixed up. We forget how good we've got it these days."

"He appreciated you listening to him, making him feel valued. It's hardest for his generation, I think. He lived half his life in one place, half in another. He's neither here nor there."

"Like you?" Gideon guesses Zoe's greatest fear.

She denies it with all the vigor such unspoken truth deserves. "No! Of course not! I'm fine. My life is easy compared to what they went through." She quotes Gideon, to drive her point home. "We forget how good we've got it these days."

"'Cause, you know"—Gideon lets her homage pass without comment—"I wouldn't understand feeling like you don't belong in any one place, with any one group."

"You wouldn't."

Zoe expects Gideon to laugh at her. He doesn't. He continues sitting there, patiently waiting to hear what uninformed, offensive nonsense will sprout from her mouth next. But Zoe's not being glib or ignorant or culturally insensitive. She's seen Facebook posts and tweets about black men needing to "act white" in order to get ahead, the lack of diversity in tech, code-switching, cultural appropriation. She can recite all the latest buzzwords. She's woke. Ish.

"It's not the same." Zoe gives up the ghost of her lie in order to make him see the truth. "You're comfortable anywhere."

"I made myself that way."

"How?" Her query bursts like the xenomorph from John Hurt's chest in *Alien*.

Gideon asks, "Why do college kids go to bars?"

Is this a trick question? "To get wasted?"

"I went to listen. Not at the bars around Caltech. Caltech is, shockingly, not a cross section of the American public. I went farther out, where the regular people go. I'd sit there with my drink, and I'd listen to the conversations going on around me. It was like an anthropology project."

"And that worked?"

"Enough that I could avoid being like my dad."

"What's wrong with your dad?"

"Keeping jobs wasn't his thing. He's a smart guy. Too smart, according to popular consensus. They call him Cassandra at work, always predicting what will go wrong. Folks don't like that. Makes them feel stupid. My dad may have been smart, but he never quite learned what to say when. Or how. Or to whom. My dad went on a lot of job interviews. My mom would give him a kiss for luck before each, and she'd remind him, 'Don't be yourself!' "

"Your mom should meet my family. They're constantly telling me how nobody wants to hear what you really have to say. Or what you really think."

"Until you find somebody who does." Gideon one-eighties.

"That's totally going to happen." Zoe saves her greatest scoffs for matters she most wants to believe are true.

"My mom and dad used to talk for hours. About everything."

"My grandparents can not talk for hours. About everything."

Gideon laughs. He has a great laugh. He doesn't let it out in trial balloons, as if waiting for permission. He doesn't stop if no one joins him. He doesn't hold anything back.

"So tell me, how does one go about finding someone who actually wants to listen to you, like your mom and dad?" Zoe is teasing.

He answers as if she's not. "You listen to them. Especially to the things they don't say."

"Are you for real?" Zoe does her speaking-without-thinking bit again. And then she takes it a step further. She puts her money where her mouth is. She doesn't just speak without thinking; she acts without thinking, too.

She kisses Gideon. For real.

Chapter 41

===

Gideon doesn't break off their kiss like Zoe expects him to. He kisses her back, not tentatively or politely, like a man taken by surprise and acting on instinct, but enthusiastically. Alas, their current positions aren't conducive to grand passion. They're sitting on office chairs. With wheelies. Which means their bodies drift side to side in opposite directions while their lips remain plastered together. They're bent at the waist, cutting off a good amount of necessary airflow. If they remove their hands from the plastic armrests, they risk the chairs twisting even farther apart.

In spite of that, it's still a hell of a kiss. One that starts at the lips, but snakes down to the stomach, from which it branches off in all directions, reaching as far as the tips of Zoe's fingers and toes, while turning her ears bright pink.

Zoe's the one who finally breaks it off. While kissing in general, and this kiss in particular, is awesome, breathing is kind of a vital function, too.

"You didn't break it off," Zoe accuses, as if Gideon had violated a previously agreed upon social contract.

"I figured you would, when you wanted to."

"Stop treating me like an adult who knows her own mind."

When Gideon fails to grasp the gravity of the situation, Zoe extrapolates, "What if the decisions I make for myself are wrong? What if I'm a huge disappointment? As long as I'm following other people's expectations for me, I have somebody else to blame my screwups on."

"You'll figure it out." Gideon swivels back to his computer, smiling.

He expects her to leave his cubicle. That's what she stopped by to tell him she was about to do. Before they got . . . distracted. Instead, Zoe asks, "Want to do something crazy?"

Gideon turns back around, looking at Zoe with what she hopes is newfound—if undeserved—respect. "Always."

FLYING A PLANE, scaling a mountain, driving a race car, slicing fruit with a ninja sword . . . These are all things Zoe wants to do. As soon as she gets up the courage. In the meantime, she'll settle for checking out a Midtown Virtual Reality place where yellow bellies like her can attempt all of the above, only with goggles strapped to their heads and feet planted squarely on the floor.

"No one ever wants to go with me," Zoe confesses to Gideon as they pay their admission and are issued their gear. Gideon helps himself to the Wet-Naps on offer and wipes down first her equipment, then his. "All my friends said, quote, lame, nerdy, and pathetically lame."

"Leaves more Fruit Ninja for us." Gideon flourishes his weapon dramatically. In real life, it's a black plastic stick with a censor on it. But on the VR screen, it's a mighty sword meant to slash any and all fruit that comes flying their way.

So they gleefully slash fruit. They climb the Matterhorn using disembodied metal hands that periodically lose their grip and send them tumbling. They race cars and crash into walls without dying fiery deaths. They blow the heads off zombies and maneuver spaceships through asteroid fields while improvising a pilot-to-pilot dialogue that goes like this:

HIM: You've got a Bogey on your six.

HER: You've got a Bacall on your five thirty.

HIM: Great, kid, don't get cocky.

HER: I shot first.

HIM: I'm Spartacus.

HER: I'm Brian!

HIM: I am the walrus, goo goo g'joob.

HER: I'm Mrs. Robinson.

HIM: I'm the entire Swiss Family Robinson.

HER: I'm the Swiss Miss.

HIM: You are the sun, I am the moon.

HER: That's no moon; that's a space station.

Did somebody say lame, nerdy, and pathetically lame?

Ha! Zoe slices them with her ninja sword like so much airborne banana!

Zoe has never closed down a bar, had sex in public, or done anything similarly cool in her life. But she's getting the impression that's what the staff fears she and Gideon are doing as they climb into the airplane simulator . . . and decline to come out. (What's the problem? Nobody else is in line. It's the middle of the day, and they're the only ones playing hooky.)

There's something mesmerizing about sitting in a room designed to look like a real cockpit, pushing buttons and twisting dials, watching the view outside their windshield as it turns from clear blue skies to lightning storms to an image of the ground coming at them at many miles per hour to the Himalayas popping up out of nowhere, all the while knowing that, even if you make a mistake and send your plane plummeting, everything will turn out fine.

This is how Zoe likes her danger, behind a screen and as far away from reality as possible. When she was little and scared to get shots, Baba commanded Zoe to be a brave partisan—did she want to be a coward all her life? Zoe would make a lousy partisan.

Because the bravest thing she's ever done—or ever expects to do—in the cockpit of a plane that isn't even real—is, after multiple false starts and second-guesses, reaching out and resting her hand atop Gideon's.

She's ready to spring back and claim a mere slip of the wrist at the first hint of disapproval. Or visible revulsion. Instead, Zoe sees Gideon smiling. So she just sits back.

And dares to fly.

ZOE SHOWS UP in Brighton for dinner the following day without calling or texting. No one is surprised to see her. Reporting for debriefing was understood. Baba didn't get her chance to offer Zoe the customary twenty-minute recap of her sins during their visit with Alex.

Deda finishes eating, kisses the top of Zoe's head, and says he's stepping out to take a stroll on the boardwalk, so they might have girl talk.

Mama clears the dishes and carries her stack to the kitchen. A waist-high island separates it from the dining room, so she can see and hear everything. Baba gathers the edges of the tablecloth and takes it to the balcony to shake off the crumbs. A glass door separates it from the dining room, so she can see and hear everything. Balissa is left sitting at the table with Zoe.

Zoe figures she can do this the Soviet way—pretend she has no interest in the subject she has the most interest in and spend thirty minutes discussing everything but—or she can go all-American, like squeezing a pimple before it's ready to burst. It's painful, and half the time it gets infected and takes longer to heal, but at least you've done something rather than wait passively.

"So." Call her a Yankee Doodle Dandy. "What did you think of Alex?"

The three women somehow manage to exchange glances without looking at one another.

"He is a very nice boy," Mama says.

"Shrewd," Baba adds. "Ambitious. Enterprising. Dynamic."

"An excellent young man for you," Mama concludes.

"Not the right man for you," Baba says at the same time.

Zoe's head swivels. She's used to Baba contradicting anything anyone says out of principle. And she's certainly used to Baba disapproving of anything Zoe does, out of habit. But Zoe honestly thought, this time, she'd gotten it right. Finally done something her entire family could approve of, maybe even praise! Her shock is seen and raised by her confusion. How in the world has she managed to screw up *again*?

Baba finishes cleaning off the tablecloth and folds it while reentering the dining room. Mama takes off her apron, hangs it on a hook, and leaves the dishes to soak, then reenters the dining room. They stand on either side of Zoe.

"Why would you say such a thing, Mama?" Zoe's mother seems as confused as Zoe. She, too, must have hoped this would be that rare Baba-condoned situation. "Alex is precisely the sort of man you've always held up as an example. It's what you loved about Eugene!"

"And how did that work out?" Baba reminds her.

"That was my fault, not his."

Zoe can't believe it. Might Mama, at long last, let slip what drove her to leave her marriage? Maybe Zoe has finally done something right, after all!

Julia continues, "I know I disappointed you, Mama. You may not have been happy with Papa all these years, but at least you stuck it out."

And now Mama is admitting the forty-fifth anniversary she's been so insistent on is in celebration of a less-than-ideal couple? Zoe sneaks a peek at Balissa to check if Zoe is hearing what she thinks she's hearing, but her great-grandmother appears as serene as if they were discussing a grocery list. No, she'd be more invested in a grocery list. Balissa claims Baba buys the wrong kind of sunflower seeds. She says they never taste like the ones back home. The ones back home, she says, tasted as sweet as candy.

"Papa and me is Papa and me," Baba says, "and you and Eugene is you and Eugene. The difference is, I failed with a good man. You failed with a bad one."

"What was wrong with him?" Zoe bursts out, pissed that a conversation that was supposed to be about her has bypassed her completely.

"Tell her," Baba commands with a dismissive sweep of her arm. "Keeping it secret only makes Zoya imagine the worst."

She's right. When Zoe was little, she imagined her father as a literal monster. As a sophisticated, know-it-all teen, she cynically assumed there'd been an affair. Now that she's older and knows a whole lot less, she's actually afraid to hear about physical abuse or assault.

"Insurance." Mama sighs, her voice a combination of embarrassment and defeat. She sinks into a chair and buries her face in her hands. She's gone beet red, and there are tears in her eyes.

"Insurance?" Zoe repeats numbly.

"Insurance," Baba repeats, scoffing.

That, most definitely, is not what Zoe imagined.

Mama's eyes peek out between her fingers. She mutters, "You know I met your papa when I went to work in his office, bookkeeping."

Zoe did know that.

"After we married, he promoted me from part-time to full-time."

Baba corrects, "He fired his regular man and put Mama in, this time without paying her."

Mama flops back in her chair, hands by her sides, fingers twitching nervously, like she's playing an imaginary keyboard. Balissa cocks her head, notices, and smiles. She does it when she gets anxious, too. Zoe proudly broke herself of the family habit years earlier.

Mama says, "Doing his books, I saw where Eugene was being dishonest. He would bill insurance companies for procedures he didn't perform. Or he would use one person's Medicare number to treat another. Most of his patients were on welfare, so it was easy to cheat. He would sign papers saying a person deserved disability payments. The government doesn't look closely."

"Exactly!" Baba crows. "If Eugene hadn't done this, somebody else would have. And it is not as if he hurt his patients, only the idiot government. They deserve this. Why should bureaucrats decide who needs what procedure, when, and how much doctor should charge for it; why bureaucrats decide who should work and who should not? Why should he play by the rules when no one else does? Why should he be the fool?"

So the big secret is Zoe's dad was . . . no different from most of the dads she'd known growing up? If they weren't doctors signing disability claims, they were office managers stealing software and selling copies of it at half-off retail price, or store owners who didn't charge tax, or piano teachers who accepted cash only for lessons while collecting welfare. Baba was right. In Brighton, playing by the rules was considered being a chump. Why in the world had Mama chosen to break from the pack and take a stand there, of all places?

"Because it's the right thing to do!" Mama insists, her tears as bitter now as Zoe imagines they must have been then. Zoe can also imagine Baba's disapproval, Eugene's confusion, and the entire neighborhood's contempt. And yet, Mama—Zoe's soft-spoken, conflict-averse, peacemaker Mama—stuck to her guns and did what she thought was right, regardless of the consequences. She didn't let anybody cow her. She didn't care what anybody thought. Another family member whom it turns out Zoe hardly knew. At least this secret was a good thing. Something to be proud of.

"I could not stay married to a man who would be so dishonest," Mama continues.

"Because you were scared you'd be caught," Baba begs to differ. "You're just like your father!"

"I already said I was sorry for disappointing you. I know you think I never should have divorced Eugene!"

"You never should have married him!" Baba amends, which comes as much of a surprise to Mama as it does to Zoe.

"But you liked Eugene," Mama practically whimpers. "You said he was shrewd, ambitious, dynamic, enterprising."

Now where has Zoe heard those words before?

"Good for him," Baba says. "Not good for you. Or for our Zoya."

"No such thing as good man," Balissa unexpectedly speaks up. "Only man in a good time. If Eugene is living in USSR, what he does, it is to provide for his family. He would be hero. But in America, he is criminal who puts family at risk." Balissa says to Baba, "I love your papa, yes?" referring to the great-grandfather with the eye patch Zoe has seen only in photographs.

"I suppose . . ." Baba falters.

"I love him. He is good man. Drinks too much, talks too much, works maybe too little, still good man. There are many good men where we live in Siberia. But your papa, he is a soldier, he is there temporarily, and he has *propiska*, permission to live in Odessa. I want to return to Odessa."

Balissa lets that sink in. It does.

Baba begins, "You married Papa for . . ."

"Many reasons," Balissa insists. "Odessa *propiska* is one of them." She goes on, instructing Baba, "Your grandfather Edward was good man, too. He loved my mama. He loved me and my sister. But the right man must also be in the right place, at the right time, for the right purpose." She looks meaningfully at Baba, and something passes between them that Zoe can't identify. "You know this, don't you, my Natashenka?"

Baba clearly knows this.

"Alex is the perfect man for me at the perfect time." Zoe is unsure how this happened. She thought they'd be the ones selling Alex to her, not the other way around! Her extant terror of making the wrong call, thanks to her family's continued expectation of Zoe doing precisely that, flares with a vengeance. The less confident

Zoe is of her choices, the more she feels compelled to defend them. By putting the onus on somebody else.

"You told me I should find a nice Brighton boy. Alex is from Brighton! And he's nice. Enough. You said the problem with your husband, Balissa, is he worked too little. No one could say that about Alex. And everything he's doing is legal. I saw the paperwork, Mama; you don't have to worry he's too ambitious. Alex inspires me to be a better person. Isn't that why you're constantly criticizing me, telling me how to behave? Because you want me to be a better person? Alex is on your side! He already sees me as the person I want to be. You told me not to be myself when we went out? I wasn't. I did what you said to land the kind of guy you want who believes I already am the girl you think I should be!"

Zoe's great-grandmother speaks Russian—and some German. Zoe speaks English—and some Russian. Zoe's grandmother and mother speak both Russian and English.

Right now, Zoe doesn't think any of them are speaking the same language.

Which, as her family learned almost one hundred years ago, is a sure path to disaster.

That no one could figure out how to stop.

Chapter 42

═══

"Did you convince them?" Lacy asks when Zoe calls post-tribunal.

"I convinced myself," Zoe says. Unconvincingly.

ALEX AND ZOE are eating in a restaurant tonight, not juggling finger foods alongside business cards. Zoe notices that Alex deliberately doesn't eat European-style, with the knife in the right hand, fork in the left, but the American way, where he switches his fork from side to side, even though it goes against the way he was taught. It comes off awkward, like he has to remind himself to do it before every bite. It's the first chink she's noticed in his ultra-smooth armor. It's reassuring. Alex isn't perfect, either.

It gives Zoe the courage to blurt, "My grandparents' forty-fifth wedding anniversary is next weekend. Will you come?"

He considers the question much longer than Zoe thinks should be necessary, then asks an equally unnecessary, to Zoe's view, follow-up. "Do you even want me there?"

"What? Of course I do. Why would I invite you if I didn't want you there?"

"Come on, tell the truth, Zoe, are you even all that into me?"

This is not the way any of this was supposed to go. Zoe's family was supposed to fall in love with Alex, and Zoe was supposed to fall in love with Alex, and, most important, Alex was supposed to know he'd been fallen in love with! Deep, meaningful like, at least. Did Alex think Zoe just went around kissing anybody? (Wait, strike that.) Did he think she invited just anybody to intimate family gatherings? It was one thing for Zoe to have moments of uncertainty, but how dare Alex feel the same way? And after how she'd defended him! How dare Alex doubt Zoe when she'd gone out on such a limb for him, not only with her family but with herself. Did he think that level of self-delusion was easy?

"Of course I'm into you," Zoe defends for the benefit of all assembled. And then the perfect excuse comes to her so expeditiously, she must have been subconsciously anticipating whipping it out all along. "It's just—I—It's—It's the evil eye!"

The evil eye is why you spit three times when something good happens. It's why you stick your thumb through two fingers and hide the *doolya* in your pocket when a stranger compliments your kids. To keep the evil eye from seeing and ruining everything.

Alex scoffs. "You don't believe that superstitious nonsense, do you?"

"I just don't want to screw this up." It's the most honest thing Zoe has said to Alex, possibly ever. "I really appreciate how great you were with my family. They really liked you." That part might have been a little less honest. "So will you come? To Brighton? Saturday?"

Alex leans back in his chair, scratches his nose, looks everywhere but at Zoe. "I don't know. Weekends aren't any easier than weekdays. So much work to do. I had this idea." Now he leans forward, eyes blazing. "What if we combine the translation app with a dating app? Everybody wants to know what the person they're out with is thinking, right? What if we could calibrate the app to pick up nuances not just in language but in tone of voice, inflection, hesitation, pitch? You'd be talking to someone, and right there, on your phone, you're getting subtitles. How amazing would that be? Think of the partnership opportunities! The cross promotion!"

He goes on in this vein for over an hour. Zoe doesn't need any subtitles to know that he also manages to avoid answering her question.

AS THEY LINGER at the top of the subway steps, much to the chagrin of those running to catch a train on either side, Alex asks if Zoe would like him to escort her home, as a gentleman should.

Before she left her studio that morning, Zoe gave it a thorough cleaning, including a scrub under the toilet seat, should Alex care about such things. She was ready for the inevitable offer to shepherd her home. She was ready to accept it with enthusiasm. It was the least Alex had earned after spending the afternoon with her family.

Yet now, Zoe hears herself ducking. "Rain check?"

Considering how he's asked it of her, Alex can't very well object, can he?

Alex looks like he realizes that's the case. But he doesn't have to be happy about it.

Zoe waits for Alex to hop in a cab and speed away. After a perfunctory hesitation to pretend this wasn't what she'd been thinking about all through dinner, Zoe takes out her phone and, before she can change her mind—channeling Lacy insisting everything will be fine—she types a text to Gideon, asking if he'd like to be her date for Baba and Deda's anniversary party. She hits Send and descends toward the platform, away from Wi-Fi as soon as she sets foot on the train and the possibility of an answer. Or a rejection.

She'd planned to wait until she was in her apartment before peeking, but then she decides waiting until she's out of the subway is enough. If Zoe gets a connection, it would be God's way of telling her she was right to jump the gun. And to have sent the invite in the first place.

She has bars.

She has a reply.

Gideon texted back, Sure.

Zoe smiles without thinking about it. And then she slips her thumb between her two fingers. To keep the evil eye from seeing and ruining everything.

OBVIOUSLY, LACY NEEDS to hear about this. Obviously, Zoe's family doesn't.

Zoe tells Lacy she invited Gideon to be her date for Baba and Deda's anniversary party.

"That's great!" Lacy gushes. Which, like the reason Zoe's great-grandmother married her great-grandfather, isn't the sole grounds for calling Lacy, but it's definitely one part of it. Lacy can be counted on to gush about anything.

"Does that mean I've screwed things up with Alex for good?"

"If that's what you want." Lacy can also be counted on to be supportive about anything. Even if it is confusing.

"I don't want to screw things up with Alex!"

"So why did you invite Gideon?"

"Because he's fun. And he makes me laugh. And I like being around him. And when we're together, I don't feel like I'm constantly being judged. I can be myself with him. Which is why he's the wrong guy for me."

"That makes sense," Lacy says. Zoe doesn't know if she's being sarcastic or sincere.

"You understand, right? With Gideon, I'm just me. And who the hell needs me?"

"Um . . . I'm going to guess . . . Gideon?"

"My family really likes Alex," Zoe tells Lacy what she wishes would be the truth, already. It'd make all of this so much easier.

"I thought you said they liked Gideon, too."

"He was nice to Deda," Zoe concedes. "But it doesn't matter. They'd never accept Gideon."

"So what?" asks Lacy, the American girl whose parents have celebrated her every turn since the womb. "How you feel is the only thing that matters."

So, so American.

"I've told you how I feel. Alex is the guy I should want to be with. I will never, ever find anyone better for me."

"And Gideon is . . ."

"Gideon is . . ." It's been years since Zoe allowed herself to twitch her fingers when she gets nervous. She's twitching them now. "Gideon is the guy I'm taking to Baba and Deda's anniversary party."

GETTING DRESSED FOR said anniversary party, however, turns into a minor crisis. Zoe weighs the formal requirements of a Brighton Beach gathering versus her distaste for anything that crowd considers fashionable versus Mama calling her disrespectful versus Gideon thinking she dressed up for him and/or feeling underdressed himself. The latter is the tiebreaker when Zoe convinces herself black dress pants and an aquamarine sweater that sparkles not-excessively are acceptable. She also puts on a pair of gold hoop earrings Baba bought for Zoe's sixteenth birthday. She wished her Zoyenka luck in breaking family tradition and managing to hold on to them.

Zoe is ready with defenses for what she anticipates will be her family's mortification at Gideon's appearance in casual wear (as if Gideon's taste in clothes will be their biggest gripe), when he shows up, right on time, and looking more Brighton-appropriate than Zoe.

Not that he's wearing a red velour tracksuit with white racing stripes, a *Miami Vice* neon knockoff, or a costume rejected from a high-school production of *Guys and Dolls*. Gideon is wearing beige slacks; a jewel-tone orchid dress shirt, the sleeves rolled up to his forearms; and a tie in a darker orchid hue. He's carrying a flat package wrapped in silver paper with a matching bow.

"You look terrific," Zoe blurts out.

"Thanks." Gideon doesn't try to deny, Brighton-style, how, no, he really doesn't. It leaves Zoe without a traditional conversation pattern to follow.

"You brought a gift." She points out the obvious, stunned and touched.

"My grandmother would disown me if I didn't. I've had home training."

"My grandmother would never disown me," Zoe says. "Who would she criticize?"

As they walk from the train toward the boardwalk restaurant, Zoe offers Gideon an overview of her family tree, including the great-great-uncle visiting from Israel, as well as all the folks she's not related to but still calls aunt or uncle—no Russian-speaking youth would dare address an elder by only their first name—and their children, whom Zoe had been friends with when they were little because her family was friends with theirs.

"Play cousins." Gideon says he has those, too. He asks, "Do your grandparents hang out with the same people here they did back in the USSR?"

"No. It's pretty strange, actually. They call Brighton Little Odessa. You'll be walking down the boardwalk and run into the girl you sat next to in first grade. Or getting your nails done and, hey, the manicurist once lived in the same courtyard as your second cousin. Most people love it. It's why they congregated here in the first place. My grandmother hates it. She goes out of her way to avoid everyone and anything that reminds her of the past."

Chapter 43

The party is in full swing when Gideon and Zoe enter. Zoe timed it so the space would be full and dimly lit, and they wouldn't attract too much attention. There's a nightclub stage at the farthest end of the floor Mama rented. A band named Russian Spirit, composed of a piano, bass, drums, and tambourine, is plugging away, fronted by a dude in his forties, sweating through his black dress shirt and matching fedora, and backed by three busty women of the same age, but dressed as if they'd raided their teenage daughters' closets—in the 1980s. Baba isn't the only one refusing to give up on figure-flattering fashions.

There's a dance floor in front of the stage. A handful of couples, a few Mama's age, most Baba and Deda's, are getting down. The old guys have serious hip action going. The women match them in wild head tosses and wanton shoulder shaking. Those without partners dance in groups, gyrating their legs, swooshing their skirts, waving their hands beneath the disco ball, a Soviet-inspired *hora*.

Four rows of tables are set up in semicircles around the dance floor. Each seats four. Each bears two bottles of vodka. The buffet is in the corner, featuring sculpted mountains of beet and potato salad, pickles, olives, caviar, black bread, shredded cabbage, deviled eggs, meat pastries, veal tongue with a dab of mayonnaise on every slice, and herring so dry you have to hit it against the table—that's how you tell it's good. And, of course, the *pièce de résistance*, a whole roasted pig, complete with an apple in its mouth.

Baba and Deda sit at the head, sharing a table with Balissa and Mama. They aren't dancing. Not in the designated area, anyway. Deda has turned his chair to face the action and is kicking his legs, cancan-style, and raising his arms, torquing his wrists as if screwing in two lightbulbs. Baba is doing her best to ignore it.

The room is flickering with strobe lights bouncing off the mirrored walls and gilt-edged furnishings. But it's not so blinding as to distract from Gideon's presence. He's being stared at. Some are doing it discreetly, taking quick peeks, then whipping their heads away innocently. Some are pretending to study an object right next to him, while their eyes shift surreptitiously for a better look. Others are blatantly gaping.

Zoe turns to Gideon and whisper-shouts over the pounding music, "Are you okay?"

"I'm used to it," Gideon reassures her.

"To . . . this?" Zoe can't think of any other way to describe . . . this.

"Looks like any other room of white people to me."

Right. Where Zoe sees the cringeworthy culture she tries to distance herself from, he sees . . . white people. It's like when Zoe has to explain to those who'd call her Russian that she's not; she's Jewish. Soviet Russians didn't consider Jews to be Russian, and Zoe's family never thought of themselves that way . . . until Americans insisted they were. "But weren't they born in Russia?" Americans would ask. Actually, they weren't, they were born in Ukraine, except those who were forcibly passed through Siberia. They speak Russian, though, not Ukrainian, because that's what the Jews of

Odessa spoke, since they weren't considered Ukrainian, either. That nuance is even more difficult to grok. Zoe's standard reply used to be, "If you were born in Japan, would that make you Japanese?" But then she gave up and, when asked if she was Russian, shrugged and replied, "Sure."

"Wanna dance?" Gideon asks.

Zoe's about to shock herself and say yes when the music scrapes to an abrupt halt, and the singer, also their emcee for the evening, announces it's time for the festive toasts Baba and Deda's friends have prepared. One toupee-wearing gentleman announces that, on this joyous occasion, he is moved to muse about how marriage is like the following Russian verse:

> *When you're first hit in the eye*
> *You'll let out a mighty cry.*
> *Hit you once, hit you twice*
> *You'll learn to find it very nice.*

The crowd roars.

The next tribute comes in song. An elderly couple share a microphone to warble an original composition that begins, "People sing a beautiful song of you, wise and dear . . ." They've taken the patriotic dirge and rewritten the lyrics, so that, instead of Stalin, it's the happy couple who are being saluted. They've replaced Soviet landmarks with Brighton's, so "mountain heights" become "B train heights" and "where eagles take flight" is "where JFK planes take flight." When they get to the line about soldiers gearing up for one final battle, everyone hoots in Baba and Deda's direction. Deda takes his ribbing in good-natured stride, ruefully shaking his head to agree that yes, yes, there have been some great battles between them.

Then there's another poem that the reciter thinks is hilarious for the occasion, Pushkin's "I Am in Chains." Fearing Gideon might be feeling a bit trapped himself, surrounded by a language he doesn't understand, Zoe tries to include him, translating what's being said, then offering, "Pushkin was black, you know. His great-grandfather was taken from Cameroon and given as a present to Peter the Great when he was a boy. Peter took a liking to the little guy and raised him in the Imperial Court as his godson. He sent him to France to learn math and engineering, then put him in charge of major government projects."

"A Russian using a black man for his engineering skills?" Gideon raises an eyebrow. "I can't imagine such a thing."

Zoe doesn't laugh until Gideon laughs. And not until after he whispers, "Relax, Zoe, I'm fine. This is really something."

That's easy for him to say. He's enjoying himself, as opposed to cringing at how lame it all is. Adults—old people!—acting like idiots, thinking they're being clever with their rhymes and their puns and their references to songs from a time and place nobody cares about. Zoe watches through Gideon's eyes, which makes the furniture even shabbier, the music even more Eurotrash, the food even more gluttonous, and the people even more cheap, tacky, and foreign. She regrets inviting him. If Alex were here, they could've made fun of the proceedings together. They could've rolled their eyes and muttered droll comments to prove how above this, how American they were. They'd be having an appropriately miserable time. As opposed to Gideon, who insists on having a blast, no matter how strenuously Zoe tries to make clear he shouldn't—he's even bobbing his head along to the atrocious music! It's not fair. Gideon having a good time is making Zoe have a good time. And that wasn't the plan.

Neither was Alex showing up.

He walks in like he was invited. Which he was. Technically. He blinks through the smoke, scanning the room. He spies Zoe and waves. He takes note of Gideon. He barely breaks his stride. Did Alex know Gideon was coming? Zoe never bothered to ask

Gideon if he'd told Alex. No. Zoe deliberately never asked. Because she was too scared to find out. She didn't want to know if Alex was upset by it. Or if he wasn't.

There's a woman with Alex, a few years older, beautifully put together, tastefully dressed (nothing sparkling), her hair up in a classy chignon. Zoe wonders if Alex brought a date to her grandparents' anniversary party.

He's guiding the woman over to Baba and Deda for an introduction. Zoe figures she should be part of that conversation, if only so Mama can whisper, "I told you so," regarding Zoe letting Alex slip through her fingers. Gideon follows.

But Alex isn't content to present his new and improved girlfriend in private. He'd like to introduce her to the world. Alex pushes his way to the front of the tribute line, ignoring those already waiting—luckily, being ex-Soviets, they merely sigh resignedly. Alex takes the mic and introduces himself from the stage. He pauses, expectantly, for applause. This mob has been toasting for over a good hour now so, yeah, sure, they'll applaud.

"The forty-fifth wedding anniversary," Alex intones, "is the sapphire wedding anniversary. Not as well known as the gold or silver, but, to this gathering, even more meaningful. The sapphire is a holy stone, first mentioned in the Bible, in the book of Exodus. Exodus," Alex repeats. "What could be more meaningful to us than that?"

Alex takes a breath, suggesting this isn't close to being over, and goes on to lavishly praise the bravery of those first Jewish emigrants from the USSR, those daring groundbreakers of the 1970s, the ones who took a leap of faith before the trail was blazed, the ones who stepped into the abyss of their own Exodus and set a course to be followed by thousands of grateful others. The ones without whom people like him would have nothing.

That is such a load of insincere, pandering crap and—Is Baba crying? When Lacy's mother said the same thing, Baba couldn't wait to make fun of her for being a naive romantic, one of Lenin's useful idiots. But at Alex's words, Baba is seriously crying?

Gideon leans over to whisper, "Damn, he's good."

Zoe nods in stunned agreement.

"Of all the humiliations our people suffered in the USSR, which was the greatest one?" Alex barely pauses to offer a chance for guesses before elucidating, "Marriage! It was marriage!"

The crowd, primed to applaud and agree, nod their collective heads sagely. Yup, marriage. Marriage was the greatest humiliation they suffered, that's just what they were about to say, Alex simply didn't give them the chance.

"We're celebrating forty-five years of marriage. But what sort of marriage was it?" Again, Alex answers his own question. "It was a Soviet marriage!"

If he means a situation forced on you by outside powers that you initially struggled against then accepted in defeat, trudging through your gray days, resigned and hollow, because extracting yourself wasn't an option, and, in the end, it was your sole source of food and shelter, then, yes, the marriage of Natalia Crystal and Boris Rozengurt was pretty darn Soviet.

That's not what Alex means. "It was a marriage sanctioned by Soviet authorities, because the true sanction, the holy sanction, a Jewish wedding ceremony, was forbidden. Such a *shanda* must not be allowed to stand. Especially not on this foremost anniversary, the sapphire anniversary, the Exodus anniversary."

Wow. Alex really burned up the Google search for this one.

"This is my friend Rose." Alex beckons his date forward. Zoe finally recognizes her as one of the cultural advisers Alex hired for his app, to translate idioms. "Rose is a rabbi."

Zoe feels the urge to throw herself over the roast pig. Just because Zoe judges her family doesn't mean she wants anyone else doing it. Baba doesn't deserve to be lectured condescendingly—or, worse, sympathetically—about how she's doing Judaism wrong.

Baba knows she's doing Judaism wrong. She also knows she's suffered more for her Judaism than some American-born rabbi whose idea of anti-Semitism is that time in college when the Upper East Side girl made a JAP joke. Just like Zoe itched to lecture Mama about her racism, she's ready to fight for Baba's honor. It'll go a long way toward assuaging her own guilt.

Alex explains, "I brought Rose here tonight so she could perform an authentic Jewish wedding ceremony and our guests of honor might finally be married in the eyes of God."

Once again, Alex pauses for his applause.

During which time Baba leaps out of her seat, shaking her head, waving her arms, the napkin she used to dab at her eyes a few moments earlier still crumpled in her palm.

"No," she insists. "This is unnecessary. No."

"Don't be shy," Alex says.

"I do not want this," Baba reiterates. Then, remembering that it takes two to temper, she swats her hand in Deda's direction. "We do not want this."

"But we do!" Alex includes himself in the watching audience. And then he starts a chant: *"Gorko! Gorko!"*

The word itself means bitter. It's a tradition to shout it when you want the bride and groom to kiss. To get rid of the bitterness.

If there's one thing a youth spent in the USSR conditioned this group to do it's to pick up a rousing cry and keep repeating it until the only objective is to make sure you aren't the first to stop. Overwhelmed by his friends' fervor, Deda hefts himself from his chair, smiling awkwardly, like someone caught on a stadium kiss-cam during a blind date that's going badly. He catches Baba's wildly gesticulating hands in his and strains his neck to try to get her to look up at him, shouting something that gets lost in the din. She refuses to be appeased.

Out of the blue, Gideon says, "Give her my gift."

He never got a chance to place it on the designated table. It was too crowded with guests jostling to make sure theirs was in primary position, its price tag hanging out casually, so Gideon has the box handy to thrust at Zoe. "It'll calm her down, you'll see."

Zoe trusts him. She can't explain why, she just does. Zoe shoves her way toward the stage, through the cheering crowd. Balissa watches with a look suggesting that nothing surprises her anymore as Mama tries to play peacemaker and keep Baba from making more of a scene.

"Open this." Zoe inserts the present between her arguing grandparents.

"What is it?" Alex asks, miffed at another unscheduled interruption to his grand gesture.

Since she doesn't know, and Baba, as is her custom, is in no mood to follow instructions, Zoe goes ahead and tears open the package herself. Inside is a sapphire-colored glass picture frame—Alex wasn't the only one hitting Google. It surrounds a document of rich, fancy paper, inscribed with a bunch of calligraphic flourishes. In Hebrew.

"It's a *ketubah*," Rabbi Rose says, delighted to spot something familiar.

"It's your *ketubah*," Gideon arrives to tell Baba. "This proves you're already married by Jewish law—you don't have to do it again."

"Where'd you find this?" Alex asks the question everyone is thinking.

Cries of *"Gorko!"* have died down, replaced by murmurs of confusion and splashes of vodka being poured.

Alex demands, "How could you have gotten your hands on their Jewish wedding license?"

"It was part of their immigration file," Gideon says. "To prove they were Jewish, to prove they were married. I went online, did a little digging, a little backdooring, and I downloaded—"

Baba's night-long frown fades, replaced with bewilderment.

Baba, who prides herself on remaining in control and on top no matter what the situation, suddenly looks helpless and lost.

She turns to Zoe and whispers, "Why would you to do this?"

Without waiting for an answer, right there, in front of all her guests, Baba raises the frame above her head and hurls it to the floor.

Epilogue

===

"Wait!" Gideon dives heroically and catches the framed *ketubah* that Baba is about to shatter. He scrambles to his feet and again offers his gift. "This is still your original marriage license—I just prettied it up. There are your names, and here is your wedding date, July 18, 1974. That's almost exactly one year before you left the Soviet Union, right?"

Baba stares at the *ketubah* as if everything on it is new to her. And then she does the most surprising thing of all. She grabs Gideon's face in her hands. She kisses him—first one cheek, then the other. She pulls him into an embrace. She murmurs, "Thank you, thank you, you lovely boy."

This is definitely not how Zoe expected this night to go. Alex clearly didn't, either. That was his "Thank you, you lovely boy" going astray. Zoe can't figure out if Alex looks more pissed or confused. Everyone else looks befuddled.

Baba takes a break from embracing Gideon to approach the microphone. A respectful hush falls over the room.

"Life has never given me what I wanted," Baba commences her version of an anniversary toast. Some people grin, waiting for the punch line. Deda shifts from foot to foot. He's already heard it. "But it has, once in a while, given me what I needed."

Deda's head bobs up, his eyes wide. This part is new.

Baba looks over her shoulder at Balissa. "It's been that way for all the women in my family. My grandmother, Daria." The assembled titter, so Baba explains. "It was Dvora. Her mother made her change it. She thought it would make a difference." Now the crowd really laughs. There's a Russian expression: *They don't punch your passport; they punch your face.* No name change could pass a Dvora off as a Daria. "Baba Daria didn't want to be banished to Siberia. But it shielded her from the war. She left Odessa just in time. Baba Daria got what she needed, not, maybe, what she wanted, because of two men. My grandfather, Edward Gordon." Baba says the name with meaning. After Stalin's death and Khrushchev's exposure of his butchery, Edward Gordon was rehabilitated. His recordings were again available, and every Jewish child forced to suffer through piano lessons had been compelled to listen to them. "He's one of us!" their parents touted. Edward's name was returned to a place of honor at the conservatory where he'd trained, the metal plaque reinstated to the wall where it had once been ripped off by crowbar, his death date added after his birth date. The ballet school where he'd accompanied the dancers put up a plaque, too. According to Baba, Balissa attended the ceremony because she had been required to. But she never set foot in the school again and forbade her Natasha from taking lessons there.

"Mama didn't want her cherished papa to die." Baba puts words in Balissa's mouth, though the tears in Balissa's eyes suggest Baba knows what she's talking about. "But his sacrifice saved her life. His sacrifice, and the actions of her stepfather. Whom Mama certainly didn't want. Whom Mama certainly didn't like. But whom she needed, nonetheless. Not to mention, this stepfather, he gave Mama her beloved baby brother!"

Baba waves to an elderly man standing off to the side, clutching the hand of his nurse—the one with the chatty relatives. Despite pushing eighty, and having shrunk some, he's still the largest member of the family, not in height—Deda is tall, though slight—but in width. Plus, he has an amazing head of hair. White now, but they say it was a bright red in his youth.

Uncle Igor waves back at Baba, playing along with her shout-out. But his eyes are not playful, they're worried, and they're not on her. His attention is focused on Balissa. She smiles sorrowfully over the guests' heads, followed by a melancholy shrug in Uncle Igor's direction. It confirms the verity of what Baba said about the man who whisked them from Odessa, and the man who made their departure possible. How much Balissa didn't want it, despite needing it desperately.

"It was the same for me," Baba continues. "A man." She points at Deda. "This man, my Boris, he showed me that life does eventually give you what you think you want. Except maybe not in the way that you think you want it."

Is that a compliment? No one is sure. Baba is not known for her compliments. Zoe hears a few whispers, a few tentative claps. A few raised glasses and murmurs of "Hear, hear!" Deda takes a step toward Baba, his lips puckered to kiss her, but whether it will be mouth, cheek, or air isn't yet clear.

She's not done. Before Deda can zero in on his target, Baba abruptly turns to where Zoe is standing, between Alex and Gideon, one of whom understood her words, but seems eager for her to wrap it up already, and one who hasn't understood a thing, but appears in no hurry to escape. "I hope my granddaughter learns from my example. I hope, when it comes to choosing the right man to spend her life with"—because any other option isn't an option, obviously—"she will have what she wants and what she needs, both." Baba hesitates for so long that some believe her speech over and start to clap. She cuts them off with a terse shake of the head. Quickly, before she changes her mind, Baba adds, "I hope she will be brave, also. You must be brave. So you can know truth about yourself. So you can to tell difference between the wanting and the needing, my Zoyenka."

Everyone is looking at Zoe now. A response is required. She

can't stay planted at the edge of the stage, blinking in confusion. So she reverts to propriety. Zoe finally understands why Mama and Deda are committed to following rules. It makes coming to a decision in difficult situations simpler. Zoe does what is expected of her. She steps forward and kisses Baba, then Deda. Mama actually looks pleased. Finally, it would seem Zoe has done something right.

The band begins playing again, prompted by the emcee, who knows an emotional cue when he hears one. At Baba's stern urging, the dancing resumes, more frenzied than before. Mama rises to join the group hug. Everyone is happy.

There is no way it can last.

Zoe takes advantage of the fleeting truce to disentangle herself and make a run for it, Alex and Gideon following.

They get far enough up the scarlet velvet stairs, past the mirrored walls and toward the front door, that they can hear each other without screaming and English is no longer a foreign language. Rabbi Rose sweeps by, barely calling goodbye to Alex and best wishes to Zoe and Gideon before she's on the boardwalk, speed-walking toward Coney Island Avenue for a cab.

Alex grumbles in Rose's wake, "Your grandmother could have shown a little gratitude. I went through a lot of trouble to get Rose here."

"Nobody asked you to. Baba didn't want a Jewish wedding. You blindsided her."

"Please. She was just doing that keep-saying-no-so-they'll-keep-asking bit."

"Maybe instead of constantly talking about your app, you should use it to really listen to what people are saying. Or"—Zoe looks at Gideon, wondering if he remembers—"what they're not saying."

Gideon smiles. He definitely remembers.

And another thing. "What are you doing here, anyway, Alex?"

"You invited me!"

"You never accepted!"

"I didn't know until the last minute if I'd be available."

"You mean you didn't know until the last minute if something better would come along."

"I tried to make it up to you. Why do you think I went through this nonsense?"

"To show off."

"Isn't that what these parties are for? Everyone tries to come up with the better song, the best poem. I knew you wouldn't have anything prepared like you're supposed to. Your family would be so disappointed, you'd never hear the end of it. I thought I'd help you out. Get everyone talking about how great the Rozengurts' granddaughter was, earn you a ton of Brownie points. Honestly, you could stand to be a little grateful, too."

How can somebody be so right—because Alex is totally right about everything—and yet so wrong at the same time?

"And I certainly didn't expect you to bring another date."

Alex sighs. Not for his sake, but for Zoe's. He feels sad for her, making such an avoidable mistake, choosing an obvious outsider over an ideal candidate like him. Doesn't Zoe realize what she's setting herself up for? The hysteria from family, the gossip from neighbors, the censure from kids she grew up with, the community cold shoulder. He knows she'll come to regret it. He tried to save Zoe from herself. She was just too foolish to listen.

Except Zoe knows something Alex doesn't. If Mama could survive it, so can Zoe. Because it's the right thing to do.

At the same time, Zoe realizes why Alex was ever interested in her. It's not the financing. Financing, he can get anywhere. It's because dating an on-paper ideal candidate like Zoe made his life easier, too. She wonders how many times a day his mother texts him about not letting Zoe slip through his fingers.

"Sorry you came all the way out here," is the closest Zoe will get to apologizing.

Alex shrugs. "It's cool."

Zoe believes him. Alex won't hold a grudge. Not against her, not against Gideon. To hold a grudge, you'd have to care.

Just before he takes off, Zoe taps her phone against Alex's. "That's my friend Lacy's number. You should give her a call. You guys will really hit it off." Zoe pictures them being optimistic about everything. Even Lacy's mother regaling Alex's parents with how great socialism is. "Tell her I said so."

Alex salutes two fingers against his hairline and melts into the crowd. Like he belongs there.

Zoe realizes Gideon hasn't said anything. She realizes he trusted her to handle Alex. And he isn't haranguing her about doing it wrong. Zoe meets his eyes. "What happened in there? Why did my grandmother—"

"Let's go outside," Gideon says.

On the boardwalk, they are instantly surrounded by shirtless guys zipping around on bikes; polyglot families wrapped in towels with clumps of sand clinging to their butts; couples clutching cheap trinkets won on Coney Island; Russian-speaking pamphlet wielders insisting Jesus was the Jewish messiah; and electric organs, guitars, and drum sets erected without permits to blast amateur compositions and wring coins from softhearted visitors. Also dozens of elderly couples strolling, arm in arm—women, men, long-marrieds, and lifetime friends. Some have gone native, making their evening appearances in tracksuits and windbreakers. Others stick to the old ways, dressing up for a promenade, skirts, hose, silk scarves, salon-styled hair tucked under jaunty berets, heels, and makeup. Children pedal alongside on miniature BMWs and Mercedes, the girls with huge bows in their hair and the boys in vintage Red Army caps their great-grandfathers died to earn, which now can be bought on every Brighton corner.

Zoe and Gideon walk over to the metal barriers keeping the beach from the boardwalk. The air smells of the sea. It's why so many love it here. "Like Odessa," Deda says.

Zoe and Gideon sit on a wooden bench, looking both ahead and at each other.

Gideon says, "You told me your grandmother didn't want an anniversary party. She offer any hint why?"

"Beyond general disdain for anything and everything, no."

"Forty-fifth, right?"

"Right. Sapphire, Exodus, you heard Alex."

"When your grandfather visited our office, we talked about a programming language he once used. Ratfor. He said he dabbled in it before he got married."

"So?"

"Ratfor was invented in 1975. Forty-four years ago."

Zoe sees what he's getting at, but . . . "Isn't it possible he just got the year wrong?"

"Of course. It's also possible that your grandparents got married in 1975, not 1974. Which would make your mother . . ."

"A touch illegitimate."

Zoe realizes she should feel shocked. And she does. But not in a bad way. She's actually kind of tickled at the idea of Baba, who just a few minutes ago described Deda not as something she wanted but as something she needed, so overwhelmed by passion that she'd break the ultimate good-*Komsomolniks*-don't-engage-in-such-activities taboo, and that Zoe's very righteous Mama was the result of it. Of course, Zoe could be the naive romantic of the moment. The actual situation could have been more prosaic. Baba could have been bored, or scared she'd end up an old maid at the ancient age of twentysomething, or a whole host of other reasons to which Zoe would never be privy. But whatever Baba's motives, it led to Mama, which led to Zoe, which led to sitting here now. With Gideon. As Baba mused: "What happened is what happened, no going back for anyone. What's the point of combing through the past? That's not the direction time moves in."

Gideon speculates, "I figured your grandma didn't want to deal with your mother finding out. Not to mention the rest of Brighton Beach."

"But that's . . . so . . . stupid."

"To you and me, sure. Around here, though, sounds like a pretty good reason not to want to draw attention to your wedding anniversary, doesn't it?"

"So you dummied up that *ketubah*."

"I thought your grandma would like concrete proof of the date she's been lying about for forty-four years."

Now Zoe wants to kiss Gideon on the cheek and call him a lovely boy.

"Funniest part is, Alex and I were on the same track to show off for you; we just went about it in different ways."

A lovely boy kiss on the cheek isn't enough. Not for Zoe, not now. She leans in and kisses Gideon on the lips. She's not expecting him to pull away this time. She's actively hoping he won't.

He doesn't. He kisses her back like this is the kiss Gideon's been expecting Zoe to initiate all along. Like he's been waiting patiently. And like it's been worth the wait. He kisses her like he doesn't think there's anything wrong with what they're doing, like he can't imagine anyone finding anything wrong with what they're doing, and, if they do, how sad that will be for them. He kisses Zoe like he never intends to stop.

Then there's a tap on their shoulders.

Balissa is standing there, leaning on Baba for support. It's several yards from the restaurant to their bench, so it couldn't have been easy for her to navigate. But when Zoe's great-grandmother has something to say, nothing can impede her. And Balissa has quite a bit to say to Zoe and Gideon.

Thanks to Alex's earlier sigh and Zoe's understanding of what it meant, she braces herself for the tirade that must follow, especially when Zoe spies Mama in hot pursuit of the runaway pair. But it's Baba who speaks first.

"You have never listened to me, my Zoyenka."

She's speaking English, so Gideon can comprehend her disapproval. Will Baba open with the general inappropriateness of Zoe making out with a near-stranger in public (lovely boy aside), or will she zero in on who exactly the near-stranger is? What he is. Which will come first, stories of how Mama was treated in school by those hooligans, or the time a *mamzer* ripped Balissa's purse off her shoulder and skateboarded away? Maybe Baba will trend political. African revolutions. Savages, that's what those people are. Not because of the bloodshed, but for thinking Communism could be the solution to anything. Not merely savages, fools, too. Then again, Baba might settle for highlighting what people will say about Zoe. Doesn't Zoe care what people might say about her?

"Listen to me now. Please." Baba points to Gideon. "This is very good boy."

Perhaps Baba took the *ketubah* incident into account, after all. But as Balissa lectured, "No such thing as good man. Only man in a good time." Zoe presumes that applies to good boys, too. And now is definitely not a good time for a good boy like Gideon to be standing next to a could-always-be-better girl like Zoe. Now is the time for Baba's compliment to be followed by "but not here, not now."

"Good, yes, so important," Mama echoes.

"Especially when life not so good," Baba struggles to explain. "The Alex boy, he is . . . he is . . ." She makes a shape with her hands like she's encircling a balloon. "He is empty. He flies high; he flies away. He has many big dreams, and that is where he will always be first. This boy"—she pats Gideon on the shoulder—"this boy stays on ground."

In America, land of "give a child wings so he can fly," her metaphor would be an insult. But to Zoe's family, dubbing someone strong enough to tether you to the ground so that you don't disappear in the middle of the night into a Chaika limousine is the height of compliments.

"My Boris," Baba tells Gideon, "is man who does no fly away.

He like you. He sees problem, he fixes. I not smart enough, too stubborn, too proud, to ask for help; he fixes anyway. And he does not, at the end, say I told you so. Can you believe this? Not once does he say this to me. That is what real man is, yes?"

Zoe realizes Mama is the only one on this stretch of boardwalk oblivious to the problem Gideon fixed for Baba. Zoe realizes they all intend to keep it that way.

"Zoya's papa," Baba, after knowing Gideon a few minutes, fills him in on family history Zoe pried out of her only the other day, "if born in USSR, what he do with his little deceits, it would be necessary. He like Balissa's stepfather, man who can do favors, get favors. In America, is not time and place for these things, we do not need same. Time and place, my mama tell me, they matter when it come to what man is good and what man is bad. She is right. I realize this after too long."

Zoe sneaks a peek at Mama to check how she's responding to Baba's declaration. Mama's face remains neutral. It's not the time or place to push.

"I no have choices when I am younger. I no can choose job, I no can choose man, I no can choose life." Baba turns her attention to Zoe. "But like Balissa also say, sometimes no choice is best choice. No choice gives me Deda, and he is what I need. You, Zoyenka, you are not like me. You have many choices. So many choices in America. You will to make wise one, yes?"

"You trust me to make wise choices?" Zoe double-checks. "On my own? Without your input?"

Gideon says, "Listen to your grandmother, Zo-yay-enka."

His attempt to pronounce her nickname the Russian way makes everyone laugh.

"And you will be brave, yes? You will not look at outside of person." Baba rubs Gideon's arm appreciatively. "You will look at inside. Inside yourself, too. Look honestly, see what is really there, not what you wish to be there."

Hearing Baba echo the words Zoe's babbled at Lacy how many

times over the past few weeks brings Zoe up short. The idea of Baba understanding something Zoe assumed was unique to her is disconcerting. She thinks back to the day she first realized there might be more to her family than she previously believed. Between the fudged wedding date and now this, Zoe's oblivion is starting to feel embarrassing.

But then Baba continues issuing instruction on how Zoe should live her life, and she's back on familiar ground. "You must to look that other person will give you what you really need. Even if you not know what you really need and ask for nonsense you think you want. Do you to see this?"

Zoe smiles at Gideon. Zoe smiles at Baba. Zoe says, "I to see this."

"Good." Baba leans back, studying them both happily. "You will be better than me. Braver than me. Smarter than me. Better and braver and smarter than all of us." And then, of course, she has to add, "Do not make fun of my English. When you are old woman, we will listen how you speak language you must to learn as adult."

Balissa nudges Baba. The rise of her eyebrows reminds Baba of why they came out in the first place. And it wasn't so Baba could chastise Zoe. Baba takes the plate Balissa is holding in her hands and offers it to Gideon. "My mother, she was to be worried you leave party with no food. She bringing this for you."

On the plate is a little bit of everything from the buffet. Including a potato.

Acknowledgments

━━

This book—not to mention every other aspect of my life—would not have been possible if my parents, Genrikh and Nelly Sivori-novsky, hadn't decided to leave the Soviet Union in 1976.

I thank them for bringing me to America and for understanding when I wanted to be a writer—and not a computer programmer.

Thanks to them and to the Khait family for their stories, many of which appear in this book. Any errors are my own.

Thank you to my brother, Martin, who speaks my language, and to his wife, Rachel, who doesn't mind when we do—endlessly.

Thank you to my in-laws, who opened my eyes to a whole new America.

Thank you to my agent, Allison Hunter, who said, "You obviously know how to write, so go ahead and just write this story."

Thank you to my editor, Sarah Stein, who took that writing and made it readable.

Thank you to my children, Adam, Gregory, and Aries, who contained their emergencies to when I wasn't writing.

And thank you to my husband, Scott, who is the answer to the question, "How can a woman have it all?"

About the Author

===

Alina Adams is the *New York Times* bestselling author of soap opera tie-ins, romance novels, and figure skating mysteries. She has worked as a creative content producer for *As the World Turns* and *Guiding Light*; was part of the *All My Children* and *One Life to Live* reboot; and has been a writer, producer, and skating researcher for ABC, NBC, TNT, ESPN, and Lifetime TV. Alina immigrated to the United States with her family from Odessa, USSR, in 1977. She lives in New York City with her husband, Scott, and their three children. Visit her online at AlinaAdams.com.